Writing Lives in China, 1600–2010

# Writing Lives in China, 1600–2010

## Histories of the Elusive Self

Edited by

Marjorie Dryburgh and Sarah Dauncey
*School of East Asian Studies, University of Sheffield, UK*

palgrave
macmillan

First published 2013 by
PALGRAVE MACMILLAN

Palgrave Macmillan in the UK is an imprint of Macmillan Publishers Limited,
registered in England, company number 785998, of Houndmills, Basingstoke,
Hampshire RG21 6XS.

Palgrave Macmillan in the US is a division of St Martin's Press LLC,
175 Fifth Avenue, New York, NY 10010.

Palgrave Macmillan is the global academic imprint of the above companies
and has companies and representatives throughout the world.

Palgrave® and Macmillan® are registered trademarks in the United States,
the United Kingdom, Europe and other countries.

ISBN 978–1–137–36856–0

This book is printed on paper suitable for recycling and made from fully
managed and sustained forest sources. Logging, pulping and manufacturing
processes are expected to conform to the environmental regulations of the
country of origin.

A catalogue record for this book is available from the British Library.

A catalog record for this book is available from the Library of Congress.

# Contents

# Figures and Tables

## Figures

## Tables

# Preface

The origins of this volume lie in conversations conducted over many years that led us to consider the meanings and uses of life stories written in China or about Chinese people, past and present. Many of these conversations were not, at first, about life writing in its own right, but about the ways in which life stories of self or others featured in our work – as illustrations of social change, eye-witness accounts of historical events, challenges to hegemonic narratives or supplements to fragmentary archival records – and the challenges inherent in drawing these personal stories into understandings of wider changes. The advice offered to scholars on the use of these life narratives was often cautious, and sometimes discouraging. Life narratives – whoever their authors or intended audiences – might be of some interest, but they were to be understood as lesser sources: less robust, less objective and less 'representative' as historical sources than the archival record; of less 'literary' value and interest than fiction, drama or poetry; less revealing, because of distinctively Chinese generic traditions, of lives and selves than auto/biographical work produced elsewhere.

However, the volume of extant works – some now available in translation, others not – pointed to powerful personal, social and political interests that underlay auto/biographical production; and the relatively recent proliferation of critical and theoretical studies of life narrative across cultures offered increasingly sophisticated tools for disentangling those interests. Despite those warnings, therefore, it seemed more productive to engage with those supposedly imperfect auto/biographical artefacts, to understand how and why they were produced and what effects they were designed to achieve, than simply to set them aside or lament their shortcomings. The new conversation that this work stimulated led more or less directly to the interdisciplinary international workshop, Writing Lives in China, held in March 2008 at the University of Sheffield, UK, and thence to this volume.

The contributions to this volume were all presented at the 2008 workshop, and we would like to express our sincerest gratitude to all workshop participants for their interest in extending the boundaries of our understanding of life writing in China, and to the contributors for their continued commitment to the book. The workshop was made possible by generous support from the British Academy, the Chiang Ching-kuo Foundation for International Scholarly Exchange and the White Rose East Asia Centre, as well as the School of East Asian Studies and the Humanities Research Institute at the University of Sheffield, which helped to host the workshop.

In addition to the authors included in this volume, we would like to thank those workshop participants who made significant contributions to our discussions, but whose work it was sadly not possible, for a variety of reasons, to incorporate in the present volume. These include Katherine Carlitz (University of Pittsburgh), Lynn A. Struve (Indiana University, Bloomington), Margaretta Jolly (University of Sussex), Tan Tian-yuan (School of Oriental and African Studies, London), Yvonne Schulz Zinda (University of Hamburg), Sarah Schneewind (University of California, San Diego), Jennifer Eichman (Lehigh University), Yi Jolan (National Taiwan University), Karin-Irene Eiermann (acatech, Berlin), Jeremy Taylor (University of Nottingham), Lena Henningsen (University of Freiburg) and Jesse Field (University of Minnesota). Our research and ideas were further honed by discussants Tim Wright (University of Sheffield), David Pattinson (University of Leeds) and Naomi Standen (University of Birmingham). We would also like to thank Ms Mary Jo Robertiello, Professor Wu Pei-yi's long-time companion, who made possible his attendance at the workshop.

Finally, we would like to dedicate this volume to Professor Wu Pei-yi, best known for his seminal work *The Confucian's Progress*, who gave a keynote paper at the workshop but unfortunately passed away a year later in April 2009. An enthusiastic participant, we remember him for the breadth and depth of his knowledge of Chinese biography and autobiography that informed our discussions and for his intellectual curiosity that stimulated further enquiry in us all. This volume is all the richer for his insight and observations, and it is a shame that he was unable to see it completed.

# Contributors

**Sarah Dauncey** is Lecturer in Chinese Studies at Sheffield University, UK and co-convenor of the dis/abilitystudies@sheffield network. She is currently working on a British Academy-funded monograph that will provide the first comprehensive study of changing literary and cultural representations of disability in China since 1976. Key publications include 'Screening Disability in the PRC: The Politics of Looking Good' (*China Information* 21:3, 2007), 'Three Days to Walk: A Personal Story of Life Writing and Disability Consciousness in China' (*Disability and Society* 27:3, 2012) and 'Breaking the Silence? Deafness, Disability and Education in Two Post-cultural Revolution Chinese Films' (in *Different Bodies: Disability in Film & Television*, ed. Marja Mogk, forthcoming).

**Marjorie Dryburgh** is Lecturer in Modern Chinese Studies at the University of Sheffield, UK. Her research focuses on the multiple social and political histories of twentieth-century China, and she has a longstanding interest in the tensions between personal histories – memoirs, autobiographies and diaries – and national or nationalising historical narrative. She is the author of *North China and Japanese Expansion, 1933–1937* (2000) and is now working on a study of memories of empire, war and their aftermath in north-east China, and their mediation between generations, genres and national communities.

**Alison Hardie** is Senior Lecturer in Chinese Studies at the University of Leeds, UK. She holds undergraduate degrees in Literae Humaniores (Ancient History and Greek and Latin Literature) from the University of Oxford and Chinese from the University of Edinburgh, UK. After a 16-year career in China trade, she studied for a doctorate in the history of Chinese garden design at the University of Sussex before becoming an academic. She is currently completing a monograph on identity and authenticity in the life and work of Ruan Dacheng, and is researching dramas written about politics and current affairs during the Ming-Qing transition.

**Isabelle Henrion-Dourcy** is Associate Professor of Anthropology at Université Laval, Canada. She has conducted extensive fieldwork among Tibetans, first in Lhasa (Tibet Autonomous Region), then among exiles in Dharamsala (India) and in Belgium. Recent publications include "Ache Lhamo: Jeux et enjeux d'une tradition théâtrale" (*Mélanges chinois et bouddhiques*, 2013); "Une rupture dans l'air: la télévision satellite de Chine dans la communauté tibétaine en exil à Dharamsala" (*Anthropologie et Sociétés*, 2012); and "Le théâtre tibétain ache lhamo: Un contenu d'héritage indien dans des formes d'héritage chinois?" (in *Théâtres d'Asie à l'œuvre: circulation, expression, politique*, ed. H. Bouvier-Smith and G. Toffin, 2012).

**Nicola Spakowski** is Professor of Sinology at the University of Freiburg, Germany. She previously held positions at the Free University of Berlin and at Jacobs University Bremen. Her research is dedicated to twentieth-century and contemporary China, in particular concepts of time, history and the future; feminism and women's studies; and the internationalisation, globalisation and regionalisation of China. She is the author of *'Mit Mut an die Front'. Die militärische Beteiligung von Frauen in der kommunistischen Revolution Chinas (1925–1949)* ('Courageously to the front': Women's military participation in the Chinese Communist revolution, 1925–1949, 2009).

**Chloë Starr** is Assistant Professor of Asian Theology and Christianity at Yale University Divinity School in the US. She is currently working on a volume on Chinese intellectual Christianity and a translation anthology of Chinese theology. Publications include *Red-Light Novels of the Late Qing* (2007), the edited volumes *China and the Quest for Gentility* (co-edited with Daria Berg, 2007) and *Reading Christian Scripture in China* (2008), and a textbook, *Documenting China: A Reader in Seminal Twentieth-Century Texts* (2011).

**Harriet T. Zurndorfer** is an Affiliated Fellow of the Leiden Institute of Asian Studies. She is the author of *Change and Continuity in Chinese Local History* (1989), *China Bibliography: A Research Guide to Reference Works about China Past and Present* (1995), editor of the compilation

*Chinese Women in the Imperial Past: New Perspectives* (1999), and has published more than 100 articles and reviews. From 1992 to 2000, she served as editor-in-chief of *The Journal of the Economic and Social History of the Orient*; she is also founder and editor-in-chief of the journal *Nan Nü: Men, Women and Gender in China*. She has been a Visiting Fellow at All Souls College (Oxford), Visiting Professor at the Sorbonne and a participant in the London School of Economics-sponsored project Global Economic History Network (2003–2006).

# Introduction: Writing and Reading Chinese Lives

*Marjorie Dryburgh*

China has long and rich traditions of life writing that run from its earliest historical records to the contemporary blogosphere. Biography was, for centuries, a central strand in historical writing, and this official, public life narration co-existed with 'social' biographies, necrologies, hagiographies, diaries, poetry, letters, essays and other genres that contained a wealth of reflection on character, experience, identity and the life course. These were preserved in personal collections, exchanged to cement friendships and social alliances, published to promote or challenge hegemonic values, or to enhance individual or communal reputations. China scholars have drawn on this work to supplement or interrogate the orthodox historical record and have mined life narrative for insights into shifting representations of ideas or practices, into generic conventions, and into changing modes of self-representation and identity formation.[1]

Despite this extensive and intensive use of life narrative texts in research, Chinese life writing practices received, until recently, relatively little scholarly attention outside China. Aside from Wolfgang Bauer's magisterial work on the *longue durée* of self-narrative, the bulk of work on the subject appears as sharply focused case studies on specific eras or genres, most notably by Wu Pei-yi's ground-breaking study of early autobiography or Lynn Struve's collection of personal accounts of seventeenth-century dynastic change.[2] In exploring highly exceptional lives and writings – works that were more candid and more personal than the majority – those studies have offered sophisticated insights into Chinese life writing practice and products, and have done much to inspire and inform later studies.

Common to these specialised studies are the observations that, first, much Chinese life writing was bound by strict conventions; second, that these conventions were at many times more assertively stated than those obtaining in Europe and North America; and third, that the distance between the life-as-lived and the life-as-written was, more often than not, greater in Chinese than in European traditions as convention was often privileged over reference.

In our own work, we have found the first empirical observation – that Chinese auto/biographers often confronted a set of firm generic and interpretive conventions – to be sound; we also observe, however, that the boundaries to these conventions were at times negotiable or otherwise mutable. Similarly, it is hard to deny that these conventions differed in many ways from those obtaining in Europe and North America: while the impulse to write an 'I', a 'she' or a 'he' may be international, expectations in China of how that storied subject was to be conceived and written were not only culturally situated but also often critically scrutinised by reading elites and, at times, policed by the state. That said, we note that recent scholarship has explored more purposefully the 'rules-based' dimensions of life writing and self-representation in European and North American contexts.

It is the third observation, though, that forms the major point of departure for the works in this collection. Here, we propose an understanding of life writing – as ordinary and extraordinary practice – that considers the gap between the life-as-lived and the life-as-written as a space that is productive both of insights and of further questions, and thus as a focus of enquiry in itself, rather than as a flaw in the Chinese work. Our contributors demonstrate in this volume that the conventions were far from being the whole story: that these might be observed, exploited, subverted or evaded to serve a range of personal and communal ends; that we may find the social meanings attached to written Chinese lives in the dialogue – and often in the tension – between formal convention and auto/biographical construction; and that this tension is not confined to subaltern genres or subjects, but may be observed across the range of life writings and writers. That understanding, that convention may be a resource as well as a constraint, offered (and continues to offer) both opportunities and challenges to the writers and readers of Chinese lives.

In producing this collection, we have examined life writings of self and others, men and women, exemplars and outcasts, from the seventeenth to the twenty-first centuries; while there is much of interest to be learned from earlier works, the record from those later centuries is particularly rich, and offers greater opportunities for working with a range of records of one life, comparing autobiographical with biographical work, official with personal records, and earlier or later renditions of life narrative. Within that longer period, we have aimed to question the conventional periodisations of dynasties, regimes or 'transitions to modernity', and our assumptions of their implications for genre and content in life writing practice. Examining those works, we ask what life narrative was designed to do – Whose lives are written, and why? Is the subject of the life narrative public or private, social or interior? How far are life stories understood as 'history-telling' as well as personal narratives? – and consider the implications of those questions for our reading of auto/biographical texts. We have adopted an inclusive definition of life writing, and chapters therefore explore not only biographies for a range of audiences but also autobiographical narratives, fictions and drama, diaries and blogs. Finally, we have aimed to avoid treating the works examined *a priori* as distinctively Chinese forms or as Chinese variations on other forms of life writing: only by calling those conventional categories into question can we develop a more nuanced understanding of the practices and processes of life writing (and indeed life reading) in any cultural context.

Chapter 1 critically explores the existing literature on Chinese life writing, highlighting the competing social, political and personal interests that shaped life narratives and that subtly destabilised the elite-centred traditions that formed the focus of most early studies. Chapters 2 and 3 analyse late imperial or early modern life writings, in Alison Hardie's comparison of competing biographies of official Ruan Dacheng (1587–1646) with Ruan's own efforts to challenge orthodox interpretations of his life in his dramatic composition, and Harriet Zurndorfer's exploration of the shifting terms on which lives were written and obscured and the role that self-conscious twentieth-century modernisers played in erasing the life history of the female scholar Wang Zhaoyuan (1763–1851) from the record. Chapters 4 and 5 examine the shifting relation between life writing and normative personae in the mid- and late twentieth century: Marjorie

Dryburgh highlights the use of the personal diary by calligrapher and wartime collaborator Zheng Xiaoxu (1860–1938) to reassert a moral self, and Nicola Spakowski reveals the deployment of self-narrative by women who took part in the Communist revolution in the 1930s and 1940s to destabilise later official Party renderings of political lives. Chapters 6, 7 and 8 analyse the life narratives produced by 'marginal' subjects in the reform era (1978–): Chloë Starr's study of the diaries and autobiographical fiction of Zhang Xianliang (b.1936) deconstructs the multi-layered self-exploration of a political outsider; Sarah Dauncey maps Zhang Haidi's (b.1955) journey from voiceless official exemplar to novelist and blog writer; and Isabelle Henrion-Dourcy analyses the reworking of autobiographical narratives by prominent Tibetans born in the 1910s as a form of 'history-telling' between Tibetan and Chinese audiences.

This introduction, however, focuses more sharply on three themes that have hitherto marked, possibly constrained, our reading of Chinese lives: how effectively *can* we read socially situated texts of this kind across cultures? How, and how far, did the conventions and prestige of officially sanctioned biography inhibit the emergence of other forms and other conventions of life writing and dictate the form of other work? Where is the subject in Chinese life narration and 'self'-narration, and what are its audiences? The chapters in this volume demonstrate the scope that exists for reading life narratives across culture as well as across time, while pointing to some of the specific challenges that this delicate navigation presents to readers of Chinese lives. They offer robust challenges to rooted assumptions of generic stasis, as they demonstrate the knowing deployment of genre – sometimes strategic, sometimes playful – by Chinese writers. Finally, while noting the common charge that the subject of life narrative in China was a construct existing at several removes from the writing or written individual, they propose a set of strategies for decoding the sometimes elusive subject in Chinese life writings.

## Reading across cultures

Philippe Lejeune has noted the tendency of critical works on autobiography and the diary to draw on a single national or linguistic body of material, and posed the provocative question, 'Is the "I" international? Is it possible to construct a theory of autobiography...without its carrying the mark of a specific culture or a particular ideology?'[3] and the question applies equally to biographical writing in its various forms. Lejeune's question poses an important challenge to anyone reading life and self-narratives produced outside the Euro-American context in which the majority of the analytical frameworks commonly deployed in auto/biographical studies were developed: can those frameworks lead us towards a better understanding of storied Chinese selves? We suggest that, while the Euro-American literature does not offer a precise map of the Chinese textscape, it may nonetheless offer useful navigational strategies.

True, it was once commonplace to treat genres such as autobiography as products of a peculiarly 'western' consciousness; and the editors of a new collection of essays on Chinese women's biography concluded that even 'recent innovations in scholarship and critical theory on the Romanticism-inspired Western biographical tradition...rarely offer methods applicable to the Chinese tradition'.[4] However, rising international scholarly dialogue, the rapid diversification and heightened reflexivity manifested in auto/biography studies, and greater attention to life writing practice beyond European and North American territory and traditions has considerably eroded that earlier certainty.[5] In China, Yang Zhengrun's ambitious project that attempts to establish a theoretical framework for understanding Chinese biography in comparative perspective reveals a similar interest.[6]

Thus the reification of the distance in 'culture' between narratives of lives lived and written in China, and a critical literature largely produced in Europe and North America risks creating artificial barriers to understanding, and obscuring the equally important distances in moral and material environment that might separate lives lived, lives written and lives read across time, even within a narrower spatial or social framework. As China scholarship has become more sensitive to the changes over time and space within Chinese histories, and to their connections with global frameworks, these assumptions of essential difference cannot hold.[7] If we are to follow Maureen Perkins in thinking beyond the east–west binaries that once shaped understandings of life writing work, we must also be sensitive to the variations within Chinese practice.[8] To apply the analogy to another category: a superficial reading of, for example, early modern English religious lives might inspire some vague sense of community in a

British reader today, through the recognition of local details and a distant familiarity with the struggles of the time between church and state. Yet the mentalities that produced the sixteenth-century martyrdoms documented by John Foxe and the seventeenth-century emergence of Puritanism were not only unfamiliar to many twenty-first-century audiences but also quite distinct from each other, and the demands made of individuals at different points in that shifting politico-religious landscape might be documented in very different ways for profoundly different purposes.[9]

Examining Chinese practice in a similar spirit, we should be sensitive to the distorting effect of twentieth-century upheavals on later understandings of earlier lives, values and life writing practice. As Dorothy Ko has pointed out, both the May Fourth/New Culture movement of the 1910s and 1920s – styled variously as an 'intellectual revolution' or a 'Chinese Enlightenment' – and the Communist movement relied heavily for legitimation on a construction of imperial China as a monolithic Other, gripped by rigidly formalistic, feudal and patriarchal values. Just as this construction combined in historical writing with ethnocentric feminist discourse to produce a powerful but under-nuanced image of women as the 'wretched ones' of Chinese history,[10] so too in studies of life writing is there a risk that our understanding of Chinese life writing may be obscured by reductive readings both of auto/biography theory and of the complexities of Chinese social and writing practices as these are shaped by time, space and regimes of gender, class and ethnicity. Clearly, we cannot simply pour Chinese evidence into one end of theories formed in other cultural environments and expect to see rigorous scholarship dispensed at the other; yet it is nonetheless worth asking seriously what questions these bodies of work raise about each other. The Chinese academy offers no easy answers to these questions, though that is not to say that the Chinese work is of no interest. Margaretta Jolly, writing in 1999, noted the diversity of approaches then visible within the Chinese scholarship, from the search for the 'true and real' in biography to the exploration of interpersonal devices in autobiographical writing, and the assumption by many Chinese scholars of profound differences between Chinese and Western traditions of life writing,[11] and these tendencies still mark the range of newer work.

At one end of the range, Chinese-language studies maintain their long-standing focus on genre theorisation and material classification, but also consider questions of 'accuracy', 'impartiality' and ways to consider occasions when authors might 'deliberately turn their back on the truth'.[12] Consequently, texts are often assessed purely in terms of their empirical content – as a marker of their historical value – rather than as social artefacts. The pre-occupation with the 'true and real' in life writing is both deeply rooted and strikingly ironic. The claim to offer moral lessons drawn from true life stories was central to the legitimacy of traditional historical biography, and anxieties over that core truth claim haunted official biographers. The rejection of those truth claims in the early twentieth century, and the charges of formalism and instrumentalism levelled at traditional biography, promised newly authentic modes of auto/biography, yet much of this work was in practice heavily influenced by newer, but equally instrumental and equally formalist concepts of 'truth and reality'. The tensions between understandings of truth and reality as absolutes that can be detached from the frameworks of values (now super-seded or discredited) within which earlier life narratives were created, and assumptions that later narratives must nonetheless reflect truth and reality within a proper framework of values appear impossible to resolve. While the terms on which lives are written may be reworked to encompass 'truth, virtue, beauty ... and the national spirit' in the abstract, in place of other moralities that might be labelled specifi-cally 'Confucian' or 'socialist', the insistence on values remains, as does the predictable obsolescence of once-usable life narratives as those values shift.[13]

At the other end of the range, close studies of the construc-tion of self-narratives, as seen in the work of Li Zhanzi, offer new directions and opportunities to explore the uses and the claims to authenticity of individual narratives and of wider, changing prac-tices. Li's published work explores the relation between language and self-narrative, in nuanced studies of the interpersonal mode in autobiographical writing and of autobiographical treatments of language-learning and identity formation.[14] Yet it is striking, first, that Li's case studies for these works all come from European or American writings and, second, that these or similar approaches are not widely reflected in the analysis of Chinese life writing practice: Li's work is cited by scholars working on a range of texts in pub-lic communication, but has only rarely been taken up within auto/ biographical studies.

That said, the textscape is changing in ways that challenge us to rethink the Chinese auto/biographical. Even relatively conservative scholars writing in China on traditionally published work point to changes in understandings of who gets a life, with celebrities and ordinary people joining state and business leaders, scientists and cultural figures as biographical subjects,[15] and the increasing visibility of oral history in both scholarship and social activism, or of online life writing, is extending these understandings still further. There has been growing interest in more private or ephemeral forms of life writing, such as diaries, travel journals, letters, blogs and images; yet there is a significant difference in the way in which these materials are approached.[16] All of the above appear in Yang Zhengrun's comprehensive list of genres; yet all are classed as 'marginal autobiography', 'sub-autobiography' or 'experimental autobiography', which raises intriguing questions about the perceived value of writing by non-professionals.

The space devoted to the deliberation of who or what makes an appropriate biographer, subject or writing style highlights this further. Guo Jiulin, for example, asserts that successful biographers require qualities including 'a devotion to the truth', 'integrity', 'the skill of a historian', 'the mind of a philosopher' and the 'the pen of an author'.[17] While this reveals both an interest in historical reflection and a concern for the direction of future biographical writing in China, the question of exactly *whose* values are being applied in these analyses begs consideration.

We may suggest, as a first step, that the most adaptable analytical tools are those that allow processes – of imagining or narrating, self-fashioning or self-criticism – to be decoupled from content, and from specific values, ambitions and audiences. In Spakowski and Dryburgh's essays, narrative theory and the notion of 'autobiographical living' offer lenses through which the revolutionary struggles of Communist women and the anxieties of wartime collaborators may be scrutinised. These approaches offer frameworks for reading, but demand also that we ask (rather than assume) how our subjects might have chosen to fill in those frameworks. Both authors acknowledge the questions that these approaches leave unanswered, yet in highlighting the silences that remain in documented lives, they emphasise the distance between the life-as-lived and the life-as-written – which is surely an inherent feature of life writing, rather than a localised shortfall in the Chinese literature.

## Reading genre

Life writing is marked by generic diversity. As Hermione Lee demonstrates, even within a 'very short introduction' to British literary biography it is possible to accord equal weight to observance *and* violations of convention; Sidonie Smith and Julia Watson identify 52 sub-types of autobiographical narrative, from apologia via memoir to *testimonio* and beyond; and Lejeune's work on diary covers diaries spiritual and secular, diaries inflected by gender and generation, diaries written with a goose-feather quill and at a keyboard,[18] each freighted with distinct generic convention. As for China, Joan Judge and Hu Ying's list of forty-odd traditional biographical genres is clearly not exhaustive.[19] A critical understanding of genre and its implications is central to the reading of life narratives and to the pursuit of the elusive selves packaged therein.

The earlier critical literature on China focuses above all on the official biography of dynastic history,[20] a form often marked by elite interest and didactic zeal. While we have been taught to see this form as hegemonic, this existed from its inception in uneasy relation to other life stories written for different audiences and interests. Chinese lives were written intensively across a range of genres: if we confine our attention to explicitly marked auto/biographical texts, we risk missing the life narration or self-narration – the 'auto/biographical living' – packaged into poetry, essays, diaries, prefaces or postfaces to longer works, drama, funerary and other occasional writings and the visual arts. If we are to map this complex generic landscape we must probe the messages of genre and the factors informing the strategic, instrumental decisions taken on genre by writers of lives; and the task here is possibly not so different to the task facing scholars of early modern European life writing.[21]

The commonly cited conventions of the orthodox biographical form did not apply with equal weight to all auto/biographical writings. While biographical works were often more concerned with didactic functions and were relatively respectful of the conventions, and while studies of early autobiographical writing and more recent oral history have argued that official biography often exerted a stifling influence on self-narration,[22] other studies – including some chapters in this volume – have found in autobiographies a purposeful and artful exploitation of generic possibilities, rather than a resigned submission to generic constraints. This is particularly striking where third-person and first-person narratives of the same lives illuminate differing authorial choices. Spakowski's study of the biographies and autobiographies of revolutionary women demonstrates the ways in which strategies of self-narration may decentre an orthodox tale. Similarly, Dauncey reveals that, if we remove the biographical filters from Zhang Haidi, we find someone who wrote her own life more authoritatively and more creatively than her edited, 'biographised' self might lead us to expect.

Within the broad categories of biographical and autobiographical, sub-categories proliferated. Taxonomic anxiety appears as comedic device in Lu Xun's classic 1920s novella *The True Story of Ah-Q*: – 'What kind of a biography was it to be?...You really do have to be so darned careful about titles. But there are so many! Why, just for biography alone there are enough titles hanging around to make your head swim: *narrative biography, autobiography, private biography, public biography, supplementary biography, family biography, biographical sketch...*'[23] – yet generic distinctions and choices were serious matters. Zurndorfer underlines the differing conventions of the standard biography, with its well-established didactic freight, and the chronological biography (*nianpu*), which appealed to early twentieth-century, self-consciously modernising intellectuals as a more factual, 'scientific' and authoritative mode of writing; the choice of genre here implied simultaneously a judgement on the subject and an act of self-fashioning by the author. Hardie's work on Ruan Dacheng reveals the diverging interests underlying personal, local and official biographies: each form was considered the proper domain of writers who differed in their relation to the biographical subject and represented different interests, and each produced very distinct portraits of the person.

Additionally, the conventions of genre might change over time and according to the conditions within which lives were written. In the 1930s, the diary form was lampooned by novelist Qian Zhongshu: '...spiritual narcissism had prompted him to write an autobiography and keep a diary...to prove from every angle and with every kind of fact [his] noble character. Now whenever he said or did something, he was thinking at the same time how to record it in his diary or in his record of deeds and sayings.'[24] Yet the diarists examined in this volume – collaborationist premier Zheng Xiaoxu and novelist Zhang Xianliang – reveal the multiple possibilities and problems of self-narration. Whereas diary practice for some earlier diarists[25] was marked by the drive to discipline the moral being and to fit it for action, Dryburgh proposes that Zheng used the diary to reassemble on the page a moral persona that he was unable to realise in practice, with little overt commentary on the political challenges that he faced in life and his inability to rise to them. Zhang Xianliang, Starr argues, writing in the early People's Republic, when self-narration was almost inescapably public, created in his diary not a life story that could be judged as more or less candid or authentic, but a string of prompts that did not immediately disclose – possibly did not determine – their associated memories, from which Zhang later reconstructed in fiction his diaried life. Here, the reworking in the novels of experiences foreshadowed in the diary flagged the writing of a life as a work in constant progress. In each case the diary is not a life-made-text, but stands at one or more removes from the acting self.

As well as revealing what was politically prudent and artistically satisfying to Zhang in different genres at different times, this suggests also that life narration was above all an iterative practice, rather than summative. This applies also to Wang Zhaoyuan as she shifted in and out of the biographical gaze, or to Zhang Haidi as she struggled to snatch subjectivity from the jaws of socialist spiritual civilisation. In some contexts, such as late imperial social biography, the costs of violating generic and moral convention were intangible, possibly negligible; in other times, places or moral environments – notably in the coerced self-narration of the 1950s and 1960s, as Starr has indicated – failure adequately to account for oneself or others might attract severe sanctions. Yet the knowledge that self- and life-narration were scrutinised by the powerful did not deter all attempts to take ownership of the narrative: Henrion-Dourcy's analysis of Tibetan auto/biographical narratives reveals the purposeful manipulation both of indigenous Tibetan forms and of Chinese, state-sponsored history-telling as history-tellers adapted their tales to different audiences and to the narrative needs of different times. The essays in this volume demonstrate that while many of those who wrote lives for themselves or others recognised the power of the text, few were willing slaves to its conventions.

## In search of subject

Such is the weight accorded to convention and trope in many accounts of Chinese life narratives that convention itself – rather than the lives recorded within conventional frameworks – may appear to be the true subject of Chinese life narrative. Instead of the 'discovery of a human soul',[26] the task of a biographer appeared to have been to pack the fragments of a life or of a career into a mould formed by value and precedent; the task of an autobiographer, more often than not, was to mimic that work. Of the lives and narratives examined in this volume, many were written to affirm community; to assert shared identity; to declare adherence to collective values; or to address an imagined audience. While themes of community – political, intellectual, social, familial – are well represented in the literature of early modern Europe, later auto/biographical writing was for decades more typically held to be marked indelibly by a distinctively 'western' notion of the autonomous, individualised self,[27] and the apparent centrality of community to Chinese life writing traditions has thus been taken as a key marker of difference.

This assumption has been challenged on two fronts. First, newer scholarship offers a more nuanced approach to practices of self-narration in extra-European and postcolonial societies.[28] Second, auto/biography theory itself is shifting: Paul John Eakin noted in 1999 that '... autobiography criticism has not yet fully addressed the extent to which the self is defined by – and lives in terms of – its relations with others', and his more recent work has explored in greater depth the social rules that surround self-narration in Europe and North America.[29] Recent work on memoir – distinct from autobiography in its tendency to focus on episodes within a life, rather than on the whole, and in the use of the term to include relational lives and lives of others – also reminds us of the often porous boundaries in auto/biographical work.[30]

Given the role that 'paradigms of collectivity' have had in discouraging scholarly attention to life histories and life writing beyond Europe and North America, Eakin's analysis of relational western lives is instructive; and David Arnold's formulation of the 'self-in-society' in the study of Indian life narratives appears to offer more sophisticated insights both into life narratives and into the societies in which these were produced than the traditional binary oppositions of individualism and collectivism.[31] And the reading of auto/biography for social insight is by no means unique to the Chinese work: Denis Twitchett's argument that Chinese biographical writing 'not only throws into relief the motives, preoccupations and interests of its authors, but also illuminates the relationships existing between the individuals who provide its subjects and society as a whole' echoes Robert Sayre's comment that 'Autobiographies … may reveal as much about the author's assumed audience as they do about him or her, and this is a further reason why they need to be read as cultural documents, not just as personal ones.'[32]

Most significantly, Eakin draws on recent strands of work in philosophy and cognitive psychology that conceptualise the self variously as the product of speech or narrative acts, or as an effect of 'multiple registers of self-experience' that may exist 'ecologically' (in relation to the physical environment), 'interpersonally' (in interaction with others), 'in extension' (in memory of the past and expectation of the future), 'privately' (through experience that is not accessible to others) or 'conceptually' (through socially constructed roles, identities and theories of self).[33] The self of autonomy and interiority occupies a small territory indeed within these registers; and to return to one of the ur-texts of the 'modern' self-narrative, while Rousseau presented his *Confessions*[34] as a new and naked self-narrative, the self that first grabs our attention is not the self 'honestly' told within the main text, but the self of the opening paragraphs, in bravura performance to the author's peers.

## 'Our public needs us': The self in society

Community, values and audience played central roles in the production and circulation of life narratives in China, and any reading of storied selves depends on an understanding of that social context. While communities might be defined by kinship or shared place of origin, they were also intimately bound to assumptions of shared values. More often than not, writers wrote as if for their peers, engaging purposefully with the communities into which they wrote their own or others' lives, and with the potential or imagined audiences of those life histories. That engagement need not be read in every case as a submission, and the self was not invariably subsumed into society. For some who aimed to avoid scrutiny or censure – notably Ruan Dacheng in the seventeenth century and Zhang Xianliang in the twentieth century – their reticence was prompted more by an aware-ness of the reputational or judicial consequences of differences in values than by an assumed distinction between 'public' and 'private' domains and writings.[35]

Community mattered, nonetheless, at the simplest and most prac-tical level, as the longevity of texts often depended on familial, social or intellectual networks. This was particularly the case for life writing produced in troubled times;[36] however, if we consider auto/biographical 'survival' to include the wider visibility and rep-utation of the subject, as well as the physical survival of the text, we find subtler modes of erasure at work. We should, for example, be mindful of the relations of power within which life stories were produced, received and circulated. While neither biographical nor autobiographical subject could expect to retain control over his or her life story, its audiences and their interpretations of that story, the bio-graphical subject was by some margin in a weaker position than the autobiographical. Biographers had – or could at least reach for – the power to embed individuals in the historical record or to erase them from it, and to shape audience understanding of values through the carefully crafted and filtered messages of those biographies. The bio-graphical subject was rarely in a position autonomously to demand or command an audience's attention, or to negotiate the terms of the subject–reader relationship, but depended instead on the mediation of the biographer to reach that audience, and was vulnerable to the biographer's understanding and representation of his/her life.

Hardie's analysis of Ruan Dacheng's drama shows one contentious subject's efforts to escape that predicament. The canonical biogra-phies of Ruan Dacheng reflect the hostile views of those whom he had alienated in his lifetime; Ruan's packaging of self-narrative into drama suggests an assertive quest for other audiences beyond the highly educated elite who controlled official biographies, and is con-sistent with the expansive and impulsive character described by his contemporaries. As well as challenging the status of the educated elite as primary author and audience for his life narrative, Ruan questioned the very basis on which biographical judgements were made, building his plots on misapprehensions, misrepresentations and mistaken identities to highlight the fragility of understandings of character, motive and action. In this Ruan appears as a mirror image of Zheng Xiaoxu, who used his diary to record, meticulously, the traces of an orthodox life, despite his transgressive political choices. Auto/biographical survival might be threatened as communities rose and fell in status and understandings of who was an exemplar worthy of public attention shifted across time. As Zurndorfer shows, Wang Zhaoyuan's reputation as a talented scholar was established in the nineteenth century, at a time when women's learning was valued by elite families, only to be eclipsed in the early twentieth century, first because of her association with those discredited traditions and then because of her sex, even as other women, whose lives were more fitted to the exemplary categories of post-May-Fourth China, achieved acceptance as legitimate auto/biographical subjects through their explorations of fiction and explicitly auto/biographical genres.[37]

Moreover, the doors opened by officially sponsored or hegemonic biography might remain open to autobiographical writing and memoir, allowing self-narrators access to an established audience; and Spakowski's study in this volume suggests that neither the audience nor the commissioning authority necessarily determined autobiographical performance. While we may assume a shared audience for auto/biographical stories of revolutionary women, as those women reasserted control over their life stories, they produced accounts that were subtly but quite insistently distinct from the orthodox narratives into which earlier biographers had packaged their lives. In Henrion-Dourcy's contribution, too, we see that, even as the state worked to co-opt individual life histories by commissioning auto/biographical works, Tibetans such as Lhalu Tsewang Dorje and Lobsang Tenzin gently subverted the terms of the state project to produce life narratives that spoke to Tibetan audiences in China on quite different terms.

Dauncey's analysis of auto/biographical writing and disability points to a similar shift. While Chinese people with disabilities were until the 1980s rendered virtually invisible by discourses that valorised physical labour and physical vigour,[38] some, most famously Zhang Haidi, were subsequently elevated to model status, provided that their moral ambitions and achievements offered compensation for their impaired bodies. While the imagined audiences of this new exemplary biography may well have overlapped with the intended audience of Zhang Haidi's autobiographical fiction or her blog, the unmediated Zhang is strikingly more authoritative than the plucky but disabled heroine of official representation.

Thus the relation between texts and contexts, between lives, communities and values, between auto/biographical authors or subjects and their audiences, and between convention and referentiality undoubtedly shape many written Chinese lives. Yet these relations are not fixed: they are often tense, or fractious, or subject to repeated renegotiation, and an informed reading of Chinese lives demands that we consider the precise configurations within which a given life was written, rather than taking these relations as given or transparent. At the same time, while the Chinese literature is substantial and increasingly sophisticated, it is important to consider also what use we can best make of the analytical work generated by scholars working outside China, in studies of other traditions of life writing. The chapters in this volume suggest a range of approaches that may be taken to the problem; they also highlight the work that remains to be done in developing our understanding of Chinese life writing work.

## Notes

1. Recent work that relies heavily on auto/biographical material to explore late imperial and twentieth-century society includes Joseph Esherick, *Ancestral Leaves: A Family Journey through Chinese History* (Berkeley: University of California Press, 2011); Beata Grant, *Eminent Nuns: Women Chan Masters of Seventeenth-century China* (Honolulu: University of Hawaii Press, 2009); Joan Judge and Hu Ying, eds., 'Introduction,' in *Beyond Exemplar Tales: Women's Biography in Chinese History* (Berkeley: University of California Press, 2011); Susan Mann, *The Talented Women of the Zhang Family* (Berkeley: University of California Press, 2007); William T. Rowe, *Saving the World: Chen Hongmou and Elite Consciousness in Eighteenth-century China* (Stanford: Stanford University Press, 2001).
2. Wolfgang Bauer, *Das Antlitz Chinas: die Autobiographische Selbstdarstellung in der Chinesischen Literatur von ihren Anfängen bis heute* (The face of China: autobiographical self-representation from its origins to the present) (Munich: Carl Hanser Verlag, 1990); Wu Pei-yi, *The Confucian's Progress: Autobiographical Writings in Traditional China* (Princeton: Princeton University Press, 1990); Lynn Struve, *Voices from the Ming-Qing Cataclysm: China in Tigers' Jaws* (New Haven: Yale University Press, 1998). For a fuller

discussion of the state of the field, see Chapter 1 and the works cited therein.

3. Philippe Lejeune, 'Le Moi est-il International?/Is the I International?,' tr. Jean Yamasaki Toyama *Biography* 32.1 (2009): 1–15.

4. Judge and Hu, 'Introduction,' 7; the very rich essays contained in this volume are a model of scholarship based on the chosen methods of close, interpretive reading, the search for non-canonical sources and the emphasis on texts authored by women. Elsewhere, Wang Jing quotes Georges Gusdorf and Roy Pascal to this effect; while she rejects their assertion in its strongest form she nonetheless holds that China had no meaningful autobiographical tradition before the early twentieth century. *When 'I' Was Born: Women's Autobiography in Modern China* (Madison: University of Wisconsin Press, 2009), 3, 16–26.

5. Compare, for example, Phyllis E. Wachter, 'Annual Bibliography of Works About Life Writing, 1999–2000,' *Biography* 23.4 (2000): 695–755 (listing around 360 works) with 'Annual Bibliography of Works About Life Writing, 2009–2010,' *Biography* 33.4 (2010): 714–846 (listing around 680 works); yet note that, in each case, fewer than 10% of those works address practice beyond Europe and North America.

6. Yang Zhengrun, *Xiandai zhuanji xue* (A modern poetics of biography) (Nanjing: Nanjing daxue chubanshe, 2009).

7. For a concise and lucid account of Chinese history that takes seriously both internal changes and global connections, see Paul Ropp, *China in World History* (Oxford: Oxford University Press, 2010).

8. See the essays, collected in Maureen Perkins, ed., *Locating Life Stories: Beyond East-West Binaries in (Auto)biographical Studies* (Honolulu: University of Hawaii Press, 2012), on practice in Australia, Hawaii, India, Indonesia, Malaysia and South Africa.

9. See John Foxe's *The Unabridged Acts and Monuments Online* or TAMO (HRI Online Publications, Sheffield, 2011), especially the editors' prefatory comments in 'About TAMO'. Available from: http://www.johnfoxe.org/ (accessed 28 July 2011), and compare that layered polemic with the intimacy of the Puritan diaries discussed by scholars such as Margo Todd, Tom Webster and Theodore de Welles; see Todd, 'Puritan Self-Fashioning: The Diary of Samuel Ward,' *Journal of British Studies* 31.3 (1992): 236–264; Webster, 'Writing to Redundancy: Approaches to Spiritual Journals and Early Modern Spirituality,' *The Historical Journal* 39.1 (1996): 33–56; de Welles, 'Sex and Sexual Attitudes in Seventeenth-Century England: The Evidence from Puritan Diaries,' *Renaissance and Reformation* 24.1 (1988): 45–64.

10. Dorothy Ko, *Teachers of the Inner Chambers: Women and Culture in Seventeenth-century China* (Stanford: Stanford University Press, 1994), 1–5.

11. Margaretta Jolly, 'Approaching the Auto/biographical Turn,' from 'The First International Conference on Auto/Biography' held at Peking University, 21–24 June 1999. Unpublished Conference Report (accessed 8 October 2012).

12. Yang Zhengrun, *Xiandai zhuanji xue*. The new challenges faced in a rapidly changing China in the quest for 'authenticity' and a proper moral stance, in biographies of historical or contemporary figures, are discussed by Sang Fengkang: 'Zhuanji zaoyu shuangrenjian – zai shichang jingji tiaojian xia de zhuanji xiezuo' (A double-edged sword – writing biography in a market economy), *Jingmen zhiye jishu xueyuan xuebao* (Journal of Jingmen Technical College) 20.2 (2005): 1–5.

13. Quan Zhan, 'Minzu jingshen, minjian lichang, pingminhua shijiao: xin shiji pingmin zhuanji zonglun' (National spirit, grassroots standpoint and common people's perspective: a review of common people's biographies in the new century), *Zhejiang shifan daxue xuebao* (Journal of Zhejiang Normal University) 31.6 (2006): 7–13.

14. Li Zhanzi, 'Di er ren cheng zai zizhuan de renji gongneng' (The interpersonal function of second-person address in autobiography), *Waiguo yu* (Journal of Foreign Languages) 6.6 (2000): 51–56; 'Zizhuanzhong fenshen biaoda de renji yiyi' (The interpersonal significance of reflexive expression in autobiography), *Waiyu jiaoxue* (Foreign language education) 22.3 (2001): 7–13; 'Xianzai shi zai zizhuan huayu zhong de renji yiyi' (The interpersonal significance of the present tense in the language of autobiography), *Waiyu yu waiyu jiaoxue* (Foreign languages and their teaching) 154 (2002): 3–7; '<Fayu ke> yuyan xide, wenhua shenfen he zizhuan sucai' (French lessons: language acquisition, cultural identity and autobiography) *Sichuan waiyu xueyuan xuebao* (Journal of the Sichuan Institute of Foreign Languages) 21.4 (2005): 70–74.

15. Quan Zhan, 'Shiji zhi jiao: Zhongguo zhuanji wenxue de liu da redian' (At the turn of the century: six key points in Chinese biographical literature) *Huaibei zhiye jishu xueyuan xuebao* (Journal of the Huaibei Professional and Technical Institute) 1.1 (2002): 34–36.

16. This difference was noted by Margaretta Jolly in her conference report 'Approaching the Auto/biographical Turn'.

17. Guo Jiulin, 'Zhongguo zhuanji wenxue fazhan gailun' (Introduction to the development of Chinese biography), *Wenyi baijia* (Arts Forum) 7 (2010): 107.

18. Hermione Lee, *Biography: A Very Short Introduction* (Oxford: Oxford University Press, 2009); Sidonie Smith and Julia Watson, *Reading Autobiography: A Guide for Interpreting Life Narratives* (Minneapolis: University of Minnesota Press, 2001), 189–207; Philippe Lejeune, *On Diary*, tr. Jeremy D. Popkin and Julie Rak (University of Hawaii Press, 2009). See also, of course, Margaretta Jolly, ed., *Encyclopaedia of Life Writing*, 2 vols., (London: Routledge, 2001).

19. Judge and Hu, *Beyond Exemplar Tales*, 5–6, 287–290.

20. Denis Twitchett, 'Chinese Biographical Writing,' in W.G. Beasley and E.G. Pulleyblank, eds., *Historians of China and Japan* (London: Oxford University Press, 1961), 95–114. On dynastic history, see On-cho Ng and Q. Edward Wang, *Mirroring the Past: The Writing and Use of History in Imperial China* (Honolulu: University of Hawaii Press, 2005).

21. Kevin Sharpe and Stephen Zwicker, eds., 'Introducing Lives,' in *Writing Lives: Biography and Textuality, Identity and Representation in Early Modern England* (Oxford: Oxford University Press, 2008), 1–28.
22. Wu, *The Confucian's Progress*, 3–7; Gail Hershatter, 'Getting a Life: The Production of 1950s Women Labor Models in Rural Shaanxi,' in Judge and Hu, eds., *Beyond Exemplar Tales*, especially 49–51.
23. Lu Xun, *Diary of a Madman and Other Stories*, tr. William Lyall (Honolulu: University of Hawaii Press, 1990), 101–102.
24. Qian Zhongshu, *Fortress Besieged*, tr. Jeanne Kelly and Nathan K. Mao (London: Penguin, 2004), 142.
25. Lynn A. Struve, 'Self-Struggles of a Martyr: Memories, Dreams, and Obsessions in the Extant Diary of Huang Chunyao,' *Harvard Journal of Asiatic Studies* 69.2 (2009): 343–394.
26. Critic and biographer Emil Ludwig, writing in 1936 and quoted in Laura Marcus, 'The Newness of the 'New Biography',' in Peter France and William St Clair, eds., *Mapping Lives: The Uses of Biography* (Oxford: Oxford University Press, 2002), 196.
27. Sharpe and Zwicker, eds., *Writing Lives*; Stephen Greenblatt, *Renaissance Self-Fashioning: from More to Shakespeare* (London: University of Chicago Press, 1980); Georges Gusdorf, 'Conditions and Limits of Autobiography,' in James Olney, ed., *Autobiography: Essays Theoretical and Critical* (Princeton: Princeton University Press, 1980), 28–49.
28. See, for example, Ronald P. Loftus, *Telling Lives: Women's Self-writing in Modern Japan* (Honolulu: University of Hawaii Press, 2004); David Arnold and Stuart, eds., *Telling Lives in India: Biography, Autobiography and Life History* (Bloomington: Indiana University Press, 2004); Nawar Al-Hassan Golley, ed., *Arab Women's Lives Retold: Exploring Identity through Writing* (Syracuse: Syracuse University Press, 2007); David Huddart, *Postcolonial Theory and Autobiography* (London: Routledge, 2008); Bart Moore-Gilbert, *Postcolonial Life-writing: Culture, Politics and Self-representation* (London: Routledge, 2009).
29. Paul John Eakin, *How Our Lives Become Stories: Making Selves* (Ithaca: Cornell University Press, 1999), 43.
30. Thomas Couser, *Memoir: An Introduction* (Oxford: Oxford University Press, 2011), 9; Ben Yagoda, *Memoir: A History* (New York: Riverhead Books, 2009).
31. Eakin, *How Our Lives Become Stories*, 43–99; David Arnold, 'Introduction: Life Histories in India,' in *Telling Lives in India*, 2–3, 19–20.
32. Twitchett, 'Chinese Biographical Writing,' 95; Robert Sayre quoted in Smith and Watson, *Reading Autobiography*.
33. See Eakin's discussion of the work of Antony Paul Kerby and Ulric Neisser in *How Our Lives Become Stories*, 21–25; quoted phrase from 22.
34. Jean-Jacques Rousseau, *Les Confessions de J J Rousseau. Tome Premier*, London, 1786. Online via Eighteenth Century Collections Online (accessed 1 August 2011).
35. Understandings of 'privacy' are explored in Bonnie S. McDougall and Anders Hansson, eds., *Chinese Concepts of Privacy* (Leiden: Brill, 2002).

36. Life writings from the late Ming – the late sixteenth and early seventeenth centuries – for example, were threatened after the 1660s by the efforts of the newly established Qing dynasty to assert dynastic legitimacy, manage Chinese elites and suppress anti-Qing and anti-Manchu expression, manifested in the assertive scrutiny, collection and censorship of literary works. See R. Kent Guy, *The Emperor's Four Treasuries: Scholars and State in the Late Ch'ien-lung Era* (Cambridge: Harvard University Asia Center, 1987), especially 17–30. The destruction of potentially incriminating personal documents is a common trope in memoirs of the late twentieth century.

37. Zhu Xichen, 'Zhongguo xiandai nüzuojia zhuanji xiezuo zongshu' (Overview of biographies of women writers in modern China), *Xueshujie* (Academics in China) 5 (2006): 270–274.

38. As well as the sources cited by Dauncey, see Andrew D. Morris, *Marrow of the Nation: A History of Sport and Physical Culture in Republican China* (Berkeley: University of California Press, 2004), and Susan Brownell, *Training the Body for China: Sports in the Moral Order of the People's Republic* (London: University of Chicago Press, 1995).

# 1
# Chinese Life Writing: Themes and Variations

*Marjorie Dryburgh and Sarah Dauncey*

The critical literature on Chinese life writing has expanded rapidly in the past two decades: while only a handful of studies were produced before the 1990s, the past two decades have seen the publication of specialised monographs and essay collections, several dozen scholarly articles and a growing body of translations. That has produced a collection of very rich and scholarly works that, in their individual insights, do much to advance our understanding of categories of life narratives as historical sources, life narratives as artefacts and life writing as social practice. The growth of that corpus of specialised studies challenges our understanding of the wider context of life writing practice and life writing texts, and has produced a divided literature in which more general studies that tend to emphasise the 'rules of the game' (and in China, as elsewhere, life writing is a rules-based practice[1]) exist in uneasy tension with more specialised works that highlight variations on, and departures from, those established patterns.[2] Whereas, once, it was possible to understand Chinese auto/biography as overwhelmingly 'Confucian',[3] didactic, state-centred and masculine, more recent work has highlighted frequent departures from that apparent norm.

The cumulative effect of recent research has been to populate the field with so many exceptions that the 'rules' are sometimes obscured; it is time, we suggest, to look again at those rules and their place within the wider range of life writing practice. In this chapter, therefore, we offer a critical reappraisal of the existing literature on Chinese life writing that aims, first, tentatively to map the landscape in which our own chapters are sited and, second, to point to some of the unresolved questions raised by that literature. We will also suggest some of the challenges inherent in drawing general conclusions from a body of diverse, fragmentary material that was produced across many centuries, and whose porous boundaries are not yet fully charted. We would not argue that life writing practice across the smaller territory of western Europe had remained unchanged across a comparable period and do not think it wise to suggest the same of China, despite the rather greater efforts expended by state and elites in maintaining the appearance of a unified, empire-wide (later, nation-wide) culture.

To set that reappraisal in context, we will begin by highlighting some of the factors in strategies of composition, selection and preservation that have shaped and filtered the life writing corpus as it now survives and that thereby shape our understanding of life writing practice. The remainder of the chapter is structured along loosely chronological lines, addressing first the early traditions from which many assumptions on the nature and development of life writing in China were formed, before examining other work on the period covered by the later chapters in this volume. First, the critical literature on early life narratives reveals the assumptions on the power of orthodoxy in historical and biographical writing that are reflected in much of the existing scholarship; at the same time, it shows the inherent tensions and internal variations in those developing traditions, and the external pressures created by other, competing narrative forms, and suggests that those traditions and that assumed orthodoxy may have been less robust than once supposed. Second, work on life writing practice between the fourteenth and early twentieth centuries shows that social changes and new intellectual stimuli prompted changes in the authorship, audiences and uses of life narrative, as social biographies and personal memoirs were deployed in the negotiation and articulation of personal and group identities and values, and thus reflected shifting currents of change. Finally, studies of auto/biography from the late twentieth century highlight the efforts of the state to control the content and circulation of life narratives, the reception of those efforts and their complex legacies as the state becomes less assertive. Thus the literature reveals, on one hand, that state and non-state elites harboured powerful ambitions to manage the production and publication of life writings on terms that served their own interests but, on the other hand, that neither those interests, nor the conventions developed to defend them, were fixed, and that these were repeatedly re-appropriated, recast or rejected by others seeking new ways of storying lives and building communities.

Here, as in the specialised chapters that follow, we have adopted an inclusive definition of 'life writing'. It is of course possible to query the treatment of certain works as life narrative – there is much in the poetry of the imperial era, for example, that sits between self-expression, self-portrait and self-narrative – and some narratives were necessarily spoken, rather than written, 'speaking bitter' in the early People's Republic being the most striking example. Inspired by Thomas Couser's recent work on memoir,[4] we have chosen to focus on *clarification* of the development and uses of Chinese work, rather than devoting space to *classification* and to determining which works used in China can be categorised as specific 'life writing' genres, which can not and on what terms that decision is made.

## Considering the archive

Before considering the insights that we can take from the critical literature, it is instructive to consider how the extant archive of life writing was created. Our understanding of Chinese life writing work and practice is shaped by multiple, layered selections, and we see the work of composition only through those lenses of selection. Although conventions of composition and strategies of preservation offer important insights into the social context in which they are deployed, they may also obscure detours, alternative traditions and the work involved in the negotiation of generic norms. The work to which we now have access is best understood not only as a residue, a passive accretion of life writing work by Chinese across the centuries, but also as the product of repeated triage, sometimes through historical accident, but often also through human agency, informed variously by principle, generic convention and sectional or personal interest.

The physical survival of texts was challenged periodically[5] by the devastating upheavals that accompanied domestic rebellion, foreign invasion and dynastic change, as well as by flood, fire and family financial crisis when the empire as a whole was nominally at peace. The work of Lynn Struve[6] has recovered and analysed vivid personal accounts of some of these traumas from the seventeenth century, and highlighted the role that local scholarly, religious and commercial networks played in preserving and circulating such work – in some cases rushing to press memoirs and eyewitness accounts of the Manchu invasion and Ming-Qing dynastic transition of the 1640s for audiences outside the occupied zones – yet it would be unwise to assume that little of interest was lost.

In addition to these external interventions, decisions on composition and on preservation were shaped by judgements on individuals' value as biographical subjects; and while conventions shifted over time, some lives were much less readily marked as subjects for recording than others. Subjects of official biographies were consciously selected in the first instance for their utility as positive or negative exemplars; subjects of social biography were chosen to reaffirm networks, alliances, kinship and status. Thus, the influence of official and social biography encouraged attention to orthodox behaviours and patriarchal attitudes, and hierarchies of gender and generation often combined to valorise the lives of adult males and consign those of women and of children to a formulaic hinterland. The conventions of life narrative were assertively championed by official and non-official actors, assumptions on the fit form and content of a life story offered powerful discouragement to those who might produce or preserve unorthodox accounts, and the power of these filters is suggested by references to 'lost' or suppressed works, the only trace of whose existence is a comment that they should never have been written.

Even for Chinese of some status, acceptable forms of self-narration were limited by custom. Before the seventeenth century, for example, confession as a mode of spiritual self-discipline was neither common nor orthodox, and apologetics were treated with outright distaste. Condemning an unrepentant confession, historian Liu Zhiji (661–721) grumbled, 'Although the episode may well have been true, there is nothing commendable about it. Is it not shameful to include such an episode in an autobiography?', and other apologetics are known to us only through similarly disapproving commentaries.[7] This heavily loaded the dice against anyone who – like Alison Hardie's subject in this volume, Ruan Dacheng – might hope to salvage a compromised reputation; and even once self-scrutiny and self-criticism became a requirement (rather than a taboo) under Communist rule in the twentieth century, the power to decide how a life was to be scrutinised, criticised and given meaning lay in the hands of the state and elites, and not of the self-critic.

While defenders of orthodox life narrative worked to keep out deviant narrators, the converse also applied: the auto/biographical form was not the primary vehicle for much life or self-narration, and this often appears as 'auto/biographical moments' in poems, para-texts and other occasional genres. While it is probably not useful to define every poem or essay that reflected a mood or a moment as 'life writing', amongst the reflections on conventional subjects such as flower viewing, temple visiting and examination success or failure, it is worth noting works such as Du Fu's (712–777) 'Journey North' and 'Seven Songs written while living at T'ung-ku in 759' that link the poet's personal history to the fate of the empire, Gao Qi's (1336–1374) verse commemoration of his daughter's brief life, essays such as Gui Youguang's (1506–1571) 'The Xiangji Studio' that packages personal and family narrative into a description of Gui's study, or Zhang Dai's (1597–1689) rueful pastiche, 'An Epitaph for Myself.'[8] Nor should we ignore the accumulation of this work across a writing lifetime: the private summary auto/biography may not have been a common form in some eras, but literate Chinese lived auto/biographically, and the work of life/self-narration was deeply embedded in study and sociability.[9]

Undoubtedly, this material is harder to track than canonical works. The growth of commercial publishing after the fourteenth century allowed circulation of a massive range of works on history and phi-losophy, popular almanacs and 'how-to' works, as well as collections of *belles-lettres* containing material of this type; yet the markets for such work were fluctuating, fickle and often localised.[10] While the survival of official biographies was secured by the resources of the state, the longevity of works outside the canon depended on the will and resources of social networks; even minor occasional works pro-duced by persons of recognised status were preserved, yet we know much less of what many literate Chinese chose to commit to paper.

The case of one early nineteenth-century work raises intriguing questions about the distance between the production and preser-vation of life narratives. *Six Chapters from a Floating Life* charts the precarious existence on the fringes of official and gentry life of one Shen Fu, native of Suzhou in Qing China's prosperous heart-land. Completed probably between 1809 and 1816, the *Six Chapters* remained in obscurity until 1877, when four chapters were discovered in manuscript in Suzhou and subsequently published.[11] Shen Fu's was an unexceptional life: in his repeated failure to progress through the examinations that governed access to official posts, his struggle to secure a respectable living, and in his leisure pursuits, he appears wholly typical of men of his social background; he does not try to present himself as exceptional. That said, *Six Chapters* is an exceptional work; yet it is hard at this distance to determine whether this strikingly intimate self-portrait was quite as exceptional a composition in 1809 as it was a survivor in 1877.

These cases challenge us to ask *what we are looking for* as we explore traditions of life narrative. Are we seeking to explore what writers chose to write? Or do we confine ourselves to what others chose to preserve and publish? How do we account for slippages between composition, preservation and circulation? How does awareness of these slippages shape our understanding of life writing work? Finally, how far can we confidently generalise on the basis of a body of work that we know to be fragmentary, and whose contours – as recent work continues to demonstrate – are still emerging?[12]

## Reappraising 'Chinese traditions' in early life narrative

Much of the critical literature on early life writing practices focuses on biographical, rather than autobiographical work. This accounts for the bulk of the surviving Chinese material, and it is this tradition that is commonly treated as hegemonic. Denis Twitchett argues that the didactic conventions of 'official biography', produced for dynastic histories, influenced other life narratives to the extent that these 'share[d] many formal characteristics and form[ed] a single tradition'.[13] Yet, the political, social and intellectual contexts within which these early traditions emerged were shifting and uncertain. The earliest documented works date from the last centuries BCE and were produced as a central state was forged, in what is now northern central China, out of smaller warring regimes. As auto/biographical traditions developed, they grew in a China that was expanding in territory; that was ruled at times by a single, stable central authority (as was the case for much of the Han (206 BCE–220 AD), Tang (618–907) and northern Song dynasties (960–1126)); but that also saw periods of disunion and rule by foreign conquest (for example, in the Six Dynasties (220–589) and the Mongol Yuan (1279–1368)). These centuries saw a transition from largely aristocratic rule in the first century to more bureaucratic government by the eleventh; fierce competition between major philosophical systems – most visibly Confucianism, Daoism and Buddhism – for primacy as the bases of statecraft or social practice; significant economic and commercial expansion that tied coastal China to global trading networks; and dramatic shifts in regimes of kinship, gender and social status.[14]

Thus, the context in which early lives were lived and written changed markedly across time and space. It is true that the categorising of lives by status and by attributed exemplary qualities marked many works; that early works were refreshed and reinvented to suit changing times; and that even biographies from outside official traditions took on some of this strong exemplary flavour.[15] However, official biography and its imitators were not, even in this early period, the only vehicles used for writing lives. An examination of the literature to date on earlier life writing practice reveals first, that the field was marked, even from its earliest stages, by generic diversity and by the 'poaching' of official biographical convention by the writers of non-official lives; and second, that official traditions were beset by internal and external pressures. The conventions, therefore, were powerful and highly visible; but they were not uncontested.

The earliest extant Chinese writings that are conventionally held to be 'biographical' form part of Sima Qian's *Records of the Historian* (*Shi ji*), composed around 104–91 BCE; these were roughly contemporaneous with Plutarch's *Lives of the Noble Greeks and Romans* and Suetonius' *Lives of the Caesars*. They suggest, in their form and number, a tradition of writing lives that was already well established.[16] Sima Qian's work established biography of the influential and the exemplary as a core feature of the official dynastic history; this bound the writing of lives both to political interest and to morally inflected processes of imperial legitimation.[17] The didactic function is neatly illustrated in Sima Qian's biography of rebel general Han Xin (d.196 BCE):

> ...Had Han Hsin [Han Xin] followed the Way...and been more modest instead of boasting about his achievements and glorying in his ability, all would have been well...But instead he attempted

to revolt when the empire was united. To have his family wiped out was no more than he deserved.[18]

With the progressive bureaucratisation of historical writing, the drive to underline the exemplary exerted an increasingly stifling influence. Official biographies were presented as carefully selected stock types – categories might include 'Compassionate Officials' and 'Assassin-Retainers' – described in tightly regulated language, as positive or negative examples to the governing classes in service of dynastic legitimation and social reproduction; biographical material might be distorted or fabricated to make a case, so that the moralising text risked obscuring the life from which the moral was drawn.[19] However, if we consider the work involved in creating usable biographies out of raw lives, those traditions appear more fragile.

Historiographical and biographical practice was no simple process of packing complex lives into a mould of uniform, 'traditional' interpretation, and recent work suggests that the monolithic appearance of biographical traditions was deceptive. Grant Hardy notes that the content of Sima Qian's biographies was varied, that the historian's commentary was 'brief and inconsistent [and] difficult to weave... into a coherent philosophy', and suggests that this reflected a dissonance recognised by the historian between ethical vision and historical fact.[20] Catherine Parke notes that the Han Xin biography quoted above illustrates also the historian's concern with evidence and verification of the tales transmitted by others:

> *When I visited Huaiyin, the local people told me* that even while a common citizen Han Hsin [Han Xin] was not like ordinary people. At the time of his mother's death he could not afford to give her a funeral, yet he found a high burial ground with room enough for ten thousand households to settle. *I visited his mother's grave and confirmed that this was true...*[21]

Within decades of its composition, Sima Qian's *Records* co-existed with other life writing genres, including orthodox compendia such as Liu Xiang's *Traditions of Exemplary Women* (*Lienü zhuan*), composed in the first century BCE, which consisted of biographies of women grouped by their virtues, and (rather later) with its 'dissenting... counterpart' *A New Account of Tales of the World* (*Shishuo xinyu, ca.* 440). By the Tang dynasty, these jostled for attention with Buddhist and Daoist hagiographies, social and occasional works including epitaphs and necrologies, and forms of self-narration, as well as brief lives and pseudo-auto/biographical fragments embedded in cultural forms from folk opera to scholars' occasional writings.[22]

Early life writing was thus marked by diversity both in genre and in values; while we see some sharing of 'formal characteristics' as Twitchett suggested, we cannot easily treat this work as components within a 'single tradition'. The ownership of exemplary traditions was not exclusive: the compiler's preface to the sixth-century Buddhist *Lives of the Nuns* declared that

> These nuns ... whom I hereby offer as models, are women of excellent reputation, paragons of ardent morals, whose virtues are a stream of fragrance that flows without end. That is why I take up my ink brush ... to record the women's biographies to hand on to later chroniclers ... to encourage and admonish later generations ... I did not embellish the material; rather I worked to preserve the essentials, hoping that those who seek freedom from the world of suffering will emulate the nuns' virtue.[23]

Here, the orthodox biographical form, with its assertive claims to audience in posterity for unembellished, exemplary lives was poached to embed counter-traditions within the textscape; if this was a triumph for didactic convention, it was not undiluted.

Beside the lives of others recorded in these ways were emerging traditions of self-narration. These received little attention until Wu Pei-yi's pioneering study in 1990; while Wu notes that autobiography was often treated as a later, 'lesser' and largely imitative practice, his meticulous readings of late imperial autobiographical texts have remained central to the field and have sparked questions that can be asked of earlier and later works alike. Relatively few self-narratives survive from the early imperial era – though Wu highlights numerous references to lost works – but even that fragmentary record reveals diversity in life writing practice. Wendy Larson sets autobiographies across Chinese history on a continuum between 'circumstantial' narratives, that located the individual within social and temporal frameworks and borrowed to some extent from biographical tradition, and 'impressionistic' works, that mocked these orthodoxies, instead asserting the author's autonomy through detachment from social ties and the indulgence of personal tastes for wine and poetry.[24] Thus, Sima Qian opened his own life story with a sober and detailed genealogy, whereas the poet Tao Qian (also Tao Yuanming, 365–427) began, 'No-one knows where he comes from or is clear about his name';[25] and while Daoist master Ge Hong (*ca.* 250–330) was strikingly self-deprecating: '[he] was rustic and obtuse. Inarticulate and ugly, he never tried to justify himself with words or to embellish his appearance...'; philosopher Wang Chong (27–*ca.* 100) was unabashed in his self-celebration: 'Every time he wielded a pen the mass of readers marvelled.'[26]

On the whole, the surviving early works emphasised the circumstantial over the impressionistic, the life over the self and the social over the interior. Wu notes Ge Hong's relative inattention to spiritual matters and 'internal transformations', and Stephen Durrant argues that these early works reveal selves 'at the intersection of traditions', commenting of Sima Qian's self-narrative that, '[its] most pervasive feature...is the degree to which the individual repeatedly disappears into the patterns of traditions. It is almost as if [he] could not...interpret his own most intense experiences outside a network of historical relations and precedents.'[27] Yet, Matthew Wells's study of Ge Hong proposes, instead, that early Chinese self-narratives are better read as 'metaphors of the self' and as 'socially-bounded act[s] of self-creation', and finds in Ge Hong's self-narrative a critical, personal reworking of archetypes that aspired to 'create a durable name beyond the authority of state-sanctioned historiography'.[28]

The institutionalisation of official historical work and of biographical conventions between the seventh and tenth centuries, produced an abundant historiographical literature, but did relatively little to mitigate the internal and external tensions that beset historical and biographical writing. Dynastic histories produced during the Tang dynasty by teams of bureaucrats betray less of the personal quest for meaning that scholars have found in the work of Sima Qian; yet while some biographies suggest the freedom that biographers had to rework obscure lives into exemplary tales, others underline the constraints that they confronted in representing better documented and politically more sensitive lives. Two biographies from the official history of the Sui dynasty (581–618) make the point. The exemplary Mrs Lu was commemorated as a model mother, and as resolute in defence of her virtue, and her life was neatly packaged into conventional story:

> The mother of Yuan Wuguang was the daughter of a Mr Lu of Fanyang. As a child she loved to study...She was widowed in her prime, while her children were still young and weak. She was poor and could not afford to have them educated, so Mrs Lu schooled them herself, taught them right from wrong, and was widely praised for this. Towards the end of the Renshou reign [*ca.* 604], Prince Liang of Han raised an army and rebelled; Qi Liang was sent to occupy the land east of the mountains, and appointed Wuguang his scribe. When Liang was defeated, Shangguan Zheng, the Cizhou prefectural governor, registered Wuguang's household, took a liking to Mrs Lu and tried to assault her; Mrs Lu swore she would rather die. Zheng, a fierce man, was furious, and burned her with candles. Mrs Lu held fast and would not yield to him.[29]

We may read the biography of the unfortunate Mrs Lu as a warning of the sacrifices demanded by convention, and as symbolic compensation for those sacrifices – lose a real life, gain a written one – but, through the veil of orthodox values, we see little of the girl who loved to study, or the mother who passed on moral understanding to her children.

The biography of rebel official Yang Xuangan was less successful in closing off the alternative interpretations that complex lives might evoke, and thus points to some of the internal tensions affecting official biography. It opened with a glowing exposition of Yang's personal and official merits:

> Yang Xuangan was the son of Situ Su. He was imposing in appearance and handsome. As a child, he was slow to develop, and many people thought him foolish, but his father always said to his friends: 'This boy is no fool.' As he grew older, he loved to study, and was a skilled rider and archer. His father became a key official because of his military exploits, and he was truly his father's son...Later, when [the first Sui emperor] ordered his promotion to the first rank, Xuangan thanked him, saying, 'I had not expected to receive such favour...' First, he served as prefectural governor of Yingzhou. When he took up the post,...he understood every

detail, recognised the good officials and the corrupt, and pursued his work energetically; no-one dared deceive him. Officials and people respected and praised him . . . Although proud by nature, he loved scholarship, and famous men from across the empire flocked to his door . . .[30]

Like Han Xin, Yang combined admirable qualities with pride and ambition that led him to confrontation with his emperor and to rebellion. Later sections of the biography explain Yang's rise and fall by reference both to the external circumstances of declining imperial rule and to Yang's own flawed character, showing him ignoring the advice of his associates that revolt was futile, and disastrously overestimating his own strength compared to the imperial forces.

However, the possible, orthodox lessons of Yang's defeat – that pride goes before a fall; that power is received by heaven's mandate, not seized by force of arms – are stated neither in the biography proper, nor in the historian's coda to the chapter. Instead of the explicit *ad personem* moralising that marks the Han Xin life quoted by Parke, the commentary focused on imperial rulership, emphasising the part that the second Sui emperor, Yangdi, played in leaving the empire vulnerable to rebellion.[31] Yang Xuangan's abortive revolt was problematic for biographers, as it was followed a handful of years later by a successful rising led by a high official who was subsequently recognised as the legitimate founder of the new Tang dynasty. Unable to argue forcefully that rebellion was wrong in the 610s, Tang historiographers suggested instead that Yang was the wrong rebel, and his biography became a commentary on imperial responsibilities rather than on a dissident life.[32]

Official biographical work involved more than just a negotiation of abstract values. It required that officials navigate fraught power relations at court;[33] beyond that bureaucratic machinery, official historians were heavily dependent on private and family records, and the exemplary project could be served only if the mass of material produced by the relatives, friends and pupils, peers and rivals of biographical subjects could be marshalled and disciplined to approved ends. Elite families, alert to the uses of biographical writing in the building of individual and familial reputation, had a strong sense of the audience for private and public writings, and some worked above all with an eye to securing recognition such as a posthumous title for the deceased. Yet, other families failed to maintain complete records, or simply refused to release them to biographers, apparently relishing the powers that came from granting or withholding access to biographical work.[34]

Newer forms such as the 'chronological biography' (*nianpu*), and the 'account of conduct' (*xingzhuang*), popularised between the seventh and eleventh centuries, suggest a methodical approach towards that business of securing official recognition and creating a usable basis for biographical work; these combined records of activity and achievement with extracts from personal and official writings and correspondence, and often look very like templates for an 'authorised' biography.[35] Faced with this proliferation of interested sources, historians feared that sober accounts of individual conduct might be obscured by 'false interpolations ... luxuriant composition ... [and] insubstantial verbiage',[36] and private materials were subject to official verification and approval.

At other times, shifts in the social and political landscape between the life and its uses destabilised the biographical edifice, and while late mediaeval scholars such as Zhu Xi (1130–1200) appeared confident in categorising acts and actors and defining a language for biography,[37] critical examination of biographies has revealed that these reflected the uncertain moral and political environment in which they were written. Naomi Standen's work on frontier officials who switched allegiances between the Chinese Song state and the non-Chinese Liao during the tenth century illuminates the changing meanings attributed to complicated lives, and the interplay of borrowing and editing in the compilation of official biographies. The border-crossings and transfers of allegiance examined by Standen were not uncommon in the tenth century, but they were hard for later historians to incorporate into a morally satisfying retrospective history without considerable selection and amplification. Hence, the writers of an eleventh-century chronicle described one frontier-crossing official as a drinker to cast doubt on his character, and the fourteenth-century writer of another's official biography emphasised his post-crossing espionage activities to underline his continuing 'Chinese' loyalties.[38] Even within the court and within a shorter time span, the available resources and the messages that might be taken from them were diverse, as Patricia Ebrey reveals in a thoughtful juxtaposition of the official biography of the eleventh-century Empress Xiang with other contemporaneous palace sources.[39]

Aside from this wrangling over the proper content and meaning of official biography, we see alternative uses of biographical forms: reading the biographies of artist Li Cheng (916–967) against the grain of conventional expression, Charles Lachman finds both a coded portrait of a man and his artistic and personal values and an assertion by Li's biographers of the value of a life that did not qualify for commemoration on orthodox terms.[40] Other variant uses of standard genres remind us that the storying impulse could not always be accommodated within conventional practice. While mourning rituals for adults were elaborate and included the production or commissioning of epitaphs and necrologies,[41] young children rarely received such recognition. However, a minor tradition of infant necrology mirrored the commemorative life narratives produced for adults. The earliest examples are found in scattered poems and essays from prominent and prolific mediaeval writers, such philosopher Han Yu (768–824); fuller commemorative writings produced later by more obscure scholars suggest that this became more commonplace, and that records became more personal, in later dynasties. Epitaphs for women, written by male relatives, suggest some frustration with exemplary convention in its disregard for the personal and affective, and its tendency to reduce whole lives to one single quality.[42]

Thus while early orthodox biography had the practical and symbolic resources of the state behind it, and was emulated in other life narrative forms, its grip on the allegiance of the writing classes was less certain than some earlier work has suggested. Earlier academic literature concluded that power in defining meaning through biography lay with the historiographical establishment, yet practitioners clearly felt at times that the boot was on the other foot, and the work of interpretation and composition was complicated by sectional interests and the tensions inherent in the discipline of biography. Some imitators of orthodox biography used its forms to extend the reach of, for example, Confucian values and exemplars; others poached those forms, or recycled them to plant alternative or dissenting traditions in the spaces created for the conventional. In other genres such as epitaphs, even writers closely associated with the traditions of orthodox biography at times felt it inadequate to record whole lives; and the fragmentary record of early self-narrative reveals an eclectic and often playful approach to the adaptation of biographical convention to autobiographical work.

## Life writing in a changing China

Between the fourteenth and the early twentieth centuries, China appeared in some ways more stable under the Ming and Qing dynasties (1368–1644 and 1644–1912, respectively) than in the earlier imperial era. Yet, the bureaucratic and authoritarian imperial governments of those centuries ruled a China marked by astonishing levels of commercial expansion, unprecedented population growth, social fluidity and cultural experimentation; that was periodically shaken by domestic rebellion, and traumatised by foreign invasion and violent dynastic change in the 1640s; and that saw the extension of Qing influence towards central Asia in the eighteenth century and suffered imperialist encroachment by Western powers on the south and east coasts in the nineteenth and twentieth. The security of traditionally educated elites was threatened by the growing difficulty of achieving the government posts on which their status depended and by status competition from an increasingly assertive merchant class.[43] As elite identities were destabilised, social biography – in essays, sketches, prefaces and epitaphs – became an important strategy in the recording of personal and communal achievements and the affirmation of social networks and values. A growing publishing industry facilitated the circulation of this work, revealing a range of life writings of which official biographies formed only a small part.

The traumatic events of this period offered a powerful stimulus to life narrative: Lynn Struve notes a 'phenomenal outpouring of memoir-like personal accounts' from the mid-seventeenth century Ming-Qing dynastic transition, which was marked by epidemic, famine, rebellion and war. Some of these works, like the autobiographies cited by Wu Pei-yi, were written by intensively educated officials; others were produced by people of more modest backgrounds, working through personal and communal experiences of turmoil. Although memoir records of earlier dynastic transitions were fairly common, the seventeenth-century works focused to an unprecedented extent on personal experience rather than on the fate of the empire.[44]

However, narratives of self or others were also shaped by slower economic or social changes, or by shifts in mentalities, as intellectual leanings once considered unorthodox – notably interest in late Ming China in Buddhism and in Wang Yangming Confucianism – became more popular. This fostered a more introspective tone in literary forms including the auto/biographical, and it is this period that Wu Pei-yi has characterised as a 'golden age of Chinese [male] autobiography'.[45] Other works looked outwards towards society, and while social biography may appear simply to amplify the functions of canonical works, its potential uses were more complex, as life narratives offered an anchor in text against shifting currents of social change. By the fifteenth century, the provision of a preface for published work, or epitaphs for a deceased relative, as commercial transaction or social favour, might enhance the reputation of consumer and producer alike, and these therefore became important markers of status and community for elite males and their families. While some might be content with a highly conventional product, for others the value of the work lay in the demonstration of a thoughtful, personal relationship between subject and author; and the content of some of this work thus offered sophisticated biographical insights as the fact of its transmission mapped the social and commercial networks within which it was circulated.[46]

These life stories reflected the porous social boundaries between the traditionally distinct status groups of gentry and merchants. Some recorded social mobility, upward and downward, some served to affirm core virtues and cement reputations; others, such as local history biographies, commemorated conventional worthies including upright officials and filial sons, and the selfless behaviour of merchants, binding them into a wider textual and moral community. Other works were more personal: as Yang Xunji (1456–1544) packed a tale of study, bibliophilia and rueful judgement on his family into thirty lines, he offered a commentary on his times and snapshot of a life lived between classes:[47]

> Mine was a trading family,
> Living in Nanhao district for a hundred years.
> I was the first to become a scholar,
> Our house being without a single book.
> Applying myself for a full decade,

I set my heart on building a collection.
...
I'll do my best by these books all my days,
And die not leaving a single one behind.
There are some readers among my friends –
To them I'll give them away.
Better that than to have my unworthy sons
Haul them off to turn into cash.

Cultures of reading and writing remained highly gendered; yet tensions within those traditions were increasingly visible. Official narratives of women's lives continued to emphasise the exemplary. The cult of female chastity and widow suicide that gathered momentum during the fifteenth and sixteenth centuries created new categories into which female behaviour could be packaged: as the 'chaste widow' biography became a standard element in local histories, memorial arches dedicated to these women were common features of local landscapes, and the production of stylised exemplar biographies became a site of competition between families and communities.[48]

Yet, even as women's lives were written by men, the traditions of exemplarity were questioned. Two biographies by the eighteenth-century scholar Zhang Xuecheng, one of a relative by marriage, another written for a local history, suggest that a concern for family reputation and moral message need not preclude vivid depiction of personality. Lu Weijing argues that widow biographies became a device by which male biographers questioned the cult of widow chastity: in writing biographies and necrologies for women of their own families, educated men confronted the dissonances between the comforting tropes of virtue and the troubled lives of which they had personal knowledge.[49] At the same time, rising literacy gave some elite women new status and new opportunities to narrate themselves and each other. As Dorothy Ko notes, 'In the seventeenth century ... in every Jiangnan city, and in every generation there were women who wrote, published and discussed one another's works';[50] and these women wrote their own lives – as scholars, wives, sisters, Buddhist devotees – on more varied and more personal terms than the formulae of orthodox biography.

Life writing conventions continued to shift under Qing rule through the late seventeenth and eighteenth centuries. Some traditions appeared solid: friends and families recorded the achievements and built the reputations of notable men and women, and the Qing authorities produced an official history of their predecessors, with the conventional accompaniments of official biography.[51] However, the intense self-scrutiny that marked late Ming life narrative disappeared, and writings formally designated as auto/biographical became generally less revealing of the inner life. Martin Huang attributes this retreat to the Qing state's assertive claims to interpretative authority, and to the association in the elite mind between the emphatic subjectivity of late Ming intellectual culture and dynastic decline. However, he points also to the popularisation of self-allegorising and self-metaphoring rhetorics in fiction, and to the markedly more autobiographical flavour of the novel, 'whose avowed fictionality seems to have provided a safer medium for continued exploration of the self'. Self-scrutiny was not dead, but had sought refuge in a genre that was relatively new, relatively low in status (and therefore relatively well camouflaged), and well adapted to narratives of self-criticism, wish-fulfilment and auto/biographical redemption.[52]

The grand narratives of modern Chinese history suggest that we should see the nineteenth and early twentieth centuries as a period in which past traditions (and their associated social personae and conventions of life and self-narrative) were rejected in the search for a new order. Challenges to traditional values, and to the traditional social and governmental order, took in both literary and historiographical traditions and understandings of the relation between individual and community. These processes of intense revaluation were hailed by their supporters as a liberation from confining tradition and a celebration of individual and collective possibility. While these shifts have been widely attributed to developments emerging during the 'May Fourth era' of the 1910s and 1920s, as educated Chinese encountered new political, social and literary ideas through study overseas or through works translated in China,[53] it is also possible that they have deeper roots.

Visible cracks within apparently monolithic traditions, shifts in concepts of self and in autobiographical conventions, dating from the eighteenth and early nineteenth centuries, suggest slower underlying processes of change;[54] and the existing literature reveals a notable absence of consensus on the meaning of late nineteenth and early twentieth-century Chinese life writing. As China struggled from the mid-nineteenth century to confront the threats presented by western imperialism and domestic rebellion, criticism from within of textually centred traditions delegitimised both the principles of government that these encoded and important elements of the elite persona; and this was reflected in practices of self-narration. Whereas the authorial persona of the circumstantial autobiography, as identified by Larson – socially engaged and embedded in familial, local and official networks – could be reinvented to meet new challenges, the figures of the impressionistic autobiography – eremitic, abstract and devoted to pure scholarship – were less adaptable.[55]

The new conventions of the early twentieth century favoured social and political engagement in action and as a theme in self-narration: if the emergence of 'the individual' is commonly associated with passages to modernity, the moral and social imperatives of China's nineteenth and twentieth centuries insisted on self-conscious dedication to collective goals and thus favoured the 'self-in-society' as auto/biographical subject. This suggests that we should resist the temptation to consider those transitional decades as an era of new, untempered freedoms in life narration. True, the discussion of new freedoms in hitherto lesser-used forms is a salient theme in the academic literature: Brian Moloughney has argued that the growing independence of biography from history legitimised closer attention to individuality and to personality, and Janet Ng has identified autobiography as 'one of [China's] most widely-used literary forms'.[56]

Autobiographical writing was deployed, notably by women, to 'chart and enact the escape from trope and tradition',[57] and that escape led writers in different directions. Some turned to explicitly marked autobiography as a refuge from the orthodoxies of literary production whose proper business was increasingly taken to be national salvation and social reform, rather than emotional matters, and worked to re-map the personal and intersubjective realms, for example, exploring the mother–daughter bond to decentre both patriarchal tradition and the new teleologies of post-May-Fourth radicalism.[58] Others played with the possibilities of the genre, selecting, omitting and reconstructing at will. Wang Jing has argued that, 'Chinese women's autobiography ... disassociated from femininity by eliminating conventional details of women's lives such as love, marriage, domesticity and roles as mothers and wives ...', though, as she shows, those details survived in other genres. Thus, novelist Lu Yin recounted her own unhappy childhood in great detail but neglected to mention her own children in her autobiography; and she cast herself as a devoted wife and amanuensis in her biography of her deceased husband, Guo Mengliang, despite her 'abrupt dismissal' of him as she wrote her own life.[59]

That said, not all self-narration showed quite this subversive impulse, and we see also the trading of old hegemonies for new. Authoritative (typically, male) voices such as Hu Shi and Liang Qichao proposed a new didacticism, calling on famous Chinese to write their life stories to inspire the young, and offering privileged access to autobiographical space to those already recognised by critics and readers.[60] 'Exemplary lives' – ancient and modern, Chinese and foreign – were appropriated and contested from diverse ideological positions throughout the twentieth century.[61] China's early tabloid press energetically mined the lives of celebrities, assassins and suicides for social meaning;[62] and the war years saw a search for heroic biographies aimed at elite and popular audiences.[63] Yet, other work suggests an ongoing reconsideration of the form and function of life and self-narrative: Qu Qiubai's *Superfluous Words*, completed in prison shortly before his execution in 1935, shows a life in transit from his family's gentry roots towards revolutionary activism. Qu's early classical education, and a sojourn in Moscow in his twenties, would have exposed him to both traditional Chinese and revolutionary modes of life narrative, yet the voice of *Superfluous Words* shifts as Qu cast himself variously as errant gentry son, doubtful friend and ambivalent revolutionary, before concluding with a wistful reference to the everyday: 'Tofu is delicious, the best food in the world. Farewell!'[64]

## The hand of the state: Life narrative in the People's Republic

With the establishment of the People's Republic in 1949, the new state asserted its authority over auto/biographical work. The ambitious reworking of social hierarchies, economic organisation and structures of authority was underpinned by a drive also to transform the people – to make new Chinese for a new China – as both practical reforms and ideological campaigns involved new ways of exerting control over lives-as-lived, and categorising and defining those new Chinese. Recent scholarship has pointed to the artificial, even arbitrary, nature of many of those categories but their force, once assigned, was undeniable. The Land Reforms of the late 1940s and early 1950s required the assignment of class status to all rural Chinese – landlords, rich, middle and poor peasants – as well as redistributions of farmland, and these defined individuals and families in social, economic and experiential terms; the Hundred Flowers and Anti-Rightist Movements of 1956–1959, designed first to encourage and then to quash debate on official policy, brought to the fore definitions of (mostly urban) Chinese based on their perceived ideological orthodoxy; in 1958–1961, the Great Leap Forward required that Chinese enact those new identities in service of industrialisation and agricultural growth; and the Cultural Revolution dramatised the inclusion and exclusion implied by those multiple categorisations in the very public humiliation, beatings or killings of those deemed enemies of the revolution.[65]

State control extended also over lives-as-written. Writing in 1962, William Ayers commented, 'Biography in the People's Republic of China...is a highly purposeful craft, but rarely, if ever, is its primary purpose to portray an individual personality for his [*sic*] own sake...Biography is didactic, hagiolatrous, or propagandistic....'[66] The reappraisal of one's own or others' life history within the sweep of the revolution was central to the education of Party members before 1949, and that exemplary drive was manifest in Party-sponsored collections of biographies and memoirs that enshrined personal experiences of revolutionary and other historical events and figures, such as those discussed by Nicola Spakowski in this volume.

Self-narrative was also central to the re-education of outsiders: framed as self-criticism, it became a test of rehabilitation for transgressors such as former supporters of Jiang Jieshi's Guomindang, and Chinese who had collaborated with the occupation forces in Manchuria after 1931 and during the Second Sino-Japanese War. Their experiences, and those of others outside the Party, were compiled in series such as *Selected Materials on History and Culture* (*Wenshi ziliao xuanji*), launched in the early 1960s. The *Materials* originated from a request by Premier Zhou Enlai for eyewitness accounts of key events and historical figures between 1911 and 1949. The first volume of the national edition contained works focusing on lives in history: personal recollections of the outbreak of war with Japan in 1937 were followed by an evaluation of Jiang Jieshi's handling of anti-Japanese resistance; eyewitness accounts of the regional wars of the early Republic were accompanied by reminiscences on prominent actors in national politics.[67] As well as portraying the self-in-society through the lens of historical developments, some of these pieces incorporate or reproduce prison self-criticisms, revealing the formulaic terms on which errant selves were written into the new society. Yet other, later examples – as Isabelle Henrion-Dourcy demonstrates in this volume – address personal experience and ambition despite the constraints of the form and its semi-official audience.

The contours of new official life narrative were most visible in mass communication, where the state promoted a new generation of socialist exemplars, most famously the model revolutionary Lei Feng, whose selfless desire to serve the people and the revolution spawned posters, slogans, school textbook chapters and a host of dedicated works.[68] The mass of the Chinese people were not expected simply to be a passive audience for these narratives, but were instructed on how these were to be understood and how their own new lives were to be storied, as self-narrative – focused, edited and delivered on approved terms – became a key strategy for embedding revolution in popular consciousness.

This self-storying required active personal engagement, as mass movements such as Land Reform were conducted not simply with reference to economic redistribution, but also through the practices of 'speaking bitter' (*suku*), by the rural poor against former landlords.[69] 'Speaking bitter' was state-orchestrated 'history-telling'[70] produced variously in the community setting of small groups or in the more coercive 'struggle' meeting. Apparently ephemeral, as an oral form, but nonetheless powerful for its association with state power and projects of inclusion and exclusion, speaking bitter simultaneously publicised local and personal stories of exploitation, binding the personal histories of the speakers into national narratives of revolution, and presented an often violent challenge to the status and sense of self of those targeted by the speaking.[71] Charlene Makley argues that speaking bitter in eastern Tibet created a rupture in personal and communal practices of history-telling, as it forcibly displaced traditional modes of life and self-narration yet failed to establish itself as a legitimate and usable alternative. While the Tibetan encounter with the Communist revolution was clearly not representative of the wider People's Republic, the core experience of 'drastic split between narrating and narrated selves' that speaking bitter required, and the subsequent delegitimation of politicised (and other) self-narration are conceivably not unique, and her thoughtful study raises questions that might usefully be asked of other communities and modes of life narrative across China.[72]

The very marked influence of the state in these practices, and the frequency with which memoirs of the period refer to the burning of personal papers, letters, photographs and diaries in order to avoid incrimination during political campaigns, do not encourage us to assume that great auto/biographical treasures from this period are lurking undiscovered. Yet, some continued to write: the diaries of eminent literary critic Wu Mi (1894–1978) may form one of the most extensive published personal records of the time, but other diaries, collections of letters and memoirs are extant. In her essays on family, Yang Jiang stood back from what Spakowski describes below as narratives of 'capitalised Revolution', embedding self-narrative in a longer time-frame and more complex social and personal relations; as was the case with early modern auto/biographical work, her essays became a site for reflection and dialogue on the affective life and everyday community of the family.[73] The recent publication of growing numbers of other life narratives suggests that it may be some time before the detailed textures of life writing practice in the early People's Republic become visible.[74]

From the late 1970s, the social and economic context in which life stories were told, written and published was transformed, with the adoption of economic reforms and the slow beginnings of the state's withdrawal from the very assertive interventions in personal life that had marked early Communist rule. While a mass of new, 'approved' biographies of public figures appeared – with over sixty works on the late premier Zhou Enlai alone[75] – the life writing of the very late twentieth and early twenty-first centuries is possibly best understood as the increasingly pluralist product of tensions and creative frictions rather than of dominant conventions. In examining life writing in China today, therefore, we find few certainties, and it is probably more productive to frame that enquiry in terms of the challenges and questions that we face.

First, how do the writers of Chinese lives locate lives in history and selves in society? Personal experience of dramatic public changes remains an important strand in life writing, and some examples of this work may owe much to earlier conventions of history-telling. Collections of 'testimony' (*jianzheng*) or personal experience (*qinli*) of war and revolution[76] allow personal memories to be marshalled in service of hegemonic narratives, though that is not to say that the motives of commissioners, collectors and contributors are necessarily identical for any such collection. While the ambitions of the collectors may appear orthodox, the risks to narrators in telling dissonant or resistant personal histories have declined dramatically, and as Spakowski's analysis of revolutionary women's self-narrative demonstrates below, a careful reading of these works often reveals a more personal, less national tale than similar, earlier collections would have offered.

Second, what interests are now served by exemplary lives? The discursive conventions of the early People's Republic survived into the reform era, in efforts in the 1980s to reframe personal writings such as Yu Luojin's autobiographical novel, *A Chinese Winter's Tale*, as 'safe' political memoir, in the repeated revivals of the Lei Feng cult, and in biographies of national figures such as Qian Xuesen, one of the authors of China's space programme.[77] It is easy to dismiss exemplarity as a narrow, state-driven project, yet recent work suggests a more complex dynamic. On one hand, Wang Ning's analysis of Qian's many biographies and Gail Hershatter's work on female labour models suggest that the exemplary narrative might be a source of material, professional or political security, or was powerfully constitutive of personal identity.[78] On the other hand, the exemplary mode is flexible enough to accommodate new, reform-era values, and recent best-selling commercial biographies have included celebrities and tycoons as well as more conventional subjects such as writers and statesmen.[79]

Third, how does Chinese life writing speak to global audiences? Some of the works most visible to audiences outside China – a wave of memoirs charting the sufferings of the Cultural Revolution years – might at first sight suggest a new autobiography of resistance, possibly even of individuation in reaction to totalitarian mobilisation.[80] Yet, Peter Zarrow has pointed to the shared narrative trajectory of many of these works, which fit rather neatly into a 'Revolution 2.0' narrative of lives constrained under Mao-era socialism and subsequently liberated under market reform, as they reframe personal experience of the Cultural Revolution and its aftermath against suffering, moral dissonance and exile; his analysis has highlighted the ideological assumptions underpinning a sub-genre that often declares itself as sharply sceptical of ideology in its Cultural Revolution formations.[81]

The journey of Chinese lives to foreign audiences may be an uncertain one, as Margaretta Jolly has demonstrated. Her analysis of Li Zhisui's *The Private Life of Chairman Mao* reveals a web of interests, assumptions over the proper nature of biography, and understandings of the authority of eyewitnesses that governed the transformation of Li's narrative into a ghost-written, published work and its reception by reviewers and readers. Yet, Jolly points elsewhere to other works – less contentious and less intensively processed – that show the possibility that such life stories may disrupt both 'Chinese' and 'western' conventions: Anchee Min's Cultural Revolution memoir, *Red Azalea*, recalled her erotic life more candidly than was typical of Chinese life stories, while declining to package her lesbian relationship into a coming-out narrative.[82]

Finally, what are the implications of wider popular access to the means of life narrative production in China? While the decline in state control over public discourse has allowed lives and selves to be narrated on different terms, the recent explosive growth of internet use in China has allowed many more Chinese – though by no means all – access to new fora of auto/biographical living. The roles played by Chinese online activity and our understandings of its potential impact are constantly shifting, with the expansion of the Chinese blogosphere and the more recent dramatic rise of microblog (*weibo*) platforms. State manipulation and suppression of some strands of online debate is well documented; some of the most popular current blogs deal with practical matters such as stock market tips; and the costs of access still bar many from regular internet use.[83] At the same time, though, these fora are flexible enough to accommodate activists such as Zhang Haidi, celebrity and provocateur bloggers such as Han Han and Muzi Mei, and socially networked urban professionals and older users whose postings of family and personal memoir, poetry and calligraphy are strikingly reminiscent of more traditional everyday life narrative.[84] It will take time for scholars to map China's netscape, and the shifting debate on the wider implications of internet use suggests that a robust model of online life writing in China is still some way off.[85]

## Conclusions

On one hand, therefore, to deny the rules that surround Chinese life writing would be to distort our understanding of a practice that is still largely rules-based: assumptions over what life writing should do, and what interests it might serve, may be more varied now than was once the case, but are still very visible. On the other hand, to assume that those rules are fixed in time and in social or geographical space, and that contemporary or historical life writing practice can be wholly encompassed within them, would be equally misguided. As recent research has demonstrated, the meanings and social uses of Chinese life writings may be asserted in more or less subtle resistance to the constraints imposed by those rules, or articulated through creative or selective exploitation of the possibilities that they offer. An appreciation of these meanings and uses therefore depends on our understanding of the context of life writing work, and of the reception of life writing products as well as of their content. While the cumulative effect of the best work done in the past two-and-a-half decades may have been to prompt further, nagging questions, rather than to offer neat answers, this is a function of vitality in the field, and it presents a powerful challenge for future scholars.

## Notes

1. Paul John Eakin, *Living Autobiographically: How We Create Identity in Narrative* (Ithaca: Cornell University Press, 2011), 17.
2. Compare, for example, the earlier essays by Denis Twitchett and Yang Lien-sheng, the essays collected in the Summer 1962 special issue of *Journal of Asian Studies*, and Di Feng and Shao Dongfang's meticulous 1994 charting of conventions, with works such as Wang Jing's *When 'I' Was Born: Women's Autobiography in Modern China* (Madison: University of Wisconsin Press, 2008); see Twitchett, 'Chinese Biographical Writing,' in W.G. Beasley and E.G. Pulleyblank, eds., *Historians of China and Japan* (London: Oxford University Press, 1961), 95–114; Yang, 'The Organization of Chinese Official Historiography: Principles and Methods of the Standard History from the T'ang through the Ming Dynasty,' in W.G. Beasley and E.G. Pulleyblank, eds., *Historians of China and Japan*, 44–59;

Di and Shao, 'Life-writing in Mainland China (1949–1993): A General Survey and Bibliographic Essay,' *Biography* 17.1 (1994): 32–55; Wang, *When 'I' Was Born*. Wang's thought-provoking study of women's autobiography points to a flowering of the genre in the mid-twentieth century, but a comparison with the essays collected by Joan Judge and Hu Ying suggests that she considerably overstates the formulaic nature of the auto/biographical work of earlier periods; Judge and Hu's collection is a powerful demonstration of the plurality and fluidity of women's auto/biographical traditions, yet the editors still refer in passing in the introduction to the 'unique' challenges they present. Wang, *When 'I' Was Born*, 16–22; Judge and Hu, eds., *Beyond Exemplar Tales: Women's Biography in Chinese History* (Berkeley: University of California Press, 2011), xiii.

3. This is not the place for a detailed history of Confucianism, but it is worth noting that (despite the durability of values identified as 'Confucian') practical and philosophical Confucianism co-existed and competed with other schools of thought and sources of values such as Daoism and Buddhism; and, like Christianity, 'Confucianism' was repeatedly reappraised and reinvented between the earliest forms expressed in the *Analects* (*ca.* 500 BCE) and those of the nineteenth century.

4. G. Thomas Couser, *Memoir: An Introduction* (Oxford: Oxford University Press, 2011), 9.

5. While not every rebellion or invasion accompanying dynastic change affected the whole empire, there were no peaceful transitions; destruction of property, loss of life and displacement of population often extended across the most prosperous regions of China and those surrounding the imperial capital and thus disproportionately affected those areas rich in personal writings and literary collections.

6. This includes the groundbreaking collection of translations, *Voices from the Ming-Qing Cataclysm: China in Tiger's Jaws* (New Haven: Yale University Press, 1993); 'Confucian PTSD: Reading Trauma in a Chinese Youngster's Memoir of 1653,' *History and Memory* 16.2 (2004): 14–31; 'Dreaming and Self-search during the Ming Collapse: The Xue Xiemeng Biji, 1642–1646,' *T'oung-pao* 92 (2007): 159–192; 'Self-Struggles of a Martyr: Memories, Dreams, and Obsessions in the Extant Diary of Huang Chunyao,' *Harvard Journal of Asiatic Studies* 69.2 (2009): 343–394; *The Ming-Qing Conflict, 1619–1683: A Historiography and Source Guide* (Ann Arbor: Association of Asian Studies, 1998).

7. Wu Pei-yi, 'Self-examination and Confession of Sins in Traditional China,' *Harvard Journal of Asiatic Studies* 39.1 (1979): 16; the association of confessions with Daoist and Buddhist healing rituals in the early imperial era may have fed distrust of the confessional mode. The work that offended Liu, a self-narrative by poet Sima Xiangru (d. 118), has not survived. Also Matthew Wells, *To Die and Not Decay: Autobiography and the Pursuit of Immortality in Early China* (Ann Arbor: Association of Asian Studies, 2009), 12–13.

8. Works by Du Fu and Gao Qi (Kao Ch'i) in Victor Mair, ed., *The Columbia Anthology of Traditional Chinese Literature* (New York: Columbia University Press, 1994), 209–216, 264–265; by Gui Youguang in David Pollard, tr. and ed., *The Chinese Essay* (London: Hurst & Co., 2000), 75–77; by Zhang Dai in Yang Ye, tr. and ed., *Vignettes from the Late Ming: A Hsiao-p'in Anthology* (Seattle: University of Washington Press, 1999), 98–101. See also collected translations including Ellen Widmer and Kang-I Sun Chang, eds., *Writing Women in Late Imperial China* (Stanford: Stanford University Press, 1997); Kang-i Sun Chang and Haun Saussy, eds., *Women Writers of Traditional China: An Anthology of Poetry and Criticism* (Stanford: Stanford University Press, 1999); Susan Mann and Yu-yin Cheng, eds., *Under Confucian Eyes: Writings on Gender in Chinese History* (Berkeley: University of California Press, 2001); Wilt L. Idema and Beata Grant, eds., *The Red Brush: Writing Women of Late Imperial China* (Cambridge: Harvard University Press, 2004).

9. On this point, see Wilt L. Idema, 'The Biographical and the Autobiographical in Bo Shaojun's *One Hundred Poems Lamenting My Husband*,' in Judge and Hu, *Beyond Exemplar Tales*, 231–232 and 336.

10. Lucille Chia, *Printing for Profit: The Commercial Publishers of Jianyang, Fujian (11th–17th centuries)* (Cambridge: Harvard University Press, 2002); Kai-wing Chow, *Publishing, Culture, and Power in Early Modern China* (Stanford: Stanford University Press, 2004); Joseph McDermott, *A Social History of the Chinese Book: Books and Literati Culture in Late Imperial China* (Hong Kong: Hong Kong University Press, 2006).

11. Milena Dolezelova-Velingerova and Lubomir Dolezel, 'An Early Chinese Confessional Prose: Shen Fu's *Six Chapters from a Floating Life*,' *T'oung Pao* 58.1/5 (1972): 137–160. English translations include those by Leonard Pratt and Chiang Su-hui, *Six Records of a Floating Life* (London: Penguin, 1983) and by Graham Saunders, *Six Records of a Life Adrift* (London: Hackett, 2011).

12. Both Yao Ping and Ann Waltner's chapters in Judge and Hu, *Beyond Exemplar Tales* point to sources that have only recently come to scholarly attention: Yao, 'Women's Epitaphs in Tang China (618–907),' 139–157; Waltner, 'Life and Letters: Reflections on Tanyangzi,' 212–229.

13. Denis Twitchett, 'Problems of Chinese Biography,' in Arthur Wright and Denis Twitchett, eds., *Confucian Personalities* (Stanford: Stanford University Press, 1962), 24; also 'Chinese Biographical Writing,' 95–96.

14. Paul Ropp, *China in World History* (Oxford: Oxford University Press, 2010).

15. Harriet Zurndorfer's subject, Wang Zhaoyuan (Chapter 4), built her scholarly reputation in the early nineteenth century through commentaries on canonical early works such as the first century BCE compilation *Exemplary Women*; Harriet Zurndorfer, 'The *Lienü zhuan* Tradition and Wang Zhaoyuan's (1763–1851) production of the *buzhu* (1812),' in Judge and Hu, eds., *Beyond Exemplar Tales*, 55–69.

16. Catherine Parke, *Biography: Writing Lives* (London: Routledge, 2002), xxi; Twitchett, 'Chinese Biographical Writing,' 95–96; Brian Moloughney,

'From Biographical History to Historical Biography,' *East Asian History* 4.4 (1992): 2–6. A looser definition of 'biography' might encompass also texts such as the *Analects* (*Lun yu, ca.* 500 BCE), the *Mencius* (*ca.* 300 BCE); these were cast as collections of anecdotes and conversations between teacher and disciples and were credited by some Chinese scholars as influences on historian-biographers such as Sima Qian. Hu Shi, *Hu Shi yanjiang lu* (The lectures of Hu Shi) (Shijiazhuang: Hebei renmin chubanshe, 1999), 230; Di and Shao, 'Life writing in Mainland China,' 32, point to earlier works such as the *Yanzi Chunqiu* (third century BCE).

17. While practices of writing and transmission changed over time, the association of official historiography with 'statecraft and morality...legitimation and propaganda' was a durable one. For a longer view, see On-cho Ng and Q. Edward Wang, *Mirroring the Past: The Writing and Use of History in Imperial China* (Honolulu: University of Hawaii Press, 2005).

18. Quoted in Parke, *Biography*, 2; the translation used by Parke carries the interpolation 'Had Han Hsin followed the Way *[of Confucius]* and been more modest...'; the comments by Hardy, noted below, on Sima Qian's 'inconsistency' suggest that this may not have been the full intention of the original.

19. Harriet Zurndorfer, *China Bibliography: A Research Guide to Reference Works about China Past and Present* (Leiden: Brill, 1995), 137; David Nivison, 'Aspects of Traditional Chinese Biography,' *Journal of Asian Studies* 21.4 (1962): 458.

20. Grant Hardy, *Worlds of Bronze and Bamboo: Sima Qian's Conquest of History* (New York: Columbia University Press, 1999), 39, 150–153; see also Wells, *To Die and Not Decay*, 108–112 for discussion by early Chinese critics of Sima Qian's 'moral ambiguity'.

21. Original source quoted in Parke, *Biography*, 2; emphasis in Parke's translation.

22. While the *Lienü* and *Shishuo* were produced centuries apart, they were subsequently read at times as complementary – if conflicting – traditions; see Qian Nanxiu, '*Lienü* versus *Xianyuan*: The Two Biographical Traditions in Chinese Women's History,' in Judge and Hu, eds., *Beyond Exemplar Tales*, 70–87; on the *Lienü zhuan*, see also Anne Behnke Kinney's University of Virginia website at http://www2.iath.virginia.edu/xwomen/intro.html# (accessed 15 August 2012).

23. Kathryn Ann Tsai, tr. and ed., *Lives of the Nuns: Biographies of Chinese Buddhist Nuns from the Fourth to the Sixth Centuries. A translation of Pi-ch'iu-ni chuan, compiled by Shih Pao-ch'ang* (Honolulu: University of Hawaii Press, 1994), 15–16. Buddhist *auto*biographies are discussed in Wu Pei-yi, *The Confucian's Progress: Autobiographical Writings in Traditional China* (New York: Columbia University Press, 1990), 71–92, 142–159. Beata Grant's work *Eminent Nuns: Women Chan Masters of Seventeenth-century China* (Honolulu: University of Hawaii Press, 2009) relies heavily on the self-narration of female Chan clerics.

24. Wu, *The Confucian's Progress*, 56–57; Wendy Larson, *Literary Authority and the Modern Chinese Writer* (Durham: Duke University Press, 1991), 11–24.
25. Larson, *Literary Authority*, 13, 19; Wu, *The Confucian's Progress*, 42–43, 15–18; Janet Ng describes Tao's narrative as 'antibiographical' in *The Experience of Modernity* (Ann Arbor: University of Michigan Press, 2003), 6.
26. Both quoted in Wu, *The Confucian's Progress*, 45, 47.
27. Wu, *The Confucian's Progress*, 47; Stephen Durrant, 'Self as the Intersection of Traditions: The Autobiographical Writings of Ssu-ma Ch'ien [Sima Qian],' *Journal of the American Oriental Society* 106.1 (1986): 33–40, quotation from 36.
28. Wells, *To Die and Not Decay*, 21, 55, 84, 92 93.
29. 'Liezhuan 45: Lienü' (Biographies 45: virtuous women) in Zheng Wei, comp., *Sui shu* (History of the Sui) (Beijing: Zhonghua shuju, 1973), 1810. The Sui history (581–618) was compiled in the first decades of Tang rule and completed in 656.
30. 'Liezhuan 35: Yang Xuangan' (Biographies 35: Yang Xuangan) in Zheng, *Sui shu*, 1615. For an English-language sketch of Yang's career, see Howard J. Wechsler, 'The Founding of the T'ang dynasty: Kao-tsu (reign 618–26),' in Denis Twitchett, ed. *Cambridge History of China 3: Sui and T'ang China, 589–906, Part I* (Cambridge: Cambridge University Press, 1979), 152–153.
31. Zheng, *Sui shu*, 1636–1637.
32. Denis Twitchett, 'Introduction,' in Denis Twitchett, ed., *The Cambridge History of China Vol. 3: Sui and T'ang China, 589–906 AD, Part 1* (Cambridge: Cambridge University Press, 1980), 42.
33. William Hung, 'A T'ang Historiographer's Letter of Resignation,' *Harvard Journal of Asiatic Studies* 29 (1969): 7–8.
34. Hung, 'A T'ang Historiographer,' 7–8; on the processes of selection involved in producing official biographies at a later time, see Sarah Schneewind, 'Reduce, Re-use, Recycle: Imperial Autocracy and Scholar-Official Autonomy in the Background to the Ming History Biography of Early Ming Scholar-Official Fang Keqin (1326–1376),' *Oriens Extremus* 48 (2009); Twitchett, 'Problems of Chinese Biography,' 27; Denis Twitchett, *The Writing of Official History under the T'ang* (Cambridge: Cambridge University Press, 1992), 66–67.
35. Di and Shao, 'Life Writing in Mainland China,' 33; Mouloughney, 'From Biographical History,' 11. The 'chronological biography' genre is not always engaging reading but it remains a common form for recording individual lives, works and times: it typically includes a detailed (for more recent lives, sometimes daily) listing of personal activities, that may be supplemented variously by records of local/national/ institutional events, personal writings, official documents and the like. Recent examples include works on third-century scholars Lu Ji and Lu Yun, distinguished Buddhist monk Xu Yun (1840–1959) and military leader Zhang Xueliang (1901–2001). Yu Shiling, ed., *Lu Ji, Lu Yun nianpu* (Chronicle of Lu Ji and Lu Yun) (Beijing: Renmin chubanshe, 2009); Zheng Hui, ed., *Xu Yun*

*heshang nianpu* (Chronicle of the monk Xu Yun), 5 vols. (Zhengzhou: Zhongzhou guji chubanshe, 2009); Zhang Youkun et al., eds., *Zhang Xueliang nianpu* (Chronicle of Zhang Xueliang), 2 vols. (Beijing: Shehui kexue wenxian chubanshe, 2009).

36. Twitchett, *The Writing of Official History under the T'ang*, 72–74.

37. See Zhu Xi's (1130–1200) overview in William T. de Bary and Irene Bloom, eds., *Sources of Chinese Tradition*, vol. 1. (New York: Columbia University Press, 2000), 662.

38. Naomi Standen, *Unbounded Loyalty: Frontier Crossing in Liao China* (Honolulu: University of Hawaii Press, 2007). The official histories of the Liao (907–1115) and the Song (960–1279) were both completed in the 1340s. On the range and filiation of sources, see 35–40; on two officials, Li Huan and Wang Jizhong, and their treatment in official biographies, see 149–171, especially 168–171. A central element of Standen's argument is that the idea of 'China' was less robust at the time of the crossings than the later biographies were designed to make it appear.

39. Patricia Ebrey, 'Empress Xiang (1046–1101) and Biographical Sources beyond Formal Biographies,' in Judge and Hu, eds., *Beyond Exemplar Tales*, 193–211; see 194–195 for the full text of the formal biography.

40. Charles Lachman, 'On the Artist's Biography in Sung China: The Case of Li Ch'eng,' *Biography* 9.3 (1986): 189–201.

41. See Beverly J. Bossler, *Powerful Relations: Kinship, Status, and the State in Sung China (960–1279)* (Cambridge: Harvard University Press, 1998), 10, and translations of twelfth-century epitaphs in Mann and Cheng, eds., *Under Confucian Eyes*, 71–84.

42. Wu Pei-yi, 'Childhood Remembered: Parents and Children in China, 800–1700,' in Anne Behnke Kinney, ed., *Chinese Views of Childhood*, (Honolulu: University of Hawaii Press, 1995), especially 148–152; Ping Yao, 'Women's Epitaphs in Tang China (618–907),' in Judge and Hu, eds., *Beyond Exemplar Tales*, especially 145–148.

43. Timothy Brook, *The Confusions of Pleasure: Commerce and Culture in Ming China* (Berkeley: University of California Press, 1998).

44. Wu, *The Confucian's Progress*, xii; Lynn Struve, 'Confucian PTSD,' 14–15, 29, n.10 (note that the 'ego-document' central to this article survived only by personal transmission; Struve, *Voices from the Ming Qing Cataclysm*; Paul Jakov Smith, 'Impressions of the Song-Yuan-Ming transition: The Evidence from *Biji* Memoirs,' in Paul Jakov Smith and Richard von Glahn, eds., *The Song-Yuan-Ming Transition in Chinese History* (Cambridge: Harvard University Press, 2003), 71–110; Lynn Struve, 'Chimerical Early Modernity: The Case of 'Conquest-generation' Memoirs,' in Lynn Struve, ed., *The Qing Formation in World-Historical Time* (Cambridge: Harvard University Asia Center, 2004), 335–380.

45. Wu, *The Confucian's Progress*, xii.

46. Katherine Carlitz, 'Lovers, Talkers, Monsters, and Good Women: Competing Images in Mid-Ming Epitaphs and Fiction,' in Judge and Hu, eds., *Beyond Exemplar Tales*, 177–183; Chow Kai-wing, *Publishing, Culture, and*

*Power*. Sharpe and Zwicker have noted the status performance function of life writing and self-representation among the high elites of early modern England, and we may see many of these impulses pursued to different audiences on a wider scale among families of more modest means in auto/biographical practice in late imperial China; Kevin Sharpe and Stephen Zwicker, 'Introducing Lives,' in *Writing Lives: Biography and Textuality, Identity and Representation in Early Modern England* (Oxford: Oxford University Press, 2008), 1–28.

47. Yang Xunji, 'Written on the Doors of My Bookshelves,' translated in Mair, ed., *The Columbia Anthology of Traditional Chinese Literature*, 273. See also 'Biography of Zhu Jiefu,' in Patricia Ebrey, ed., *Chinese Civilisation: A Sourcebook*, 2nd ed. (New York: Free Press, 1993), and, on the Confucianisation of the trading classes, Richard Lufrano, *Honorable Merchants: Commerce and Self-Cultivation in Late Imperial China* (Honolulu: University of Hawai'i Press, 1997).

48. On the cult of female chastity and its biographical manifestations, see Katherine Carlitz, 'Shrines, Governing-Class Identity, and the Cult of Widow Fidelity in Mid-Ming Jiangnan,' *Journal of Asian Studies* 56.3 (1997): 612–640 and Mark Elvin, 'Female Virtue and the State in China,' *Past and Present* 104 (1984): 111–152; Mann and Cheng, eds., *Under Confucian Eyes*, 135–148.

49. See Zhang's biographies in Mann and Cheng, eds., *Under Confucian Eyes*, 217–230; Lu Weijing, 'Faithful Maiden Biographies: A Forum for Ritual Debate, Moral Critique, and Personal Reflection,' in Judge and Hu, eds., *Beyond Exemplar Tales*, esp. 100–103.

50. Dorothy Ko, *Teachers of the Inner Chambers: Women and Culture in Seventeenth-Century China* (Stanford: Stanford University Press), 29; Ellen Widmer, 'Women as Biographers in Mid-Qing Jiangnan', in Judge and Hu, eds., *Beyond Exemplar Tales*, 246–261; Idema and Grant, *The Red Brush*, 414–421, 553–557.

51. L. Carrington Goodrich, *The Literary Inquisition of Ch'ien-lung* (New York: Paragon, 1966 [1935]) notes periodic imperial orders to suppress or destroy heterodox works as well as direct imperial interventions in the biographical sections of the Ming history. See also Yang, 'The Organization of Chinese Official Historiography,' 48. Huang Zongxi's *Records of the Ming Scholars* (1676) followed established traditions of tracing intellectual histories through biographical sketch and commentary and may be read both as a defence of his own intellectual genealogy and – conceivably – of the scholar's prerogative to interpret both letters and lives. See Lynn Struve, 'Huang Zongxi in Context: A Reappraisal of His Major Writings,' *Journal of Asian Studies* 47.3 (1988), esp. 481–484, and Huang Zongxi [Tsung-hsi], tr. Julia Ching, *Records of the Ming Scholars* (Honolulu: University of Hawaii Press, 1987).

52. Martin Huang, *Literati and Self-re/presentation: Autobiographical Sensibility in the Eighteenth-century China Novel* (Stanford: Stanford University Press, 1995), 2–8, 10–12.

53. Vera Schwarcz, *The Chinese Enlightenment: Intellectuals and the Legacy of the May Fourth Movement of 1919* (Berkeley: University of California Press, 1986); and Lydia Liu, *Translingual Practice: Literature, National Culture, and Translated Modernity – China, 1900–1937* (Stanford: Stanford University Press, 1995).

54. Moloughney argues that the school of 'evidential research' (*kaozheng xue*) had launched a challenge to traditional historiography from within the Confucian establishment; 'From Historical Biography,' 13–14.

55. Larson, *Literary Authority*, 31–60.

56. Moloughney, 'From Biographical History,' 1–2; Ng, *Experience of Modernity*, vii.

57. Ng, *Experience of Modernity*, 54–64.

58. Wang Lingzhen, *Personal Matters: Women's Autobiographical Practice in Twentieth-century China* (Stanford: Stanford University Press: 2004), 1, 17; on mothers, see Chapters 2–3.

59. Wang, *When 'I' was Born*, 30–32, and Chapter 4, especially 114–120; quotation from 77.

60. Ibid., 30–32, and Chapter 4, especially 114–120; Ng, *Experience of Modernity*, 96, 100.

61. Moloughney, 'From Biographical History,' 1–2; Joan Judge, *The Precious Raft of History: The Past, the West and the Woman Question in China* (Stanford: Stanford University Press, 2008); Paul Cohen, *Speaking to History: The Story of King Goujian in Twentieth-Century China* (Berkeley: University of California Press, 2009).

62. Bryna Goodman, 'The New Woman Commits Suicide: The Press, Cultural Memory, and the New Republic,' *Journal of Asian Studies* 64.1 (2005): 67–102; Eugenia Lean, *Public Passions: The Trial of Shi Jianqiao and the Rise of Popular Sympathy in Republican China* (Berkeley: University of California Press, 2007); Anne Kerlan-Stephens, 'The Making of Modern Icons: Three Actresses of the Lianhua Film Company,' *European Journal of East Asian Studies* 6.1 (2007): 43–73.

63. Arthur Waldron, 'China's New Remembering of World War II: The Case of Zhang Zizhong,' *Modern Asian Studies* 30.4 (1996): 958–961.

64. Qu Qiubai, *Superfluous Words*, tr. Jamie Greenbaum (Canberra: Pandanus Books, 2006), 172.

65. Philip C.C. Huang, 'Rural Class Struggle in the Chinese Revolution: Representational and Objective Realities from the Land Reform to the Cultural Revolution,' *Modern China* 21.1 (1995): 105–143; the practical implications of those class categories and the embedding of life stories in local history and memory are explored in Jiangsui He, 'Death of a Landlord: Moral Predicament in Rural China, 1968–1969,' in Joseph W. Esherick, Paul G. Pickowicz and Andrew G. Walder, eds., *The Chinese Cultural Revolution as History* (Stanford: Stanford University Press, 2006).

66. William Ayers, 'Current Biography in Communist China,' *Journal of Asian Studies* 21.4 (1962): 477.

67. *Wenshi ziliao xuanji (Selected Materials on History and Culture)* 100 parts in 40 vols. (Beijing: Zhongguo wenshi chubanshe, 1986). When the original request was made to older members (over 60 years old) of the China People's Political Consultative Conference (Zhongguo renmin zhengzhi xieshang huiyi, CPPCC), manuscripts totalling 2 million characters were submitted within months. *Wenshi ziliao xuanji*, vol. 1, 1–5. These were originally produced for limited *(neibu)* circulation between 1960 and 1984. Provincial, city and county editions are also published, and the scope of collection has been extended to the post-1949 period. The *Materials* are discussed more fully below by Henrion-Dourcy.

68. For a typology of exemplars, see Di and Shao, 'Life Writing in Mainland China,' 34–35; on the use of models, see Mary Sheridan, 'The Emulation of Heroes,' *China Quarterly* 33 (1968): 47–72; Uradyn Bulag, 'Models and Moralities: The Parable of the Two "Heroic Little Sisters of the Grassland",' *China Journal* 42 (1999): 21–41; for visual narratives of Lei Feng, Qian Xuesen (discussed below) and several dozen other exemplars, see IISH, *Models and Martyrs*, http://chineseposters.net/themes/models. php (accessed 8 April 2013).

69. David Apter and Tony Saich, *Revolutionary Discourse in Mao's Republic* (Cambridge: Harvard University Press, 1994), 264–284. The best-known example of these narratives of rehabilitation is the life story of China's last emperor: Aisin Gioro Pu Yi, *From Emperor to Citizen*, tr. W.J.F. Jenner (Oxford: Oxford University Press, 1987); Ann Anagnost, *National Pasttimes: Narrative, Representation and Power in Modern China* (Durham: Duke University Press, 1997), 28–38.

70. The phrase comes from Alessandro Portelli, 'History-Telling and Time: An Example from Kentucky,' *Oral History Review* 20.1&2 (1992): 51–53, though Portelli's work shows very different power relations between interviewer and narrator.

71. For an account of Cultural Revolution struggle from the accused's point of view, see Jesse Field, 'Taking Intimate Publics to China: Yang Jiang and the Unfinished Business of Sentiment,' *Biography* 34.1 (2011): 88–92.

72. Charlene Makley, ' "Speaking Bitterness": Autobiography, History and Mnemonic Politics on the Sino-Tibetan Frontier,' *Comparative Studies in Society and History* 47.1 (2005): 59.

73. Wu Mi, *Riji* (Diary) 10 vols and *Riji xu bian* (Diary: second series) 10 vols (Beijing: Sanlian, 1998–2006) covers the years 1910–1974; Field, 'Taking Intimate Publics to China,' esp. 87.

74. Some works – such as diaries and letters of 'educated youth' sent to the countryside – fitted the political mood of the moment: see Lu Rong, *Yige Shanghai zhiqing de 223 feng jiaxin* (223 letters home from a Shanghai educated youth) (Shanghai: Shanghai shehui kexue chubanshe, 2009). Some may have survived simply because their authors avoided political talk: the post-1949 diary of Xu Baoheng (1875–1961) who, like Zheng Xiaoxu, had worked for the Japanese in Manchuria during the war, focused firmly on the everyday; others – such as the diaries kept by Zhang Xianliang

(discussed in Chapter 7 of this volume by Starr) and playwright and novelist Chen Baichen (1910–1994) – cover experiences of persecution and were kept covertly. Chen Baichen, *Xiankou riji* (Keeping-mouth-shut diaries, 1966–1972, 1974–1979), (Zhengzhou: Daxiang chubanshe, 2005).

75. Di and Shao, 'Life Writing in Mainland China,' 39–40, 43.
76. Recent collections include works such as *Wode jianzheng: 200 wei qinli kangzhan zhe koushu lishi* (My testimony: 200 oral histories based on personal experience of the War of Resistance) (Beijing: Jiefangjun wenyi chubanshe, 2005); Ding Chen, ed., *Qinli Zhongguo Gongchandang de 90 nian* (Personal experiences of 90 years of the Communist Party of China) (Beijing: Renmin chubanshe, 2011); Zhang Shujun et al., eds., *Jianzheng lishi: Zhongguo 1975–1976* (Historical testimony: China 1975–1976) (Changsha: Hunan renmin chubanshe, 2009). It is possible that, as oral history as a sub-field takes root in Chinese universities, a wider agenda may emerge.
77. Wang Lingzhen, *Personal Matters*, esp. 140–150; of the nine hundred-odd works on Lei Feng listed in the National Library catalogue, 109 were published (or reprinted) in 2012 alone. On Qian, see Wang Ning, 'The Making of an Intellectual Hero: Chinese Narratives of Qian Xuesen,' *China Quarterly* 206 (2011): 352–371.
78. Wang Ning, 'The Making of an Intellectual Hero'; Gail Hershatter, 'Forget Remembering: Rural Women's Narratives of China's Collective Past,' in Ching Kwan Lee and Guobin Yang, eds., *Re-envisioning the Chinese Revolution: The Politics and Poetics of Collective Memory in Reform* China (Stanford: Stanford University Press, 2007), 69–92; and Hershatter, 'Getting a Life: The Production of 1950s Women Labor Models in Rural Shaanxi,' 36–54.
79. Emily Huiching Chua, 'The Good Book and the Good Life: Best-selling Biographies in China's Economic Reform,' *China Quarterly* 198 (2009): 364–380.
80. The best known of these is probably Jung Chang's *Wild Swans* (London: Harper Press, 2012), but there are numerous others, including Heng Liang, *Son of the Revolution* (London: Fontana, 1984); Nien Cheng, *Life and Death in Shanghai* (London: Grafton, 1986); Rae Yang, *Spider Eaters* (Berkeley: University of California Press, 1997), He Liyi, *Mr China's Son: A Villager's Life* (Boulder: Westview Press, 1993), as well as collections of shorter pieces such as Feng Jicai, *Ten Years of Madness: Oral Histories of China's Cultural Revolution* (San Francisco: China Books and Periodicals, 1996). Less well known overseas but nonetheless significant are the (often heavily auto/biographical) fictional genres of 'scar' and 'roots-seeking' literature that sought to process the Cultural Revolution experience and reassert personal over collective identity.
81. Peter Zarrow, 'Meanings of China's Cultural Revolution: Memoirs of Exile,' *positions: asia critique* 7.1 (1999): 165–191.
82. Margaretta Jolly, 'The Exile and the Ghostwriter: East-West Biographical Politics and the Private Life of Chairman Mao,' *Biography* 23.3

(2000): 481–503, and 'Coming Out of the Coming Out Story: Writing Queer Lives,' *Sexualities* 4 (2001): 474–496.

83. China had an estimated 513 million internet users (38.3% of total population) at the end of 2011, of whom 136 million were located in rural areas; an 'internet user' is defined here as 'a Chinese citizen over the age of 6 years who has used the internet in the past six months'. China Internet Network Information Center, *[29th] Statistical Report on Internet Development in China,* 2012, online via http://www.apira.org, 4–6, 11.

84. For a snapshot of Han Han that highlights the persona built on the blog, see David Pilling, 'Lunch with the FT: Han Han,' *Financial Times* 21 April 2012; on Muzi Mei and others, see Liu Jianxin, 'Gendered Performances and Norms in Chinese Personal Blogs,' *Gender Forum* 30 (2010), online via http://www.genderforum.org/; elsewhere, compare IT entrepreneur Wang Jianshuo's Chinese/English blog at http://home.wangjianshuo.com/ (accessed 17 September 2012) with the personal site kept by retired doctor Wang Daxiang at http://www.wangdxx.com/ (accessed 15 September 2012).

85. Michael Keren's usefully sceptical ideal-typology of bloggers is intriguing in this context: 'Blogging and Mass Politics,' *Biography* 33.1 (2010): 110–126; James Leibold, 'Blogging Alone: China, the Internet, and the Democratic Illusion?' *Journal of Asian Studies* 70.4 (2011): 1023–1041, offers the bleaker view 'that the Sinophone blogosphere is producing the same shallow infotainment, pernicious misinformation, and interest-based ghettos that it creates elsewhere in the world'.

# 2

# Self-representation in the Dramas of Ruan Dacheng (1587–1646)

*Alison Hardie*

Ruan Dacheng (1587–1646), known to his friends as Stone Nest (Shichao) or the Woodcutter of Baizi Hill (Baizi shan qiao), and to his enemies as Beardy Ruan (Ruan huzi), Hirsute of Anqing (Wan ran) and ultimately as Hairy Heirless (Ran jue), is most notorious as the associate of Wei Zhongxian (1568–1627), chief eunuch of the Tianqi court and as the vengeful sidekick of Ma Shiying (1591–1646/7) in the faction-ridden Southern Ming regime, sharing with Ma a joint biography in the 'Treacherous Officials' section of the official *Ming History*.[1] But he was also a distinguished poet, regarded by Yuan Zhongdao (1570–1623) as a worthy follower of his brother Yuan Hongdao (1568–1610), the leader of the Gong'an School in literature,[2] and a phenomenally successful dramatist, described by the historian and drama aficionado Zhang Dai (1597–1680) as 'extremely talented' as both playwright and director,[3] whose dramas were greatly admired even by his bitterest enemies

Accounts of Ruan by himself and others form an interesting case study of life writing, partly because the views taken vary so widely, and are often extreme. I will discuss these accounts in some detail in the section on sources below. Ruan's role in the Ming-Qing transition was a significant one, whatever view is taken of his character and behaviour. He was faced with a series of choices in his life and career, and generally made what turned out later to be the wrong choices. But many of his experiences were shared with others in his social class, and in many ways he can be regarded as typical of members of the scholar-official class in the late Ming.

Ruan's self-presentation, therefore, is of some interest in under-standing the self-image of late-Ming scholar-officials, and when that is compared or contrasted with the views of his contemporaries, an even greater depth of understanding can be achieved. Because Ruan was such a controversial figure, moreover, a wide variety of people at the time had things to say about him, and we can gain a many-faceted view which would be unobtainable by relying only on official sources such as the *Ming History*, in which he appears as a somewhat one-dimensional villain. The fact that Ruan's own view of himself is completely different again reminds us that our view of historical people and events is inevitably coloured not only by what evidence survives but also by the time at which that evidence was compiled.

Much of the most hostile writing about Ruan (such as the *Ming History* biography) appeared after his death, and it is arguable that many people with guilty consciences chose to use someone who was already unpopular, and now conveniently dead, as a scapegoat onto whom they could shift the blame for the ignominious collapse of the Ming dynasty. But he was the target of attacks during his lifetime also, notably in the Revival Society's 'Proclamation of Nanjing' of 1638.[4] Contemporaries believed that his dramas represented an attempt to defend himself against his detractors. It is clear too that many of his approximately 2,000 poems are concerned with self-justification. The fact that Ruan Dacheng's literary output springs from his own experi-ences is not surprising. Ruan was associated with the Gong'an School of writers; strongly influenced by Wang Yangming's concept of innate knowledge, they believed writers should express their 'native sensi-bility' rather than imitating the style and subject-matter of earlier masters.[5] What is surprising is the extent to which he incorporated personal material into his dramas, rather than just his poetry. Because his dramas were likely to be seen, or read, by a wider audience than his poetry, the dramas also worked to shape his image for a wider public.

In this chapter, I will first discuss the main contemporary accounts of Ruan's life, and compare them briefly with the image of Ruan pre-sented in his poetry, and in more detail with the image of himself and his family that he presents in his plays. I argue that his plays contain an unusually large element of personal content – the author does not normally appear so prominently in *chuanqi* drama[6] – and that this is facilitated by the fact that he created his own plots rather than using pre-existing stories. By examining Ruan's self-representation, we can appreciate how the same life could be understood so differently from within and without, and thus perceive how unsympathetic or actively hostile life writing may have distorted our understanding of a significant late-Ming individual; we may consequently recover a more impartial view.

## Ruan's life and career

Ruan Dacheng was born in 1587 into a wealthy and influential family in Anqing, on the Yangtze in the Southern Metropolitan District, Nanzhili (Anqing is now in Anhui province).[7] The city of Anqing, the prefectural capital, was also the county seat of Huaining; the Ruan family had been resident in Tongcheng County, to the north-east of Anqing, but had moved to Huaining in a previous generation. The family claimed descent from the third-century poet Ruan Ji (210–263), and had been officials for many generations. Ruan Dacheng's great-grandfather was Ruan E (1509–1567, *jinshi* 1544), one of the more prominent adherents of Grand Secretary Yan Song (*jinshi* 1505, died *ca.*1565); a great-uncle, Ruan Zihua (*jinshi* 1598), was well known as a poet and had some influence on the young Dacheng.[8] Ruan Dacheng became an Elevated Person (*juren*, the second level in the imperial examination system) in 1603, at the early age of 17 *sui* (16 by Western count).[9]

After obtaining his Presented Scholar (*jinshi*) degree in 1616 (the highest level of the imperial examinations), Ruan became a Messenger (*xingren*, rank 9a); this was a normal first post for Presented Scholars who had not attained the dizzy heights of appointment to the Hanlin Academy. Ruan's official career proceeded in a fairly routine way until he came up for promotion in 1624 to the post of Chief Supervising Secretary of the Ministry of Civil Offices (*like du jishizhong*, rank 7a). At this point the Eastern Grove (Donglin) faction, who styled themselves as the 'righteous tendency' in the internecine conflicts of late-Ming officialdom, strongly pushed their own candidate for the post, Wei Dazhong (1575–1625). Up to this point, Ruan Dacheng had never been an opponent of the Eastern Grove; in fact he had been associated with them, and his wife's grandfather, Wu Yuexiu (*jinshi* 1580), was a member.[10] It is not clear why the faction turned against Ruan, except that they seem to have found him insufficiently serious and potentially unreliable as regards confidentiality.[11] Eventually the appointment went in Ruan's favour, as it should have done all along, but he felt under so much pressure that he soon resigned.

It seems to have been this experience which drove him to associate himself with Wei Zhongxian, the powerful chief eunuch of the Tianqi Emperor's court. However, Ruan's association with Wei Zhongxian cannot have been as intimate as it was later represented to be since, when the Tianqi Emperor died in 1627 and Wei Zhongxian was shown the door, Ruan did not immediately suffer; he was in fact promoted to Vice-Minister of the Court of Imperial Entertainment (*guanglu shaoqing*, rank 5a) in 1628. He was, however, removed from office in 1629 or 1630, and the following year was convicted of involvement in the 'Treason Case' (i.e. of association with Wei Zhongxian). He returned to Anqing as a commoner (having paid a fine in lieu of hard labour), and it seems to have been at this time that he seriously took up dramatic writing, publishing *Spring Lantern Riddles*, the first of his surviving plays, in 1633. In 1635, bandit activity in the Anqing area became so serious that Ruan and his family moved to Nanjing, the 'secondary capital' of the Ming empire and capital of the Southern Metropolitan Region.

Ruan, an energetic man now in his forties, evidently found it hard to do nothing; he composed poetry, wrote and directed plays, published his own and others' work, and continued to take an interest in public affairs, with a particular interest in military and frontier issues. Reputedly he aimed to use his claimed expertise in frontier affairs as a way of being recalled to office. In pursuit of this aim, he kept open house for various military men and martial arts practitioners, as well as people with personal experience of China's frontiers, such as Kuang Lu (1604–1650), the Cantonese writer and adventurer who wrote about his experiences with monsters and savages in Guangxi.[12] Kuang Lu acted as editor of Ruan's poetry collection, *Poems from the Hall of Chanting what is in my Heart*, published from 1635 onwards.[13] Despite Ruan's official disgrace, he socialised actively with the officials of the Southern Capital. All this activity provoked the Revival Society, successors to the Eastern Grove faction which had suffered under the ascendancy of Ruan's former patron Wei Zhongxian, to issue in 1638 a 'Proclamation to Prevent Disorder in the Secondary Capital' (*Liudu fangluan gongjie*, known in English as the 'Proclamation of Nanjing'). This makes some wild accusations against Ruan, claiming that Ruan's plays contained 'hidden slanders against the emperor's wisdom, and satire on society'[14] and implying that his association with martial artists could be interpreted as sympathy with the peasant uprisings then widespread in China. There was not a shred of solid evidence for this, and it is noteworthy that no one in authority saw fit to follow up the allegation. Until the fall of the Ming, however, Ruan never returned to office. The *Ming History* states that throughout this time 'he was melancholy because he could not realise his ambitions',[15] and this is certainly borne out in many of his poems.

When Beijing fell in 1644, and the Southern Ming resistance government was set up in Nanjing with the Prince of Fu as its figurehead, Ruan was finally able to obtain an official post – against much opposition – through the influence of the powerful Ma Shiying, with whom Ruan had been on friendly terms since they had taken the Metropolitan Examinations together in 1616 (though Ma did not take the Palace Examination to become a Presented Scholar until 1619). Ruan ultimately became Minister of Defence in the Southern Ming, but his supposed military expertise stood him in little stead, and when the Manchus conquered Jiangnan in 1645 Ruan was one of many officials who decided to throw in their lot with the invaders. He did not do so immediately on the fall of Nanjing, as many did, because he happened to be away from the city at the time, but he joined the Qing army not long afterwards. He could be categorised as one of the 'Romantics' of this time, in Wakeman's definition: like several of Wakeman's Romantics, he was a follower of the Gong'an School of poetry.[16] According to the historian Zhang Dai,[17] on joining the Manchus he issued a public statement expressing his gratitude to the Great Qing for their recognition after his mistreatment under the Ming.[18] Zhang quotes this example of brazen cheek without comment, but it may have been one of a number of reasons why Ruan was singled out for particular execration by his contemporaries.

Ruan followed the Qing army on campaign towards Fujian, and died suddenly, in somewhat mysterious circumstances, while crossing the Xianxia pass, in the mountains on the Zhejiang–Fujian border. He was about 60 years old, and left two daughters but no male heir, so there was no one to defend his interests once he was dead. It must be said that his servants were remarkably loyal to his memory: one of them went to great lengths to retrieve his body from the roadside (under wartime conditions, we must remember),[19] and later the former lead actor of his household troupe refused offers of employment acting in revivals of his plays, on the grounds that 'whenever one of [Master Ruan's] plays is performed, he is ridiculed and abused in every way; it makes one upset all day long'.[20]

## Contemporary sources for Ruan's life

There is a wide variety of contemporary or slightly later sources for Ruan's life, which can be categorised as neutral, hostile or scandalmongering to a greater or lesser degree. The two best-known hostile sources, which have had the most impact on Ruan's later reputation, are the joint biography of Ruan and Ma Shiying in the official *Ming History*, and Kong Shangren's (1648–1718) dramatic account in his much-loved historical play *The Peach-blossom Fan*. This play was completed in 1699, half a century after Ruan's death, but Kong based it on extensive research and interviews with survivors of the Ming who had known the real people in the drama. However, in the interests of dramatic representation, Kong took some liberties with strict historical accuracy. Ruan Dacheng as a character in *The Peach-blossom Fan* is really a caricature villain, and I will not discuss here how he is presented in the play.[21]

The *Ming History* biography is obviously based on authoritative sources, including official records, but the compilers of the *Ming History* were extremely hostile to Ruan and his associates, so where this account offers interpretation of Ruan's activities it has to be regarded with some scepticism. The *Ming History* was compiled largely by former adherents of the Eastern Grove or Revival Society factions under the Ming, who had been co-opted to a greater or lesser degree into the service of the Qing dynasty. They or their relatives had suffered under Wei Zhongxian and had been sidelined during the Southern Ming: they chose to blame all this on Ruan Dacheng, who was no longer around to defend himself, rather than acknowledging the role of the Eastern Grove in exacerbating factional conflict.

Another 'official' but neutral account of Ruan is a short biography in the Kangxi-era local gazetteer of Huaining, published in 1686. This shows how differently Ruan's life could be presented when the writer was not hostile to him, but its publication in a local gazetteer meant that it did not circulate widely and therefore had little influence on the general view of Ruan. It appears in the section devoted to literary men of the Qing dynasty (thus acknowledging his surrender to the invaders). It is concerned with Ruan's status as a man of letters and his personality, and touches very lightly on his official career, merely alluding to things 'repeatedly going wrong' for him. Clearly the editors of the *County Gazetteer* did not wish to get involved in discussing the rights and wrongs of Ruan's political career, but simply wished to include whatever cast the most reflected glory on their locality. Though published 40 years after his death, the biography seems to have been written by someone who knew him, or at least to be based on such a source. It does not appear to derive from any of the other extant sources on Ruan of which I am aware. Although other writers have plenty to say about what Ruan did and why, they generally (with the exception of Qian Chengzhi [1612–1693], whom I discuss below) treat him as a stock villain and give very little sense of what he was like as an individual, so the *County Gazetteer* is an interesting supplement. It describes a rather exuberant personality, 'forceful and outgoing' (*kangshuang*), with whom it might have been difficult for an interlocutor to get a word in edgeways: 'He would twirl his beard and discuss the affairs of the empire, in a torrent of speech to which no boundaries could be perceived.'[22]

Two more hostile but none the less persuasive accounts of Ruan by people who knew him well are Qian Chengzhi's 'Ruan Dacheng benmo xiaoji' (Notes for a full account of Ruan Dacheng), and Zhang Dai's biography of Ruan in the *Supplement to Book for a Stone Casket*, his monumental study of the fall of the Ming, together with other material by Zhang. Qian Chengzhi's 'Notes' is also known in a slightly different version as 'Wan ran shimo' (Hirsute of Anqing; from start to finish); it seems to have been one of the sources for the *Ming History* biography. Qian did at least have personal justification for his bitter resentment and hostility towards Ruan. The Qians were distantly related to the Ruans, and in Qian's youth, Ruan – who was certainly an arrogant, domineering and no doubt thoroughly annoying personality – had attempted to patronise and manipulate him.[23] Then, after the fall of Beijing, and the subsequent collapse of the Hongguang regime in Nanjing, Qian remained extremely active in the Southern Ming resistance, and he had every reason to despise those like Ruan who had switched to the winning side as soon as the going got tough. Qian Chengzhi's account is the most detailed and openly hostile of those by various writers during the early Qing, who were concerned to demonstrate how the pernicious influence of Ruan and his associates such as Ma Shiying and Feng Quan (1595–1672) had undermined the Ming dynasty. It does not merely criticise Ruan but aims to make him a figure of ridicule, especially towards the end of his life.

Qian's account is, however, interesting and in many ways persuasive, because he gives the impression of telling what he believed to be the truth about Ruan, rather than relaying any and every bit of scurrilous gossip that came his way. For instance, two famous anecdotes in later sources claim that Ruan acted as Wei Zhongxian's adoptive son,[24] and that he hung a couplet in his house stating, 'To have no son means one's person is light, to hold office means that all things are satisfactory' (*Wu zi yi shen qing, you guan wan shi zu*),[25] but Qian Chengzhi says nothing about either of these thoroughly implausible allegations. Qian clearly knew Ruan and describes his personality in similar though less flattering terms to the *County Gazetteer*. He says that he was a 'superficial' person, whose reactions to the most trifling occurrences were visible in his facial expression.[26] (This hardly supports the *Ming History*'s accusation of cunning and deviousness, which is probably a standard criticism of 'treacherous officials'.[27]) Qian makes a point of noting his sources for Ruan's brief career with the Qing military, citing names or native places of his informants.[28] He remarks on Ruan's ability to arrange a very high standard of catering even amid the devastation of war, and gives a sardonically amusing account of Ruan's efforts to raise cultural standards in the army, as a sort of one-man armed forces' entertainment troupe:

> The officers had heard about his [Ruan's] plays *Spring Lantern Riddles*, *The Swallow Messenger* and so on, and asked him whether he himself could perform. He sprang up and seized the clappers, tapped his feet and sang, to entertain the officers as they drank. The officers were northerners and could not understand the music or dialect of Wu, so it was only when he changed to singing in the Yiyang style that they nodded and applauded, exclaiming, 'What a talented chap Mr Ruan is!' Every night he would sit in the officers' tents talking expansively; his listeners would grow weary and

go to bed, but he would not leave until he heard them snoring. He did this through every single tent. In the morning, before it was even light, he would be back sitting in the tents, blethering on at them, or reciting a poem that he had composed during the night. The officers were worn out, and could not stand this disturbance to their time off-duty.[29]

This description certainly supports the reference to a 'torrent of speech' in the *Huaining County Gazetteer* biography, and incidentally underlines the importance that Ruan attached to dramatic performance. Ruan Dacheng seems to have been quite oblivious of the effect he had on people, and it may have been this lack of awareness as much as anything that got him into trouble.

Zhang Dai, in the *Stone Casket Supplement*, says very little about Ruan's life prior to the establishment of the Southern Ming regime. He gives the impression of regarding Ruan's activities during the Tianqi reign as relatively unimportant, suggesting that he did not really believe that Ruan had significant responsibility for the persecution of the Eastern Grove adherents, but he places a great deal of emphasis on the bitter debate over the appointment of Ruan at the Hongguang court, and criticises Ruan sharply for concentrating his energies on factional strife rather than defending the state against invasion.[30]

From his other writing we know that Zhang, who shared Ruan's passion for the theatre, had a very high regard for Ruan as a playwright and theatrical director. Zhang had visited Ruan in 1638 (showing support when he was under pressure from the Revival Society)[31] and had watched his private opera troupe performing then and perhaps on other occasions also. One of the short essays in his *Dream Memories of Joyous Hermitage* extols the brilliance of Ruan's work,[32] and he also mentions him approvingly in a letter to the dramatist Yuan Yuling (1592–1674).[33] Zhang believed that Ruan's dramas reflected his life experiences: in his words, '[Ruan's plays are] 70% cursing society, and 30% venting his own frustrations; broadly attacking the Eastern Grove, and defending the Wei faction.'[34] Zhang had written two poems to Ruan on the occasion of his 1638 visit, and Ruan wrote poems to Zhang then too.[35] We can see, therefore, that Zhang Dai's attitude to Ruan changed over time in response to Ruan's own behaviour and to external events.

A sympathetic, though very brief, account of part of Ruan's life is given at a fairly early stage by Zhang Dai's friend and distant relative Wang Siren (1575–1646), the distinguished scholar-official from Shaoxing, who seems to have become acquainted with Ruan while serving as an official in Jiujiang, not very far from Anqing. In the preface, which he wrote for Ruan's 1633 drama, *Spring Lantern Riddles or Ten Cases of Mistaken Identity*, Wang states:

> The trend of the times was misdirected, and he [Ruan] met with opprobrium and aroused fear and opposition, so that right and wrong changed places. As a result he gave up his ambitions and returned to the countryside, holding himself aloof, and devoted himself solely to dramatic composition.[36]

Even earlier, Yuan Zhongdao (also a Presented Scholar of 1616) socialised with Ruan in Beijing in 1617[37] and describes him in a preface as a poetic successor of his brother Yuan Hongdao, but does not clarify whether Ruan ever met Yuan Hongdao in person (which is unlikely) or to what extent Ruan presented himself as an Gong'an adherent.[38]

More hostile accounts of Ruan's activities, in tune with Qian Chengzhi's narrative, can be found in the unofficial histories written by those involved in the Southern Ming resistance, including Ji Liuqi's *Mingji nanlüe* and Li Qing's *Sanyuan biji*.[39] However, these do not contain systematic biographies of Ruan, but simply refer to him in the course of their narrative of wider events. Space does not permit an exhaustive discussion of all the subsequent accounts of Ruan's life and character, and in any case the formation of his later image has already been studied by other scholars.[40] I have highlighted here the most notable sources, in order to give a sense of the range of opinions about himself which Ruan faced.

Ruan is quite remarkable for the richness and range of sources for his life. He was evidently someone to whom it was impossible to be indifferent. As we have seen, he does not seem originally to have been very deeply involved in the sufferings of the Eastern Grove under Wei Zhongxian; the opprobrium which he incurred for his factional activities in the Hongguang court seems to have been reflected back on to his earlier activity, so that this only subsequently became notorious. We should bear in mind therefore that the view which many of his contemporaries held of him at the time when he was active as a writer – even if they disliked him intensely – was not as virulent as it became in retrospect, after his surrender and death.

To highlight how exceptional is the treatment of Ruan, we may also contrast how he is depicted in early Qing sources with the treatment of others who, arguably, behaved just as badly during the Ming-Qing transition. Qian Qianyi (1582–1664), for example, took a leading role in organising the surrender of the Southern Ming officials on the capture of Nanjing by the Manchu army, but – at least until the Qianlong Emperor took against him – his treatment in historical sources is largely sympathetic, partly because of the romantic aura surrounding his concubine Liu Rushi (1618–1664), the celebrated courtesan.[41] Another figure whose career more closely paralleled Ruan Dacheng's was his friend Feng Quan. Feng, whose home was in the north, surrendered when Beijing fell to the Manchus and subsequently held high office in the early Qing government. Perhaps because he was not famous for anything else – as Ruan was for his dramas – he never suffered the degree of opprobrium which attached to Ruan.[42]

## Ruan's literary output

For Ruan's own reflections on his activities and experiences, we are largely dependent on his poetry and drama. Apart from the brief prefaces to his dramas, some writing on poetry, and a short travel diary, no prose exposition of his views on anything survives. Chinese poetry (*shi*) was traditionally expected to reflect the life experiences of its writers. In this sense, the fact that Ruan puts so much of himself into his poetry is much less surprising than in the case of his dramatic composition. Ruan's earliest surviving poetry collection, *Harmonising with the Flute* (*Hexiaoji*), has a preface dated 1614, before his success in the Metropolitan and Palace Examinations of 1616. This collection survives in a unique copy in the Tianyige Library in Ningbo. The poems mainly relate to Ruan's travels in the Huguang area, when he and like-minded friends established a poetry society named the Harmonising with the Flute Society. The tone of the poems is light-hearted and often humorous, though there is also a more solemn reference to the death in 1610 of Yuan Hongdao, the leader of the Gong'an School of literature, of which Ruan was an adherent.[43]

Ruan Dacheng's later poetry, published from 1635 onwards as *Poems from the Hall of Chanting what is in my Heart* (*Yonghuaitang shiji*), is better known, although still undervalued. The title, referring to Ruan's studio in Anqing, is a direct reference to Ruan's famous ancestor, the third-century poet Ruan Ji, one of the Seven Sages of the Bamboo Grove. Ruan Ji's sequence of 82 'Poems chanting what is in my heart' (Yonghuai shi), commenting by innuendo on current events, but also concerned with ultimate values, constitute his masterpiece, and the phrase became the name of a poetic genre.[44] By using this phrase both for his studio and for his major poetry collection, Ruan Dacheng was clearly signalling an identification with Ruan Ji, both as frustrated official and as poetic genius.

I have written in detail elsewhere about Ruan's self-representation in his poetry as hermit and agriculturalist.[45] I will summarise briefly here by saying that, in his enforced retirement from officialdom, Ruan depicts himself as living a virtuous life close to the soil, rubbing shoulders with farmers, fishermen and woodcutters (he called himself the Woodcutter of Baizi Hill, owning a country house on Baizi Hill, just outside Anqing). This was particularly the case when he was living in Anqing, but even in Nanjing, where he lived on the outskirts, mostly on Patriarch's Hall Mountain (Zutang shan) to the south of the city, he emphasised the rustic simplicity and withdrawal of his life. There is a perceptible conflict between his expressed commitment to the hermit's life and his continuing interest in current affairs and evident desire to return to office. His self-portrait as a virtuous hermit, only distantly concerned with affairs of the day, is very different from the picture given by Qian Chengzhi and others of an ambitious man who never gave up plotting and pulling strings to return to office. The pose of the hermit is a conventional one; in Ruan's case he did actually spend much of his time in rural surroundings, so it is not a pure affectation, but it is certainly intended to counter those who saw him as hungry for power and office.

Ruan was also a prolific dramatist. At least 11 plays by him are known, of which only four survive: *Spring Lantern Riddles or Ten Cases of Mistaken Identity* (*Shicuoren chundengmi ji*, 1633), *The Sakyamuni Pearls* (*Mounihe*, undated), *Double Examination Success* (*Shuangjinbang*, undated) and *The Swallow Messenger* (*Yanzi jian*, 1642).[46] Ruan's dramas appear to contain an unusually large personal element for late Ming *chuanqi* drama, although we do have the example of Xu Wei

(1521–1593), writing within the *zaju* tradition, whose dramas could be said to reflect aspects of his life and personality. We may recall that Xu Wei's writing was much admired by Ruan's poetic model, the Gong'an leader Yuan Hongdao.[47]

It is interesting too that, as far as we know, all the surviving dramas have plots which were creations of Ruan's own fertile brain. He makes a great point of this in the case of *Spring Lantern Riddles*, emphasising his creativity in his own preface to the drama:

> The story is entirely made up, and was not taken from vernacular story-telling; of course, vernacular story-telling is made up too, but I much prefer a story made up by myself.[48]

Wang Siren's preface also makes much of the fact that the plot was Ruan's own creation. As Wang says:

> As a result [of 'misunderstanding'] he [Ruan] gave up his ambitions...and devoted himself solely to dramatic composition...Then he stopped setting old stories, and instead related his own original concepts, bringing thunder from a clear sky and building structures out of thin air. In just one month, *Spring Lantern Riddles* came into being[49]

Wang is evidently implying that Ruan created the plot of *Spring Lantern Riddles* specifically in order to reflect his reaction to his political misfortunes.

Zhang Dai, in his letter to Yuan Yuling, also refers to Ruan's originality (*lingqi*). He writes of lesser dramatists' 'quest for mindless action with no rhyme or reason, [their] desire for surprising effects with no regard for literary art', adding, 'Among the dramatists of recent days, scarcely anyone can be found who even approaches Ruan Yuanhai's originality or Li Liweng's [Li Yu, 1610–1680] ingenuity.'[50]

It has been argued that Ruan's final play *The Swallow Messenger* has a pre-existing source, but the evidence for this appears unconvincing.[51] Strangely enough, one of the most far-fetched elements in *The Sakyamuni Pearls*, the villain Ma Shumou's cannibalism, is taken from a Tang dynasty narrative, Han Wo's *Record of Opening up the Waterway*, which had been edited by Wu Guan (*jinshi* 1571?) in the late Ming,[52] but the rest of the plot seems to be Ruan's own invention.

*Spring Lantern Riddles*, the earliest surviving drama, is the one most explicitly concerned with injustice and mistaken identity, and therefore the one that contemporaries most often saw as self-justification on Ruan's part. The final scene contains a line urging the audience to 'think earnestly and carefully about this play',[53] certainly implying that the author intended to convey a deeper meaning. The play has the alternative title *Ten Cases of Mistaken Identity*, and the plot is an elaborate structure of mistakes, misunderstandings, gender-switching, name-changing and general confusion. To summarise briefly, a young scholar, Yuwen Yan, and a young lady, Wei Yingniang (disguised as a man), meet while solving riddles at the Lantern Festival and exchange poems. In darkness, each mistakenly boards the other's boat (their fathers are both travelling to their respective official posts). Yingniang is adopted by Mr and Mrs Yuwen, but Mr Wei has Yan thrown overboard; he is taken for a bandit and put in prison, where he is befriended by a perceptive jailer. The Yuwens are misled by the discovery of Yingniang's maid's body into thinking their son is dead. Meanwhile, their older son achieves success but his name has been accidentally changed from Yuwen Xi to Li Wenyi; he marries Yingniang's sister. Yan, released from prison, discovers he is believed to be a spirit; he changes his name and accompanies his former jailer to the capital, where he comes first in the examinations and is betrothed to the Yuwens' (now the Lis') 'daughter'. Once he meets his prospective father-in-law, actually his real father, all is gradually revealed; in a happy ending, Yan and Yingniang are finally united, and a grand celebration takes place.

The second of the surviving plays is *The Sakyamuni Pearls* (*ca.*1635–1638); set in the Sui and very early Tang dynasties, the plot relates the misadventures of Xiao Siyuan, a descendant of the Liang royal family, who is falsely accused of sedition by an official whom he has offended. After he is forced into hiding, his young son is seized as food for the cannibalistic barbarian general Ma Shumou, but rescued and adopted by a childless merchant. Xiao, under a false name, ends up coaching his own son to examination success. Finally, by means of the pair of pearls given to his ancestor by the Zen patriarch Bodhidharma, the plot is resolved and everyone lives happily ever after (except the villains, who are executed).

The third play, *Double Examination Success* (*ca.*1638–1642), tells the story of a poor scholar of Luoyang, Huangfu Dun. Pirate chief

Mo Cifei 'borrows' Huangfu's robe as disguise to steal a holy pearl from the White Horse Temple; Huangfu is consequently convicted of the theft and exiled to Canton, leaving behind his young son by his deceased first wife, to be adopted by a neighbour. In Canton, Huangfu meets the beautiful young Lu Ruoyu. They marry and have a son, but because of Huangfu's connection with the criminal but chivalrous pirate chief, the family gets into further trouble, and Huangfu spends many years in exile in South-East Asia, bringing Confucian culture to the natives. Eventually both sons grow up to achieve the eponymous double examination success; after further misunderstandings, everyone's identity is established, Huangfu's name is cleared, and the pirate chief is reconciled with the authorities.

Ruan's final play, *The Swallow Messenger* of 1642, is his best known, and one of its comic scenes is occasionally still performed (it remains in the repertoire of the Jiangsu Province and Suzhou *kunqu* troupes). The hero is a talented young scholar, Huo Duliang, who is in love with a courtesan, Hua Xingyun (Strolling Cloud). Through a mix-up at the mounter's shop, a joint portrait which Huo has painted of himself and Strolling Cloud is exchanged with a painting belonging to a young lady, Li Feiyun (Floating Cloud), who closely resembles Strolling Cloud. Floating Cloud takes a fancy to the young man in the portrait and writes a poem about her feelings, which is snatched up by a flying swallow and dropped at the feet of Huo Duliang. Through jealousy of his exam success on the part of the villain Xianyu Ji, Huo gets into trouble and escapes from Chang'an to take refuge with a general, whom he helps to crush the rebellion of An Lushan. In the confusion of war, Floating Cloud is adopted by Huo's patron, while Strolling Cloud is adopted by Floating Cloud's parents. Strolling Cloud is able to unmask the villain; Huo's name is cleared, he is given a high official position and ends up married to both the beautiful young women. This play, perhaps because it is so purely romantic and has much less overt concern with injustice or mistaken identity than the earlier plays, was a howling success when first performed, being much admired even by those who most disapproved of Ruan Dacheng.[54]

It should be noted that the surviving plays all pre-date the Southern Ming, and as far as we know *The Swallow Messenger* of 1642 was the last play that Ruan wrote, so none of them can reflect the most notorious period of their author's life; they were all written in the aftermath of the Treason Case or the 'Proclamation of Nanjing'.

## Self-representation in the dramas

Ruan's first surviving play, *Spring Lantern Riddles*, is particularly interesting, not just for the themes of mistaken identity, injustice and the failings of human society, but for the many ways in which Ruan inserts himself and his family into the action. As we have seen, the prefaces by Wang Siren and by Ruan himself indicate that it was the first play for which he himself invented the plot. It is possible that Ruan himself acted as the Narrator of the Prologue (a *mo* role, equivalent to Beijing opera bearded scholar [*xusheng*] – Ruan himself was noted for his bushy beard). The first lines of the Prologue are as follows:

> [Narrator/*Mo*:] In this sage era literature has value, fragrance flows from the bard's pen and ink. In a place deep amid flowers, the Hall of Chanting what is in my Heart, we paint a miniature of the Bamboo Grove. The elder Ruan's reputation stood high in the Southern Office; his young descendant ventures to emulate Dongfang Shuo. Please indulge yourselves from the goblets in your hands, and don't bother to worry in vain over celestial omens.[55]

The Bamboo Grove here alludes to the family's ancestor Ruan Ji. Coincidentally, in both Ruan Dacheng's father's and his own generation, there were seven male cousins,[56] and there must have been many family jokes about Seven Sages. The reference to emulating Dongfang Shuo (*ca.*160–*ca.*93 BCE), the famous strategist, seems to allude both to Ruan's interest in military strategy and to the play's ingeniously constructed plot.

There is also the reference to the Hall of Chanting what is in my Heart, Ruan's own studio and presumably the location where he composed the play. The insertion of a reference to the playwright's own studio seems to be a convention of *chuanqi* drama at this period; it also occurs, though much more briefly, in three of Tang Xianzu's (1550–1616) four 'dream' plays.[57] The first of the set of woodblock print illustrations drawn by Ruan's friend Zhang Xiu (dates unknown) for the published edition of the play is captioned 'A place deep amid flowers, the Hall of Chanting what is in my Heart', quoting from this Prologue. Zhang Xiu seems to have visited Ruan in Anqing about the time when the play was published, when he must have produced the illustrations, so we can assume that Ruan had some personal input into how they were designed, and therefore that they reflect his own intentions.

The first illustration shows an elegant young man in official dress, holding what seems to be a *ruyi* sceptre, standing outside an open-sided garden building, within which can be seen a standing screen with a landscape painting, and a low table with writing implements. In the foreground an arching pine tree and a rock overhang a pond, which is separated from the ground around the building by a low balustrade. A variety of flowering plants is visible, and a crane appears in the background. The building is obviously identified as the Hall of Chanting what is in my Heart, but the man seems too young to represent Ruan Dacheng, who was in his mid-forties when *Spring Lantern Riddles* was published. He seems to be an idealised literary man; he may be intended as Ruan Ji, but in that case one would expect bamboo to be more in evidence (there is some half-concealed behind the rock). If the play's hero, Yuwen Yan, is intended to 'be' the much misunderstood Ruan Dacheng himself, it is more likely that the figure represents the play's hero, transposed into its author's garden.

In the interpolated scene 36a 'Watch this space', there is a quite post-modernly self-referential discussion between another Narrator (a *za* role this time) and a 'voice off' about why the author has not completed the script for this scene, and a promise that he will do so when his parents reach the age of 100:

> (Narrator/*Za:*) Dear audience, in this scene, the 37th, we ought to show the Third Metropolitan Graduate Li Wenyi, on his way back to court after defeating Yiluohe, passing by Huangling Temple, where he happens to meet Doulu Xun who's there on official business... [A summary of the plot development follows.]... This is another remarkable sequence of events. However, the gentleman responsible for writing the script hasn't actually written it yet.

> (A voice within:) Why hasn't he completed it yet?

(*Za*, striking gong:) This play is really far too complicated; he's afraid if he wrote the script for this scene he would get into trouble.

(Voice within:) Trouble with who?

(*Za*:) Trouble with Chaos. So he's leaving this bit for now, and he'll fill it in later on.

(Voice within:) How much later on?

(*Za*:) All in good time; just wait till the time when his parents have reached the venerable age of 100, and then he'll complete the old lyrics and write some new ones.[58]

The final illustration of the set is also intriguing. The caption reads 'Strings and pipes in the spring breeze and the fragrance of a hundred flowers,' followed by the words 'Zhang Xiu, [your] disciple from Changzhou, drew [this] for Master Mountain Woodcutter' (Woodcutter of Baizi Hill/Mountain was one of Ruan's cognomina). The quotation is a line from the final scene, 'Mistakes expounded', in which official musicians from the imperial music office (*Jiaofang si*) present a performance to the assembled *dramatis personae* to celebrate their reunion and the official success and marriages of the Yuwen sons.[59] This shows a much more lively and active scene than most other illustrations. In a garden setting, a young woman is dancing on a carpet such as was used to define the stage area in the days before residences were provided with purpose-built theatres. To one side, three musicians are playing: a stout, heavily bearded man playing the clappers between a flautist and a percussionist. At one level this represents the *Jiaofang si* performance – the play within the play – but it could also represent the performance of *Spring Lantern Riddles* itself. My contention is that the bearded man with the clappers is Ruan Dacheng himself. Ruan was famously hirsute: his nicknames were 'Whiskers' or 'Beardy' Ruan (Ruan huzi) or 'Hirsute of Anqing' (Wan ran). His friend and fellow-graduate Cao Lüji (?–1642) wrote a poem referring to his beard and to the strong resemblance between himself and his equally bearded father.[60] We know from Qian Chengzhi's account of Ruan's last days with the Manchu army that he was in the habit of playing the clappers. The personal terms in which Zhang Xiu's 'signature' is expressed would also be appropriate for a portrait rather than an impersonal set of illustrations. I know of no other instance of an author appearing within a scene illustrating his own creation. This may give us a hint of the extent to which Ruan did intend his plays to embody, not just self-expression, but self-representation.

As previously indicated, Ruan's family was a distinguished one. Ruan's great-grandfather, Ruan E, was a senior official in the Jiajing reign-period, and Ruan's great-uncles Zisong (*jinshi* 1556) and Zihua were both well known, Zisong being famous for righting cases of injustice (he is said to have saved 200 people from prison), and Zihua both as a poet and as a strategist; he was known for decisive action taken against pirates when he was an official in Fujian. Ruan E had also been noted for strategic ability, and Chen Jiru (1558–1639) wrote a biography of him strongly emphasising this aspect of his career.[61] It is not clear why Chen wrote this biography; presumably he was commissioned to do so, perhaps even by Ruan Dacheng. Dacheng had a great interest in military matters and strategy himself: he had been involved in armed attempts to suppress banditry in Anqing, and when living in retirement in Nanjing, he is said to have discussed military matters and border affairs, and to have surrounded himself with freelance swordsmen, with a view to returning to office on the basis of his expertise.

Military strategy plays an important part in the plots of both *Spring Lantern Riddles* and *The Swallow Messenger*. In the former, the hero's brother Yuwen Xi succeeds in the imperial examinations on the basis of an essay on military strategy, and is then despatched to accept the surrender of the bandit Hailaipi's rebel army and lead them to crush the Mongol invaders, which he does with resounding success, thanks to Hailaipi's cunning plan to lure the Mongols into a river bed and then release the water to drown them. In *The Swallow Messenger*, when the hero Huo Duliang flees from the capital he takes refuge with the general charged with putting down the An Lushan rebellion, and assists him with strategic advice, including an ingenious plan to sow dissension in the rebel ranks (all this despite the fact that Huo Duliang has never previously shown any sign of being anything other than a rather weedy young scholar). The author seems here to be reminding us of his family's distinguished military pedigree. Similarly, when Yuwen Xi in *Spring Lantern Riddles* investigates doubtful cases of imprisonment in his capacity as a judge, and releases his (unrecognised) brother, we are probably supposed to be reminded of Ruan Dacheng's great-uncle Zisong, who was noted for righting wrongs as an official.

Wrongful accusation and unjust treatment are recurring themes in all Ruan's surviving dramas. In *Spring Lantern Riddles*, Yuwen Yan is accused of banditry. In *The Sakyamuni Pearls*, Xiao Siyuan is accused of plotting to restore the previous dynasty, of which he is a descendant, his friend Wang Xian is pursued by the police for having rescued a child from the cannibal official Ma Shumou, and Xiao is murdered by pirates when he refuses to become their leader (he is later restored to life by magic). In *Double Examination Success*, because of misleading evidence, Huangfu Dun is wrongly convicted of sacrilegious theft and exiled to Canton, where he is then accused of collusion with pirates; later, Huangfu Dun's two sons, unknown to each other, quarrel and accuse each other of backstabbing, deception and treason. In *The Swallow Messenger*, Huo Duliang's semi-literate classmate plots to take over his successful exam results by accusing him of an immoral relationship with the Chief Examiner's daughter. All these plot features have been seen by commentators as symbols of Ruan Dacheng's own suffering under what he considered to be false accusation.[62]

Mistaken identity is the most noticeable recurring theme, and it was this that Ruan's contemporaries picked up on as representing his claim that he had been misjudged. The plot of *Spring Lantern Riddles* is one case of mistaken identity after another, as suggested by the alternative title *Ten Cases of Mistaken Identity*: the heroine Wei Yingniang visits the temple *en travesti* as 'Mr Yin'; the hero's brother's name is accidentally changed (by a deaf examination official) from Yuwen Xi to Li Wenyi; the drowned corpse of Chunying, Wei Yingniang's maid, is mistaken for that of the hero Yuwen Yan (her body has been dressed in his clothes); and Yuwen Yan himself, having changed his name once to Yu Jun, finally achieves exam success under the name of Lu Gengsheng (Born-again Lu). There is also a farcical scene where he goes to consult a spirit medium and gets a message in automatic writing signed with his own name; when he protests that he is still alive, he is shown, as proof of his death, the grave which is supposed to be his. In *The Sakyamuni Pearls*, the hero Xiao Siyuan and his wife assume the identities of Mr and Mrs Liang Zude ('Ancestral Virtue of the Liang Dynasty') while in hiding from the authorities; their son

Xiao Fozhu, having been rescued from the cannibal Ma Shumou's larder and adopted by a childless merchant, grows up as Linghu Foci and is unknowingly tutored by his birth father. In *Double Examination Success*, the hero's misfortunes are triggered when pirate chief Mo Cifei 'borrows' his clothes to commit theft, so that it appears that the hero is guilty, and in *The Swallow Messenger*, the heroine's mother mistakes Strolling Cloud, the tart with a heart of gold, for her own daughter.

Despite all this confusion, one of the features of *Spring Lantern Riddles* is that true identity is perceptible to the positive characters: whereas the heroine's disagreeable father Wei Chuping immediately jumps to the conclusion that Yuwen Yan is a bandit, and that his own daughter is no better than she should be, Mrs Yuwen recognises Wei Yingniang as a lady, the jailer Doulu Xun recognises that Yuwen Yan is not a bandit but a gentleman, and his brother Yuwen Xi/Li Wenyi, investigating the case of 'Yu Jun', recognises that he is a scholar rather than a criminal.

As a natural counterpart to the focus on mistaken identity in *Spring Lantern Riddles*, there is also much concern with issues of reputation, face and disgrace: when caught on board the wrong boats, both Yuwen Yan and Wei Yingniang give false names to avoid disgracing their families. Mr Wei assumes the worst of his daughter on finding her poem in Yan's possession, and Yingniang, knowing her father will assume the worst, decides to stay with the more open-minded Yuwens. When Mr Wei covers up his daughter's 'elopement' to preserve his own reputation, this sets off all the confusion over Yuwen Yan's supposed drowning, while the resulting reputation for Yuwen Yan's 'manifestation' as the husband of the goddess Purple Maiden (the patron of lavatories) leads to Zigu Temple's prosperity. Yuwen Yan twice tries to commit suicide as a way out of disgrace, while, on a more positive note, the bandit leader Hailaipi is given the opportunity to surrender because of his honest reputation (he has turned to banditry out of desperation rather than evil intent).

Another theme which recurs in the four surviving dramas is adoption. In *Spring Lantern Riddles*, the heroine Wei Yingniang is adopted by the hero's parents after boarding their boat by mistake. In *The Sakyamuni Pearls*, the hero's son Fozhu is adopted by the childless merchant Mr Linghu and brought up as Linghu Foci. In *Double Examination Success*, Huangfu Dun's elder son is adopted by his neighbour and brought up as Zhan Xiaobiao. In *The Swallow Messenger*, Floating Cloud is temporarily adopted by General Jia Nanzhong, who has lost his own family in the sack of the city of Xingzhou; at the same time, the courtesan Strolling Cloud is adopted by Floating Cloud's parents. Ruan Dacheng himself was adopted, as the heir to one of his uncles, who had no son.[63] However, he remained close to his birth father, and when his adoptive father died relatively young, he seems to have reverted to regarding his birth father as his social father also (though presumably he continued to perform the appropriate rites for his adoptive father). The *Poems from the Hall of Chanting what is in my Heart* collection includes many referring to his birth father simply as his father; these references sound genuinely affectionate. The positive effects of adoption in the plots of the dramas presumably reflect Ruan's own positive experience of this life event; again we see the occurrence of a personal element within the dramas. The freedom to invent the plots allows such elements to be included, though the effectiveness of these references depends on the audience knowing about the author's family; this reminds us of the relatively restricted social circle in which such knowledge, and such literary works, circulated.

Another instance of Ruan Dacheng drawing, in this case vicariously, on real-life experience, is the exotic atmosphere of Canton in the far south, where *Double Examination Success*'s hero Huangfu Dun is exiled after the unfortunate misunderstanding over his old clothes. Local marriage customs are represented as requiring the couple to sit on the ground and sing alternately (something still associated with south-western 'minority' peoples). Huangfu, coming from Luoyang in the Chinese cultural heartland, finds this deeply embarrassing.[64] In the late Ming, although the area around Canton was regarded as quite civilised, outlying parts of Guangdong, and still more Guangxi, were still in the process of being settled by Han Chinese. Ruan Dacheng's student Kuang Lu was able to tell tall tales about his experiences among barbarians and monsters in Guangxi, and included a description of local courtship and marriage customs in his *Customs of the South* (*Chiya*).[65] It may well be that Ruan owed some of the exotic atmosphere of *Double Examination Success* to Kuang's stories, after Kuang's arrival in Jiangnan in 1635. Ruan moved to Nanjing in the same year, and this was presumably when Kuang became Ruan's student (Hu Jinwang believes *Double Examination Success* was written sometime between 1638 and 1642).[66] In addition, some of the Cantonese characters in the play have typically Cantonese surnames which might well sound strange to northern ears: in addition to pirate chief Mo, the maiden name of the heroine's mother, Widow Lu, is Kuang, like that of the Cantonese Kuang Lu, and her neighbour is Mrs Ou. This local colour was presumably intended both to make the drama more vivid and to display Ruan's knowledge of 'frontier affairs'.

It is possible also to see the villainy of Ma Shumou in *The Sakyamuni Pearls* as a sort of projection, on to the repulsive figure of a barbarian, of Ruan Dacheng's resentment against the fallen chief eunuch Wei Zhongxian. Even at the height of Wei's power and influence, Ruan seems to have regarded him with considerable distrust. Like Wei, Ma Shumou is a corrupt and overweening figure exercising unsupervised power. The position of the barbarian, beyond the pale of Confucian propriety, can be seen as analogous to that of the eunuch, excluded by his physical condition from full participation through the family in Confucian society. This may be another instance of Ruan's dramatic output reflecting his life experiences.

Ruan sometimes exhibits a very cynical view of human affairs, no doubt as a result of his own bitter experience. For example, the final chorus of *Double Examination Success* includes the lines:

> Right and wrong, others and ourselves are all laughable, just going out of your way to make yourself miserable. Why cover it up? [?? – text corrupt] It's all just fleas hopping around in your pants. Could even a dreamer say this was any good?[67]

Interestingly, the metaphor of fleas in one's pants is a reference to Ruan Ji: in a prose essay, Ruan Ji compares 'worldly gentlemen' to the lice in people's trousers.[68] Here the chorus is speaking for the dramatist rather than for any of the characters in the play. While subscribing to the conventional idea that an official career is the proper goal of all right-thinking people (and this was certainly his own ambition), Ruan Dacheng suggests in this final chorus that the efforts which the protagonists have put into their careers are ultimately a waste of time. This indicates the extent to which Ruan had been disillusioned by his experiences during the Tianqi and Chongzhen reigns.

## Conclusion

We have seen that, although some contemporaries such as Yuan Zhongdao, Wang Siren, Zhang Dai, and the author or source of the *Huaining County Gazetteer* biography wrote approvingly about aspects of Ruan Dacheng's life and abilities, most contemporary or near-contemporary accounts of his life and activities, including the Revival Society's 'Proclamation', Qian Chengzhi's 'Notes', and the *Ming History* biography, were extremely hostile, while others, like Zhang Dai's in his *Stone Casket Supplement*, were highly critical. It was the hostile accounts, and their dramatic presentation in Kong Shangren's *Peach Blossom Fan*, which formed later views of Ruan to the present.

Ruan's own views on his life and experiences can be seen only indirectly through his poetic and dramatic writing. We can see that Ruan uses his plays – as he does his poems – not to tell a story as an impartial narrator but to project his own image. He constantly reminds the reader or spectator that this is not just any old entertainment but a play by Ruan Dacheng which reflects his particular interests and concerns (whether with military strategy or mistaken identity). There is nothing 'confessional' in the way that Ruan presents himself;[69] he never seems to be less than pleased with himself, even if he is not pleased at how others have treated him. He is rather drawing attention to his own importance (in his own estimation), and the injustice of being misunderstood. This is all of a piece with the statement he issued on going over to the Qing, stating his position without any real attempt to justify it morally.

However, although we may be aware that Ruan is making a point about his own status and about how he has been treated, this is so well integrated into his ingeniously constructed plots that it never outweighs the interest of the drama itself. To some extent the personality that emerges from his self-representation supports his enemies' accusations: clearly he was arrogant, overbearing and insensitive to others. We may also deduce that his literary fluency was a counterpart to his real-life inability to keep his mouth shut. But at the same time we can see that he was a man who felt – with considerable justification – that he had been grievously wronged: as the intellectually brilliant scion of a family with a very long tradition of public service, he might have been given the benefit of the doubt and allowed to serve his sovereign without incurring such relentless hostility. As it was, he could only project his own ambitions on to the figures of his theatrical heroes, who all, either personally or through their sons, finally achieve official success and position.

## Notes

1. Zhang Tingyu, ed., *Mingshi* (Ming history) (Beijing: Zhonghua shuju, 1974), vol. 26, 7937–7945. There is a full translation and discussion of the joint biography of Ruan Dacheng and Ma Shiying in Robert Crawford, 'The Biography of Juan Ta-ch'eng,' *Chinese Culture* 6.2 (1965): 28–105.
2. Yuan Zhongdao, 'Ruan Jizhi shi xu,' (Preface to the poems of Ruan Jizhi) *Kexuezhai ji* (Collected works from the Kexuezhai), Qian Bocheng, ed. (Shanghai: Shanghai guji chubanshe, 1989), vol. 1, 462.
3. Zhang Dai, 'Ruan Yuanhai xi,' (Plays of Ruan Yuanhai), in Li Ren, ed., *Tao'an mengyi, Xihu mengxun* (Dream memories of Tao'an, Dream recollections of West Lake) (Beijing: Zuojia chubanshe, 1995), 157.
4. Wu Yingji, 'Liudu fangluan gongjie' (Proclamation to prevent disorder in the secondary capital), in *Guichi ermiao ji* (Records of two notables of Guichi), *juan* 47 (Qing edition in Bibliothèque Nationale, Paris).
5. On the Gong'an School, see Jonathan Chaves, *Pilgrim of the Clouds: Poems and Essays by Yüan Hung-tao and His Brothers* (New York and Tokyo: Weatherhill, 1978), 15–21, and Chou Chih-p'ing, *Yüan Hung-tao and the Kung-an School* (Cambridge: Cambridge University Press, 1988), chap. 2.
6. *Chuanqi* (literally 'transmitting the strange') is the form of drama or opera popular with the educated class in the late Ming; it eventually developed into what is now known as *kunqu*. Extracts from late Ming *chuanqi*, including one of Ruan's own, can be found in Cyril Birch, *Scenes for Mandarins: The Elite Theater of the Ming* (New York: Columbia University Press, 1995).
7. There is a thorough study of Ruan's family background in Liu Zhizhong, 'Ruan Dacheng jiashi kao,' (Family history of Ruan Dacheng) *Wenxian* 3 (2004): 193–204.
8. Qian Qianyi includes Ruan Zihua in his *Liechao shiji* (Poems from all the reigns [of the Ming dynasty]) and appends a few sentences on Ruan Dacheng: Qian Qianyi, *Liechao shiji xiaozhuan* (Brief biographies of poets from all the reigns) (Shanghai: Zhonghua shuju, 1961), 645–647. Ruan also says he studied with his great-uncle: Ruan Dacheng, *Ruan Dacheng xiqu sizhong* (Four plays by Ruan Dacheng), Xu Lingyun and Hu Jinwang, eds. (Hefei: Huangshan shushe, 1993), 5.
9. Liu Yun et al., eds., *Huaining xianzhi* (Gazetteer of Huaining County) [1686], in *Zhongguo fangzhi congshu: Huadong difang* (Taipei: Chengwen chubanshe, 1985), vol. 730.
10. Liu Zhizhong, 'Ruan Dacheng jiashi kao,' 200–201.

11. This is the explanation given by Qian Chengzhi, 'Ruan Dacheng benmo xiaoji,' (Brief record of Ruan Dacheng) in his *Suo zhi lu* (Record of what I know) (Hefei: Huangshan shushe, 2006), 149. Qian also seems slightly puzzled by the Donglin's volte-face, despite his own dislike of Ruan.

12. On Kuang's adventures in Guangxi, see Duncan Campbell, *Kuang Lu's Customs of the South: Loyalty on the Borders of Empire* (Wellington: Victoria University of Wellington, 1998) and Steven B. Miles, 'Strange Encounters on the Cantonese Frontier: Region and Gender in Kuang Lu's (1604–1650) *Chiya*,' *Nan Nü: Men, Women and Gender in China* 8.1 (2006): 115–155.

13. Two editions of Ruan's *Poems from the Hall of Chanting what is in my Heart* are available: Ruan Dacheng, *Yonghuaitang shi* (Taipei: Taiwan Zhonghua shuju, 1971 [facsimile of 1928 edition]); Ruan Dacheng, *Yonghuaitang shiji*, ed. Hu Jinwang and Wang Changlin (Hefei: Huangshan shushe, 2006). I refer here to this later edition.

14. See Xie Guozhen, *Ming Qing zhi ji dangshe yundong kao* (On factional activity in the Ming-Qing transition) (Shanghai: Shanghai shudian, 2004), 124. The charge of 'satire on society' is a fair one, but not the others. The only surviving plays dating from before the 'Proclamation' are *Spring Lantern Riddles* and *The Sakyamuni Pearls*.

15. Zhang Tingyu, *Mingshi*, 7938.

16. See Frederic Wakeman Jr., 'Romantics, Stoics, and Martyrs in Seventeenth-Century China,' *Journal of Asian Studies* 43.4 (1984): 631–665.

17. On Zhang Dai's life and work, see Jonathan Spence, *Return to Dragon Mountain* (London: Quercus, 2008).

18. Zhang Dai, *Shikuishu houji: Ma Shiying Ruan Dacheng liezhuan* (Supplement to Book for a Stone Casket: biographies of Ma Shiying and Ruan Dacheng), in Ruan Dacheng, *Yonghuaitang shiji*, 511–512.

19. Qian Chengzhi, 'Ruan Dacheng benmo xiaoji,' 155.

20. Jiao Xun, *Jushuo* (On theatre) [1805], in Zhongguo xiqu yanjiuyuan, ed., *Zhongguo gudian xiqu lunzhu jicheng* vol.8 (Collected works on classical Chinese theatre) (Beijing: Zhongguo xiqu chubanshe, 1980), 201–202. I owe the reference to Grant Guangren Shen, *Elite Theatre in Ming China, 1368–1644* (London: Routledge, 2005), 63–64, but I have slightly altered his translation.

21. For studies of *The Peach-blossom Fan* and the presentation of Ruan and other characters in it, see Richard E. Strassberg, 'The Authentic Self in 17th Century Chinese Drama,' *Tamkang Review* 8.2 (1977): 61–100; Lynn A. Struve, 'History and *The Peach Blossom Fan*,' *Chinese Literature: Essays, Articles, Reviews* 2.1 (1980): 55–72; Wai-yee Li, 'The Representation of History in *The Peach Blossom Fan*,' *Journal of the American Oriental Society* 115.3 (1995): 421–433; Tina Lu, *Persons, Roles, and Minds: Identity in Peony Pavilion and Peach Blossom Fan* (Stanford: Stanford University Press, 2001).

22. Liu Yun et al., *Huaining xianzhi, juan* 25 (Renwu: wenxue [Guochao]).

23. Qian Weilu, 'Qian gong Yinguang fujun nianpu,' (Chronological biography of Mr Qian Yinguang) in Qian Chengzhi, *Suo zhi lu*, 180.

24. This accusation occurs in, for example, *The Peach-blossom Fan*.
25. Nansha sanyushi (Wang Zhongqi), *Nan Ming yeshi* (Unofficial history of the Southern Ming) (Shanghai: Shangwu yinshuguan, 1930), 1.8b.
26. Qian Chengzhi, 'Ruan Dacheng benmo xiaoji,' 149.
27. Zhang Tingyu, *Mingshi*, 7938.
28. Qian Chengzhi, 'Ruan Dacheng benmo xiaoji,' 153–155.
29. Ibid., 154.
30. Zhang Dai, *Shikuishu houji*, 509–511.
31. Ruan Dacheng, *Yonghuaitang shiji*, 406.
32. Zhang Dai, 'Ruan Yuanhai xi,' 157.
33. Zhang Dai, 'Da Yuan Tuo'an,' (Replying to Yuan Tuo'an) *Langhuan wenji* (Langhuan anthology) (Changsha: Yuelu shushe, 1985), 143–144.
34. Zhang Dai, 'Ruan Yuanhai xi,' 157.
35. Huang Shang, 'Guanyu Zhang Zongzi,' (On Zhang Zongzi) *Haoshou xueshu suibi: Huang Shang juan* (Essays by senior scholars: Huang Shang) (Beijing: Zhonghua shuju, 2006), 88, refers to two poems entitled 'Spending the night with Ruan Yuanhai at the Ancestor's Hall', in Zhang's *Langhuan shiji*. Ruan's two poems are in Ruan Dacheng, *Yonghuaitang shiji*, 406.
36. Wang Siren, 'Shicuoren chundengmi ji xu,' (Preface to the *Spring Lantern Riddles or Ten Cases of Mistaken Identity*) in Ruan Dacheng, *Ruan Dacheng xiqu sizhong*, 169–170.
37. Yuan Zhongdao, *Youju feilu* (Notes made while travelling and at repose) (Shanghai: Shanghai yuandong chubanshe, 1996), 280–281.
38. Yuan Zhongdao, 'Ruan Jizhi shi xu'.
39. Ji Liuqi, *Mingji nanlüe* (An outline history of the Southern Ming) (Beijing: Zhonghua shuju, 1984); Li Qing, *Sanyuan biji* (Notes from the three government departments) (Beijing: Zhonghua shuju, 1982).
40. For example, Wang Ying, 'Shi lun Ruan Dacheng xingxiang de suzao', (On the portrayal of Ruan Dacheng) *Shenyang Shifan Xueyuan xuebao: sheke ban* (Journal of Shenyang Normal College: social science edition) 1 (1995): 64–67.
41. For Qian's life, see Arthur W. Hummel, ed., *Eminent Chinese of the Ch'ing Period (1644–1912)* (Washington DC: United States Government Printing Office, 1943–1944), 148–150.
42. Hummel, *Eminent Chinese*, 240–241.
43. Ruan Dacheng, *Hexiaoji* (Harmonising with the flute) (hand-copied facsimile of Ming edition, Tianyige Library), 4a.
44. Donald Holzman, *Poetry and Politics: The Life and Works of Juan Chi, AD 210–263* (Cambridge: Cambridge University Press, 1976), 1.
45. Alison Hardie, 'Conflicting Discourse and the Discourse of Conflict: Eremitism and the Pastoral in the Poetry of Ruan Dacheng (*ca.*1587–1646),' in Daria Berg, ed., *Reading China: Fiction, History and the Dynamics of Discourse. Essays in Honour of Professor Glen Dudbridge* (Leiden: Brill, 2007), 111–146.
46. Ruan Dacheng, *Ruan Dacheng xiqu sizhong*. *Yanzi jian* is sometimes translated as *The Swallow's Message*, but this sounds as though the

message originates from the swallow, whereas the swallow merely delivers it. Cyril Birch (*Scenes for Mandarins*) translates it as *The Swallow Letter*; however, what is written on the paper in question is not a letter but a poem.

47. Yuan Hongdao, 'Xu Wenchang zhuan,' (Biography of Xu Wenchang) in Li Ren, ed., *Yuan Zhonglang suibi* (Random notes by Yuan Zhonglang) (Beijing: Zuojia chubanshe, 1995), 216–218.

48. Ruan Dacheng, 'Zi xu,' (Author's preface) in *Ruan Dacheng xiqu sizhong*, 5.

49. Wang Siren, 'Shicuoren chundengmi ji xu', 169.

50. Zhang Dai, 'Da Yuan Tuo'an', 143.

51. Liu Yihe, 'Qianyan,' (Foreword) in Ruan Dacheng, *Yanzi jian* (The swallow messenger) (Shanghai: Shanghai guji chubanshe, 1986), 7.

52. Han Wo, *Kai he ji* (Record of opening up the waterway) in Wu Guan, ed., *Jingming keben Gujin yishi*, vol.35 (Ancient and modern unofficial histories, facsimile edition) (Shanghai: Shangwu yinshuguan, 1937).

53. Ruan Dacheng, *Ruan Dacheng xiqu sizhong*, 168.

54. Mao Xiang, *Yingmeian yiyu* (Reminiscences from the Shaded Plum Study), in Shen Fu, *Fusheng liu ji (wai san zhong)* (Six records of a floating life), Jin Xingyao and Jin Wennan, eds. (Shanghai: Shanghai guji chubanshe, 2000), 13–14; cf. Xu Zi, *Xiaotian jinian fukao* (Annals of an era of small prosperity, with annotations), ed. Wang Chongwu (Beijing: Zhonghua shuju, 1957), 191.

55. Ruan Dacheng, *Ruan Dacheng xiqu sizhong*, 7.

56. Liu Zhizhong, 'Ruan Dacheng jiashi kao'.

57. Tang Xianzu, *Tang Xianzu xiqu ji* (Collected plays of Tang Xianzu), ed. Qian Nanyang (Shanghai: Shanghai guji chubanshe, 1978), 9, 233, 509; references to Yuming tang appear in the first scenes of *Zichai ji* (The purple hairpin), *Mudan ting* (The peony pavilion) and *Nanke ji* (The southern bough).

58. Ruan Dacheng, *Ruan Dacheng xiqu sizhong*, 153.

59. Ibid., 165.

60. Cao Lüji, 'Shou Ruan Zhuweng nianbo (qi san)', (For the birthday of 'uncle' Ruan Zhuweng, no. 3) in *Bowang shanren gao* (Manuscript by the mountain man of Bowang), in Siku quanshu cunmu congshu biancuan weiyuanhui ed., *Siku quanshu cunmu congshu*, vol.185 (Jinan: Qilu shushe, 1995–1997), 605.

61. Chen Jiru, 'Hanfeng Ruan Zhongcheng waizhuan', (Unofficial biography of Minister Ruan Hanfeng) in *Chen Meigong xiansheng quanji* (Complete works of Chen Meigong) Chen Ming, ed. (Shanghai Library), 38.12a–38.19b.

62. For example, in Wu Mei's (1884–1939) Afterword to *Double Examination Success* in Ruan Dacheng, *Ruan Dacheng xiqu sizhong*, 479–480.

63. Liu Zhizhong, 'Ruan Dacheng jiashi kao'.

64. Ruan Dacheng, *Ruan Dacheng xiqu sizhong*, 398.

65. See Campbell, *Kuang Lu's Customs of the South* and Miles, 'Strange Encounters'. Kuang Lu, *Chiya* (Customs of the South) (Haixuetang edn., preface dated 1769), 1.7b–1.8a, 1.8b.

66. Hu Jinwang, *Rensheng xiju yu xiju rensheng: Ruan Dacheng yanjiu* (The comedy of life and a life in comedy: a study of Ruan Dacheng) (Beijing: Zhongguo shehui kexue chubanshe, 2004), 175.

67. Ruan Dacheng, *Ruan Dacheng xiqu sizhong*, 477.

68. Ruan Ji, 'Daren xiansheng zhuan' (Biography of the great man) *Ruan Ji ji jiaozhu* (Annotated works of Ruan Ji), Chen Bojun, ed. (Beijing: Zhonghua shuju, 1987), 165–166.

69. On the 'confessional' theme in Chinese autobiographical writing, see Wu Pei-yi, 'Self-Examination and the Confession of Sins in Traditional China,' *Harvard Journal of Asiatic Studies* 39.1 (1979): 5–38.

# 3
# How to Write a Woman's Life Into and Out of History: Wang Zhaoyuan (1763–1851) and Biographical Study in Republican China

*Harriet T. Zurndorfer*

## Writing biographies: Forms and changing norms

In Chinese historical writing before the twentieth century, the genre of biography included several distinctive forms, of which the two most common were the standard biography (*zhuan*) and the chrono-logical biography (*nianpu*). In addition, epitaphs, either in the style of tomb epitaph (*muzhiming*), grave notice (*mubiao*) or sacrificial ode (*jiwen*) also provided information, sometimes in great detail, about a person's life.[1] The standard or official biography became a staple liter-ary form in imperial China. These were highly formal, and whatever anecdotes they did feature were often stereotyped and might even be false. This genre of life writing was intended to reveal the character of the person, because the entire purpose of biography in traditional historiography was didactic: the subject's success (or failure) was an illustration for future generations to follow, or as the case may be, to avoid. The emphasis was on a person's virtue and, most commonly, how that virtue related to administrative success.[2]

The tradition of *liezhuan*, or writing 'exemplary lives', was to domi-nate formal Chinese historical writing until the end of the nineteenth century. Recent studies of Chinese biography underline how this genre is about 'performance': the authors of Chinese biographies were not documenting the selfhood or individual identities of their subjects but their actions.[3] In other words, what a person *did* was what a person *was*. In imperial China, the tradition of writing 'exemplary lives' was codified already during the Han dynasty (202 BCE–AD 220) into the *liezhuan* format which basically had three parts: an introduction that identified the person through specific details such as time, place and family background; second, the biography written in narrative form; and third, an epilogue that appraised the second part through meta-narrative comments by the author, or other authorities.[4] Men and women who merited a biography were those whose life stories could be identified with social and moral ideals. In the case of women's lives, biographies tended to classify and depict individuals as exemplars of normative social types, whether 'evil queen', 'wise counsellor' or 'virtuous wife'.

On the other hand, in imperial China there were also other kinds of biographies that supplemented those in official records. These included autobiographical or semi-autobiographical writings that were often emotive and sometimes even given to exaggeration;[5] anecdotal biographies which were not necessarily based on a real person but an opportunity for the author to reflect his personal philosophy; and those biographies which share common features with *chuanqi* (strange tales) and often featured eccentrics, chaste women, aristocrats and other extraordinary figures.[6] Moreover, male literati also wrote about their female relatives not only in the form of tomb inscriptions but also in elegiac verses and accounts of conduct which sometimes conveyed in minute detail domestic relations and were occasionally voiced with emotion and tenderness.[7] Life writing in imperial China was also integrated into commerce. In the materialistic world of late Ming China (1550–1644), it was possible for a merchant 'to enter polite society' by commissioning a literatus to write his biography and that of his family members. Probably the most famous of these professional status-boosters was Chen Jiru (1558–1639), whose exploits as both 'literatus-entrepreneur' and intellectual eremite have become the subject of recent investigations.[8]

Despite this variety in biographical writing during the late imperial era, the *zhuan* biography would remain the prevailing form until the beginning of the twentieth century when the reformer Liang Qichao (1873–1929) proposed a new construction that he hoped would become a source for national and individual self-definition.

In an essay 'Lun xiaoshuo yu qunzhi zhi guanxi' (On the relation-ship between fiction and public governance), first published in the inaugural issue of *Xin xiaoshuo* (New fiction) in 1902, Liang argued for a kind of life writing that should have a social function and political purpose.[9] He repudiated traditional historiography as noth-ing more than accounts of mutual beheading or piles of epitaphs,[10] and implied that biographical writing was little more than geneal-ogy.[11] Yet, even before this publication appeared, Liang had already indulged in a certain kind of biographical study that was highly unconventional. In 1897, he wrote for the periodical publication *Shiwu bao* (Chinese progress) a biography of the first Chinese woman medical doctor Kang Aide (1873–1931), a converted Christian, who had trained at the University of Michigan. Kang originated from the small town of Jiujiang in Jiangxi province and had gone to the United States with missionary support.[12] As the modern scholar Hu Ying has written about Liang's praise for Kang: what is significant is how 'this obscure figure ... became synonymous with [Liang's idea of] the "new citizen" of China, and, more specifically, with the new Chinese woman'.[13]

Liang's praise of Kang Aide is also noteworthy in relation to another essay he composed for the same publication. In an earlier issue that same year he had published his now well-known article 'Lun nüxue' (On education for women) in which he decried the lamentable state of Chinese women whom he considered 'parasites'. In this essay, he rejected talented women (*cainü*), those who could read, write and had published literary works; he judged talented women useless and their writings worthless: 'a few trifling poems on wind and moon, flowers and grass'.[14] Liang's biography of Kang took his critique of talented women one step further as he contrasted her with two specific tal-ented women authors Wang Zhaoyuan (1763–1851) and Liang Duan (1793–1825).[15] Unlike the American-educated Kang who in his eyes was 'the modern *cai* [talent] par excellence',[16] Liang questioned the achievements of these two women who had both published anno-tated editions of the classic compilation *Lienü zhuan* (Biographies of exemplary women) by the Han dynasty scholar Liu Xiang (77–76 BCE). Although their work rested squarely within the classical schol-arship tradition of the Qing dynasty, Liang passionately 'proclaimed their learning "not real learning" '.[17] Moreover, he singled out Wang Zhaoyuan because she had, in fact, demonstrated her talent in so many genres, not just poetry writing. He wrote: 'Whereas the other talented women understood the meaning of texts and were well-versed in carving insects and capable of writing about flowers, grass and winds and the moon, Wang could read and compile her studies on the classics.'[18] Nevertheless, in Liang's view, the scholarly accomplishments of Wang Zhaoyuan could not measure up to the practical knowledge possessed by Kang Aide.

Liang Qichao was not alone in his efforts to devalue the authority and privileged status of literate women in imperial China. Fellow reformers as well as a number of overseas female students, including Kang Youwei's daughter, Kang Tongwei (1879–1974), took part in the process of reassessing the function of literate women in the past and of diminishing their achievements.[19] Also, May Fourth intellectuals added new stimuli to this debasement of Chinese women's literary heritage out of ever-increasing nationalist sentiment and, consequently, canonised all Chinese women as 'victims'.[20] In their quest to dissociate the past from the present and to boost their own 'path-breaking' ideas, they downplayed, even to the point of oblivion, what talented women had indeed accomplished.[21] And even when May Fourth intellectuals did examine the record of Ming and Qing women writers, they were unable to articulate the complex relations between men and women, modern and classical, literature and national politics.[22]

However, during the last 25 years or so, modern scholars have 'rescued' literate women from the 'enlightenment' of the May Fourth period and demonstrated how a substantial body of female-authored writing by women before the twentieth century – poetry, drama, *tanci* (ballads), religious scriptures, essays, criticism and fiction – was published, and that some female poets even enjoyed public recognition for their work.[23] Moreover, they have analysed early twentieth-century modern woman writers and their works in relation to Chinese literature in general and the complexity of the modernising Chinese nation-state.[24] Despite these achievements, one would like to know more about the historical significance of talented women, in particular, in relation to the critical perspective that Chinese historians in the Republican era adopted towards the writing of biography.

In this chapter, I focus on the life of Wang Zhaoyuan and how she was extricated from the obscurity to which Liang Qichao might have had her consigned. I demonstrate that the recovery of her life story and achievements was itself due to the renewal of interest during the early twentieth century of those subjects and research methods that had captivated her and her own generational cohort of eighteenth- and early nineteenth-century scholars. To achieve this goal, we need first to examine what historical and cultural issues preoccupied scholars in the 1920s and 1930s with regard to biographical study, and to locate Wang's biography within the historiographical practices of those decades.

## Writing biography and the new historiography in the early twentieth century

Liang Qichao's advocacy of a different kind of biographical writing, in opposition to a 'record of exemplary lives' approach, impacted other scholars, including Hu Shi (1891–1962) who saw the value of modern Western biography as not only useful for making nationalistic propaganda but also fundamental to the promotion of vernacular literature. The many biographies Liang Qichao wrote in the first decade of the twentieth century demonstrated his broad interests: from personalities as varied as Darwin, Montesquieu, Kossuth, Mazzini, Descartes, Bentham, Kidd and Aristotle,[25] to more conventional Chinese figures such as Guanzi (d.645 BCE) or the Ming explorer Zheng He (1371–1433).[26] In Shanghai, from 1904 to 1910, Hu Shi also experimented with writing a number of biographies, including one on Jeanne d'Arc and another about the legendary heroine Wang Zhaojun.[27] At this point both Liang and Hu wrestled with how to construct a 'modern' biography: both writers realised the necessity of incorporating the biographical subject into a social and historical context. In other words, they attempted to realise the tension between the 'life' and 'times' of an individual. Nevertheless, as Moloughney suggests, for Liang it was 'the subject's involvement in affairs of public importance which should be the historian's concern', and thus not, 'the interior life of the individual'.[28] While Hu Shi would admit his intellectual debts to Liang Qichao's inspiration, he himself went beyond him in his use of scholarly methods for biographical study. Liang Qichao did not concern himself with gathering evidence or arguing cogently about the contradictory facets of an individual's behaviour.[29]

Liang Qichao's extensive biographical output came to an end by the time Hu Shi returned from his American sojourn in 1917. Hu's years of study there had led him to take an even more critical stance towards traditional Chinese biographical writing which he found wanting because of its political reserve, insincerity and excessive formality.[30] And yet, Hu's first important biographical work was a chronological biography of the Qing scholar Zhang Xuecheng (1738–1801), *Zhang Shizhai xiansheng nianpu*, which was published by the Commercial Press in Shanghai in 1922.[31] The choice of Zhang Xuecheng for this kind of study was no accident. Not only did Zhang Xuecheng theorise on the nature of biographical and historical writing,[32] but he was also associated with a cluster of well-known eighteenth-century scholars reputed for their engagement in 'evidential research' (*kaozheng xue*).[33] Evidential research was a methodology that involved the meticulous evaluation of data based on exact standards of precision. Using philology, epigraphy and phonetics, practitioners were able to explicate and expurgate errors in classical texts, and thereby recover authentic works of Confucianism.[34]

A year before his chronological biography of Zhang appeared, Hu Shi had published an essay praising the scholarly methodology of these Qing textual scholars as a Chinese precedent for contemporary scientific research. This essay, 'Scholarly methods of Qing dynasty scholars' (Qingdai xuezhe de zhixue fangfa; published in *Hu Shi wencun* [Preserved writings, 1921]), expressed Hu's belief that there was in China's past evidence of an indigenous 'scientific tradition' congruent with standards integral to the modernising narrative of the West. The 1921 article also represented Hu Shi's concern with the future of Chinese historical writing that he had implemented in his project of 'reorganisation of the national past' (*zhengli guogu*), the purpose of which was 'to look at history as a means to forge new culture out of old by recovering the best of the past and integrating it with the present'.[35] And to achieve this aim, Hu Shi invoked the requirement of evidential research: subjecting historical data to 'rigorous scientific' examination before any reconstruction of the past could be attempted.[36]

Hu Shi's chronological biography of Zhang Xuecheng also conformed to his immediate goal to adapt what he believed were the requirements of modern biography (honest in tone, featuring plenty of facts and expressed in the vernacular) but in this traditional format. This work, which included a year-by-year development of Zhang's ideas and opinions, accompanied by passages of his writings, and Hu's own critical comments, both favourable and otherwise, exemplified the kind of scholarship that he and other intellectuals of the Republican era were about to pursue.[37] While a great many Chinese historians during the 1920s and early 1930s focused on issues in social and economic history,[38] and thus turned away from biography, Hu Shi continued to stimulate a critical perspective on China's cultural history that contributed to a re-assessment of traditional biographical writing, and further understanding of how eighteenth-century writers had utilised that format.[39]

One of the first intellectuals to pursue Hu's project was his student Gu Jiegang (1893–1980) who questioned the exemplary nature of traditional biographical writing by criticising the authenticity of the texts in which these biographies appeared. He also expressed his appreciation of the liberating impact of the new 'reorganisation of history' in his own autobiography: 'Our eyes have been opened to a new world of hitherto uninvestigated and unorganized materials; questions which were once believed to have no significance have now taken on entirely new meaning.'[40] Gu Jiegang's revisionist perspective stimulated dialogue with others such as the Beijing University professor Qian Xuantong (1887–1939) who, with Gu and Hu Shi, wrote a number of essays later published in the seven volume series *Gushi bian* (Critiques of ancient history) that 'doubted antiquity'. Among these studies was a critical review of the legendary bad last emperor stereotype.[41]

These Republican scholars regarded Zhang Xuecheng as a model historian from whom to draw inspiration not only because of his comments on biographical writing but also because of his controversial standpoint on the historicity of the classics that he had voiced in the dictum 'the Six Classics are all history'.[42] Interest in Zhang Xuecheng's achievements also prompted a number of Republican era contemporaries to consider his involvement in evidential research (which ironically, Zhang himself had rejected as 'excessive', on occasion) and to use their findings in their own quest to unravel (and 'reorganize') China's historical record. Zhang Xuecheng's network of patrons included Bi Yuan (1730–1797), a powerful official and well-respected scholar who stood at the forefront of the evidential research movement.[43] With his extensive connections to those who had participated in the *Complete Library of the Four Treasuries* (*Siku quanshu*) project, Bi Yuan commanded a vast network of scholars willing to participate in the kinds of ancillary disciplines of history – epigraphy, archaeology, bibliography, textual criticism, historical geography – he considered essential to the re-examination of all kinds of pre-Han and Han dynasty (pre-200 AD) texts. Thus, as Republican era historians began to familiarise themselves with the classical scholarship conducted by Zhang Xuecheng, Bi Yuan and other eighteenth-century giants, they realised that their own ambitions to de-throne the Confucianist historical canon were very much tied to the accomplishments of these Qing scholars.[44]

## Writing Wang Zhaoyuan into history

It was this interest in Bi Yuan and his scholarly network that induced the historian Xu Weiyu (1905–1951) to examine one of Bi's most important textual studies, the *Lüshi chunqiu* (Master Lü's 'Spring and Autumn Annals' [*ca.*239 BCE]), which in turn led him to consider the likelihood that other evidential scholars had also investigated this particular work.[45] When Xu Weiyu discovered Hao Yixing's (1757–1825) comments on Bi Yuan's explorations of this text, he also ascertained that Hao's wife Wang Zhaoyuan was very much involved in her husband's scholarly tasks.[46] As he researched and familiarised himself with the collected works of this 'literary couple', the *Bequeathed writings of the Hao family* (Haoshi yishu; first printed in 1879), which included, among other writings, more than 30 individual evidential studies of various classical texts, Xu Weiyu must have grasped the significance of the Hao-Wang collaboration and proceeded to compose a chronological biography of their lives. This work was published in 1936, in the periodical *Qinghua xuebao* (Journal of Qinghua University), with the title 'Hao Lan'gao (Yixing) fufu nianpu' (Chronological record of Hao Lan'gao [Yixing] and his wife).[47] Although this title may give the impression that Wang Zhaoyuan was not as important as her husband, the work in fact treats them equally and allows us to re-construct the life and achievements of this extraordinary woman.

Xu Weiyu's work on Wang Zhaoyuan satisfied those criteria that both Zhang Xuecheng and Hu Shi advocated for biographical writing.

It would have pleased Zhang because it 'reflected Wang Zhaoyuan the person',[48] and it would have met Hu's approval because it aimed to reveal the life through 'facts' and records of actions, was written in the vernacular and was straightforward. It was not excessive in detail, but worked to present the record so that the modern reader could also sense those moments identified as pivotal in Wang's life story; not least, it was devoid of explicit 'moral judgement'. Let us now read her life history, according to Xu Weiyu's study.

Wang Zhaoyuan was born on the 26th day of the ninth month in the 28th year of the Qianlong reign (4 October 1763), in the village of Hebei, Fushan county, Dengzhou prefecture, which is located on the northern side of the Shandong province peninsula and the same locale where the Hao family resided. Zhaoyuan was the only child of two locally well-known teachers. When she was five years old, her father Wang Xiwei (?–1767) died, and thereafter she and her mother (surnamed Lin) began to subsist on the latter's earnings as a teacher. Zhaoyuan became very close to her mother who instructed her in literary skills. The chronological biography records that she was a diligent student and that, with her mother's coaching and encouragement, she could recite the classic *Shijing* (Book of poetry) at around the age of 11. By age 14, she could read and write, practised embroidery, and began to read the classics and (dynastic) histories. Like her mother, Zhaoyuan would become a 'teacher of the inner chambers'.

It was in her capacity as a female instructress to Hao Yixing's eldest daughter, Gui, that Zhaoyuan entered her future husband's life. Yixing's first wife, also née Lin (b.1758), had died in 1786. Although Xu does not make clear whether Zhaoyuan had served in the Hao household before the wife's demise, by late 1787 at the age of 25 *sui* (24 years old), she became Hao's second wife in what we now know proved a compatible marriage. Yixing represented the 15th generation of the Hao lineage in Qixia, an inland district of Dengzhou prefecture. At the time of his marriage to Zhaoyuan, he was in the throes of the cycle of examination success and failure. A year into his second marriage he gained his *juren* degree, but it would take some 11 years before he passed his *jinshi*.

During the decade of the 1790s, a crucial period in the intellectual and social development of the couple, Yixing encouraged Zhaoyuan to use her literary talents to write prose commentary. In 1794, Bi Yuan became governor of Shandong, and his protégé Ruan

Yuan (1764–1849), director of education for the same province. Both these officials were in close communication with local scholars and encouraged them to engage in epigraphical study, which at this point both Yixing and Zhaoyuan began to pursue. Ruan Yuan's personal contact with the couple was well known in literati circles, and the relationship between the three strengthened in 1799 when Yixing passed (after two previous attempts) the metropolitan exam, then under Ruan's directorship. To celebrate that achievement, Zhaoyuan, accompanied by other Hao family members, journeyed to Beijing. There she met Ruan again, along with other luminaries of evidential research.

In the following year, the couple went into mourning at the death of Yixing's father, Peiyuan, and shortly thereafter for their second son, Yinghu. Earlier in 1792, they had suffered the loss of their first son, Shou'en. Although the chronological biography does not convey any feelings of grief due to this bereavement, it does indicate the happiness that Yixing and Zhaoyuan felt when in 1801 she gave birth to a third son, Yungu, and thus, we may only guess about what distress Zhaoyuan had suffered at the loss of her eldest two children. Nevertheless, it seems likely that with so much death and sorrow in the family, in such a short period of time, her decision to annotate the Han dynasty text *Liexian zhuan* (Biographies of transcendents) was not unrelated to her personal anguish and pain. Another reason Zhaoyuan may have committed herself to this specific Han work was because of its resonances with the text she and Yixing had been studying and revising around the same time, the *Shanhai jing* (Classic of mountains and seas), and in particular, its images of immortals. In any event, as the chronological biography does make clear, when news spread in literati circles that Zhaoyuan was engaged in a meticulous and critical exegesis of this collection, the renowned bibliophile Hong Yixuan (1765–1837) immediately offered to write a preface. His encomium was incorporated into the final version, the *Liexian jiaozheng* (Corrections to the 'Biographies of transcendents'), first printed in 1812, some eight years after Zhaoyuan had embarked on the project.

In early 1805, Yixing collaborated with Gu Guangqi (1776–1835) on lexographical and phonological research to the *Erya* (Examples of refined usage) while Zhaoyuan assisted them. Gu had published in 1796 an important study of the *Lienü zhuan*, the *Gu Lienü zhuan fu kaozheng* (Appended evidential research to the 'old' [version] of the 'Biographies of women'). Although the chronological biography does not communicate the direct connection between Gu's revisionist account and Zhaoyuan's interest in the *Lienü zhuan*, it does seem likely that her appreciation of this publication and her familiarity with classical text study led her to consider formulating her own annotated edition of this work.[49] It took another seven years to complete her annotations which were printed with the title *Lienü zhuan buzhu* (Supplementary annotations to 'Biographies of women') in 1812.[50] In the second of the two prefaces to the *Lienü zhuan buzhu*, Zang Yong (1767–1811), another famous evidential scholar, and a member of Ruan Yuan's inner circle, compared the intellectual bonds between Wang Zhaoyuan and Hao Yixing to those of the well-known father and son partnership Wang Shiqu (Wang Niansun [1744–1832]) and Wang Manqing (Wang Yinzhi [1766–1834]), both philology specialists. Zang made the comparison based on his observations of the couple's working relationship from the time he lodged in the Hao home in autumn 1810. The chronological biography records he had gone there to assist Yixing in the second edition of the appendices to his commentaries to the *Shanhai jing*, the *Shanhai jing jianshu* (Explanatory notes to the 'Classic of mountains and seas') and saw how Zhaoyuan helped Yixing correct more than 300 misprinted graphs and provide an updated count of the graphs for each chapter and for the book as a whole.

Both the *Liexian zhuan* and the *Lienü zhuan buzhu* were first printed in the *Shaishu tang waiji* (Secondary works of the collection 'Airing Books under a Bright Sun'). The chronological biography also indicates for the year 1812 that Liang Duan who lived in Qiantang (Zhejiang) was aware of Zhaoyuan's annotations to the *Lienü zhuan* and sometime around then began her own study of the same work. Her collation entitled *Lienü zhuan jiaozhu* (Collations and annotations to 'Biographies of women') was published posthumously in 1831 by her husband Wang Yuansun (1794–1836).[51] Also, according to the chronological biography, Wang Zhaoyuan's erudition and intellectual skills were becoming so renowned in the second decade of the nineteenth century that seven distinguished scholars commented at length on her particular amendments to the *Lienü zhuan*: Wang Niansun, Wang Yinzhi, Ma Ruichen, Hu Chenggong (1776–1832), Hong Yixuan, Mou Ting (1759–?) and Wang Shaolan's

(1760–1835) notations were included in an appendix and printed in the 1879 edition of Zhaoyuan's work. We may infer that because these individuals were also close associates of Ruan Yuan who had wide networks in the Jiangnan region and in Guangdong, they also helped spread her reputation for scholarly prowess in locales far away from Shandong.

In 1813, Yixing suffered from a hernia and asked Zhaoyuan to help him complete his analyses of the official histories of the Jin (264–419) and Song (420–477) periods. The result of this joint effort was the set of studies, *Jin Song shugu* (Notes on the Jin and Song dynasties) and *Song suoyu* (Fragmented words of the Song era). Because of Yixing's ill health, Zhaoyuan now took control over the financial and business side of her husband's work, including supervising the conservation of the printing materials, such as wooden and metal blocks.

In 1819, Yixing's and Zhaoyuan's only surviving son Yungu, then 18 years old, married. His bride was the eldest daughter of another Dengzhou literatus, from nearby Fushan (Zhaoyuan's home district), Wang Yuying (*jinshi* 1809), who at the time of the wedding held a county magistracy's post in Hunan. Two years later, Yixing and Zhaoyuan became grandparents. Their first grandson, Liansun, was followed two years later in 1825 by another grandson, Lianwei; but in that year Yixing died in Beijing in the second month, and it was only in the fourth month that Yungu was able to return to Qixia with his father's coffin. Zhaoyuan dedicated the rest of her life (another 26 years) to preserving and arranging Yixing's many research notes, papers and unpublished manuscripts. With the support of Wang Yun (1784–1834), a literatus who had collaborated with Yixing on the *Shuowen jiezi* (Explaining single-component graphs and analysing compound characters), Zhaoyuan oversaw the preparation of her husband's writings, as well as most of her own, for publication. Later, her grandson, Lianwei, finalised this groundwork and arranged for the printing of the *Haoshi yishu* (Bequeathed works of Mr Hao) in 1879.

Wang Zhaoyuan's role in Chinese history was made accessible to a wider audience by Du Lianzhe (Tu Lien-che; 1904–?) who authored a biography of her for *Eminent Chinese of the Ch'ing Period.*[52] Although Du consigned Zhaoyuan's biography to the entry for Yixing, she wrote Zhaoyuan's life history in such a way that it was integral to that of her husband, and thus she did not appear as an 'appendage' to him. Du Lianzhe, as a young motivated Yenching University student herself, had, along with her friend Fang Zhaoying (Fang Chao-ying; 1905–1985; who would later become her husband) been involved in Hong Ye (Hung Yeh; 1893–1980)'s creation of the Harvard-Yenching Institute Sinological index series.[53] Number 9 of that series, *Sanshisan zhong Qingdai zhuanji zhonghe yinde* (Combined indexes to 33 Qing dynasty biographical collections), published in Beijing in 1932, gave citations to the names of 27,000 persons, including Zhaoyuan and Yixing. Zhaoyuan had been included among those women honoured with biographies in the *Qingshigao* (Draft history of the Qing), completed in 1927.[54] Given the similarity in content between the dynastic history account and Du's biography in *Eminent Chinese*, it is not unlikely that Du had used the biography in the 'Draft history' first, to compose her study of the Qing woman scholar, and then later added materials from Xu Weiyu's work. The fact that Xu Weiyu gives much more detail than either the *Qingshigao* or *Eminent Chinese* studies, leads us to conclude that it was most probably his account of Wang Zhaoyuan that has advanced the most information about her.

## Writing Wang Zhaoyuan out of history

Some 30 years after her death in 1851, Wang Zhaoyuan was honoured by the Guangxu emperor (r.1875–1908). In 1883, he issued an edict expressing his admiration for her erudition and her contributions to scholarship, and commanded that her writings on poetry, *Shishuo* (Interpretation of poetry) and *Shiwen* (Inquiries about poetry), which she co-authored with her husband, and her study *Lienü zhuan buzhu* be housed in the imperial pavilion Shangshu for the consultation of Hanlin scholars.[55] This would be Wang Zhaoyuan's last accolade for some 50 years until Xu Weiyu reinstated her reputation.

Wang Zhaoyuan's 'fall from grace' reflects the predilections of reformists and May Fourth intellectuals rather than any foibles of Wang herself. Her situation may be likened to that about which Susan Mann has recently written concerning the talented women of the Zhang family in Jiangnan. In her book about the Zhang sisters, Mann suggests that 'talented women' in nineteenth-century China 'were not a problem'.[56] By this she means, writing women who flourished in that century were 'secure' in their intellectual and domestic spaces in Chinese society, and that it was only with the eruption of debate on the *fünü wenti* (woman problem) initiated by Liang Qichao and fellow reformers that the reputation of learned women, like the four Zhang sisters, changed. Mann attributes this disavowal of talented women to the reformers' efforts to create a modern nation-state where the two goals of 'educating women as the good wives and wise mothers of future citizens and putting them to productive work in the factories of an industrialising country' took precedence. In other words, 'women's roles in the old empire rendered them useless for the challenges facing the new nation'.[57] Also relevant to this shift in values was the new engendered role of authority. As both Hu Ying and Joan Judge have argued, Liang associated the female classical tradition with all that was obsolete and weak about China. By renouncing the (feminine) authority of classical learning and the power of its writings, Liang hoped to separate past from present and to create a modern (masculine) nation.[58]

Liang's programme to transform China into a nation was complex. In the 1890s, he considered taking distance from the past to be integral to his vision of reform,[59] but some 20 years later he busied himself with what was indeed worthy about earlier era in Chinese history. In 1920, he completed his masterpiece, *Qingdai xueshu gailun* (Intellectual trends of the Qing period), in which he documented how evidential scholarship was 'a movement in research methodology' whose impact was comparable in importance to Renaissance scholarship in the West.[60] In this book, he restored the inner world of Qing intellectuals, and emphasised how different and how 'progressive' Qing scholarship was in comparison to that of the Song and Ming eras. This about-face may be explained in terms of the strong interest Liang (as well as Hu Shi) held at this point in modern science and what it could do for China.[61] In *Qingdai xueshu gailun*, he posited that the philological scholarship of eighteenth-century academicians, with their respect for accuracy, comprehensive factual knowledge and inductive methods of verification, was proof that 'Qing scholars . . . were generously endowed with the scientific spirit'.[62]

Such thinking on Liang's part reflected another stage of his nationalist sentiment. His preoccupation now was *not* with the useless feminised past but the recovery of the record of the pragmatic past. However, as before, his gender bias outweighed deference to the requirements of historical accuracy. In *Qingdai xueshu gailun*,

Liang Qichao dutifully recorded where Hao Yixing had made major contributions to the enterprise of evidential research, but left out from this publication any mention of Wang Zhaoyuan's input, either to her husband's work, or to the world of Qing intellectual life. Thus, Liang's erasure of Wang Zhaoyuan from history was a double bill: first, he negated her for exercising her talent in classical scholarship whose authority he doubted in the 1890s; and second, he made her invisible from the male circle of evidential scholars whom he validated in his 1920 book.

Around the same time, Hu Shi made known his verdict on Qing woman writers: in his 1921 essay *Sanbai nian zhong de nüzuojia* (Women writers in the past 300 years) he assessed their contributions as 'without value'.[63] Hu's negative appraisal of women writing also extended to his analysis of Zhang Xuecheng's views on women in the historical record. Zhang, as Susan Mann observes, complained that historical biographies of women 'rarely celebrate anything but chastity'.[64] She also writes that 'Zhang's own treatment of exemplary women, ... portrays women in diverse roles', and that he took women seriously as historians in their own right.[65] For Hu Shi, however, Zhang Xuecheng's stance on writing women had another meaning. Mann refers to Hu's comments on Zhang's essay *Fuxue* (Studies on women) that he inserted in his chronological biography of Zhang: Hu concluded Zhang's tone in this essay was similar to the 'twisted talk of a Shaoxing shyster'.[66] The implication of Hu's remark is that Zhang Xuecheng's views on women were deceptive and not appropriate.[67] One may conclude that Hu Shi's lack of appreciation of learned women of the late imperial era was indicative of the kind of scholarship both he and Liang Qichao were endorsing at the start of the 1920s. Neither of them was willing to confront the 'facts' which might tamper with the narratives they and their fellow cultural revisionists had constructed, and thus, neither man did anything to restore the role of talented women in history, nor to promote the modern biographical study of Chinese women.[68]

## Coda

Modern China scholars often proclaim the two decades between 1917 and 1937 as a golden age of Chinese historiography.[69] And yet, for all the emphasis on new methodologies, new data, and so on, the genre of biography does not seem to have advanced as much as other forms of historical study.[70] Although the *Eminent Chinese* project was a major breakthrough, in particular for its recognition of the role of women (wives, daughters, daughters-in-law and mothers) in the historical record, Chinese women's lives did not capture the interest of the majority of biographers. Even those Republican scholars who did the most to disseminate Western biographies and related theories, Yu Dafu (1888–1944), Zhu Dongrun (1896–1988) and Sun Yutang (1911–1985), did not include the problems of women's biographies in their agendas.[71]

This assessment leaves us to contemplate two ironies. First, that it has been the 'traditional' chronological biography format, one may argue, which has contributed most markedly to the promotion of modern biographical writing. Whatever its limitations, due to its 'disjointed narrative', this form still provides a wealth of information, including exposition of the main events in a subject's life.[72] As recent bibliographical catalogues of extant works attest, the genre's popularity has never really expired, and so, for those scholars wishing to pursue the intricacies of writing the lives of talented women, such as Wang Zhaoyuan, the chronological biography remains an indispensable tool.[73]

The second paradox concerns the role of Chen Yinke (1890–1969) in the promotion of biographies of women active in imperial China. Chen may be considered the first historian to probe the personalities of women in Chinese history. Beginning with his portraits of the Tang dynasty figures Empress Wu (Wu Zetian [r.690–705]) and Yang Guifei, followed by studies of 'long-suffering genteel wives of impoverished literati', and culminating in his 'magnum opus', *Liu Rushi biezhuan* (An ulterior biography of Liu Shi [1618–1644]; 1959), Chen's scholarship gave a prominent place to women.[74] The biography of the courtesan Liu Shi, and then his study of the woman writer Chen Duansheng (1751–1796), author of *Zaishengyuan* (Karmic bonds of reincarnation) which he found comparable to the great Greek and Indian epics,[75] communicated his appreciation of how women could and did achieve literary proficiency, and entrance into circles of male literati discourse. Yet, Chen Yinke himself, according to Yu Yingshi, was the most 'traditional' of the great Republican era historians, because he found the Western ideas associated with the New Culture movement and so on, an 'anathema'. For all his training in Europe and at Harvard, he revelled in the time-honoured values of 'old-style' Chinese scholarship, including textual criticism and other facets of philological research.[76]

Chen Yinke excepted, biographical study of Chinese women would have to wait until the late twentieth century. We should, therefore, consider Xu Weiyu's chronological biography of Wang Zhaoyuan an exceptional achievement for its time, and an example of how biographical study contemplates the problematic of measuring the interaction between the occlusion of the historical record and contemporary social thought, and between the reverence for the past and the impact of modern historiographical inquiry.

## Notes

1. Women were not excluded from epitaph writing. Recent analyses of Tang era epitaphs written specifically for women include the studies by Josephine Chiu-Duke, 'Mothers and the Well-being of the State in Tang China,' *Nan Nü: Men, Women and Gender in China* 8.1 (2006): 55–114 and Yao Ping, 'Good Karmic Connections: Buddhist Mothers in Tang China,' *Nan Nü: Men, Women and Gender in China* 10.1 (2008): 57–85.
2. For references in Western languages that focus on Chinese biographical writing, see those publications discussed in Harriet Zurndorfer, *China Bibliography: A Research Guide to Reference Works about China Past and Present* (Leiden: E.J. Brill, 1995), 137–141.
3. Susan L. Mann, '*AHR Roundtable*: Scene-setting: Writing Biography in Chinese History,' *American Historical Review* 114.3 (2009): 637; Bret Hinsch, '*Review Article:* The Genre of Women's Biographies in Imperial China,' *Nan Nü: Men, Women and Gender in China* 11.1 (2009): 103.
4. Hinsch, '*Review Article*,' 104.
5. See Wolfgang Bauer, 'Time and Timelessness in Premodern Chinese Autobiography,' in Lutz Bieg, Erling von Mende, Martina Siebert, eds., *Ad Seres et Tungusos: Festschrift für Martin Grimm zu seinem 65. Geburtstag am 25. Mai 1995* (Wiesbaden: Harrassowitz, 2000), 19–31; Wu Pei-yi, *The Confucian's Progress: Autobiographical Writings in Traditional China* (Princeton: Princeton University Press, 1990).
6. Chen Shaotang, *Wan Ming xiaopin lunxi* (Discussion and analysis of late Ming 'xiaopin') (Hong Kong: Bowen shuju, 1980), 36–38.
7. See Weijing Lu, 'Personal Writings on Female Relatives in the Qing Collected Works,' in Clara Ho, ed., *Overt and Covert Treasures: Essays on the Sources for Chinese Women's History* (Hong Kong: Chinese University Press, 2012), 411–434; Susan Mann and Yu-yin Cheng, eds., *Under Confucian Eyes: Writings on Gender in Chinese History* (Berkeley: University of California Press, 2001). Also relevant are the essays by Martin Huang, Katherine Carlitz, Lynn Struve, and Allan Barr in the theme issue

'Remembering Female Relatives: Mourning and Gender in Late Imperial China' in *Nan Nü: Men, Women and Gender in China*, 15.1 (2013).

8. Jamie Greenbaum, *Chen Jiru (1558–1639): The Background to, Development and Subsequent Uses of Literary Personae* (Leiden: Brill, 2007); Ōki Yasushi, 'Textbooks on an Aesthetic Life in Late Ming China,' in Daria Berg and Chloë Starr, eds., *The Quest for Gentility in China: Negotiations beyond Gender and Class* (London and New York: Routledge, 2007), 179–187.

9. Theodore Huters, *Bringing the World Home: Appropriating the West in Late Qing and Early Republican China* (Honolulu: University of Hawai'i Press, 2005), 112, considers this essay 'a key document of modern Chinese literary criticism'.

10. Tang Xiaobing, *Global Space and the Nationalist Discourse of Modernity: The Historical Thinking of Liang Qichao* (Stanford: Stanford University Press, 1996), 206. Brian Moloughney observes that despite Liang's criticism of the traditional biography, he himself wrote *zhuan*, albeit of those persons he considered influential (Li Hongzhang [1823–1901] and Kang Youwei [1858–1927] in 1901; and Wang Anshi [1021–1086] in 1908); see 'From Biographical History to Historical Biography: A Transformation in Chinese Historical Writing,' *East Asian History* 4 (1992): 16.

11. Moloughney, 'From Biographical History,' 15.

12. Republished in Liang Qichao, *Yinbing shi heji: wenji* (Writings from the ice-drinker's studio: collected works), vol. 1 (Shanghai: Zhonghua shuju, 1936), 119–120.

13. Hu Ying, 'Naming the First 'New Woman',' in Rebecca Karl and Peter Zarrow, eds., *Rethinking the 1898 Reform Period: Political and Cultural Change in Late Qing China* (Cambridge: Harvard University Asia Center, 2002), 180.

14. Republished in Liang Qichao, *Yinbing shi heji*, 37–44. See also Hu Ying, *Tales of Translation: Composing the New Woman in China, 1899–1918* (Stanford: Stanford University Press, 2000), 7–8; Joan Judge, 'Reforming the Feminine: Female Literacy and the Legacy of 1898,' in Rebecca Karl and Peter Zarrow, eds., *Rethinking the 1898 Reform Period: Political and Cultural Change in Late Qing China* (Cambridge: Harvard University Asia Center, 2002), 158–179.

15. For brief biographies of Wang Zhaoyuan and Liang Duan, see Harriet Zurndorfer, 'Wang Zhaoyuan,' in Clara Ho, ed., *Biographical Dictionary of Chinese Women* (Armonk: M.E. Sharpe, 1998), 27–30, and Liu Fengyun, 'Liang Duan,' in Ho, *Biographical Dictionary of Chinese Women*, 127–128, respectively. See also Xu Xingwu, 'Qingdai Wang Zhaoyuan *Lienüzhuan buzhu* yu Liang Duan *Lienüzhaun jiaozu duben*' (Wang Zhaoyuan's 'Commentary on the "Biographies of women"' and Liang Duan's 'Annotated reader of "Biographies of women"' during the Qing period), in Zhang Hongsheng, ed., *Ming Qing wenxue yu xingbie yanjiu* (Studies of literature and gender in the Ming Qing periods) (Nanjing: Jiangsu guji, 2002), 916–931.

16. Hu Ying, 'Naming the First "New Woman",' 186.

17. Ibid., 187.
18. Liang Qichao, *Yinbing shi heji*, 119.
19. Joan Judge, 'Blended Wish Images: Chinese and Western Exemplary Women at the Turn of the Twentieth Century,' *Nan Nü: Men, Women and Gender in China* 6.1 (2004): 118–124.
20. Dorothy Ko, *Teachers of the Inner Chambers: Women and Culture in Seventeenth-century China* (Stanford: Stanford University Press, 1994), 2.
21. Susan L. Mann, *Precious Records: Women in China's Long Eighteenth Century* (Stanford: Stanford University Press, 1997), 222–224.
22. Ellen Widmer, 'The Rhetoric of Retrospection: May Fourth Literary History and the Ming-Qing Woman Writer,' in Milena Doleželová and Oldřich Král, eds., *The Appropriation of Cultural Capital: China's May Fourth Project* (Cambridge: Harvard University Asia Center, 2001), 193–221. Here Widmer investigates what motivated May Fourth scholars such as Liang Yizhen (1900–?), Tan Zhengbi (1901–?) and Zheng Zhenduo (1898–1958) to write women into the literary record.
23. See Ellen Widmer and Kang-i Sun Chang, eds., *Writing Women in Late Imperial China* (Stanford: Stanford University Press, 1997); Wilt Idema and Beata Grant, *The Red Brush: Writing Women of Imperial China* (Cambridge: Harvard University Asia Center, 2004); and Ellen Widmer, *Beauty and the Book: Women and Fiction in Nineteenth Century China* (Cambridge: Harvard University Asia Center, 2006). Hu Wenkai, *Lidai funü zhuzuo kao* (Research on Chinese women's writings through the ages) (Shanghai: Guji chubanshe, 1985) is the starting point for Chinese sources to this literary retrieval. See also essays in Clara Ho, ed., *Overt and Covert Treasures*, which investigate how standard histories, medical texts, epitaphs, paintings, local gazetteers, encyclopaedias, modern periodicals, women's memories, as well as literary works (fiction and poetry) are important sources for Chinese women's history.
24. Tani E. Barlow, ed., *Gender Politics in Modern China: Writing and Feminism* (Durham: Duke University, 1993); Amy D. Dooling and Kristina M. Torgeson, eds., *Writing Women in Modern China: An Anthology of Women's Literature from the Early Twentieth Century* (New York: Columbia University Press, 1998); Wendy Larson, *Women and Writing in Modern China* (Stanford: Stanford University Press, 1998); Wang Lingzhen, *Personal Matters: Women's Autobiographical Practice in Early Twentieth Century China* (Stanford: Stanford University Press, 2004).
25. Tang Xiaobing, *Global Space*, 11.
26. Richard C. Howard, 'Modern Chinese Biographical Writing,' *Journal of Asian Studies* 21.4 (1962): 472. On Liang Qichao's changing historiographical discourses in the early twentieth century, see Harriet Zurndorfer, 'China and "Modernity": The Uses of the Study of Chinese History in the Past and the Present,' *Journal of the Economic and Social History of the Orient* 40.4 (1997): 473–476.
27. Shao Dongfang, 'Transformation, Diversification, Ideology: Twentieth Century Chinese Biography,' in Stanley Schab and George Simson, eds.,

*Life Writing from the Pacific Rim: Essays from Japan, China, Indonesia, India, and Siam, with a Psychological Overview* (Honolulu: East-West Center, 1997), 21.

28. Moloughney, 'From Biographical History,' 20. Nigel Hamilton, *Biography: A Brief History* (Cambridge: Harvard University Press, 2007), 129–167, argues that it was only in the early twentieth century that life writing by Western authors shed the Victorian (hypocritical), hero-worship requirements that had inhibited biographers from sharing information on the intimate lives of their subjects. For an overview of biography in Western language writing, see Catherine Parke, *Biography: Writing Lives* (New York and London: Routledge, 2002), 1–34.

29. Zhang Pengyuan, 'Hu Shi and Liang Qichao: Friendship and Rejection between Intellectuals of Two Different Generations,' *Chinese Studies in History* 37.2 (2003–2004): 39–80.

30. Howard, 'Modern Chinese Biographical Writing,' 473.

31. Around the same time, another historian He Bingsong (1890–1946) also 'discovered' Zhang Xuecheng. See Q. Edward Wang, *Inventing China Through History: The May Fourth Approach to Historiography* (Albany: State University of New York Press, 2001), 112–120. Hu Shi's study of Zhang was criticised almost immediately by Paul Demiéville; see his 1924 review: 'Hou Che. Tchang Che-tschai sien cheng nien p'ou,' *Bulletin de l'École française d'Extrême Orient* 23 (1924): 478–489. Joshua Fogel questions Hu Shi's motives 'to canonize Zhang Xuecheng'; see his 'On the "Rediscovery" of the Chinese Past: Cui Shu and Related Cases,' in Joshua Fogel, ed., *The Cultural Dimension of Sino-Japanese Relations: Essays on the Nineteenth and Twentieth Centuries* (Armonk: M.E. Sharpe, 1995), 16–17.

32. Paul Demiéville, 'Chang Hsüeh-ch'eng and his Historiography,' in W.G. Beasley and E.G. Pulleyblank, eds., *Historians of China and Japan* (London: Oxford University Press, 1961), 167–185; David Nivison, 'Aspects of Traditional Biography,' *Journal of Asian Studies* 21.4 (1962): 457–463; and David Nivison, *The Life and Thought of Chang Hsüeh-ch'eng (1738–1801)* (Stanford: Stanford University Press, 1966).

33. By 'associated', I mean that he knew many evidential research specialists and their writings, but one should also appreciate Zhang held critical views of their works, for example, what he considered was their 'mechanical approach to human understanding'.

34. On the evidential research and its impact on eighteenth-century scholarship, see Benjamin Elman, *From Philosophy to Philology: Intellectual and Social Aspects of Change in Late Imperial China* (Cambridge: Council on East Asian Studies, Harvard University, 1984).

35. Irene Eber, 'Hu Shih and Chinese History: The Problem of *Cheng-li Kuo-ku*,' *Monumenta Serica* 27 (1968): 169–208. Yeh Wen-hsin, *The Alienated Academy: Culture and Politics in Republican China, 1910–1937* (Cambridge: Council on East Asian Studies, Harvard University, 1990), 26, assesses the significance of this expression. She writes ' "ordering the national past" ... left open the possibility of modern innovations without

radical disjuncture with the past... [and] neatly reconciled the philological study of Chinese classics to the challenge of Western sciences on the
one hand, and the spirit of cultural iconoclasm on the other'.

36. Yu Yingshi, 'Changing Conceptions of National History in Twentieth-
    Century China,' in Erik Lönnroth, Karl Molin, Rognar Björk, eds., *Con-
    ceptions of National History: Proceedings of Nobel Symposium 78* (Berlin and
    New York: Walter de Gruyter, 1994), 168.

37. Howard, 'Modern Chinese Biographical Writing,' 474. Hu Shi's chrono-
    logical biography of Zhang Xuecheng was revised and re-issued under the
    editorship of Yao Mingda (1905–1942) in 1929: see Yao Mingda. *Zhang
    Shizhai xiansheng nianpu* (Chronological biography of Zhang Xuecheng)
    (Shanghai: Shangwu yinshuguan, 1929).

38. Timothy Brook, 'Capitalism and the Writing of Modern History in China,'
    in Timothy Brook and Gregory Blue, eds., *China and Historical Capitalism:
    Genealogies of Sinological Knowledge* (Cambridge: Cambridge University
    Press, 1999), 130–157.

39. Elman, *From Philosophy to Philology*, 197–198, notes that evidential
    research scholars considered the chronological biography genre a means
    'to recreate the lives of important figures' and thereby 'to cut through the
    legends that surrounded men who lived in the past'... and 'to avoid the
    didactic biographies compiled for the *Dynastic Histories*'.

40. Gu Jiegang, tr. Arthur Hummel, *The Autobiography of a Chinese Historian*
    (Leyden: Brill, 1931), 161. See also Laurence A. Schneider, *Ku Chieh-kang
    and China's New History: Nationalism and the Quest for Alternative Traditions*
    (Berkeley: University of California Press, 1971), 19–20.

41. Moloughney, 'From Biographical History,' 21.

42. Demiéville, 'Chang Hsüeh-ch'eng,' 178.

43. Ibid., 173.

44. For a recent study of Bi Yuan's contributions to Chinese historiography,
    see Chang Woei Ong, *Men of Letters Within the Passes: Guanzhong Literati
    in Chinese History, 907–1911* (Cambridge: Harvard University Asia Center,
    2008). The *Complete Library of the Four Treasuries* project was a massive,
    imperially sponsored, eighteenth-century re-codification of the Chinese
    literary canon; see R. Kent Guy, *The Emperor's Four Treasuries: Scholars
    and State in the Late Ch'ien-lung Era* (Cambridge: Harvard University Asia
    Center, 1987).

45. Xu Weiyu's study of Lü Buwei's text was published as *Lüshi chunqiu jishi*
    (Collected notes to 'Master Lü's "Spring and Autumn Annals" ') (Beijing:
    Guoli Qinghua daxue, 1935). Xu Weiyu began his academic career at
    Qinghua University in the 1930s when he was an instructor there in
    the Institute of Sinology (Guoxue yanjiu jikan) founded in 1925 by
    Liang Qichao, Wang Guowei (1877–1927), Zhao Yuanren (1892–1982)
    and Chen Yinke (1890–1969). During the Sino-Japanese War he moved to
    Kunming and worked at Lianda (Union University). There he continued
    his compilation of a comprehensive commentary on the *Guanzi*, incorpo-
    rating the studies of both Qing-era and contemporary scholars, including

Wen Yiduo (1899–1945). Xu never saw his commentary published for he died of cancer in 1951. His work was completed by Guo Moruo (1892–1978) who published it in 1955 as *Guanzi jijiao* (Collected annotations to the 'Guanzi') (Beijing: Kexue chubanshe) in recognition of the collaboration with Xu and Wen. See W. Allyn Rickett, *Guanzi: Political, Economic, and Philosophical Essays from Early China* (Princeton: Princeton University Press, 1985), vol. 1, 42–43; and John Israel, *Lianda: A Chinese University in War and Revolution* (Stanford: Stanford University Press, 1998), 202. On Wen Yiduo's interest in classical studies during his time at Qinghua, see Hsü Kai-yu, *Wen I-to* (Boston: Twayne Publishers, 1980), 128–134.

46. These comments were compiled in their two studies, *Chunqiu bi* (2 *juan*) and *Chunqiu shuolue* (12 *juan*).

47. Xu Weiyu, 'Hao Lan'gao (Yixing) fufu nianpu,' (Chronological record of Hao Yixing and his wife) *Qinghua xuebao* (Qinghua Studies) 10.1 (1936): 185–233.

48. Moloughney, 'From Biographical History,' 22–23, writes about what Zhang considered 'problems' in classical prose in general and biographical writing in particular, including 'literary embellishment, distortion, exaggeration and fabrication' that detracted from 'the reflection' of the person.

49. This conjecture is confirmed by what the Tongcheng scholar Ma Ruichen (1782–1853) wrote in the first of the two prefaces to the *Lienü zhuan buzhu*, that Zhaoyuan's research on the *Erya* inspired her towards making these annotations.

50. Wang Zhaoyuan was the first woman to annotate the *Lienü zhuan* in more than a 1,000 years. See Bret Hinsch, 'The Textual History of Liu Xiang's *Lienüzhuan*,' *Monumenta Serica* 52 (2004): 107. On Wang's annotations to the *Lienü zhuan*, see Harriet Zurndorfer, 'The *Lienü zhuan* Tradition and Wang Zhaoyuan's Production of the *Lienüzhuan buzhu*,' in Joan Judge and Hu Ying, eds., *Beyond Exemplar Tales: Women's Biography in Chinese History* (Berkeley: University of California Press, 2011), 55–69 and 305–308.

51. Liang Duan's study was prefaced by her great aunt, the famed Hangzhou woman scholar Liang Desheng (1771–1847). The elder Liang was married to Xu Zongyan (1768–1819) who was also a member of the 1799 *jinshi* class. Thus, we may surmise that Wang Zhaoyuan's reputation was known within the elite clique of Jiangnan female writers, as well as in Ruan Yuan's male circles.

52. Arthur W. Hummel, ed., *Eminent Chinese of the Ch'ing Period* (Washington DC: Government Printing Office, 1943–1944), 277–279.

53. On Hong Ye and the Harvard-Yenching Sinological Series, see Susan Chan Egan, *A Latterday Confucian: Reminiscences of William Hung (1893–1980)* (Cambridge: Council on East Asian Studies, Harvard University, 1987), 140–143.

54. Zhaoyuan's biography in that dynastic history may be found in the 1977 edition in *juan* 501: 14051–14052. Unlike her husband, Wang Zhaoyuan was not awarded a biography in the *Qingshi liezhuan*. On the

connections between the biographies in the *Qingshigao* and the *Qingshi liezhuan*, see Wang Zhonghan, *Qingshi xinkao* (New studies on Qing history) (Shenyang: Lianning daxue, 1990).

55. Hu Wenkai, *Lidai funü zhuzuo*, 244. Hanlin scholars were a specially designated group of successful examination candidates chosen to work within the inner core of the government as litterateurs committed to document preparation and the compilation of imperially sponsored historical and literary works.

56. Susan L. Mann, *The Talented Women of the Zhang Family* (Berkeley: University of California Press, 2007), 196–197.

57. Ibid., 197.

58. Hu Ying, 'Naming the First "New Woman",' 185–186; Judge, 'Reforming the Feminine,' 165.

59. Huters, *Bringing the World Home*, 4, 7; Hu Ying, *Tales of Translation*, 8; Prasenjit Duara, *Rescuing History from the Nation* (Chicago: University of Chicago Press, 1995), 66–67.

60. Liang Qichao (Liang Ch'i-ch'ao), tr. Immanuel C.Y. Hsü, *Intellectual Trends in the Ch'ing Period* (Cambridge: Harvard University Press, 1959), 22.

61. On Liang's 'intellectual turns', see Zurndorfer, 'China and "Modernity",' and Harriet Zurndorfer, 'Regimes of Scientific and Military Knowledge in Mid-Nineteenth Century China: A Revisionist Perspective,' (paper presented to the Ninth Meeting of the 'Global Economic History Network', Wen-chou College, Taipei, 2006).

62. Liang Qichao, *Intellectual Trends*, 14.

63. Published in *Hu Shi wencun* (Preserved writings) (Taipei: Yuandong tushu gongsi, 1953).

64. Susan L. Mann, 'Women in the Life and Thought of Zhang Xuecheng,' in Philip J. Ivanhoe, ed., *Chinese Language, Thought, and Culture: Nivison and His Critics* (Chicago and La Salle: Open Court, 1996), 111.

65. Ibid., 112.

66. Ibid., 115, n.58.

67. David Nivison, 'Replies and Comments,' in Philip J. Ivanhoe, ed., *Chinese Language, Thought, and Culture*, 296.

68. Even institutions of higher learning at this time were not always 'woman intellectual-friendly'; see Harriet Zurndorfer, 'Gender, Higher Education, and the "New Woman": The Experiences of Female Graduates in Republican China,' in Mechthild Leutner and Nicola Spakowski, eds., *Women in China: The Republican Period in Historical Perspective* (Münster: Li Verlag, 2005), 450–481.

69. Yu Yingshi, 'Changing Conceptions of National History,' 170; see also Yeh Wen-hsin, *The Alienated Academy*.

70. Shao Dongfang, 'Transformation, Diversification, Ideology,' 25. Howard, 'Modern Chinese Biographical Writing,' 475, comes to the same conclusion. Interestingly, a recent compilation on Republican era historiography contains no studies on the genre of biographical writing. See Brian Moloughney and Peter Zarrow, eds., *Transforming History: The Making of*

a Modern Academic Discipline in the Twentieth Century (Hong Kong: The Chinese University Press, 2011).

71. Shao Dongfang, 'Transformation, Diversification, Ideology,' 23–25. On the other hand, one should not discount the achievements of these scholars. The modern scholar Ch'en Shih-hsiang had enormous praise for Zhu Dongrun's 1944 biography of Zhang Juzheng (1525–1582), entitled *Zhang Juzheng dazhuan* (A major biography of Zhang Juzheng). See Chen Shih-hsiang, 'An Innovation in Chinese Biographical Writing,' *Far Eastern Quarterly* 13.1 (1953): 44–62, and Moloughney, 'From Biographical History,' 29.

72. Moloughney, 'From Biographical History,' 28.

73. For a catalogue of *nianpu* compilations, see Xie Wei, *Zhongguo lidai renwu nianpu kaolu* (Catalogue of chronological biographies of historical personalities) (Beijing: Zhongguo shuju, 1992). For a collection of women's chronological biography, which includes reproduction of Xu Weiyu's publication, see Zhang Aifang, *Lidai funü mingren nianpu* (Chronological biographies of famous women in history) (Beijing: Beijing tushuguan chubanshe, 2005).

74. Yeh Wen-hsin, 'Historian and Courtesan: Chen Yinke and the Writing of *Liu Rushi Biezhuan,' East Asian History* 27 (2004): 64–65. Liu Rushi was the *zi* of Liu Shi. Idema and Grant, *The Red Brush*, 374, consider Chen Yinke's three-volume monograph of her life, 'one of the greatest monuments of twentieth century Chinese philology'. Liu Shi also has her own entry in Hummel, ed., *Eminent Chinese*, 529–530.

75. Later, Guo Moruo also picked up on the significance of Chen Duansheng and wrote about her and her epic.

76. See Yu Yingshi, 'Changing Conceptions of National History,' 171.

# 4
# The Fugitive Self: Writing Zheng Xiaoxu, 1882–1938

*Marjorie Dryburgh*

Bureaucrat, calligrapher and – latterly – wartime collaborator Zheng Xiaoxu kept a diary between 1882 and his death in 1938. In daily entries that run to nearly 2,000,000 characters,[1] he charted a life that encompassed service in the imperial bureaucracy before the 1911 revolution, retirement and then a return to officialdom as premier of the Japanese puppet state of Manzhouguo. At first reading, the diary offers a wealth of fragmentary insights into the political and social life of one elite Chinese male in the late empire and early Republic. At the same time, the trajectory of Zheng's career allows us to examine his progress from the public service, structured by largely Confucianised values, that was expected of his generation, through the shocks and disappointments of his middle age, to the transgressive and highly stigmatised political choices that led him to wartime collaboration with the Japanese.

The diary thereby challenges us also to consider how we may understand the meaning of these fragments, and read a whole life through the incremental text. This reading is complicated, not only by the turbulent times in which Zheng lived, and by the shifting distance between norms of public behaviour and his life and work, but also by the content of the diary, which is uneven in the depth of descriptive detail and interpretation that Zheng offers. Struve has noted that the conventions surrounding the content of life writings are historically situated, that the traditions of Zheng's nineteenth-century youth did not encourage the colour and intimacy that marked self-narration in some earlier periods, and that this applied to diaries with far greater force than to retrospectively constructed forms such as memoirs.[2] I will argue below that this unevenness suggests a tension between varying functions and audiences of the diary as self-narration: as Zheng wrote, he created a text that could be read in different ways by different audiences.

Lejeune has noted the distrust that marks many critics' treatments of the personal diary, and the charges levelled against the diary genre of hypocrisy, artifice, 'misrepresentation and perversion'.[3] Elsewhere, while he acknowledges that the diary 'could not possibly be more subjective', he proposes nonetheless that – unlike retrospectively composed forms such as autobiography and memoir – the diary is a form of 'anti-fiction', and that the daily discipline of diary writing makes conscious fabrication impossible or, at the very least, practically unsustainable.[4] Yet, if the private audience of the diary demands subjective truths on these terms, that subjectivity is not exercised in isolation, and other potential or fantasised audiences of the diary may have quite different requirements. As Eakin has argued, whether we are diarists or not, 'we tell stories about ourselves every day'; written life stories form only a tiny fraction of ongoing narrative practices that are not only psychologically adaptive – 'homeostatic' – but also central to our engagement with regimes of social accountability, and self-narration is therefore the product of complex and possibly contradictory pressures.[5]

Eakin points to the 'environment of social convention and constraint' in which self-narration is practiced, and suggests that, '...our sense of autonomy...is something of an illusion when talking about ourselves. The source of our narrative identities...is not some mysterious interiority, but other people.'[6] This is reflected in recent studies of Chinese diaries and diarists. In some cases, the imprint of convention appears in the close association with self-cultivation, in which diary writing becomes a form of 'embodied regulation', and a means of negotiating tensions and anxieties over role and identity.[7] In other cases – such as Bai Jianwu, known primarily for his suspect association with the Japanese armies in the years before the war – it shapes the diary as performance, as a strategy of self-fashioning and the 'crafting of a public role', with all that this implies in terms of artful self-representation and role-*playing*.[8] Whereas self-cultivation through diary writing aims to discipline the writer, diary self-fashioning appears designed above all to produce its effects on an imagined reader; both modes of writing dramatise the relation – the tension – between the diarist as subject and his or her community. The diary of Zheng Xiaoxu is particularly interesting in this respect. It reveals a diarist confronting an ever-growing divide between the norms of behaviour and self-narration that had characterised his formative years, and the emerging moral environment of his later life, and shifting his writing practice accordingly.

## A life in context

Before turning to the diary, let us begin by examining the life. Biographies of Zheng Xiaoxu tell us that, in public life, he was a loyal servant of the last dynasty (albeit, at times, a critical one); in private life he was a calligrapher and occasional poet.[9] While his alignment with the Qing court after the establishment of the Republic put him some way outside the political mainstream, his was in many ways a very orthodox form of marginality. He spent much of his adult life working his way through a system that was challenged from within and without. Born in 1860, Zheng passed through the conventional education that led to the civil service recruitment examinations – a long-established and powerful means of socialisation that shaped the elite persona as it created public servants[10] – at a time when the examination system and its products were subject to intense scrutiny and criticism, and he was in mid-career when the system was finally dismantled in 1905. From this point on, the order that he had navigated with considerable success collapsed around him, and in his later years we find him presiding over its remnants: aged 51 when the Qing dynasty was toppled in 1911, Zheng was recalled in his mid-sixties to manage the household of the former Emperor Pu Yi in 1924. After the Japanese occupation of three provinces in northeast China in September 1931, Zheng accompanied Pu Yi back to his Manchurian homeland, and served as premier of Manzhouguo, the Japanese-dominated state established there in 1932, for three years in his early seventies.

The events that shaped Zheng's life from the outside – from the reform efforts of the Qing government, through the 1911 revolution and the early Republic, and the wartime collaboration with the Japanese – are well documented. Their meaning has been the subject of intensive debate, by participants and by historians; much of what we understand about China's long twentieth century has been shaped by the progressive layering of memory and interpretation that we see in this post-war record;[11] and Zheng Xiaoxu's diary is one further, hitherto neglected layer. The focus here, however, is not the contribution of that layer to the whole, but its creation, and the processes of selection and presentation that are central to the production of the diary text and the persona of the diarist.

## Reading Zheng Xiaoxu

As noted earlier, Zheng was a dutiful diarist. The first recorded entries in his personal diary date from 1882, the year in which he achieved success within the bureaucratic examination system, the last from 1938, two weeks before his death. While serving as premier in Manzhouguo, between March 1932 and May 1935, he also kept a work diary (*yuan lu*). If we examine the personal diary as a whole, it is very clear that Zheng's writing practices, and the focus of his attention, shifted over time. The early diary blended the social and the personal, as Zheng built a career and recorded meetings, events and impressions of people, places and books. In later years, the diary became much terser. Zheng listed the people he met, the letters he sent and received, and noted in passing the major political developments that he saw, but generally offers little detailed description or commentary. Throughout, however, we see Zheng first building and then enacting a persona that acted as an anchor in difficult times and as a counterweight to his more contentious activities.

The earliest diary entries are informal and reasonably detailed: the very first entry, dated April 1882, shows Zheng in a flurry of sociability, receiving visitors and invitations, rushing from home to temple to restaurant and back as his wife busily prepared for a journey:

> Got up ..., called the servant and discovered that Ziqing [Zheng's wife] had gone to buy rice. Just as I finished washing, Ziqing's uncle Qingshan arrived. After he left, Ye Xiaolai and his nephew Xiangong came; we sat talking for a long time, and then Ziqing came back. Xiaolai invited me to Jufengyuan for a drink, but Huang Jichuan hadn't come, so Xiaolai and Xiangong went on ahead, and I agreed to follow in an hour. Huang didn't show up until after we'd eaten ... After we'd had a drink, Xiangong was set on going to the Jing'an temple, and asked me to go with him and

his uncle. So off we went... The fields were bathed in afternoon sun, and there were swarms of people... the sun had set behind the hills as we drove back. When Xiangong first invited me to go to the temple, Ziqing and I had agreed to meet at five at home; when I got there, Ziqing had gone out again on some errand. Our neighbour on the east side, Mr Ye Naili, from Quanzhou, invited me and Hong Zhuqing to go drinking at Taiheguan. Hong's from Suzhou, and works for the Changyuan wood merchant in Nantai. He's about 60 years old; he came to Fujian 37 years ago and can speak Fujianese... I couldn't get out of it, so I went, just as Ziqing came back. After we'd had a drink, Zhuqing asked me to the Shanghai opera at Sanyayuan. It wasn't particularly good, though there was one very fine young actor. Ziqing didn't join us until midnight, and then we all went by rickshaw to the docks; it was really late before we had things ready on the boat. I finally went to bed when Ziqing got home with the servant.[12]

Zheng appears to have savoured not only the activity of the day but also the novel act of recording in detail, sketching individuals' histories and their relations to him, incorporating diversions and missed opportunities (Huang Jichuan's lateness, the missed meeting with Ziqing at five, his desire to stay home rather than going drinking with Ye Naili) as well as remembered events. While few early entries in the diary are as long as this one, the chatty tone, and the attention to detail are sustained through the 1880s and 1890s, as Zheng continued to include intellectual, emotional and personal detail, copying poems that he had composed, recording his reading and response to what he had read, conversations in which he asked or offered advice, and judgements on friends and acquaintances.[13]

Later, however, the bulk of the diary becomes more prosaic, and Zheng became less inclined to record moments of explicit introspection. However, where Zheng was directly affected or threatened by the turbulence of China's early twentieth century, we see shifts in the authorial stance and narrative strategies that he adopted. These passages are a powerful reminder that, as Lejeune puts it, 'Diarists... write with no way of knowing what will happen next in the plot, much less how it will end,'[14] and at times, Zheng appears to have been hedging his narrative bets, distancing the diaried self from some of the man's more contentious actions. This introduces tensions into the diary narrative: while Zheng's first response to the republican revolution was highly conventional and rather hostile towards the new order, he nonetheless appeared intrigued at the possibility that he might 'mediate' in the developing crisis; while he showed little interest in politics in general, he observed and commented on matters that directly concerned him, such as the declining respect shown to surviving monarchies; while he often appeared to distance himself from his political patrons, he nonetheless presented himself as a dedicated official with a certain fascination with the trappings of power.

Diary entries between October 1911 and early 1912, as the Qing dynasty and the imperial order collapsed, point both to the practical challenges faced by officials in revolution, and to Zheng's efforts to fit his own conduct to them. The republican revolution seeps into the diary as a daily series of brief and conflicting reports and orders – that Zheng should in no circumstances return to his post in Hunan province, that he should go back to Hunan at once; that the provincial capital, Changsha, had fallen to rebels, that Changsha was quiet; that officials in Hunan were being executed for opposing the rebels[15] – all filtered through Zheng's uncertainties and fears for his own future.

At the same time, the diary reveals its 'homeostatic' functions, as Zheng struggled to align himself with changing political conditions and to root his responses to the crisis in familiar models proper to his official role and social identity. As befitted a public servant concerned with the future of China, Zheng noted and commented on formal political change: in late November, he recorded the establishment of a cabinet under President Yuan Shikai and listed the names of its members. As he expressed his distaste for the new order, he framed his concerns in highly traditional terms: the problem was not the new form of the Republic, but the moral inadequacy of its leaders: 'For all their grand talk of republic as the highest good, how can anyone hope that, in this relentlessly selfish and ruthless society, a republic will save us from conflict and factionalism?'[16] The following day's entry highlights the extent to which his search for a persona to fit the crisis was informed by models familiar from earlier dynastic crises. Studies of the seventeenth century transition from Ming to Qing dynasties have sketched the range of conventional official responses to dynastic collapse, from participation in the new order, through stoical withdrawal, to resolute, possibly sacrificial, resistance;[17] eschewing self-sacrifice, Zheng at first vacillated between withdrawal and engagement. At first, he stood back, lamenting the turmoil engulfing China and the grief of his peers, meditating on the moral choices that they faced and on the fragility of personal ambitions, positioning himself as a stoical but essentially passive observer:

> China is in turmoil...Wuhan, Jiangning, and Zhenjiang are dev-astated by war...in Beijing, the court is in crisis; officials sleep on brushwood and taste gall, their faces wet with tears; rebels have risen across China, and no province is spared. And I sit alone and idle in the Haicanglou [his Shanghai residence], as if it were ordained that I should not be drawn into the struggle. From Hunan, I was driven to Beijing; from Beijing, to Shanghai...In our lives, we reap what we sow...and when I built the Haicanglou, I made it fit for retirement from the world – yet how little did I expect this! As I live here, it's hardly a luxurious existence – I rise every day at dawn, exert mind and body, and can neither sleep nor eat – so am quite overwhelmed by the news of events. I tried to sow a career, and have reaped only idleness – strange indeed.[18]

As he continued, though, Zheng began to toy with the possibility of engagement, and to contemplate a path through the revolution that might be set by choice rather than by fate. He shifted his attention from the human condition to the details of plans and persons in the unfolding revolution, noted the overtures he received from the revolutionaries, and apparently set aside the distaste for revolution and republicanism that he had expressed only the previous day:

> And now, I have no responsibility at court, yet no quarrel with the revolutionary party – am I meant to be a mediator? The clouds outside my window are so dark I might think them demons...The whole Navy has mutinied, and [naval veteran] Sa Zhenbing has come to Shanghai. Lin Changmin and Pan Zuyi visited, calling themselves, 'representatives of the Fujian governor's office', and said that they had agreed with other provincial associations in Shanghai to establish a provisional government, meeting daily,

and already had a good prospect of making this work. A special envoy from Fujian, Li Sizhen, came to Shanghai, and asked to meet me – I refused, saying I hadn't yet got to Shanghai. The papers say that the cabinet has decided to meet on the 6<sup>th</sup> to announce implementation of a constitution[19]

In this entry, Zheng was not just working through the demands of survival through political upheaval: he was, in a self-consciously dramatic tone, choosing a role. While retirement was, historically, a respectable response to dynastic change, Zheng took pains to emphasise that he was not evading difficult choices by remaining in Shanghai. He acknowledged the stresses faced by officials in the capital, but declared that he had been 'driven' to Shanghai, and that his retirement was marked by personal suffering, despite the apparent comforts of his Shanghai residence; this did not prevent him from criticising other influential Chinese who sought refuge from provincial turmoil in the city.[20] He carefully presented his non-alignment as impartiality rather than as evasion, noting his own continuing interest in public affairs, and emphasising that while he was courted by contenders for power, he was still able to choose his own path through the crisis.

These musings on political engagement came to nothing. Zheng remained in Shanghai, and the focus of his writing was firmly on the everyday and on his personal circle; he showed less interest in documenting the times, and included in the diary only those events that specifically interested him. He reported on President Yuan Shikai's activities and on some of the Chinese politicking surrounding Japanese interests in Shandong province;[21] he noted the Russian revolution of March 1917 and Zhang Xun's abortive efforts at imperial restoration in China in July of the same year.[22] Other developments – despite their prominence in other histories of the early Republic – merited only a passing reference. The May Fourth demonstrations of 1919 were despatched in a couple of sentences tucked behind notes on paintings, poetry and Zheng's own position in the Commercial Press: '[May 6] . . . Students in Beijing destroyed Cao Rulin's residence over Japan's refusal to return Qingdao, and attacked Zhang Zongxiang; some say they killed him. Several dozen people have been arrested, and the universities are closed';[23] and if Zheng the poet was aware of the political debates and the proposals for 'literary revolution' carried in journals such as *New Youth* around the same time, he made no substantive comment on them.

Zheng remained in Shanghai until late 1923. We are told that, 'Only when the man he still regarded as ruler of China...summoned him to [Beijing]...did [Zheng] emerge from seclusion to begin a second career.'[24] However, as Zheng told it, this was no long-awaited return from the wilderness, but simply another opportunity to be mulled over: 'Writing practice. Letter from Xiaoqi, saying that Chen Baoshen came by on the 11th, and told him the emperor's office was reorganising its affairs. The emperor intended to order me to take up a post there, so I should consider my reply....'[25]

A couple of days after recording this cool response, Zheng reported an attack on the Japanese crown prince in Tokyo:

> The *Dalubao* reported that as the Japanese crown prince attended the Diet, the son of a Diet member fired on him, and hit the window of his car; as the crown prince escaped into the Upper House, the assailant was seized. Here in the Haicanglou, our view is that these outbursts in Japan are not caused by the insanity or perversity of individuals; there must be countless others who believe that this crime is entirely justifiable; so this person's conduct is hardly surprising. Now Japan is still a monarchy, but here it's exactly the same: although the emperor has abdicated, the rebels delight in denigrating him.[26]

By suggesting that attacks on the Japanese or Chinese monarchies were not aberrations, but products of changing times and broader decline in social support for these institutions, Zheng depicted imperial families as vulnerable to the changing times; yet, although his own future was once again associated with the deposed Qing house – as references to palace meetings, and contacts at court confirm – he declined to show much enthusiasm for this new role.[27]

Once in post in the imperial household the following year, he noted the activity of each day, typically opening each entry with, 'To work'. At times, he recorded also events beyond the daily routine, and here the carefully cultivated appearance of detachment slipped to reveal a man who apparently relished the residual prestige of the imperial institution and the material accoutrements of palace life. When Rabindranath Tagore visited the palace, one might have expected Zheng to record his interest in a fellow-poet; instead he wrote about the photo session with which the visit ended:

> To work. The emperor called me in and announced, 'Today the Indian poet Tagore will visit me, I would like to present him with a photograph; you can come too . . .' When the time came, we were called to the gardens; the emperor ordered me, 'You pose with Tagore'. The emperor sat on a stone bench, flanked by us, with the other guests standing behind. For the next shot, the photographer asked us to move over to stand by a pavilion; and then it was over.[28]

Having one's photograph taken at this time was still something of an occasion for many Chinese, but it was an experience that was more often associated with a family visit to a commercial photography studio[29] than with a private meeting between poets and emperor in a palace garden; it is easy to suspect that Zheng was a little star-struck at such times.

Zheng's work in the palace ended abruptly later that year, as a twist in China's ongoing civil wars transferred control over Beijing to armies unsympathetic to the former emperor. Pu Yi and his household were summarily evicted and found temporary refuge in the Beijing Japanese legation before settling in the Japanese concession in Tianjin in early 1925. As Pu Yi later recounted their expulsion, Zheng made only a modest contribution to the flight, and was concerned above all with securing his own position against rivals within the Imperial household by 'delicately filching' their useful Japanese connections – but was nonetheless 'very pleased with the role he had played'.[30] The narrative of Zheng's diary emphasised the calm and authority of his response, as Zheng meticulously tracked the unfolding of the Beijing *coup* that triggered the expulsion, recording press reports and open telegrams issued by the military leaders involved, and offered a dramatic account of the journey to the legation in which he shepherded an anxious emperor through a sandstorm to safety and deflected criticisms from the emperor's other supporters over the choice of Japan as host;[31] as in the account of the photographic session with Tagore there is more than a hint of self-congratulation in Zheng's telling of the tale.

Yet other, apparently more significant, political developments received far more muted treatment. In 1931, for example, Zheng appeared absorbed in the emperor's personal affairs of the imperial household, spending much of late August and early September dealing with the separation of Pu Yi from his consort Wen Xiu,[32] to the extent that the 'Manchurian incident' – the Japanese occupation of the north-east – emerged slowly into the diary from behind this smaller, domestic conflict. Zheng seems to have struggled to find a consistent way of writing about the Manchurian occupation and his own position in its aftermath. On one hand, the apparent ease with which Pu Yi's staff – Zheng included – moved to open dialogue with the Japanese authorities in Tianjin and the north-east may suggest that they were expecting the conflict and the opportunities that it presented for Pu Yi to declare a return to his ancestral homeland. On the other hand, Zheng's reports of developments were initially baldly factual; by emphasising his reliance on the Japanese press and second-hand communications from the consulate, they place Zheng firmly outside the Manchurian enterprise; and he was meticulous in recording his concerns over the emerging new order. Thus, the September 19 diary entry reads:

> The Japanese *Nichinichi Shinbun* sent a special pamphlet edition, saying, 'Telegram from Fengtian, 3.23 a.m., reports China and Japan at war.' This conflict broke out on…September 18 by the western calendar. Called in Liu Xiangye and Zheng Chui; ordered Xiangye to go to Dalian. Writing practice. Met Chen Baoshen; fear that this may end in catastrophe. Wuyuan came to ask for two letters, one for the South Manchurian Railway Company president Uchida, and one for the Japanese military commander Honjô. Zheng Chui enquired at the Japanese consulate; they say that Fengtian is occupied; the Chinese army has withdrawn and there is fighting in Changchun.[33]

Zheng's criticism of the Chinese central and regional responses to the conflict, and his advocacy of resolute resistance, regardless of its probable outcome, were also calculated to distance him from co-operation with the Japanese. On 21 September, he wrote:

Jiang Jieshi [Chiang Kai-shek] has gone back to Nanjing and protested to Japan; [Manchurian general] Zhang Xueliang has ordered his troops not to resist. These are mice, not men, and they know nothing about building the nation: what is the point of protesting to a hostile power? If they wanted to show they were serious, they would give the Japanese diplomats their passports back and give them three days to get out; get Japanese citizens and traders out within a week, then mobilise and wait for attack – do they not remember Belgium's resistance to Germany?[34]

In his contempt for Jiang Jieshi and his north-eastern ally, Zhang Xueliang, as politically inept, Zheng positioned himself as a critic of central weakness and cowardice, and echoed widespread Chinese objections to the central government.[35] It is hard to see the logic that led him from this stance to collaboration with Japan in the occupied north-east only a few months later; but while the longer narrative of Zheng's actions in these months appears replete with contradiction and evasion, any one episode taken in isolation could seem at home in the repertoire of (potentially) right actions, from suspecting the invader and condemning capitulation to safeguarding the security and interests of the deposed emperor.

Finally, Zheng expressed no optimism over the prospects for co-operation with the Japanese authorities, suggesting rather that Pu Yi was being manipulated by the Japanese armies to deceive outside observers, his own staff and other sections of the Japanese authorities:

Vice-consul Gotô visited: apparently the Japanese garrison has received a personal letter from the emperor, saying that he was not at ease in Tianjin, that he felt in danger, and hoped he could count on their protection should he decide to move. It's doubtful whether this is a personal letter. And the claims of urgency and unease are meant to force the consulate into offering protection…It looks as if this letter has been influenced by the Japanese[36]

Whereas other potential collaborators worked to present themselves as informed and independent actors in their dealings with the Japanese authorities, and while Pu Yi's memoirs show Zheng as active – if not very effective – in engaging with the Japanese authorities,[37] Zheng preferred to show their emerging co-operation as opaque and troubling, even as he was drawn into it.

This painstaking distancing became impossible once Zheng took up his post as premier of the new state of Manzhouguo, yet his apparent ambivalence over his own position remained. Writing on the first meetings of the State Council, he began with a matter-of-fact list of appointments, and a declaration of the regime's desire to alleviate popular hardship, before alluding to the internal tensions that were already evident:

> Snow. Third meeting of the State Council; Japanese officials appointed as bureau and section chiefs. Xi Xia, Zhang Yanqing and Ding Jianxiu disagreed, but gave up when Komai argued back. The Mongol leaders later came in to say that the Mongols were most disappointed that none of their people had been given posts. I consoled them, and agreed that they should propose a solution at the State Council[38]

But as well as recording this unease over the positioning of Japanese officials, he showed a brisk concern for the project of consolidating and centralising the authority of the new regime, as he continued,

> An army division has mutinied at Heihe, and Ma Zhanshan has asked to go to deal with it at once. I think this should be used to support Ma in wiping out opposition, to dismantle the provincial system and to centralise power, first in Heilongjiang and then in Fengtian and Jilin[39]

This vacillation between distaste for central aspects of the regime and observance of the logical demands of regime consolidation ran through Zheng's tenure as premier, which was marked by his efforts – thwarted for some years – to resign his post. He made his first attempt in September 1932, only six months after taking office:

> Up at half past one for the Autumn Sacrifices in the Confucian temple; finished at quarter to four... About 100 people present, including Mason, the American, and Kawasaki. Then to the palace, where I presented my resignation as premier. I wanted to take advantage of the changeover of Japanese forces to sound out

opinions; I see no good can come of hanging on over months and years just to conceal the flaws in this arrangement. Zhuzi came by and said, 'If Manzhouguo is to be secured, then the constitution must be promulgated, so that its foundations are solid; the current system cannot last'[40]

The following day's entry detailed the efforts made by senior Japanese officials to block his resignation and assert their authority over the management of his office:

To imperial residence. Komai came in, and said that Zheng Chui had been dismissed as secretary, and Zheng Yu appointed secretary to the premier's office. I said, 'Zheng Chui and Zheng Yu are secretaries to the executive; when I became premier I specifically ordered that they be appointed, and they cannot be sacked! Now that I have resigned, my sons will resign with me, and you have no grounds to transfer them.' Komai replied, 'The premier may not resign. Zheng Chui has lost his official post, but we will employ him in a senior position in the Japan-Manzhouguo Joint Company. Although you have offered your resignation, I will order the executive not to accept it...'[41]

Zheng took leave and held out for several days, refusing to attend State Council meetings – despite police surveillance of his house and visitors, and visits from an angry and abusive Komai – and agreeing to resume the post only when warned that his resignation might jeopardise Japanese recognition of Manzhouguo, and assured that he would in future be treated with respect. His recording in the following weeks of mourning ceremonies held by Chinese on the anniversary of the occupation, and of criticism by a Japanese visiting academic of army dominance in Manzhouguo, suggest that he returned only with reluctance,[42] and on 21 November, he presented his resignation for a second time. As he recorded it, he said to the emperor,

I have served as Premier for over eight months... constantly at your service, yet fearing that all my efforts are futile. If you take pity on my age and allow me to step down and return to China, it may win wider support and allow the appointment of a more talented man.

The emperor, Zheng tells us, responded sympathetically to this highly formulaic request, but asked him to stay in post until the following spring, as there was no one to replace him.[43]

Zheng's presentation of these episodes is open to differing readings. The story of his first attempted resignation presented him as a prisoner of an inherently flawed and internally unequal new order, as Japanese army officials had his house surrounded and told him bluntly that it was they, not he, who would decide when he might step down; yet it showed Zheng returning to his post out of a sense of duty, as he was reminded that the regime would be gravely weakened without him. In recording his second request, the diary emphasised Zheng's age and frailty in the face of massive political challenges, but noted that he secured not only the sympathy of the emperor, but also the recognition by Japanese officials of his dignity as premier. In both cases, Zheng shows himself setting aside political and personal concerns in return for symbolic compensation, in the form of assurances that he was indispensable to the survival of Manzhouguo.

We are reminded that the diary is only one of several possible narratives of Zheng's life when we see him described by others. Pu Yi's former tutor, Reginald Johnston, characterised him in 1934 as '...not a politician...undoubtedly one of the most learned and accomplished men of his generation...and a true Confucian gentleman', and as a dutiful and single-minded servant of his emperor; Pu Yi himself, however, writing in a Chinese prison in the 1950s and 1960s, was consistently dismissive of Zheng's political judgement.[44] Another diarist and close associate of the Japanese armies, Bai Jianwu, met Zheng in June 1933, and portrayed him in the following terms:

> We saw Zheng [Xiaoxu] at 4 today, and he said, 'Since I became Premier of Manzhouguo, my main tasks have been to reform the country, making massive loans for the relief of rural areas, turning railway revenue over to the South Manchurian Railway Company to repay loans, and encouraging landlords to exploit uncultivated land.' These policies are just what China needs, but they have only recently been implemented; it's amazing that a 74-year-old can pursue national construction on these lines.[45]

In writing so warmly of Zheng Xiaoxu, Bai was, *inter alia*, justifying his own overtures to the Japanese authorities by asserting the possibility of a Sino-Japanese collaboration that would serve Chinese popular welfare, affirming the contribution to legitimate national construction that might be made by men associated with an older political generation, borrowing the prestige of a man whose status was, culturally and politically, far better established than his own, and returning a compliment to the author of the preface for his only published work, a treatise on education, produced in 1929. As he did so, he produced an account of their meeting that was strikingly at odds with Zheng's own record of the day. Zheng's diary tells us:

> Fu Ruhuan visited. Went to State Council, and saw Mutô to discuss the choice between Sun Qichang and Cai Yunsheng as Heilongjiang provincial governor. We decided to recommend Sun and I said I would communicate this to the emperor that afternoon. Zhao Xinbo came to say that he would leave for Tokyo to consult on the constitution within the month. Then Lin told us that Mutô had just met the emperor and nominated Sun Qichang, Cai Yunsheng and Shen Ruilin [for the Heilongjiang post], the decision to be made in 3 days. Uryû Kisaburô invited me to the Daiwa for dinner; there we saw Wang Xingshan, a wealthy man from Changchun; he's just established a private school with several thousand students. Bai Jianwu and He Tingliu visited; Bai had worked with Itagaki in Tianjin to stage an uprising and seize control of Beijing and Tianjin; it failed, and so he came here.[46]

At first sight, these two diary entries reveal the terms of which collaborators were prepared to talk about collaboration, and the disjuncture between claims that Sino-Japanese co-operation offered a path towards national reconstruction, and the reverses and slights inherent in the collaborative relationship. Further to this, they show a slippage between the public and the private personae of Zheng Xiaoxu, as the man associated by Bai Jianwu with successful and benevolent Sino-Japanese collaboration appears deeply dissatisfied with his own position. Zheng did not elaborate on his morning discussions with Mutô yet; by recording the Japanese official's later disregard of their agreement, he makes it clear that these were essentially pointless. He underlines this by framing his meeting with Bai Jianwu as a further illustration of the frustrations of collaboration, rather than as an encounter in which he was able to impress the younger man with his own achievements.

Finally, the two entries reveal differing uses of the diary by the two diarists. Bai Jianwu's telling of the encounter offers explicit commentary on the meeting – the detail of Zheng's programme and Bai's admiration for him – and this highlights one of the primary uses Bai made of his diary, in the exploration of new political possibilities and models, and the reinterpretation of the day's activities to his own satisfaction. As well as Bai's personal anxieties and ambitions, it reflected also his desire to set his own interpretative stamp on the story. Zheng Xiaoxu's narrative was a more prosaic list of meetings and conversations: he recorded that he did what a dutiful and loyal official did, and is much less inclined than Bai to complete the interpretative circle.

As we look beyond the factual record, therefore, the force of Zheng's narrative becomes less clear. Zheng's reference to Wang Xingshan, for example, is much harder to read than Bai's description of Zheng. Does it hint at relief that Chinese funds were still flowing into schools? Disappointment that new schools were not being publicly financed? Approval of personal philanthropy? Concern that education was now in the hands of the merely 'wealthy'? Envy of Wang's freedom to involve himself in education? Was the reference a way of anchoring the diary persona in important matters such as education, to offset the time that Zheng himself spent mired in politicking, and in fruitless discussions with unco-operative Japanese officials? This applies to much of Zheng's diary: while Bai Jianwu was often aiming, it appears, to declare who he was, Zheng more often confined himself to recording what he did, and what he saw.

And much of what Zheng did and saw was quite repetitive: in one week in May 1933, Zheng received visits from a fact-finding group from Mie prefecture, delegations of 93 students from schools in Kagawa prefecture, 70 students from commercial schools in Japan, 50 students of Nara Girls' Normal School, with whom he had a photo taken, 180 middle-school students from Kyoto, 70 elementary school students from Ôishibashi, 160 members of the Japanese Association of Girls' School Principals, 100 students from Hiroshima Normal School and 60 from various trade and commercial academies in Japan.[47] In this context of delegations received and group photographs taken, private and emotional life was submerged in daily, official duty. Zheng only rarely expressed personal feeling, as when he quoted poems written in mourning for his son Zheng Chui, who died in February 1933,[48] and at other times, the possibility of emotion is merely glimpsed, as Zheng visited Japan in 1934, and tells us that he composed poems (that he did not include in the diary) on cherry blossom and on Hell.[49] In the poems that Zheng did record in his diary, he shows a firm sense of audience: the meditation on life and human ambition that appears in the entry for Confucius' birthday in 1934 is quite different in tone to the highly formulaic treatments of the Kingly Way – declared as the philosophical foundation of Manzhouguo – exchanged with the emperor several months later.[50]

Zheng finally succeeded in resigning as premier on 21 May 1935, and most other senior government posts were reshuffled on his departure. Zheng summoned his second son, Zheng Yu, and they went home together. As Zheng told it,

> I said to Xiaoqi, 'I've been fortunate three times in my life: first, when I resigned my regional posts and returned to Shanghai; second when I helped the emperor leave the German hospital [in 1924] for the Japanese embassy; and third when I resigned as premier after three years serving Manzhouguo. I shall not take any further official posts – I have been quite fortunate enough.'[51]

We may note that the first and third episodes of good fortune involved leaving official posts rather than serving in them, and it is tempting to read a hint of irony – and some relief – into the comment. The following day, Zheng sent a poem to his brother Zhixin, as if in celebration of his release, and passed on a comment on his successor as premier: 'According to Jiuliu, Xi Xia says, "Zhang Jinghui is no equal to Zheng Xiaoxu and will find him a hard act to follow."'[52] Resignation did not dramatically change the daily routine of the personal diary. Zheng continued to receive numerous visitors in a semi-official capacity; he was able to devote more time to discussions on the preservation of Manchuria's material heritage and to explication of the Kingly Way, though in neither case did he choose to discuss these in any depth in the diary.

The last diary entries, in 1938, note simply,

> [March 13] The papers say that Germany and Austria are to be united; things are very tense; Hitler has gone to Vienna. Britain and France are protesting but Italy has not intervened.

> [March 14] Went to Daiwa Hotel for a haircut. Took Y6,000 out of the bank, and paid back Y1,000. Anniversary of Mr Pei's passing. Letter from Jiuliu.[53]

Domestic and private routine was overshadowed by international events in the penultimate entry, returning in the last in a statement of mundane tasks completed.

## Conclusions

In attempting to read Zheng Xiaoxu through his diary, we encounter a number of challenges, notably that the diary becomes less immediately revealing of the diarist as the years pass, as Zheng tells us less of what he thought and felt and devotes more space to an increasingly bland record of action and repose. Struve's observation that diaries from the late nineteenth century onwards have tended to offer drier and less animated self-narratives than retrospective forms suggests that Zheng might have produced a more self-expressive story, had he left a memoir – but this does not explain the thinning of the narrative within the diary. Instead, it may be fruitful to return to Eakin's arguments on the dual functions of self-narrative, and to understand the rather stark diary content in this context as a series of prompts, rather than as an incomplete narrative.

Eakin's proposal that a sense of identity, rooted in self-narrative, is psychologically adaptive draws our attention to Zheng's writing choices. In his deliberations over withdrawal and engagement at the 1911 revolution, we find an emotional consideration of the roles that one might take through the crisis; latterly, instead of seeking to explain or justify his political choices, after 1911, Zheng simply recorded what he did, selectively. In the Manzhouguo years, this has the effect of domesticating and normalising a stigmatised political choice by embedding it in a daily routine that could be seen as emphatically unexceptional. The diary therefore appears as a stage on which he could enact his chosen persona, dutiful, stoical and orthodox, as recorded by the prompts within the diary.

Eakin notes also the pressure of convention upon self-narrative, and the extent to which life histories look outwards to imagined audiences as well as inwards. Here, too, it is conceivable that the spareness of Zheng's writing betrayed a growing conscious reticence, and not simply a failure of articulacy. Writing in 1911, Zheng was able to consider the choices facing a provincial official in revolution within a framework of known values; by 1931 he had noted, and reflected in diary entries, changing values that made his own political choices hard to defend, from growing opposition to imperial institutions across the world to attachment in China to concepts of national sovereignty and their accompanying responsibilities of self-management and self-defence. The wider regimes of social accountability to which Zheng's self-narrative was subject were changing rapidly, dramatically and unpredictably.

In this context, the risks attendant on thickening the diary narrative were considerable, yet the thin, bureaucratic recording that characterises the later years of the diary leaves it open to multiple readings and questions, not all of them favourable to Zheng. As Zheng recorded visit after visit from Japanese delegations, was he primarily emphasising his own regard for duty, or underlining the triviality of his official engagements? When Zheng recorded that the ceremonies at the Confucian temple that he attended in November 1932 were attended by 100 observers, including Japanese and American friends, was he simply filling the pages? Was he pointing to the cultural power of 'traditional' Chinese practices in Manzhouguo? Or – given that the ceremonies appear above all as a prelude to his resignation – was he asserting his own capacity to draw an audience? At the same time, this approach avoids closing off other, more forgiving perspectives. In reporting a State Council meeting, Zheng was able to portray Manzhouguo both as an order in which the legitimate concerns of Chinese officials were sidelined, and as an order that a conscientious official would wish to consolidate. In outline, where post-war, national historiographies have subsequently insisted that Zheng was dividing the Chinese nation and threatening its future, or that he was the puppet of an invader, Zheng reported simply that he was attending meetings, receiving visitors and managing Manchuria.

For Zheng Xiaoxu, the diary was not a confessional: we do not find in its pages the level of candour that European diarists such as Pepys may have taught us to expect in other contexts. This reticence challenges us to consider how far we expect the diary to be self-revelatory, and whether we find our diarist 'revealed' in explicit commentary, or in the incremental inclusions and exclusions of the daily record. The inconsistencies within the record of Zheng Xiaoxu's diary suggest a tension between what Zheng wrote for himself, and what he wrote for other, imagined audiences, and they suggest also an unstable relation between the written persona and the writing self. In this context, the diary persona is not a product of self-expression but a defensive carapace that stands between the fugitive self and the gaze of the reader.

## Notes

1. Zheng Xiaoxu, *Riji* (Diary), 5 vols. (Beijing: Zhonghua shuju, 1993). The originals of the diary are held in the Museum of Chinese History, Beijing.
2. I am indebted to Lynn Struve for this reminder. For a rich comparison of seventeenth- and nineteenth-century personal narratives of trauma, see Lynn Struve, 'Chimerical Early Modernity: The Case of "Conquest-Generation" Memoirs,' in Lynn Struve, ed., *The Qing Formation in World-Historical Time* (Cambridge: Harvard University Asia Center, 2004), especially 365–366.
3. Philippe Lejeune, *On Diary*, ed. Jeremy Popkin and Julie Rak, tr. Katharine Durnin (Honolulu: University of Hawaii Press, 2009), 148–149. Historians too are ambivalent: Elaine MacKay concludes that personal diaries are 'indispensable' sources for social historians but notes also familiar concerns over accuracy and the possibly unrepresentative nature of diaries produced predominantly by the literate and the affluent: 'English Diarists: Gender, Geography and Occupation, 1500–1700,' *History* 90.298 (2003): 212.
4. Lejeune, *On Diary*, 201–203.
5. Paul John Eakin, *Living Autobiographically: How We Create Identity in Narrative* (Ithaca: Cornell University Press, 2011), 22–31, 153–155.
6. Ibid, quotations from 30, 25.
7. Dorothy Ko, 'Thinking about Copulating: An early-Qing Confucian Thinker's Problem with Emotion and Words,' in Gail Hershatter et al., eds., *Remapping China: Fissures in Historical Terrain* (Stanford: Stanford University Press, 1996), quotation from 66–67; Henrietta Harrison, *The Man Awakened from Dreams: One Man's Life in a North China Village, 1857–1942* (Stanford: Stanford University Press), 12–15.
8. Marjorie Dryburgh, 'Rewriting Collaboration: China, Japan and the Self in the Diaries of Bai Jianwu,' *Journal of Asian Studies* 68.3 (2009): 689–714; on self-fashioning, see Stephen Greenblatt, *Renaissance Self-fashioning: from More to Shakespeare* (Chicago: University of Chicago Press, 1980), 2–9; note again the association of self-fashioning with 'hypocrisy or deception, [and] adherence to mere outward ceremony'.

9.  Howard L. Boorman and Richard C. Howard, eds., *Biographical Dictionary of Republican China* (New York: Columbia University Press, 1967), 271–272; Reginald Johnston, *Twilight in the Forbidden City* (Oxford: Oxford University Press, 1985), 342–343; Aisin-Gioro Pu Yi, *From Emperor to Citizen: The Autobiography of Aisin-Gioro Pu Yi*, tr. W.J.F. Jenner (Oxford: Oxford University Press, 1987), 140–162 *passim*; Xu Linjiang, *Zheng Xiaoxu qian ban sheng pingzhuan* (Critical biography of Zheng Xiaoxu: his early life) (Shanghai: Xuelin chubanshe 2003).

10. Benjamin A. Elman, 'Political, Social, and Cultural Reproduction via Civil Service Examinations in Late Imperial China,' *Journal of Asian Studies* 50.1 (1991): 7–28.

11. Aisin-Gioro Pu Yi, *From Emperor to Citizen* is one of the better known products of this process and is highly relevant here. See also the discussions below by Spakowski and Henrion-Dourcy on the processing of auto/biographies of figures within and beyond the Communist Party.

12. Zheng, *Riji*, 1. I have rendered all dates in the Gregorian calendar, as added to the published diary; the original uses the Chinese lunar calendar, with emperor reign years until 1911 and in the 60-year cyclical stem-and-branch system thereafter.

13. There is a particularly dense vein of such material in April–May 1892; Zheng, *Riji*, 258, 272–295.

14. Lejeune, *On Diary*, 202.

15. Zheng, *Riji*, 1349–1357. Zheng wrote a poem in memory of one such official, Shen Ying, on 16 November.

16. Ibid., 1357–1358.

17. On these stock responses, see Frederic Wakeman, 'Romantics, Stoics, and Martyrs in Seventeenth-Century China,' *Journal of Asian Studies* 43.4 (1984): 631–665; Lynn Struve, ed., *Voices from the Ming-Qing Cataclysm: China in Tigers' Jaws* (New Haven: Yale University Press, 1998) provides very rich personal accounts of the transition.

18. Zheng, *Riji*, 1358. Zheng refers to China as 'all-under-heaven', a conventional term for the empire.

19. Ibid., 1358.

20. Ibid., 1359.

21. Ibid., 1656 1657.

22. Ibid., 1651–1652, 1672–1673, 1689.

23. Ibid., 1781. Cao Rulin, then minister of communications, was regarded as being excessively friendly towards Japan; Zhang Zongxiang was formerly Chinese minister in Tokyo. Rana Mitter, *A Bitter Revolution* (Oxford: Clarendon Press, 2005), 3–4.

24. Boorman and Howard, eds., *Biographical Dictionary of Republican China*, 272–273.

25. Zheng, *Riji*, 1975. Xiaoqi was Zheng's second son, Zheng Yu; Chen Baoshen was imperial tutor.

26. Ibid., 1976.

27. Ibid., 1979.

28. Ibid., 1996.
29. Bai Jianwu, *Riji* (Diary) (Nanjing: Jiangsu guji chubanshe), 1215.
30. Aisin-Gioro Pu Yi, *From Emperor to Citizen*, 156–162.
31. Zheng, *Riji*, 2020–2026, 2030–2031.
32. Ibid., 2337–2343, 2575.
33. Ibid., 2341. Fengtian, now Shenyang, was also known as Mukden; the provision of a western date for a Chinese event embeds this in a global context, beyond China. In contemplating the possible end of the war, Zheng drew the comparison with the 1904–1905 Russo-Japanese War in which a resounding victory cemented Japan's position on the Liaodong peninsula and created a base for further gains on the East Asian mainland.
34. Ibid., 2342.
35. The growth of this pro-resistance discourse is the central theme of Parks M. Coble, *Facing Japan: Chinese Politics and Japanese Imperialism, 1931–1937* (Cambridge: Council on East Asian Studies, Harvard University, 1991).
36. Zheng, *Riji*, 2347. Pu Yi later claimed he had been duped into writing the letter. *From Emperor to Citizen*, 224.
37. Dryburgh, 'Rewriting Collaboration,' 704–705; Aisin-Gioro Pu Yi, *From Emperor to Citizen*, 228–238.
38. Zheng, *Riji*, 2370.
39. Ibid., 2370.
40. Ibid., 2405.
41. Ibid., 2405. Zheng Chui and Zheng Yu were Zheng Xiaoxu's first and second sons.
42. Ibid., 2406–2408.
43. Ibid., 2426.
44. Johnston, *Twilight in the Forbidden City*, 342–343; Aisin-Gioro Pu Yi, *From Emperor to Citizen*, 174–175, 261–265.
45. Bai Jianwu, *Riji*, 1110.
46. Zheng, *Riji*, 2465. Itagaki Seishirô, (1885–1948), one of the architects of the Manchurian incident and heavily involved in subversive activities in north China.
47. Ibid., 2459–2460.
48. Ibid., 2442–2443. Zheng Chui died in hospital, possibly of smallpox or scarlet fever, at the age of 47.
49. Ibid., 2520–2521.
50. Ibid., 2549, 2566; on the numerous shortcomings of the 'Kingly Way' as guiding philosophy, see Rana Mitter, *The Manchurian Myth* (Berkeley: University of California Press, 2000), 94–100.
51. Zheng, *Riji*, 2583.
52. Ibid., 2583.
53. Ibid., 2710.

# 5
# Destabilising the Truths of Revolution: Strategies of Subversion in the Autobiographical Writing of Political Women in China

*Nicola Spakowski*

During the second half of the 1980s, China witnessed an explosion of autobiographical texts dedicated to various periods in the political history of the country.[1] Most of these political autobiographies deal with the history of the Chinese Communist Party (CCP) and the Communist revolution in its various periods, places and institutions. The autobiographical texts by political women which are the focus of this essay are a sub-genre of these political autobiographies. What I mean by 'political women' is those who participated in the Communist revolution in various political, military or supporting roles, within or outside the major institutions of the revolution – party, army and Communist women's organisations – at lower or higher levels of the political hierarchy. Their texts usually fill from a few to around 30 pages in edited volumes that bear titles such as *Recollections of Women Soldiers (Nübing huiyilu)*, *Women Soldiers in the Mighty Torrent of Revolution (Da geming hongliu zhong de nübing)*, *Youth in the Flames of War (Qingchun zai zhanhuo zhong)* or *The Road to Yan'an (Yan'an zhi lu)*.

These CCP-related autobiographies, no matter which sub-genre they belong to, are typical products of post-Mao party history and serve several purposes. First of all, these texts are historical sources and as first-hand accounts of the revolution can be used to document party history at the grassroots level. Since by the mid- and late 1980s the revolutionary actors, especially of pre-1949 China, were starting to pass away, it was high time to ask them for first-hand accounts of their experience in the revolution. These autobiographical accounts, however, are also texts in their own right, albeit still within the framework of party history and with a quite ambiguous function. On the one hand, the political autobiographies of individual party members or supporters of the CCP provide abundant material for exemplifying and illustrating the general truths of party history. The details and vivid descriptions of autobiographical texts can help to give life and empirical evidence to the dry and abstract, textbook-like accounts of party history. On the other hand, they also reflect a certain trend of opening up or even 'democratising' party history. After the Cultural Revolution, the Party's rejection of Mao's leadership cult and its emphasis on collective leadership led to a greater emphasis on the Party as a collective body and also a recognition of the contribution of millions of individuals who had supported the Communist cause in a great variety of military and political roles. By giving these individuals a say, the Party had to accept a certain autonomy in these texts, which might tell stories no longer relevant for the central truths of party history and provide shifts in perspective that might cause tensions with party doctrines. These contradictory motives for allowing or even encouraging the production of political autobiographies – exemplifying general truths and representing individual experience and subjective perspectives – are also reflected in the political autobiographies by women and find expression in the tensions that characterise these texts.

In this chapter, I will demonstrate how to read these texts in order to trace the particular and subjective experience women might wish to express within the framework of a historical narrative dominated by the Party. I will do so by using a theoretical and methodological framework that relates to post-structuralist concepts of subjectivity and to strategies of signification as they have been described in narrative theory. The body of sources I use is limited to the revolutionary experience in the pre-1949 period, in particular the years between 1925 and 1949. While I have read several hundreds of these texts for a social history study of women's military participation in the Communist revolution,[2] for the purpose of this chapter I selected three texts which I found most useful for, first, exemplifying a narrative analysis that aims to discern the subjective experience of women and, second, demonstrating the variety of narrative strategies that are available to the authors. These three texts are by no way representative of the whole body of political women's autobiographies. On a continuum between subordination to the conventions of party history and the rather rare case of its explicit rejection – the two extremes that are quite easy to discern in a text – the examples I analyse stand for the fascinating 'in-between' cases of subtle tensions between the revolutionary master narrative and the representation of particular or subjective experience. By providing a close reading of three of these 'in-between' texts I want to show, first and foremost, that the potential for deviation from the truths of "capitalised Revolution" (as a master narrative of progress and transformation) does exist and that narrative analysis is a good tool to trace the more subtle forms of it.

## Theoretical and methodological foundations: Autobiographical texts in the context of capitalised Revolution

To understand how both the propositions of party history and the subjective experience of political women find their way into women's autobiographical texts and interrelate in specific ways, it is necessary to look at the role of discourse in autobiographical writing; the particular features of the master narratives employed in party history; the status of women in Communist ideology and political practice; the relation between women's autobiographical texts and the master narrative of party history; and, finally, the different modes of signification that a narrative might employ.

### Autobiography and subjectivity: The limits of representing the self

Women's studies, for a long time, saw it as their mission to retrieve the 'subjective experience' or 'authentic voices' of women that have been 'muted' in supposedly 'general' yet, in reality, male-centred history.[3] Autobiography and oral history were seen as the most useful sources for reconstructing the lives of women who were marginal if not totally missing in the more conventional sources historians use. Post-structuralism, however, questioned this search for 'experience', 'subjectivity' and 'authenticity'. Joan Scott, in her seminal article, 'The Evidence of Experience', revealed the 'constructed nature of experience'.[4] Penny Summerfield, in her oral history-based study of women's experience during the Second World War, stressed the inter-subjectivity of seemingly 'subjective' sources such as autobiography and oral history: 'Women "speaking for themselves" through personal testimony are using language and so deploying cultural constructions.'[5] Summerfield demonstrated how these personal testimonies are shaped by discourses of the past and the present, by the world the authors describe as history and by the outlook and expectations of their audience.[6] Thus, after the linguistic turn, the concept of 'subjectivity' in the sense of an 'authentic' representation of the self beyond the influence of discourse was impossible to maintain. At the same time, however, the very nature of discourse, its heterogeneity or multi-layeredness, its inclusion of both dominant and subordinate or subversive discourse traditions and subject positions also defies the notion of a *total* domination of autobiography by dominant discourse. To be sure, subordinate discourses, too, are cultural constructions. Still, the heterogeneity of discourse leaves scope for self-definitions beyond dominant discourse. Summerfield notes: 'Feminist scholars who make a special study of subjectivity suggest that subjectivities are formed by conjunctions of numerous differentiated discourses, some of which may be subordinate or even subversive and which may contain contradictory conceptualisations of identity.'[7] This more optimistic assessment of the chances of representing subjectivity – albeit still in the sense of a culturally constructed one – makes the exploration of discursive contexts and complexity the point of departure for any analysis of autobiographical texts.[8]

The post-structuralist concept of authenticity also reshapes the question of autobiographical writing in 'totalitarian' or authoritarian societies. Since cultural constructions and the dominance of master narratives are features of all societies, autobiographical writing in different political systems should be regarded as a case of 'variations of subjectivity in history'.[9] As Luisa Passerini explains: '... totalitarian systems are social systems like other ones, in the sense that their language and discourse have meaning for their protagonists, even if that meaning is unacceptable to us'.[10] To be sure, contextualisation will reveal specific discursive constraints for the representation of subjectivity in an authoritarian society. Still, models of a confrontation between the history constructed and disseminated by an authoritarian state and the 'counter-history' of repressed society, between 'official' and 'unofficial' history,[11] overlook the fact that discourse is much more fundamental and pervasive, yet, at the same time also much more open than a clear-cut distinction between the voices of state and society suggests.[12] Also, as other chapters in this volume demonstrate, various social groups in their autobiographical writing experience different degrees of constraints and different kinds of political expectations that come from the party state.[13] As will be shown below, the relationship between the Communist Party and political women in China was marked by complexity and entanglement, which is also reflected in the relation between the master narratives supported by the Party and the autobiographical texts of women.

## Communist master narratives and Communist biographies: Revolution and revolutionary lives

A discussion of the relation between Communist master narratives and political women's autobiographies has to start with the features of party history and in particular the way the relation is defined between revolution as a collective process and individual revolutionary lives. Party history in China is the history of capitalised Revolution as a master narrative of progress and transformation.[14] It demonstrates how China, guided by the CCP, progressed along the universal scheme of social development – from a semi-feudal/semi-colonial stage to socialism – and how semi-feudal/semi-colonial China, through the revolutionary activities of the Party, was transformed into a socialist society. Party history describes the Revolution as a unilinear process subdivided into clear-cut stages and marked by canonical events, some of which became the turning points in revolutionary history. Finally, party history claims an identity of collective and particular interests (such as those of women or ethnic minorities) in the revolutionary process and presents the Party as a unified agent of Revolution.[15] In the Party's perspective, participation in the Revolution is the logical way of 'liberation' for these particular interest groups also. By including women into the CCP and its affiliated institutions and by integrating their particular interests into its political agenda the Party claims to have liberated Chinese women in the process of Revolution.

Political biographies written under the auspices of party history closely follow the narrative of Revolution, progress and transformation. They depict how a person's life proceeded along the progress of Revolution, how this person participated in and contributed to a particular stage of the Revolution and its canonical events, and how he or she exemplified commitment to socialism. Political biographies are typically stories of subordination and sacrifice: a person's personal life, his or her individual will and even physical integrity are subordinated to the necessities of war and Revolution, the collective will, and the will of the Party. Since the Party is seen as the source of revolutionary wisdom, it is only natural for the Party to expect its members and supporters to become willing tools of party directives and decisions.

## The Revolution and women's participation: The conflict between 'general' and particular interests

The subordination of the individual, justified by the wisdom of the Party and the identity of general and particular interests, is a proposition that pertains to every member or supporter of the Party, men and women alike; furthermore, the need for that subordination is not unique to Chinese Communism, but is a general feature of military mobilisation throughout history.[16] It is therefore hard to claim that the conflict between 'general' and particular interests is a gender conflict alone. A general assessment of the gender-specific traits of the texts I look at would have to be based on a comparative analysis of female and male autobiographies. On the other hand, women's biographies and autobiographies are always a specific case in that they are subjected to gender discourse which determines whether and which groups of women are included in or excluded from the dominant narratives of national history.[17] (Communist) political women's autobiographies are a particularly interesting case in point due to the tensions between communism and feminism in CCP ideology. Chinese Communism, from the founding of the CCP, was a multi-layered and contradictory discourse in which women were seen as both an integral part of the Revolution sharing the general yearning for a new society, and as a particular group with particular interests and particular functions in the revolutionary process. Chinese Communism as a political movement was also multi-layered and contradictory: it forged alliances with various 'progressive' social movements such as feminism without being able to absorb them totally under the ideology and political practice of communism. It was a movement in the making which bore huge potential for individual decisions based on contradictory Communist discourse, alternative sources of 'progressive' thought or even habitual 'backward' or 'reactionary' attitudes. In the case of women's political and military participation, beneath the claim of an identity of interests we can discern constant conflict over women's roles and constant negotiations between women and their (usually) male superiors in the Party and Army.[18]

## The autobiographical texts of political women as 'nested narratives'

The autobiographical texts that form the basis of my analysis are written by women of various ranks and functions. Most of them were published in volumes edited by the Women's Federation, which participates in the recent wave of collecting political memoirs.[19] The Women's Federation, which has an interest in documenting women's contribution to the Revolution, seems to approach the authors of the individual texts through its branches at the provincial level, where most of the volumes are compiled. These volumes are usually dedicated to a particular chapter of Communist history or a specific political or military group with a substantial number of women or exclusively composed of women. The texts included are thus not autobiographies in the sense of the description of an entire life but recollections of a particular period of time in the life of an author. Given the active role of the Women's Federation as a party-affiliated institution in collecting the texts, one cannot expect entirely critical voices to be included in these volumes. Generally speaking, the authors of these texts display an affirmative attitude towards the Party which they find has shaped their lives in a positive way. This does not mean, however, that the texts are hymns of praise to the Party. Rather, they are written in a documentary mode of reporting one's experience in a specific chapter of Communist history. They assume the form of 'nested narratives', fitted into the master narrative of Revolution, and linking the micro and the macro level of revolutionary history.[20] More concretely, they describe how an author came to join the Communist movement, moved on in a political or military career, participated in a particular group, met one or more of the famous revolutionary leaders and experienced one or more of the canonical events of the Revolution. Also, the texts are not exclusively affirmative but bear traces of criticism, especially when it comes to the clash between the Party and women's interests. In some cases these conflicts are depicted quite openly.[21] In general, however, authors employ more subtle techniques of representing defiance.

### Unstable truths: The tension between different kinds of signification

My exploration of the potential for representing women's subjective experience is based on the analysis of the narrative structures of political women's autobiographies. Narrative analysis, in my view, is the best tool to detect the breaks and frictions that occur between discourses in one and the same text and thus to lay bare the instability of the truths of Revolution. The question then is how to identify certain passages as being based on a dominant or subordinate discourse, as representing the voice of the Party or the more subjective view of women.

The voice of capitalised Revolution can be found throughout the texts but its crystallisation certainly lies in explicit evaluations. The presence of this authoritative voice of the Party is most obvious in biographical texts with a close relation to party history, but political women admit this voice into their autobiographical texts as well – some of them probably as dedicated members of the Party, others just in order to signal rhetorical compliance. Explicit evaluations appear in the middle or at the end of (auto)biographical texts and can pertain to a particular experience or a person's entire life. Their function is to disambiguate the significance of an experience or a life, to fix meanings where the heterogeneous nature of discourse might suggest a variety of possible readings. Explicit evaluations provide the interpretation of an experience or the assessment of an entire life in the light of the truths of Revolution. They do so by giving outright interpretations; by drawing the demarcations and hierarchies between the stages of history, social forces and their representatives (good and bad, new and old, progressive and backward); and by offering symbolic compensation for the sacrifices a person made to the Revolution. Symbolic compensation occurs in the form of acknowledgement of an individual's contribution to the success of the Revolution or even in a promise to that the person will live on in collective memory.

In the autobiographies of political women we rarely find evaluations that would openly reject the truths of Revolution. Still, they are able to destabilise this truth with a more subtle strategy of signification, namely, detailed description. In psychological theories of memory and in narrative theory, detailed description is a technique that lends particular significance to the event or experience described.[22] As for psychology, Jay Winter and Emmanuel Sivan explain:

> The density (or weight of a memory) is shaped to a large extent by the dramatic nature of the experience, its uniqueness, its being reconsidered or reinterpreted after the fact as a turning point. Density is further enhanced by the emotional nature of the experience (quite often dramatic) and its autobiographical nature.[23]

Narrative theory confirms this observation. According to historian Ann Rigney, the 'particular choice of representative detail' has a specific function in the construction of a narrative.[24] Detailed description contributes to the concreteness and vividness of a narrative, which transforms an event into what Rigney calls 'living history'. The concept of 'living history' is of particular interest in those cases where it brings to life a position that remained subordinate in the course of history. 'Living history' thus might lead us to the 'alternative histories': '...paths not taken, the direction in which events might or could have developed had power been located elsewhere, had the desires of the narrative subject been realised'.[25]

Explicit evaluation and detailed description are two different ways of signification that can either be congruent or diverge. For the purpose of this study, divergence is the more interesting case because it is through the divergence from the authoritative voice of explicit evaluation, subtle as it may be, that political women express their subjective experience, subvert the truths of Revolution, reveal an alternative history of their own ideals and wishes, and bring to light the dark sides of revolution marked by disappointment, frustration and loss.

## Empirical examples: Narrative strategies in three autobiographical texts

To illustrate how political women willingly or unwillingly contest the authoritative voice of the Party and disclose their 'subjective' experience and perspectives through the use of particular narrative strategies, I selected three texts in which the destabilisation of the truths of Revolution are particularly obvious. As I have explained in the introduction, these texts and the strategies they use are not representative of the entire body of sources. Other texts might reveal additional strategies, blunter ways of deviation or more congruent ways of fitting an individual revolutionary life into the narrative of Revolution. What I want to demonstrate here is a way of reading these texts that might be useful for a more representative analysis of these or similar autobiographical texts.

### Li Zhen and the abstention from explicit evaluation

A first example is Li Zhen and her account of the early years of her career as a political activist in the rural revolution of the mid-1920s, where she assumed various positions in the women's movement, the CCP and the Red Army. Li Zhen was born in 1908 into a poor rural family and at the age of six was given away as a child bride.[26] Despite her origin at the margins of feudal society, Li Zhen became the best-known woman in the ranks of the People's Liberation Army (PLA): she was the first woman in the history of the PLA to be appointed general in 1955. Her outstanding career, which sharply contrasts with her social origin of poverty and oppression, made Li Zhen a paradigm of Chinese women's liberation in two respects. First, she gives evidence of women in the higher ranks of the People's Liberation Army and thus supports Communist China's claim to be a place of equal opportunity. Second, having been born in a poor family and having joined the revolution as a child bride, Li Zhen's life is an example of what women could achieve once they joined the revolution. She exemplifies the transition from feudal to socialist society and gives evidence of Chinese women's advancement from utmost oppression to full and respected members of society.

In CCP rhetoric, child brides were early paradigms of women's liberation.[27] They were living examples of women's liberation through

Communist revolution and were used by the Communists as propaganda tools. Child brides who had joined the Party usually became members of propaganda teams that were sent into the villages to convince people that the Communists were the advocates of the suppressed and the poor.[28] In public discourse, Li Zhen is usually presented in this exemplary function as the woman general who had been born as a child bride:

> History must not be forgotten. It was New China that made generations of working women who were suppressed at the bottom of life to free themselves (*fanshen*) and obtain liberation. It was the Chinese revolution that nurtured a child bride shackled by feudalism to become a female general who controlled wind and clouds (*chizha fengyun*).[29]

To what degree, then, does Li Zhen's self-narrative comply with the narrative of Revolution?

Li Zhen wrote an autobiographical essay about her life between 1908 and 1928, that is, from early childhood to the age of 20.[30] The text was published in 1987, and the very title 'From child bride to woman soldier' seems to suggest that transformation is also the dominant theme in her self-narrative. However, this assessment remains superficial unless we compare her autobiography with biographical texts written under the auspices of party history. Of particular interest is the text from which the quotation above was taken. It is a book chapter in a volume on Chinese women generals that was published in 1995 and it is obviously based on Li Zhen's own autobiographical text of 1987.[31] By comparing these two texts we can explore how the authoritative voice of party history transforms the 'raw material' of an autobiography into an exemplary life in the mode of Revolution or, to put it the other way around, how an individual can abstain from subordinating all her experience under the truths of party history. Two sections in these texts in particular show that even for the 'paradigmatic' Li Zhen there was scope to deviate from the narrative of Revolution.

The first section that is relevant here covers the moment when revolutionary activities reached the village where Li Zhen lived as a child bride.[32] Li Zhen complies with the narrative of Revolution by making this date the turning point in her life. This is how her story unfolds: Li Zhen starts with depicting the hardships and sufferings of her early years which appear as a condition without escape. At the age of six she was sent to her marital family, had to work hard, was scolded and beaten and was expected to perform tasks which were impossible to accomplish. After one such incident where she was unfairly scolded she ran away planning to drown herself. The last sentences of that paragraph which form the transition to her new, Communist life are:

> Neighbours caught me and brought me back and the grandmother of the Liu family, with tears in her eyes, comfortingly said: 'Dan Wazi,[33] women are women. Look, I am over sixty, and I still have to climb the mountains and cut firewood, I still get scolded. Women have to suffer too many hardships! Women are women...'

> Until now I still often dream of that difficult life.

> However, history is not a backwater. The storm of the First Revolutionary Civil War shook my village.[34]

Li Zhen joined the revolutionaries by becoming a member of the Women's Association. In March 1927 she entered the CCP and in the following year worked as a guerrilla leader.

What we can see in this passage is indeed a recourse to Revolution and the notion of progress ('history is not a backwater'). However, the break between feudal and revolutionary life is not as clear as one might expect. First of all, Li Zhen's old life is still present in her dreams. By including the dreams of the past – something that escapes human will – into her story, Li Zhen makes it a past in its own right. Second, the words of the old neighbour are meant as comfort; they are words of sympathy that present women's lot as an eternal, albeit shared fate. The ellipsis after the old woman's speech leaves open how Li herself evaluates the scene. Is the old woman's truth that 'women are women' too 'backward' to deserve comment or is it a truth that can claim universal validity – as the old woman herself seems to suggest? In Li Zhen's own account, the meaning of this scene of transition is ambiguous because the boundaries of time (past and present, old life and new life) and political consciousness (feudal or socialist) are blurred.

In the biography, this passage is transformed into capitalised Revolution through various changes and interpolations (in italics below):

Neighbours caught her and brought her back, and the grandmother of the neighbour family *exhorted* her: 'Dan Wazi, women are women. Look, I am over sixty, and I still have to climb the mountains and cut firewood, I still get scolded. Women have to suffer too many hardships!'

*'Why? This world is not fair!' Dan Wazi cried out into the darkness. The old society did not perceive women as human beings, but Dan Wazi wanted to be a true human being, she wanted to take a true road.*

*That day she was finally longing for!*

*War can toughen people, the battlefield can foster people. The general's badge on Li Zhen's shoulder was smelted in the flames of war.*

In spring 1926, the storm of the First Revolutionary Civil War shook Dan Wazi's village.[35]

Capitalised Revolution manifests itself, first and foremost, in explicit evaluation that stabilises the ambiguous meaning of Li Zhen's own account. Li Zhen's and the old woman's lot is explicitly interpreted as belonging to the 'old society'. It is no longer the ambiguous statement 'women are women' that concludes the old woman's words but the complaint that 'women have to suffer too many hardships'. The old woman no longer tries to appease Li Zhen but, through 'exhorting' her, prepares the ground for Li to reject the injustices of feudal society. Furthermore, in this paragraph the reader is provided with more than just the temporal information on the turning point in Li Zhen's life. Instead, war as a new theme is introduced and presented as a law of Li Zhen's (and human) development ('war can toughen people, the battlefield can foster people'). Second, the temporal structure of the story is changed. In her autobiography Li had looked back into the past (an open or even stagnant past) from the present (a present that was still filled with the past). In the biography, by contrast, the Li of the past foresees the possibility of a future as a 'true human being'. By adding Li's vision of the future and by referring to her future position as general, the *telos* of Revolution is inscribed into the past and the minds of historical actors. In the version of the biography, Li displays a truly socialist consciousness early on. In her mind she had left feudal society behind even before she entered the revolutionary movement. Whereas Li Zhen in her autobiographical text had refrained from explicating the nature of the transition from the life with her in-law family to her life as a revolutionary, the biography interpolates an interpretation and fixes the boundaries between old and new.

What follows in the autobiography is not the life of a woman who has time to ponder the course of history. Instead, Li Zhen, in a very concrete manner, depicts the dangers and hardships of her life as a guerrilla leader and the numerous conflicts she was facing. The basic difference between the autobiography and the biography is that in Li Zhen's text we find little that could help us link her experience to the progress of Revolution and the consolatory prospect of nation-wide liberation. Hardships remain hardships and are not compensated for by referring to the common good that eventually materialised in 1949.[36]

This lack of symbolic compensation can be best illustrated with an incident that seems to have severely affected Li Zhen's life. In the winter of 1928 Li experienced what she says was 'the hardest and most dangerous battle'.[37] At that time she was working for the district government of the Communists and she was in the fourth month of pregnancy. This is what happened: in the extremely unstable situation of 1928, the Communists were attacked by enemies and after one day of fighting were forced to retreat into the forests. They were able to hide there, living on what the forest provided. After one week, however, they were detected by the enemy and finally became encircled on the brink of a cliff. Having no escape route Li Zhen proposed to jump down. This was what she and her comrades did. Hitting the ground, Li Zhen lost consciousness. When she regained consciousness she found herself lying on the ground.

In her autobiography, Li Zhen uses 11 sentences to describe in great detail how she regained consciousness, lost it again, regained it, could not make sense of what had happened to her, thought she had broken her neck, discovered blood running down her legs, fainted once more and finally came to realise that she had suffered a miscarriage. The last two sentences of that paragraph read as follows:

I regained consciousness once again and only then realised that I had had a miscarriage. With the help of Zhang Wei, the child was hastily buried...[38]

Li Zhen's account is concrete and detailed. It presents the miscarriage in a scenic way and thus renders it particular significance.[39] At the same time, however, it abstains from explicitly evaluating it. What did the miscarriage mean to Li Zhen? Was it a loss nothing could make up for or did she find a way to come to terms with it? Once again, the ellipsis produces ambiguity.

The biography, on the other hand, uses only three sentences to cover that scene. It is stated that Li Zhen regained consciousness, detected the blood around her, realised that she had suffered a miscarriage and with the help of a comrade buried the foetus.[40] The story goes on with relating how she managed to escape and then provides an evaluation of the scene:

Since then, the scars of jumping from the cliff at that time remained on her left leg. Since then, Li Zhen who was only twenty years old had lost fertility. She paid a price of blood for the cause of revolution.[41]

The biography offers symbolic compensation by relating it to the cause of revolution and thus to the common good. Revolution, history and progress are evoked in order to offset personal loss by public acknowledgement. In her self-narrative, on the other hand, Li Zhen had refrained from consoling herself for the miscarriage. Through withholding an explicit evaluation, the scene remains ambiguous and destabilises the truths of Revolution.

## Zhong Fuguang: Inconsistencies between the general truths of Revolution and their illustration

The second example is Zhong Fuguang and the way she depicts her participation in the military activities during the Northern Expedition. Zhong Fuguang was born in 1903 and in 1927 became the leader of a women's team at the Central Military Academy of Wuhan, the capital of the revolution.[42] The Wuhan Military Academy existed between February and July 1927 and was a project of the more progressive forces in the coalition between CCP and Guomindang (GMD). The two parties had formed a 'united front' in a national-ist revolution that aimed to unify China, regain national sovereignty and also introduce social reforms that would transform China into a true nation-state. Feminism was on the programme of both parties based on the rationale that revolution would be incomplete without the participation of women and that China would never become a true nation-state until feudal gender relations were revolutionised.

By admitting women into a military academy, the founders of the Wuhan Military Academy signalled that they were serious about the inclusion of women into the revolutionary ranks. Around 200 women were accepted as students and formed the so-called 'women's team' (*nüshengdui*) of the academy.[43] They made up around 16% of the total number of students. This was the first time in mod-ern Chinese history that women received formal military training. However, revolutionary leaders and teachers at the academy on the one hand, and radical young women on the other hand, had differ-ent views on gender equality. In the minds of the members of the 'women's team', equality not only encompassed the idea of women's and men's equal rights but also the idea of uniformity of roles and appearance. Women's inclusion, in their view, was incomplete unless women looked like men and performed the same tasks as men. Male teachers, on the other hand, had a more moderate approach that affirmed equality in terms of rights but insisted on the special functions and appearance of women in revolution.

At first glance, Zhong Fuguang's recollections of her time in the military academy perfectly correspond with the narrative of progress and women's inclusion into the revolution.[44] She recounts how she entered the academy, met the political and military leaders of that time and participated in the canonical events in the academy's his-tory. She also sticks with the general truths of revolutionary life – revolutionary commitment and discipline. However, close reading of the text reveals contradictions between her detailed description of military life and the explicit evaluation of such scenes. These contra-dictions occur whenever Zhong refers to events in the history of the academy where the radical feminist stance of uniformity in appear-ance and role allocation and thus women's 'total' inclusion was at stake, when moderate teachers or superiors and radical students clashed in their interpretations of feminism. Here are two examples of how contradictions between detailed description and explicit evaluation reveal conflicts that do not fit the narrative of Revolution as an inclusive process.

In the section 'Life at the Military Academy', Zhong Fuguang depicts military discipline and the great demands women made on themselves. One paragraph in this section is introduced with the sentence: 'During these times the members of the women's team treated themselves with the highest standards and the strictest demands.' This is an accepted and quite conventional characterisation of a committed revolutionary. However, the text that follows to illustrate this general truth takes a quite specific direction. What Zhong actually reports are disputes between students and teachers on the question whether there should be special provisions for the uniforms and the daily life of women soldiers at the academy. Teachers insisted on the difference between women and men. They wanted the young women to wear black – instead of grey – leg wrappings and to wear armbands with the letter 'W' (for 'women'). Women were given only pistols instead of rifles; they had to wear short hair (instead of a bald head) and they were supposed to wear a red armband when menstruating, which would exempt them from military training. The women rejected all these special provisions on the grounds of gender equality: 'Since men and women are equal (*nan nü pingdeng*), why should there still be differences?'[45] Of course, these disputes can also be read as examples of the great demands female students made on themselves – they did not want to be exempted from the hardships of military life. However, the argument they employ – gender equality – raises questions of power among revolutionaries rather than exemplifying commitment to the revolutionary cause. There is an obvious inconsistency between the general principle and evaluation of the conflict (high demands on oneself) and its exemplification (demanding equality).

A second example of subverting a paradigm of Revolution without explicitly refuting it refers to a military campaign in May 1927. The women of the women's team joined the campaign as propaganda and medical personnel and were commanded by Shi Cuntong who was head of the political department and also Zhong Fuguang's husband. Zhong Fuguang was more than three months pregnant at that time.

A conflict between Zhong and her superior/husband broke out when Zhong reported to him that some women soldiers had health problems. Shi responded by ordering Zhong to lead the group of sick women home. Zhong refused to return and told Shi Cuntong that she was still able to follow the troops. She recalls how her husband 'without the slightest smile in his meagre face, with closed lips, fixed his eyes on her and said: "You have to obey orders." ' Zhong relates that she knew that there was no way for her to disobey, but that she felt unhappy and therefore wrote a note which she gave her husband. The note said that in times of fighting feudalism women must not be looked down upon. After that she led the group of sick women soldiers home. Later she asked her husband what he thought about the note. Her husband laughed and said: 'I was so busy at that time – how should I have found time to read your note?'[46] He took the note out of his pocket and returned it to Zhong – obviously without even having glanced at it. Zhong explains: 'From this one can see how scarce time is during war.'[47] This sentence also concludes the paragraph. In her evaluation of her husband's/superior's behaviour, Zhong refers to the accepted truth of scarcity of time during war. She thus refrains from directly engaging the narrative of Revolution. She does not conceal, however, that gender equality had been at stake here as well. The ambiguity of Zhong Fuguang's narrative thus does not lie in the lack of explicit evaluation as in Li Zhen's case but in the inconsistencies between explicit evaluations as bearers of the truths of Revolution and their illustration through detailed description.

### Kang Daisha and the two sides of transformation

The third example is Kang Daisha and the story of her transformation from a naïve patriot to a willing tool of the Party. Her autobiographical text 'Yan'an was calling me' pertains to the Yan'an years of the CCP, the late 1930s and 1940s – years that were dominated by ideological education. The aim of ideological education was to unify the Party and to instruct its members about the proper strategy of national liberation in a complicated ideological setting where immediate nationalist feelings had to be tempered through 'reason' represented by the Party and its long-term political strategies. The theme of transformation is particularly salient for these years and Yan'an, the 'red school',[48] became the laboratory of revolutionary transformation.[49]

Kang Daisha was born into a rich and influential bourgeois Shanghai family. After the outbreak of the Sino-Japanese War in July

1937, she followed her family to Chongqing, the capital of 'Free China'. In spring 1938, Kang decided to go to Yan'an to join the Communists. Kang's depiction of her own path and her experience in Yan'an totally complies with the narrative of transformation: 'I was continually tested in revolutionary practice and transformed myself (*gaizao ziji*).'[50] Throughout the text she praises the Party for helping her to transform and to 'overcome' her 'shortcomings',[51] and also in the concluding evaluation of her Yan'an experience, she is utterly positive in portraying Yan'an as an initiation into a life that was guided by the progress of Revolution: 'The spirit of Yan'an was the driving force for me to set out and continually advance on the road of revolution.'[52]

The truth of transformation, however, in order to become convincing, has to be illustrated, and Kang therefore describes in great detail instances of ideological education and redirection through the Party. The reason why Kang was a particular target of education was twofold. For one thing, Kang, as many other young educated women, became caught in the conflict between her own patriotism and her wish to fight on the battlefield of the Anti-Japanese War of Resistance and the CCP's women's policy that tried to channel young educated women into women's work in the villages of the 'liberated' areas.[53] Second, Kang was a particular case due to her social origin in the milieu of the Nationalists. In the eye of the Party, her family's GMD contacts predestined Kang for political work in Chongqing, a place far from Yan'an, the political centre of the Communists, and an environment which due to its political 'backwardness' Kang had deliberately left behind. In no way did her original wish to be sent to the Anti-Japanese front fit the plans the Party had for her.

In her autobiographical text Kang presents the process of transformation as a series of conflicts over her role in the revolution. She starts with shorter descriptions of instances of frustration over not being allowed to join individual classmates or entire groups of students who were sent to the front. Kang reveals her emotions: '...of course, for some days I was in a fit of depression. The political instructor wanted to see me for ideological education (*sixiang gongzuo*).' She also 'envied' a friend who was sent to the front in spring 1939.[54] In the evaluation of these instances, however, Kang turns frustration into maturation. The ideological education she received at the

Central Party School helped her to 'overcome deficiencies' such as 'being divorced from reality' or 'having ambitious plans'. Ideological training 'raised the level of [her] political thoughts and increased [her] confidence in the victory in the War of Resistance'. All in all, it made her realise that she had to 'submit to the organisation [i.e. the Party] and obey the call of the Party'.[55]

Descriptions of conflict become much more detailed when it comes to scenes where high-ranking party members tried to convince her to do political work in Chongqing. In spring 1939, Deng Yingchao, prominent party official and wife of Zhou Enlai, approached Kang to suggest that she re-establish links with her family. Kang's parents wanted her to return to Chongqing and had asked the CCP leadership to send her home. Kang started crying and said that she wanted to go to the front to fight the Japanese; she did not want to return home. Deng Yingchao expressed sympathy with her but still reminded her of the fact that it was important to get as many people as possible involved into the War of Resistance and that she would make a perfect tool in the political work among the Nationalists.[56] In spring 1940, Zhou Enlai himself called on Kang and urged her to become a member of a delegation to the GMD-controlled areas to mobilise people for the Anti-Japanese War. Kang should return to her family and use their connections with prominent people in Chongqing to foster the 'united front' between Communists and Nationalists. Kang tried to appeal to 'reason' (*liyou* – this is what in her words Zhou Enlai was also doing) and told Zhou that she hated her 'exploiting class family' and the 'corrupt rule of the GMD' – indeed a very reasonable stance for a good Communist to take. Zhou countered: 'To be a rebel against an exploiting class family is indeed praiseworthy, but since this is a revolution one has to follow the requirements of the revolution...'[57] Once again, obedience was a lesson she learned and accepted.

Kang depicts these talks with top party leaders in a scenic way, including direct quotations, which reveals the high significance she lends these scenes. She affirms this significance through explicit evaluation where she interprets them in the light of the truths of Revolution. Still, her text is ambiguous. To make her story convincing, Kang has to illustrate both ends of the transformation process, her original 'naïve' self and the matured revolutionary self. She also has to reveal her inner life: feelings of frustration and depression that are gradually overcome by 'reason'. To be sure, in her evaluation she establishes a clear hierarchy between inferior (her own) and superior (the Party's) motives and approaches. This hierarchy, however, through the detailed description of her original plans and wishes, also becomes unstable. Instead of reading her story as a process of maturation, we could also read it as a series of conflicts in which the will of the Party was imposed on the life of an individual who had developed a different idea of her place in the multi-layered struggles of revolution.

## Conclusion

The close reading and narrative analysis of three autobiographical texts reveals that political women can express their 'subjective' experience in the Chinese revolution despite the authoritarian nature of China's political system and the existence of a well-established and authoritative master narrative of the Communist revolution. After the Cultural Revolution, renunciation of the leadership cult and a turn towards collective leadership resulted in a certain opening up of party history. Political autobiographies helped to demonstrate the collective nature and also the inclusiveness of the revolution. However, as particular constituencies have won a voice in party history and begun to tell their own stories of revolutionary activism, they have diversified the master narrative of capitalised Revolution and blurred its unilinear and highly centralised plot.

This is also the central feature of the three texts analysed here. They are examples of an in-between stance towards the narrative of Revolution which they neither bluntly reject nor uncritically confirm. Rather, these texts assume the form of 'nested' narratives in that they weave an individual life story into the master narrative of Revolution. Still, the different voices that feed into these autobiographies remain distinguishable. Generally speaking, we find the authoritative voice of the Party in explicit evaluation whereas women's 'subjective' voices are represented in detailed description. Explicit evaluation relates an individual life story to the revolutionary master narrative of social progress, individual transformation and the common good. Detailed description, on the other hand, is used to express experiences that are of high subjective relevance – experiences, that in many instances represent the dark sides of the revolution, such as danger and loss, conflict and frustration. For women who have participated in the revolution, detailed description is a subtle tool of engaging and destabilising the truths of Revolution without forthrightly rejecting them. In the three examples analysed here, women used several techniques to elude total absorption by the truths of Revolution: Li Zhen refrained from explicit evaluation of her revolutionary experience and the ellipses in her text render it highly ambiguous. Zhong Fuguang confirmed a number of accepted truths but illustrated them with scenes of a quite different nature. And Kang Daisha depicted herself as an example of successful transformation by detailing all the sacrifices she had to make in order to live up to the will of the Party.

The three cases also reveal where conflicts in the representation of the revolution are most likely to appear. A first one is the Party's claim that women were harmoniously included into the revolution and that their particular interests and the 'general' interests of the revolution were one. In fact political women's autobiographies abound in instances of conflict between an author's individual wishes and the will of party and army superiors. Typically, these are conflicts over gender roles and gender equality. In our examples, Zhong Fuguang's report detailed a number of conflicts over equality. Kang Daisha exemplified the case of a revolutionary whose individual wishes were constantly frustrated by the orders of the Party. A second source of discursive clashes is the Party's claim of collective progress and individual transformation. Party publications presented Li Zhen, the child bride turned woman general, as a paradigmatic case of revolutionary progress from feudalism to socialism and of individual transformation from an object of repression to a determined revolutionary fighting for a socialist future. Her own story, however, lacks this logical sequence, the *telos* of Revolution and the clear-cut demarcation between historical and biographical stages. The young Li Zhen is not filled with the vision of socialism; the past remains present in old Li Zhen's dreams and women's oppression appears timeless. Kang Daisha's text shows that transformation is an unstable construct. To be sure, in her explicit evaluation, her former (naïve) and later (socialist) self are clearly hierarchised. Concentrating on the details of the text, however, we can easily read this story of maturation as a story of endless frustrations. The third point where the narrative of Revolution and women's individual life stories diverge is symbolic compensation for loss and sacrifice. In our texts, Li Zhen is the most telling example of this, in that she refuses to relate her miscarriage to the common good and the future victory of the revolution. By finishing her detailed report of this obviously traumatic episode in her life with an ellipsis she keeps it an exclusively personal one.

Still, we should be aware that the 'voice' of political women that was retrieved through analysing the narrative structure of their autobiographical texts is not 'authentic' in the sense of a voice independent of discourse. Rather, the contradictory nature of Communist discourse itself (for example, in the tensions between moderate and radical approaches to women's liberation, or between an immediate patriotism and a far-sighted revolutionary strategy) provided women with a variety of possible roles in the revolution which did not find their way into the one-dimensional and unilinear narratives of party history. Detailed description rendered their experience into 'living history' and highlighted their subjective interests, wishes and expectations as a potential point of departure for an 'alternative history' of women's revolutionary activism.

## Notes

1. I use the terms 'autobiographical texts' or 'autobiography' in the very broad sense of self-narration. The distinguishing features of the texts I discuss will be described later.
2. Nicola Spakowski, *'Mit Mut an die Front': Die militärische Beteiligung von Frauen in der kommunistischen Revolution Chinas, 1925–1949* (Courageously to the front: women's military participation in the Chinese Communist Revolution, 1925–1949) (Cologne: Böhlau, 2009).
3. For a discussion of these problems with regard to wartime experience, see Penny Summerfield, *Reconstructing Women's Wartime Lives: Discourse and Subjectivity in Oral Histories of the Second World War* (Manchester: Manchester University Press, 1998), 2–42.
4. Joan W. Scott, 'The Evidence of Experience,' *Critical Inquiry* 17 (1991): 777.
5. Summerfield, *Reconstructing Women's Wartime Lives*, 11.
6. Ibid., 20–32. For a similar concept of the limits of representing subjectivity and its adaptation to questions of autobiography in China, see Wang Lingzhen, *Personal Matters: Women's Autobiographical Practice in Twentieth-Century China* (Stanford: Stanford University Press, 2004).
7. Summerfield, *Reconstructing Women's Wartime Lives*, 12–13.
8. See also Gabriele Rosenthal, 'Geschichte in der Lebensgeschichte' (History within life stories), *Bios – Zeitschrift für Biographieforschung, Oral History und Lebensverlaufsanalysen* 2 (1988): 3–15.

9. Luisa Passerini, 'Introduction,' in Luisa Passerini, ed., *Memory and Totalitarianism*, International Yearbook of Oral History and Life Stories, vol. 1, (Oxford: Oxford University Press, 1992), 9.

10. Ibid., 7.

11. Rubie S. Watson, 'Memory, History, and Opposition under State Socialism: An Introduction,' in Rubie S. Watson, ed., *Memory, History, and Opposition under State Socialism* (Santa Fe: School of American Research Press, 1994), 2.

12. This idea of the pervasiveness of discourse and its entry also in those narratives that challenge dominant structures is supported, for instance, by Passerini, *Memory and Totalitarianism*, 6, who points out the 'similarities and connections in the forms of subjectivity that Fascism and anti-Fascism fostered'. For the case of China, see Gail Hershatter, 'The Gender of Memory: Rural Chinese Women and the 1950s,' *Signs: Journal of Women in Culture and Society* 28.1 (2002): 43–70 (especially 48–49, 66–68) on the memory of rural Chinese women and its intersection with state rhetoric. See also Janet Ng, *The Experience of Modernity: Chinese Autobiography of the Early Twentieth Century* (Ann Arbor: University of Michigan Press, 2003), ix, on early twentieth century autobiography as 'an efficient way to narrate the nation'.

13. See the essays by Dauncey and Henrion-Dourcy in this volume.

14. This master narrative is also the point of reference for the autobiographies examined here. For a more differentiated assessment of party historiography, see Susanne Weigelin-Schwiedrzik, 'Party Historiography in the People's Republic of China,' *Australian Journal of Chinese Affairs* 17 (1987): 77–94.

15. For integration as the basic Communist concept of women's liberation and its variations in different time periods, see Spakowski, *'Mit Mut an die Front'*. For an account of the women's movement that reflects the claim of identity of 'general' and women's interests, see Zhonghua quanguo funü lianhehui, (All China Women's Federation), ed., *Zhongguo funü yundong shi* (History of the Chinese Women's Movement).

16. Alex Vernon, 'No Genre's Land: The Problem of Genre in War Memoirs and Military Autobiography,' in Alex Vernon, ed., *War, the Military, and Autobiographical Writing* (Kent and London: Kent State University Press, 2005), 20.

17. See also Zurndorfer in this volume.

18. For the contradictory nature of Communist ideology and practice with regard to feminism, see Spakowski, *'Mit Mut an die Front'*.

19. For a long list of publications edited by the Women's Federation or affiliated institutions or individuals, see the references in ibid.

20. For the concept of 'nested narratives', see Kenneth J. Gergen and Mary M. Gergen, 'Narratives of the Self,' in Lewis P. Hinchman and Sandra K. Hinchman, eds., *Memory, Identity, Community: The Idea of Narrative in the Human Sciences* (Albany: State University of New York Press, 1997), 171.

21. See, for instance, Zhou Doubing, 'Women shi nü zhanshi' (We are women soldiers), in Xinghuo liaoyuan bianjibu (Editorial staff of the [series] Xinghuo liaoyuan), ed., *Xinghuo liaoyuan: Nübing huyilu* (A single spark can start a prairie fire: recollections of women soldiers) (Beijing: Jiefangjun chubanshe, 1987), 80–86. See also Hershatter, 'The Gender of Memory', 66.

22. For detailed description in theories of narrative, see Ann Rigney, *The Rhetoric of Historical Representation: Three Narrative Histories of the French Revolution* (Cambridge: Cambridge University Press, 1990), 77.

23. Jay Winter and Emmanuel Sivan, 'Setting the Framework,' in Jay Winter and Emmanuel Sivan, eds., *War and Remembrance in the Twentieth Century* (Cambridge: Cambridge University Press, 2000), 12.

24. Ann Rigney, 'The Point of Stories: On Narrative Communication and Its Cognitive Functions,' *Poetics Today* 13.2 (1992): 275.

25. Rigney, *The Rhetoric of Historical Representation*, 174.

26. For a full biographic account, see Cui Xianghua, 'Cong tongyangxi dao nü jiangjun' (From child bride to woman general), in Cui Xianghua et al., eds., *Zhongguo nü jiangjun* (Chinese women generals) (Beijing: Jiefangjun wenyi chubanshe, 1995), 1–36.

27. For the status of child brides as an element in the Communist ideology of emancipation during the Jiangxi period, see Tani E. Barlow, *The Question of Women in Chinese Feminism* (Durham: Duke University Press, 2004), 56.

28. For child brides and their roles in Communist propaganda teams, see Spakowski, '*Mit Mut an die Front,'* 122–130.

29. Cui, 'Cong tongyangxi dao nü jiangjun', 1. See also the title of this biography: 'From child bride to woman general'.

30. Li Zhen, 'Cong tongyangxi dao nü zhanshi' (From child bride to woman soldier), in Xinghuo liaoyuan bianjibu (Editorial staff of the [series] Xinghuo liaoyuan), ed., *Xinghuo liaoyuan: Nübing huiyilu* (A single spark can start a prairie fire: recollections of women soldiers) (Beijing: Jiefangjun chubanshe, 1987), 61–68.

31. Cui, 'Cong tongyangxi'.

32. Li, 'Cong tongyangxi', 61–62.

33. Dan Wazi (the baby who was born at dawn) was the phrase by which she was addressed in her 'old' life. She did not receive a proper name – Li Zhen – until she joined the revolutionaries. See Li, 'Cong tongyangxi', 62.

34. Ibid. Ellipsis in the original.

35. Cui, 'Cong tongyangxi', 6.

36. This contrasts with the biographical text which claims that 'the Chinese Communist Party gave Li Zhen light and a new life' (ibid., 7) and that from the moment Li had become a party member 'she understood that it was an appropriate principle to sacrifice her individual life in order to enable the millions of people who suffer hardships to lead a good life' (ibid.).

37. Li, 'Cong tongyangxi', 67.

38. Ibid., 68. Ellipsis in original text.

39. For scenic presentation as a particular relationship between narrating time and story time, see Monika Fludernik, 'Time in Narrative,' in David Herman, Manfred Jahn and Marie-Laure Ryan, eds., *Routledge Encyclopedia of Narrative Theory* (London: Routledge, 2005), 608.
40. Cui, 'Cong tongyangxi', 9.
41. Ibid. It is also noteworthy that the biography mentions only physical scars and sacrifices.
42. Strictly speaking, Wuhan was only a branch of the famous Whampoa Military Academy in Canton. For the history of the Wuhan Military Academy's 'women's team' and feminist discourse at that time, see Spakowski, *'Mit Mut an die Front,'* chap.2.4.
43. Information on the historical background can be found in Zhong Fuguang, 'Huangpu junxiao Wuhan fenxiao nüshengdui de yi duan huiyi' (Some recollections of the women's team in the Wuhan branch of the Huangpu Military Academy), in Zhonghua quanguo funü lianhehui and Huangpu junxiao tongxuehui (All-China Women's Federation and Alumni Association of the Huangpu Military Academy), ed., *Da geming hongliu zhong de nübing* (Women soldiers in the mighty torrent of revolution) (Beijing: Zhongguo funü chubanshe, 1991), 31–38.
44. Zhong, 'Huangpu junxiao'.
45. Ibid., 34.
46. Ibid., 37.
47. Ibid.
48. Kang Daisha, 'Yan'an zai xiang wo zhaohuan' (Yan'an was calling me), in Su Ping and Xu Yuzhen, ed., *Yan'an zhi lu* (The road to Yan'an) (Beijing: Zhongguo funü chubanshe, 1991), 20–35.
49. See also David E. Apter and Tony Saich, *Revolutionary Discourse in Mao's Republic* (Cambridge: Harvard University Press, 1994) on Yan'an as a discourse community and the significance of ideological education and persuasion during these years.
50. Kang, 'Yan'an', 28.
51. Ibid.
52. Ibid., 35.
53. For the conflict between patriotic women who wanted to fight and the CCP who channelled them into the women's movement, see Spakowski, *'Mit Mut an die Front,'* chap. 5.
54. Kang, 'Yan'an', 28.
55. Ibid.
56. Ibid., 29–30.
57. Ibid., 31.

# 6
# Zhang Xianliang: Recensions of the Self

*Chloë Starr*

The writings of Zhang Xianliang (b.1936) present an important case study for tracing the interplay of memory, voice and self-reflection in the first decades of the People's Republic of China (PRC). As Zhang moves between diary, short story and novel, at times rewriting earlier episodes from his own life in expanded form, at times re/presenting an episode in different form and blurring the boundaries between biography and fiction, he deliberately explores the bounds of self in self-expression. Some aspects of the process of Zhang's self-inscription are universal; others are much more darkly representative of a particular social experience. This chapter considers how these two facets – the writtenness of the self and the interposition of the state in its formation – combine as Zhang writes and rewrites his life. Zhang's work has been the subject of various studies, including social, psychological and political readings, but none has focused on the fine interplay between diary and novel forms in his life writing. The methodology is drawn from the texts: the chapter follows Zhang's hermeneutical lead in making no attempt to separate out fictional and real versions of the narrated selves. It weaves between the diaries and novels under discussion and glides over the question of whether a given character is to be read as the author or a fictional being. If biography is the history of an individual's life, then to understand the concept of self in authorial fiction, Zhang's work suggests, we need to read across and between the entire oeuvre.

Zhang's biography is well known. Much of his work refers back to the years he spent being 're-educated' in labour-reform camps and prisons in the west and north-west of China.[1] Physical and, later, mental, break-down testify to the extreme penetration of the state into human life, beginning for Zhang in the Anti-Rightist campaign of 1957 and continuing though until the pre-Tiananmen days of the late 1980s. Various stories are narrated through the eyes of a character, sometimes named Zhang, whose life story closely resembles that of the author. The extent to which the self – the physical body, the intellect and the sense of self – was formed, deformed and reformed by the state is a central theme in Zhang's work. One of the most poignant outcomes of a close reading of Zhang's writing across several decades is to trace a shift in self-understanding, from the naïve voice of the diarist as he appeases and acquiesces to official versions of himself, to the more mature novelist who painfully, and at times promiscuously, reclaims his mind and the right to his own self-depiction. Zhang's formation, and the forms in which he encrypted himself, were governed and directed by authorities to a degree which now seems incredible, and whose very transcendence Zhang wants to document. The processes of recovery in the later phases of Zhang's life, as the trope of food and hunger cedes to sex and emotion, bring new forms of expression.

Zhang's creation and re-creation of his self through writing exposes the fragmented, non-linear process of memory recall, and the multiple and shifting positions that the self can adopt. Psychological and neurological studies, which have both drawn on and fed into literary studies, have described the sedimented layering of memory, and pinpointed the various areas of the brain associated with different types of inscription and storage.[2] The relation of self to writing is attenuated by Zhang's repeated forays back to labour camp memories in different periods of his fictional characters' lives. The past is ever-present, as the still frames of the recorded past interact in characters' lives in an intertextual present. Factual and emotive recall are carefully woven together, and the passage of time allows buried traces to be reanimated and resolved in fiction. While we might expect a diary to be more intensely personal and revealing of the inner self than an abstracted fiction, in Zhang's writings the axiom is tested, because the diaries in question were terse annotations, jottings to evade the censor in 1960, while his novels are imbued with a deep autobiographical pathos.

Just as the chronology of memory is elusive, Zhang Xianliang's writings and publication dates present a complex and disordered tale. This essay focuses on four works: his volume(s) of diaries, *Fannao jiushi zhihui* (translated as *Grass Soup*) and *Wo de putishu* (My bodhi tree), originally written in 1960–1961 and expanded, annotated and published in Chinese in 1992 and 1994, respectively; *Lühua shu* (Afforestation, translated as 'Mimosa') published in 1983, and *Xiguan siwang* (Getting used to dying), completed and published in magazine format in 1989, but banned shortly after. The two diaries form volumes I and II of the same work, with later Chinese editions combining them as one. *Mimosa*, along with Zhang's celebrated camp novel *Half of Man Is Woman*, was part of the first set of an anticipated nine-part project, the 'Revelations of a Materialist' (*Weiwulunzhe de qishilu*), entitled *Ganqing de licheng* (The progress of emotion) – a meta-narrative of the author's self.[3] The desire to create intertextually self-referencing sets of works underpins the biographical emphasis of Zhang's corpus as a whole. Zhang challenges the rule that greater distance from events depicted usually results in a more homogenised depiction, and the dictum that 'autobiographers consciously shape the events of their lives into a coherent whole', with his multiple iterations, and the absence of a final, definitive textual version of an event.[4]

In their different representations of the self-in-text, the four volumes illustrate the effects of genre on the depiction of self. The two diaries provide comment, in an authorial voice, on real events. Here remembering and recreation are presented as reportage; the tenor is analytical, dispassionate. The novel *Mimosa* is set in the mid-1960s and is the most 'fictional' of the four; it recreates the period rather than particular events, with little immediate recourse to specific historicity. The later novel *Getting Used to Dying* is set in the present, and shifts back and forth between events in the narrator's life, linking the camp years of the 1960s to the 1980s. Unlike *Mimosa*, the imagined past is rooted firmly in the present consciousness of the implied author. The four works present respectively the past, the imagined past and the past-in-the-present. In each, the relationship between the remembered self and the present self is differently configured.

## The self rewritten

As Zhang notes sardonically in *Getting Used to Dying*, individuals who lived through the Cultural Revolution had a much stronger sense of self gifted to them. Life writing became a coercive experience.

They were written, and they wrote. Zhang knew his life story by heart:

> That type of investigation was particularly strict. Each and every sentence had to match up, like the serial numbers on a chain link, otherwise your life was in danger, or you faced a severe beating. The training gave me my current ability to write. The investigator had to pin down the history of the one being investigated, and the one being investigated needed constantly to compile his own history, together with a record of conversations with x and y – just like the process of reading and writing a novel. The exacting requirements of the dialogue fostered innumerable Shakespeares.[5]

Since the purpose of labour reform was to *reform* inmates, to change their view of themselves, autobiography for Zhang should be a record of the process of remoulding the self – or of his defiant resistance.[6] Wu Pei-yi has made the point that in China there was traditionally no distinction between self-written biographies and standard biographies.[7] Since Zhang writes as an observer looking at his past self, here too there is the sense that this biography is written for, and almost by, someone else. Here another tension runs between autobiography and biography: between what the self thinks of the self and what the state required one to think of oneself. The first is reflected in the published form of the diaries, in the two typefaces of original and annotated text, and the second in the constant striving to understand what the self had been.

If labour reform prisoners were profligate in their recitations of the official version of their lives, they were required to be circumspect about any private sentiments. Zhang's actual diary, which formed the basis for the later volumes of *My Bodhi Tree*, was written in the interstices of time between camp duties and recounts at the outset the detailed process of negation involved in composition. The relationship between self and diary resembles that of photographic negative to print:

> When I was writing the diary, what I first thought of was not what had happened today and whatever noteworthy thoughts I had had, but those events and those thoughts that I could not under any circumstances note down. The society we lived in at the

time did not permit anyone to have individual, private thoughts. Everybody's every private thought had to be 'handed over' to the Party, including personal diaries. The leaders used the degree of private intimacy of the thoughts handed over to determine the degree of a person's loyalty to the Party.[8]

Concoction and confabulation were common, as people competed to excel first in loyalty at exorcising anti-Party thoughts, and later in heroism at expressing in diaries and memoirs the lofty sentiments that befitted a communist citizen. Zhang was not willing to be either martyr or hero, and the brevity of the original entries, intended as aides-mémoire for an anticipated future, made reconstructing events more difficult two decades later, but ensured the diary's survival through waves of confiscation and censure. As Zhang muses, 'If I didn't have this flimsy diary, I would doubt whether that period of life were real.'[9] The laying down of a trail of catalysts, of a biographical outline to be developed in the future as circumstances permitted, shows how strongly Zhang's internal narration continued. Even the abbreviated record had a strong emotive power for the author looking back, and demonstrates why the past can never easily be separated from the effects of its recall.

The raw immediacy of the diary form, and the physical confrontation of the traces of his former self, exert a greater hold on the older Zhang than his creative writings. It is arguably this very brevity, which allows an imagined self always to form in the gaps, which make these extracts so real for Zhang. In his first annotation to the second part of the diary, Zhang writes of the past 'gushing up' at him, 'surging counter to time', images from his past transformed into 'innumerable specks of frozen spume' rushing towards him. The past 'assaults' him, leaving Zhang stranded, unable to cross the depths to safety in either past or future.[10] He has to write the diary – now, in the present – in order to link the past to the future; otherwise they will remain rent apart, with the potential not just to tear him in two, but 'to shatter the whole world into pieces'. The responsibility as a survivor, living on the yellow earth rather than 'buried deeply within it', weighs heavily, and this sense of destiny supports him in bearing the emotional costs attendant upon re-experiencing events as he writes. (The concomitant political costs Zhang could anticipate well. His initial punishment was meted out in 1957 for the publication of the poem *Da feng ge*,[11] and subsequent works entrained periods of opprobrium and exile.)

An abrupt dislocation bifurcates Zhang's life: pre- and post-incarceration. This divide figures deeply in all written recensions. His earlier life is absent from his post-camp writings, the trauma of loss banishing childhood from adult consciousness.

'A sharp knife had sliced me in half down the middle, and tossed away this part of my consciousness into some wilderness. I didn't know where the other part of me was, or whether I had ever been whole', he writes.[12] In the novel *Mimosa*, the protagonist describes a detachment in the present, a sense of floating above the ground, and asks:

> How have I ended up here?...Sometimes I felt that life before labour reform was just a huge dream, sometimes I felt the present was a nightmare, and that in the morning I would wake up again and go off to teach students Tang poetry or Song *ci*.[13]

Memory might play tricks on reality, altering daily a lost past, but the writer counters the corrosion of time with the tools of his trade. Memory and critical reflection are one continuum; the author's task in annotating the past in *My Bodhi Tree* is to re-situate himself as authentically as possible in that past, to extricate his present self and revivify his adolescent self. The re-working of autobiographical diaries is inevitably a process of associative memories. Conditions at the moment of retrieval influence the reflections made; there is no stable self, only that captured in the moment.[14] Memories are not retrieved, but constructed. In *Grass Soup* the laconic diary meets the mature writer. As the extracts present the opportunity to reconstruct the altered state of mind that incessant thought-reform induced – as the narrator considers, for example, how news of another suicide left him feeling merely a little disappointed that there would be no more visits from the wife or children – the rekindled awareness at what the self had become under oppression in turn engenders more vitriol. Yomi Braester has written of the 'unbridgeable gap' between the 1960 diaries and 1990s commentary, contesting that 'the originary experience remains impenetrable to verbal representation',[15] that the silence between the two voices is the keynote to the text. But this risks overstating the case, since however fragmented, however representative of the linguistic trauma of the intervening years, the process of writing attests to an overcoming, to the self participating in its continued recreation, a belief in the power of words to delve into and reanimate an experience.

The protagonist of Zhang's 1989 novel *Getting Used to Dying* is more at ease with the impossibility of accurate recall, but displays a corollary tendency towards psychosis. Here, the polarisation between the earlier and the later self, the written self and the recorded self, is overcome in the narrative by a bifocal narrator, two voices which seem to speak to each other, or urge the protagonist on to different ends. One voice is drawn to gunshops, weapons and annihilation, to oblivion in sex; the other is more conciliatory and gentle on himself. In a rare overt reference to the two voices, the protagonist recalls visiting a cathedral in France and seeing a statue of Christ, whose raw pain threatened to crystallise his own: 'I didn't dare stare. If I looked for too long at those stone-carved or bronze holes I would see the eyes of the one who cohabited within me. As soon as I saw those eyes, I would want to squeeze my fingers on the trigger.'[16] Elsewhere, the existential angst that the character displays is set against a blurring of fact and imagination, situated in a chronological fracturing of the self:

> I've been to this cemetery before, I vaguely remember going for a walk here with that pretty woman. But I soon realise I was mistaken. The two of us walking in the burial ground was certainly an event from a previous life…In recent years, I've often taken episodes from my past life – like our cook reporting to mother – and muddled them together with events from this life, which proves I have developed a mental illness. Perhaps being executed again might cure it?[17]

The narrator has described a mock execution scene, where he and a young girl, unbeknownst to them, are merely accompanying others to the execution ground. The Kafkaesque scene lends itself to a rejection of perceived reality. The narrator should have been shot and undergoes a vicarious death. Psychologically, he died, and writes tersely of his revivification: 'It turns out that I am still me.' A cadre tells him he must rectify himself, or next time it would be for real; 'he clarified my identity and stuffed my soul back into its shell'.[18] The disjointed narrative of *Getting Used to Dying* reinforces the confusion. 'I' refers to narrator and character, my past and my present, the lover and the lost. In Chinese, 'you' (*ni*) is used as an indeterminate 'I', or 'one'. When the referent really is second-person, it is usually an imagined interlocutor. How can I write of a coherent self, or even know if it is I who experienced events of such harrowing intensity? the narrative asks, as it segues between voices.

At times, the re-presented self threatens to engulf the writer. If Proust needed to smell the madeleine to be transported back to his childhood experiences, that stimulation of the amygdala was for Zhang achieved through the sense of touch.[19] The narrator of *Getting Used to Dying* experiences a moment of identity crisis worthy of Zhuangzi as he reinhabits a lost past, and cannot separate out one fiction, one memory, from another:

> I gently kissed those eyes edged with crow's feet. When I kissed her, I just had to shut my eyes to bring back the sparkle that she had already lost. When I kissed her, I just had to shut my eyes and could lose myself in two dreams. Was the reality that I alone out of ten convicts sleeping together in one billet was nestled up beside a female guerrilla leader? Or is the reality that I am making love on this bed, here?[20]

The repetition of events, or repeated allusions to incidents, reinforces a sense of hazy reinterpretations of a single past. Some incidents are seemingly re-remembered differently, or present slightly different versions of truth(s). One of the more significant is the 'corpse-shed scene' whose final, most vivid iteration occurs in *Getting Used to Dying*. In this novel, depiction of the protagonist waking up alive in the makeshift morgue stretches across several chapters, the painfully slow narration drawing out the awakening of the immobile body. The moonlight, the cold and the icy touch of a naked corpse add to the pathos as the narrator hovers between death and life, consciousness and dream. Again, the oneiric episode has to be re-lived to be remembered, and the writer cannot prevent the dream from taking over, demanding that he repeat yet again the experience of dying.

In the earlier novel *Mimosa* the narrator is also asked by an admiring cook: 'Are you the bastard who climbed out of a pile of corpses?'[21] But does this relate rather to an incident recounted from September

1960 in *My Bodhi Tree*? There we read not of a personal near-death experience, but of the author, on early morning kitchen duty, slipping out in the dark to investigate two large carts parked outside the camp gates. Zhang assumes that the carts must contain farm produce, and congratulates himself on his anticipated theft from the packed wicker baskets. As he feels inside, the 'frozen cabbages' turn out to be human heads, and the prize he loosens, a human arm, swings towards him. Hunger and shock numb Zhang, but his fright metamorphoses to disappointment, until he 'began to feel that these dead people were messing around with me, depriving me of the chance to steal some sugar-beets or cabbages'.[22] The dead continue to mess with him, but it is only with the passage of time that the effects of the sensory shock show their latent force, and the older diary annotator is able to link the initial event with its after-effects. Memories inscribed through heightened emotions are frequently linked to tangible triggers, and, for Zhang, the resonance is clear.

> Because the feeling when I touched them with my hand was linked to a desire for food, ever since then I've not been able to look at game or birds on sale in a butcher's window, and I've not been able to touch chicken or duck that has been plucked after slaughter. My stomach turns as soon as I look at or touch it, and I vomit bile. Since there were no such foods around during my camp years this neurosis had not become apparent.[23]

Zhang remains 'basically a vegetarian' for the rest of his adult life. This incident, recounted in the diaries rather than novels, seems to bear a generic likeness to the corpse-shed story and posit the latter as an imagined extrapolation. It is possible, of course, that both events occurred as discrete experiences in the author's mind – or even that there were two similar events; the reader is not in a position to tell.

Other incidental details crop up across the different narratives, part of the fabric of the author's remembered life that take on different forms as they are recycled or recalibrated in new fictional settings. A striking feature of the first volume of diary entries is the absence of references to the outside world, such as to families or relatives.[24] The diarist 'explains' in *Grass Soup* this omission, over four to five days of gathered entries which recall a frenzied suicide. The annotation to the entry for 4 September 1960 narrates the visit of a wife and child to the labour camp. They have come from a great distance, and wait in the fields to be allowed to see the husband. The narrator's gaze lingers on the young woman as she shakes dust off herself and erases the evidence of the journey's hardship. But when the lucky convict reached his wife, 'he neither embraced his child nor made any move to caress his wife',[25] and before she had finished speaking, snatched the bag from his wife's hand and ran off up the embankment. Some time later, the narrator hears a 'gut-rending' female cry. After wolfing down the food, the husband had slit his wrists with his scythe. The writer dismisses outsiders' theories on the suicide: it was not out of shame, nor to punish his wife or allow her to be politically free. The only explanation he can tender is that the convict had not lost his reason, but rather his emotions. Satiated, he enters oblivion. He was no longer able to, or interested in, connecting with the world.

In *Getting Used to Dying* it is the narrator himself who experiences a similar story. In his memory he is transported back to 1961, when his lover persuaded the camp guards she is his fiancée, in order to gain a visit. As she whispers sweet nothings, you 'were secretly hoping she would leave early, so you could get to enjoy a little earlier the eggs and buns she had brought'. He notes with hindsight that 'Her large eyes resolutely searched for hope in your face. But your eyes were fixed on the bag she had brought, estimating the volume of food packed inside.'[26] The inability of the hungry to do anything other than fixate on food is a leitmotif across the diary volumes. Zhang neither condemns himself nor others for this; it is a fact of life. Since we know from the diaries how infrequently Zhang himself had any visitors or food parcels, a reader who has read more of his work is likely to attribute the later redaction to the 'adapted' memories of which Zhang writes.

What is difficult to assay is the 'percentage' of the authorial self in the later fiction: whether he is more truthful about the many love affairs he describes, now that time has passed by and morality has moved on, or whether he is just more skilful at mingling fictional and others' lives with his own. As in this episode, the later novel reveals more complex layered strata than either the diaries or *Mimosa*. The split time frame allows for the interplay of event, later understanding of it and further reassessment decades on. Zhang alludes to his delight at this narrative *tour de force* in the preface. The underlying message is clear: the self is not a fixed point. At the time we experience them, we do not have the wherewithal to understand events fully. Our understanding of incidents and reflected sense of self necessarily shifts in time.

Space precludes discussion of the important question of the role of other characters in the novels in shaping the narrative subject. It is clear, as Zhang's life cycles out of the camps of the diaries, out of reform and on to rehabilitation, that it is not thought-reform, nor even labour, which redeems Zhang. It is through women, sensual rehabilitation, and love, that Zhang's healing is ultimately effected. Yenna Wu has pointed out, however, that the women in Zhang's camp novels are illusory redeemers, idealised male constructs[27] – which begs the question of how unreal, fictive women could so have moulded him. If Zhang's own process of recovery is real, are the fictive women mere literary symbols of those real women who shaped him emotionally? Is the notion of a woman enough to signify healing? A second, related question touches on the gendering of the text. Studies of English language autobiographies through to the period of Zhang's early novellas have noted a strong gender divide. 'Male' autobiographies tend towards idealisation, aggrandisement, a projection of confidence, 'female' ones towards a sifting of life's events, a need to authenticate self-image and self-worth, played out in understatement, oblique recitation and humour, in discontinued and fragmentary narratives.[28] The markedly feminine traits of Zhang's life writings show how far the repertoire of self-representation of males has shifted, and how culturally relative those traits are, or, perhaps more tellingly, point to an emasculation embedded in the narrative form itself.

## The self rehabilitated

In the most de-individuated era in Chinese history, Zhang's meagre jottings on his own life illustrate the collective experience of inmates' lives, much as 'the cook's big ladle held the fate of the entire brigade, and the small ladle used to divide the rice in our team held the fate of each of us'.[29] To write at all in the 1960s was a defiant assertion of the notion of a private individual, with an individually plotted life course. As Ng notes, autobiography presents an allegory, 'an efficient way to narrate the nation', the autobiographical form 'an ideological and political statement, reflecting one's relationship with mainstream society'.[30] The relationship of Zhang's diaries to his novels charts the course of the self in Chinese society. As Zhang fleshes out the skeletal outline of events from the original diaries, all that the self was and could be at that point in history is given body and brought into being in the new literary style he adopts when that self is later allowed to expand, to exist as a full sentient, reflective being.

The power of Zhang Xianliang's early writings derives from the lived experience of relinquishing total control over life to the state. Humans were stripped to the essentials of physiological life in Mao's experiments of the 1950s and 1960s, existing on starvation rations without family, material goods or intellectual companionship. State provision induces in Zhang a guilt that continued beyond the camp years and overshadows his rehabilitation. The novel *Mimosa* covers the period immediately following release from labour-camp in the mid-1960s. The recidivist tendencies of the main character and the other men in his half-way house detail the difficulties of adapting to being physically free. For the protagonist Zhang Yonglin, freedom also means coming to terms with the guilt at what he has become. There are two facets to this: one in probing aspects of his character that developed in order to survive, such as the ways he has procured food, another in attempting to reconcile his freedom with the political and philosophical questions it engendered. Zhang Xianliang had already shown in *Grass Soup* how thoroughgoing his reform has been, in an incident where he describes his escape from the camp and subsequent voluntary return under the aegis of his 'thought'. Outside of the camps, shades of grey and of doubt began to reappear in the protagonist's thoughtscape:

> The aim throughout life of someone from my family background was allegedly to reform oneself, but saying 'sacrifices were in order to reform the self' patently didn't accord with reality. It equated to saying that unless I died, I couldn't be properly reformed, and 'reforming oneself' then lost any meaning. Today, I was a free person, and if it punishment was to atone for sins, then when the punishment ended I could be said to have been cleansed of my sin of being a rightist. If release signified rather a temporary closure in reform, then my reform was progressing about right. How would I live from now on?[31]

Acute self-doubt following release from death sentences or terminal illnesses is a well-documented phenomenon. Zhang's contemporary Gao Xingjian, also criticised during the Spiritual Pollution campaign of 1983, expresses similar anxiety following a false-positive cancer result in his Nobel-winning novel *Soul Mountain (Ling shan)*. The narrator of *Mimosa* is under no illusions that once food and shelter are secured, the mental landscape shifts dramatically. 'I knew that once my belly was inflated, my mind would suffer a pain greater than that of hunger. Hunger hurt, a swollen stomach hurt, but pain is always easier to deal with in the flesh than in the soul.'[32] As the state attempts to subjugate both physical and metaphysical selves, strategies of resistance develop to tease back out the rational self.

The transition to manumitted convict unleashed dark existential torments. For the protagonist Zhang, the disparities of his Manichean self, and a Mencian fear of the animal forces within, were most acute at night. The reader feels the pain of the author watching his former self choose between his day and his night personae.

Mental shards splintered by pain and an incomprehensible reality all gathered up at night, and pulverised me with the sharpness of cut glass. The depths of night were when I was most awake.

By day, driven by an innate self-preservation, I fawned, I ingratiated myself, I played every last trick there was...but in the black of night, all of my various mean acts and debased thoughts shocked me...

What was most scary was not falling, but that I was well aware of how low I was falling.[33]

The guilt that Zhang experiences, some of it conveyed in religious terms, is a guilt at his inhumanity measured by conventional Confucian or Christian standards of loving one's neighbour, but behind this lies deeper probing of the question of how to judge oneself, what yardstick to use. The communist state had upended conventional morality in its incarceration of those of questionable guilt, but its invidious terms of reference were compelling.

A few chapters later in *Mimosa*, the narrator tells of the first trip of his free life, to a market outpost several hours away. He tricks an old peasant into exchanging potatoes for carrots at an advantageous rate, and is at first delighted at his mental dexterity and comprehension of the psychology of the peasant. Soon, guilt kicks in, and he asks rhetorically, dismayed, 'What sort of a person was this I?' On the ten-mile walk home Zhang loses his footing and slips into an icy stream, spilling the vegetables. Their loss, and his ensuing fever from the soaking, are acknowledged as 'punishment and retribution' for cheating the old villager. But moral guilt at a minor incident transfers itself in his feverish mind to wholesale self-condemnation. A political explanation surfaces again as the narrator links the episode to his early family life:

> I suspected that all of my various schemings had something to do with my birth into a bourgeois family background...I was shocked to realise that although I had no capital, various capitalist traits had already infused into my blood. I resisted, and doubted, criticism of me in 1957, although I later accepted it in its entirety...Although I didn't feel it myself, I really was a 'bourgeois Rightist', the reason I was not conscious of it myself is precisely because it was congenital.[34]

The character then quotes from Dante's *Comedia Divina* at this juncture, ironically underscoring his conclusion that his class is damned. The internalisation of values, even if overstated for effect, shows how far Zhang's reform has progressed. After further thought, the notion of collective guilt, or associative guilt, serves to assuage his own portion:

> As for me, I am the last of the Udegs.[35] In recognising this, I felt a bit better, and felt a certain tragic solemnity at being a sacrificial lamb at the altar of the new era. I myself had done nothing wrong, but I was responsible for the sins of several generations, like the descendents of an alcoholic or a syphilitic, who experience untold sufferings for their previous generation. This is how fate is.

Zhang's fictional works are replete with literary references – one aspect that distinguishes their narrative style from the diaries – which point, deliberately, to the author as intellectual as much as they provide an avenue of self-expression. They provide for moments of self-mockery, such as when the narrator explains how all of his bourgeois ideals have been shelved with a quotation from Yevgenii Onegin, or when Zhang takes comfort in his copy of *Das Kapital* under his pillow. It is more than faintly ironic that a volume of Marx forms his sole link to his previous life in the realm of the intellect.

The process of recognising one's own sinfulness, in communist terms, is a difficult aspect of the narratives. It is key to the narrator's self-understanding, as he mocks and despairs of the capitulation of his own class, the intellectuals. The profound effects of birth in class consciousness and in determining life course are branded onto Zhang. His background and intellect set him on an inevitable collision course with the authorities, as natural as the label attached to his family. During the corpse shed scene, an overwhelming desire to tell the doctor all that had gone wrong in his life is thwarted by his weakness, providing an analogy for the failure of his life. Autobiography *is* political biography, for all: there are no non-state actants. The brief life history that Zhang was attempting to vocalise is suffused with oblique humour, the benefit of emotional distance:

> I wanted to say that I felt awful, I felt that the sensation that all I had ever done was wrong was more frightening than any illness. I'd got the wrong womb, for a start. Before I bored my way out I should have paid a visit to check it was a poor family. Then I had become entranced by the search for truth, from Feuerbach to Hegel and on to Marx . . . By the time we realised that the bounds of our understanding of Marxism were fixed by the intellectual level of our leaders, and that to surpass their level was a crime – it was too late.[36]

The process of Zhang's reform stretches across the four narratives, in distinct stages as circumstances dictate. The diarist Zhang had entered the camp an intellectual, a classification which defines his punishment, his treatment and his group identity. Convicts could 'graduate' from labour-reform camp and were supposed to be developing towards this end: reform was not a legal, but an administrative punishment.[37] Some elements of his reform seem unfeigned, at least within the framework of a given narrative. The narrator of *Mimosa* comes to appreciate the straightforwardness of the villagers, and to value manual labour and the respect it earns. He even dreamed at night that he had become a model physical labourer, the poster-boy on the 'What's your contribution to the Motherland?' campaign. In *Grass Soup*, Zhang recreates himself as a reformed thinker; in *Mimosa* he emerges a reformed labourer. Labour's reformative effect operates only outside the camps: the de-individuation he had experienced in the work camp, where labourers were no more than tools, is gradually overcome in the village.

The fine line between thought-reform and capitulation exposes the narrator's own reasoning for, and envelopment in, new ways of thinking, and at the same time shows the protagonist castigating his fellow intellectuals for their wilful acquiescence. The fault-line runs throughout Zhang's works and lies at the centre of the problematic of self-definition. When, for example, stricter grain rationing was introduced in the camps and convicts were encouraged to ear wild grasses, the wily cadre in charge of Zhang's troop unearthed hidden food and secreted rations, haranguing the convicts for the 'sin' of their waste.

> What evil! What evil! Look at this, all of you, look! We let you eat till your bellies were bursting, and you waste food! Do you not know that every single grain is a peasant's sweat and blood?...
>
> We convicts one by one began to blame ourselves, and to blame each other. Even later, when the grain rations were increasingly small, and large numbers of people were dying, some cons on the point of death were still regretting what they had done: if we hadn't wasted so much grain then, we could eat to our fill today...[38]

Fear, prolonged uncertainty and deprivation are the explanations Zhang attempts in retrospect for this collective acceptance of the absurd.[39]

One of the most terrible scenes in Zhang's autobiographical works exploits to the full the tension between naïve, surface acceptance of Party thought and a deep subsurface irony, and stands as a comment on the reading of the past itself. The narrator of *Getting Used to Dying* returns to a faux-naïve voice to document his trip to the execution ground in a bitingly jarring, discordant description. The scene is Ningxia, the date 1970. Since he has no friends or relatives, the narrator is a compliant victim, 'grateful for their kindness in selecting him'. He admires the cadre who is combining the execution with a shopping trip for his wife, and comradeship is sealed when the cadre commends him for his level of reform. Arriving at the ground, the narrator feels pride at the huge audience of spectators, out to watch his death. A certain redolence of Lu Xun, high priest of satirical memory, is capped with a touch of pathetic fallacy and a scarcely veiled reference to chairman Mao: 'The sun shone particularly brightly that day, it was "gloriously radiant." '[40] The weight of the placard the narrator is forced to wear is neither too heavy nor too light: the Party, the reader understands, thinks of everything. The overbearing, deadpan irony continues until the reader can take no more. How right the critics were, the narrator muses, how inappropriate to have exposed children to sex in his novels, how much better for them to see educational executions instead.

Zhang Xianliang became, in his 50s and 60s, a representative on various regional and national political bodies as a leading member of the Chinese Writers' Association. The tension between criticising and reforming that had informed his own early life played itself out in reverse in his later years, as he offered up his writings as criticism in the reform era. The conflict between cowed fawning and the principled, but dangerous refutation that informed his portrayal of intellectuals in the camp returns as a motif in his own biography, as questions are levelled as to why Zhang chose to accept status and credit from the state.[41] Perry Link has called this the paradox at the heart of Zhang's work – his powerful indictment of the state and simultaneous affirmation of his loyalty to it. Link attributes this to Zhang's upbringing in the 1950s and the need of that generation to protest their innocence while avoiding the sense of wasted life that complete severance would bring, as well as to Zhang's personal ambition.[42] The complex relations of critics to state from the perspective of the state need further exploration, but it is significant that the consistency of voice and theme shown across the works discussed here suggest Zhang has not tempered his writings to reflect his changed status vis-à-vis the state. For all of his accommodation to the regime, he has remained consistently provocative in release. He was re-sentenced in 1993 for commemorating Tiananmen.

## Conclusion

Zhang Xianliang has never written an autobiography, yet has produced one of the most revealing studies of the nature of self in post-war Chinese history. The continuous recording of one's life from adolescence to senescence is entirely in keeping with traditional Chinese practices, and his sprawling intertext of autobiographical writings bears resemblance to traditional collections of dispersed life writings, a modern-day version of Sima Qian's 'additive autobiographies'.[43] In setting himself up as a guardian of memory, Zhang is taking his place in a continuous line of Chinese literati. In Zhang's case, the self that develops is fluid, and fractured, formed in response to the events in his life. This self can hide, evade, be remodelled and rethought, be unrecognisable to itself. It is perfectly attuned to the political circumstances of the 1950s and 1960s. The traumatised, damaged psyche is revealed in the lacunae, the double narration, the reworking of events, in the interplay of reportage and fictional record, of the contemporary and the re-worked. Zhang has written of his works as an indivisible, inter-related whole, revealing 'a true self, including my weaknesses and strengths, shortcomings and virtues'.[44] The circular relation between author, and author as subject of the text, is highlighted by the constant self-referentiality of the texts, as the reader's gaze directed to the [author's] act of re-reading the already-read subject. The invitation to read the entire corpus of short stories, novellas and novels as a single autobiographical project allows for the sort of self that has been described here: one narrated through captured tales and incidents, through hazy and disjointed memories, through a gentle identity theft where others' experiences illuminate a generic experience in which the self participated through shared consciousness. The passage of time, as evidenced by the diary annotations, refracts and alters memories, and the author cannot even certify the origins of incidents to which his own handwriting attests.[45] An empathetic eyewitness, experiencing an event from the side, can narrate imaginatively an episode in the first person: this is a narrative device, not an inauthenticity.

Zhang has written of his high level of self-awareness and its benefit in later life, but the self he depicts in his fictional and non-fictional works comes to that self-knowledge slowly. The protagonist/narrator is credulous, wracked with self-doubt, terrified, broken, at many points suicidal. Tempered by extremity, the metaphysical self cannot be separated from the physical self. Zhang's intellectual background in Western thought might have predisposed him towards Platonic dualisms, but the narrative knows no such disconnect: a person who is starving cannot sever the link between starvation and mental functioning. Secondary characters appear in Zhang's biography and in his fictional works, but the main excursion is deep into himself. Interactions with other humans add relatively little to his formation – until he is free and can embrace relationships with women. Zhang cannot write himself, as traditional literati did, through friendship, through poetic inscriptions and shared moments, since distrust, mistrust, isolation and fear prevent individuals of his era from opening themselves up to others. There is little friendship to speak of in the camps. There are more and less amenable convicts, but all is narrated impassively. Even with the switch to novel format in *Mimosa*, the other characters are so distant in intellectual grasp and in experience from the protagonist that they only really exist for the reader through his eyes and take on no independent being. The self that Zhang creates is a complex array of interacting selves, products both of partial memory recall and of fictional latitude.

There has been no Truth and Reconciliation Committee in China, no opening of Stasi files. The state's modes of subjection have saturated Zhang's project of remembering and rewriting himself: forcing the act of autobiography in demanding the correct recitations of life events; creating the deep traumatic schism in pre- and post-incarceration stages of his life, thus structuring his biography and shaping him; necessitating new strategies of writing to compose his memories and his sense of self; in the complication of his rehabilitated status in China. Zhang Xianliang's experience of hard labour and thought-reform during much of his adult life inspired him to adopt a prophetic role, to use his own life as a testimony against the state, as a corrective to the years of untruth. The experiences themselves cannot be redeemed, but in reflecting back on his past, he has aimed to bring understanding to others, and to militate against the impatient corrosion of forgetfulness. Zhang is a lifelong subscriber to the notion of memory as a 'cultural and ethical imperative'.[46] At the same time, recreation of traumatic events through the reliving of memory has brought a degree of catharsis.

What weight are we to give to Zhang's title for his projected compendium, Revelations of a Materialist? Is this yet another ironic distancing? Or should we recall the damning indictment of the narrator of *Getting Used to Dying*, 'By the time I realised all interpretations of Marxism had to come from our leaders … it was already much too late?' The only way for Zhang to wrest back autonomy for such a determined life was, eventually, in the recording of that life and its reinterpretation, including its philosophical basis; it is not incidental that the narrator took *Das Kapital* for a pillow. Just as he was moulded by the authorities, his identity as a materialist is taken from those who would mould him. Zhang does not philosophise directly, but leaves the interpretation to a reader. Zhang's own experiences have to be narrated in the political terminology of Mao Zedong (even if recreated ironically) because of the umbilical cord linking self perception with the words and presence of Mao.

Zhang is not a pure materialist, since he believes in much more than the proven existence of matter itself. Much as he admires Hegel he does not seem to be a dialectical materialist either, although the notion of history as the product of and process of class struggle, and a Hegelian dialectics where negativity is enveloped into the truth, would seem to accord with his lived experience. Perhaps the Hegelian sublation is apposite: the individual is both preserved and destroyed as he becomes.

The most likely referent is, however, historical materialism. Marx's 1859 preface to *A Contribution to the Critique of Political Economy* states:

> In the social production which men carry on, they enter into definite relations that are indispensable and independent of their will; these relations of production correspond to a definite stage of development of their material powers of production. The sum total of these relations of production constitutes the economic structure of society – the real foundation, on which rise legal and political superstructures and to which correspond definite forms of social consciousness ... It is not the consciousness of men that determines their existence, but, on the contrary, their social existence determines their consciousness.[47]

This 'materialist' acknowledges that he entered into, against his will, relations of production which determined the social consciousness of all around him. *Grass Soup* and *My Bodhi Tree* discuss the period of life when Zhang's labour was unpaid, when China displayed a low level of development of material forces and when the relations of production determined the totality of his existence.[48] Zhang's oeuvre can be read as a dialogue with the philosophical underpinnings of Marxist-Leninist-Maoism, and with its devastating practical application in China. His struggle against the ideological imposition of belief, and retroactive attempts to challenge the beliefs he was required to hold, represent his dialogue with Marx's dictum: 'It is not the consciousness of men that determines their existence, but, on the contrary, their social existence determines their consciousness.' The naïve young man of the diary years, who was shocked at the thought capitulation of his fellow intellectuals, develops over the course of his adult life into a broken cynic, a character whose goal was as simple as it was tragic, namely to piece together his soul and retrieve his sense of feeling. It is, perhaps, only within a Marxian frame that his life makes sense, for his life embodies an antithesis, the search to replace the language and consciousness that has been taken from him with an authentic substitute. This the character/author (the switch is central to the task) does in human warmth, in intimate relations and in the joy of the plastic bottles and cartons of everyday material life.

## Notes

1. On the evolution of the camps and the reality of camp life, as well as on Zhang's writings, its themes and structural forms, see Philip F. Williams and Yenna Wu, *The Great Wall of Confinement: The Chinese Prison Camp through Contemporary Fiction and Reportage* (Berkeley: University of California Press, 2004). vol. IV.2 of *Asia Major* in 1991 contains three notable articles on Zhang's fiction, including ones by Wu and Williams. Klaus Mühlhahn's insightful study of trauma and literary memory, ' "Remembering a Bitter Past": The Trauma of China's Labor Camps, 1949–1978,' *History and Memory* 16.2 (2004): 108–139, focuses on the relationship between historical event and written memory. Yomi Braester, *Witness Against History* (Stanford: Stanford University Press, 2003), 146–157 evaluates Zhang's diaries.
2. For a digest of some scientific literature on memory as it relates to literature, see Suzanne Nalbantian, *Memory in Literature* (Basingstoke: Palgrave Macmillan, 2003).
3. Zhang writes in the preface that the collection, one short piece, one medium-length piece and one long novel, 'records the fissures left on a poet's heart by the period when the world was shattered'. Zhang Xianliang, *Ganqing de jilu* (The record of emotion) (Beijing: Zuojia chubanshe, 1985), Preface.
4. Estelle C. Jelinek, ed., *Women's Autobiography* (Bloomington: Indiana University Press, 1980), 17; cf. Mühlhahn, 'Remembering a Bitter Past,' 115.
5. Zhang Xianliang, *Xiguan siwang* (Getting used to dying) (Hong Kong: Jiaodian wenku, 1989), 102.
6. On social reform and the personal, affective form of remoulding (*gaizao*), see Philip F. Williams, ' "Remolding" and the Chinese Labor-Camp

Novel,' *Asia Major* IV.2 (1991): 133–149. Williams notes that Zhang rarely uses the term *laogai* (reform though labour) and only ever ironically.

7. Wu Pei-yi, *The Confucian's Progress* (Princeton: Princeton University Press, 1990), x.
8. Zhang Xianliang, *Wo de putishu* (My bodhi tree) Part I (Beijing: Zuojia, 1994), 4–5.
9. Ibid., 3.
10. Ibid., 146.
11. This long poem ends with the call 'A new era approaches/Need a new life direction/Need a new struggle attitude.' It is fair to assume Zhang was not expecting his words to be fulfilled so literally in his life. *Zhang Xianliang xuanji* (Selected works of Zhang Xianliang), vol. 1 (Beijing: Baihua wenyi, 1985), 11–16.
12. Zhang, *Wo de putishu*, 3.
13. *Lühua shu* (Mimosa), in *Zhang Xianliang jingxuanji* (Best selected works of Zhang Xianliang) (Beijing: Yanshan, 2006), 17.
14. As Eakin has written, autobiographies 'are fictions about what is in itself in turn a fiction, the self. The self is properly understood as a metaphor for the subjective reality of consciousness.' Paul John Eakin, 'Autobiography, Identity and the Fictions of Memory,' in Daniel Schacter and Elaine Scarry, eds., *Memory, Brain and Belief* (Cambridge: Harvard University Press, 2000), 290.
15. Braester, *Witness Against History*, 154, 156.
16. Zhang, *Xiguan siwang*, 144.
17. Ibid., 115.
18. Ibid., 120.
19. Cf. Nalbantian, *Memory in Literature*, 135–136.
20. Zhang, *Xiguan siwang*, 38.
21. Zhang, *Lühua shu*, 5.
22. Zhang, *Xiguan siwang*, 155.
23. Zhang, *Wo de putishu*, 156.
24. For a discussion of relationships with family of concentration camp victims, see Jeffrey Kinkley, 'A Bettelheimian Interpretation of Chang Hsien-liang's Concentration-Camp Novels,' *Asia Major* IV.2 (1991): 104.
25. Zhang, *Wo de putishu*, 135.
26. Zhang, *Xiguan siwang*, 54–55.
27. Yenna Wu, 'Women as Sources of Redemption in Chang Hsien-liang's Labor-Camp Fiction,' *Asia Major* IV.2 (1991): 115–131.
28. Jelinek, *Women's Autobiography*, Introduction. Several studies discuss impotence in camp prisoners: see, for example, Williams and Wu, *The Great Wall of Confinement*, 98–102.
29. Zhang, *Wo de putishu*, 90. Hunger as a trope runs throughout Zhang's work, irrespective of genre. His relation to his physical body provides for tender moments of introspection, but the all-pervading nature of hunger and its relation to mental survival is clear.

30. Janet Ng, *The Experience of Modernity* (Ann Arbor: University Michigan Press, 2003), ix, 6.
31. Zhang, *Lühua shu*, 17.
32. Ibid., 20.
33. Ibid., 16.
34. Ibid., 32.
35. Reference to Alexsandr Fadeyev's *Last of the Udegs*, an unfinished epic written between 1929 and 1940, and set in the civil war, describing the last remaining group of Siberian partisans. The nod towards Soviet experience – in stoicism, as well as pointers to the gulags – is telling.
36. Zhang, *Xiguan siwang*, 185–186.
37. Zhang, *Wo de putishu*, 69.
38. Ibid., 23.
39. See Kinkley's social-psychological reading of the prison camp novels based on a Bettelheimian typology of German camps which sheds light on how, in the distortion of the 'extreme situation' in which they lived, prisoners underwent personality distortions, identifying with the values of their captors; 'A Bettelheimian Interpretation,' 83–113.
40. Zhang, *Xiguan siwang*, 114.
41. Zhang was rehabilitated in 1979, later becoming chair of the Ningxia branch of the China Writers' Association and a delegate to the Chinese Writer's Association Presidium. Various of his short stories and novellas in the early 1980s won national prizes.
42. Perry Link, 'A Brief Introduction to Chang Hsien-liang's Concentration Camp Novels,' *Asia Major* IV.2 (1991): 79–82.
43. Cf. Grace Fong, 'Inscribing a Sense of Self in Mother's Family: Hong Liangji's (1764–1809) Memoir and Poetry of Remembrance,' *Chinese Literature: Essays, Articles, Reviews* 27 (2005): 47; Stephen Durrant, 'Self as the Intersection of Traditions: The Autobiographical Writings of Ssu-ma Ch'ien,' *Journal of the American Oriental Society* 106.1 (1986): 34.
44. Zhang, *Zhang Xianliang xuanji*, Author's Preface, 2.
45. Cf. scientific studies, which have shown how differing aims and goals at the time of retrieval can affect recall. Michael Ross and Anne E. Wilson, 'Constructing and Appraising Past Selves,' in Schacter and Scarry, *Memory, Brain and Belief*, 233.
46. Vera Schwarcz, *Bridge across Broken Time: Chinese and Jewish Cultural Memory* (New Haven: Yale University Press, 1998), 3.
47. Karl Marx, tr. N. I. Stone, *A Contribution to the Critique of Political Economy* (Chicago: Charles Kerr, 1904), 11–12.
48. Cf. scene in Peng Xiaolian's 2009 documentary on the arch-Rightist Hu Feng, *Storm under the Sun*, where an old associate of Hu Feng is telling of his life from a hospital bed. The one thing that sends him apoplectic (and he dies soon after the filming) is outrage at the sense of injustice at his years of lost wages while he worked in reform camps.

# 7
# Whose Life Is It Anyway? Disabled Life Stories in Post-reform China

*Sarah Dauncey*

The representation of disabled people in all forms of cultural production has been shown in the Western context to have a history that closely reflects ideological changes in the perception of not just the body, but also of individuality and social relations.[1] This chapter turns our attention to the production of life stories of and by disabled people in China to demonstrate how such ideological shifts, particularly with regard to the latter two notions of individuality and social relations, are revealed and experienced in a very different cultural context. I consider here the role and motives of the Chinese state in both compiling biographical narratives about disabled people and publicising certain autobiographies written by disabled people, and demonstrate the often more creative and authoritative ways in which disabled people have begun to tell the stories of their lives and experiences as they explore the possibilities of new genres and develop new ways of engaging with their audiences.

Since the end of the Cultural Revolution in 1976 and the subsequent opening-up reforms of the early 1980s, it has certainly become increasingly common for disabled people in China to be the subjects of both fictional and non-fictional life narratives, and it is clear that there are divergences in the way in which these narratives are presented. Throughout this period, the Chinese state has played a pivotal role in encouraging the production of the life stories of a wide range of people and has used them for educational propaganda purposes as part of its wider campaign to promote 'socialist spiritual civilisation' (*shehui zhuyi jingshen wenming*). As it has moved away from promoting traditional 'picture-perfect' heroes, new models as exemplified by disabled writer Zhang Haidi (b.1955) have come to the fore. Under these new political and social conditions, the experiences of Zhang Haidi and others simultaneously provide models for idealised social roles and relations, and articulate issues relating to personal identity and community. Yet, of course, the involvement of the state, or any form of institution for that matter, in the production of life stories immediately raises the issue of authority or, as Couser speculates in his discussion of illness, disability and life writing in the West: 'Who gets a life and who doesn't: whose stories get told, why, by whom, and how?'[2] Drawing comparisons and contrasts with research undertaken by Couser and other scholars working at the intersection of Disability Studies and life writing, and using the case of Zhang Haidi as a prominent example, I highlight the processes and rationales behind the production of life writing of and by disabled people in China, revealing changes over time as government policies change, social awareness of disability increases, personal motivations revivify and new technologies come into play, all the while demonstrating how differing agenda may affect not only the form and content of such narratives, but ultimately whether the life story gets told at all.

## The complex case of narrating disability

Autobiographies, biographies and other forms of conscious and purposeful life writing by and about disabled people first began to appear in China following the end of the Cultural Revolution. This suggests a relatively late advent for what has now been recognised as a 'distinct sub-genre' of life writing in the West.[3] Yet, even in the West, such narratives only began relatively recently to incorporate disability and illness as a major theme of concern, despite the fact that human lives are intrinsically somatic. As Couser points out, while traditional biography tended to focus on physical or mental concerns only when the life of the subject is interrupted, threatened or ended by them, even autobiography, with its peculiarly privileged position to detail such matters, was for a long time reluctant to engage with issues of disability and illness in any substantial way.[4]

The more frequent appearance in the West of (auto)biographical narratives of illness and disability or (auto)pathography did not occur until the 1950s, which seems to coincide with the rise of civil rights and other liberation movements.[5] The situation has changed so much since then, however, that we now have a situation that has been described by Lee as 'warts-and-all', where seemingly no element of the body or its functions escapes scrutiny.[6] Writers have found using language an effective way to understand and work through their own and others' bodily experiences. With regard to disability, illness and other forms of bodily dysfunction, this might include dealing with pain and hardship, articulating anger against fate or the system, or merely fulfilling the need to reach out to others in similar circumstances.[7]

The various life writing genres have generally proven to be particularly accessible to marginalised individuals, to the extent that autobiography, as one example, has become recognised as 'a key revolutionary method' of cultural redress.[8] Disabled people are no exception, suggest Snyder, Brueggemann and Garland-Thomson: 'People with disabilities who write autobiographies face a conflict between self-perceptions and society's view of them. They must rhetorically narrate the vagaries of living within a disabled body while also confronting social stigmatising of bodily difference.'[9] In effect, this form of life writing offers the opportunity to counter the hegemonic narratives of the 'empire of the normal' – through raising awareness about their disability and thus reducing the stigmas associated with that particular bodily dysfunction – while at the same time providing an outlet for the articulation of more personal physical and emotional concerns.[10]

People living with impairment or illness, in particular, are often impelled to engage in these acts of self-reflection and introspection, argues Couser, and life writing, by its very nature, provides a ready outlet for this. Yet, just as easily as it impels the production of life writing, disability and illness can impede it as people may be just too ill, traumatised or disabled, both physically and/or mentally. While forms other than self-composed written narratives are possible for people under these circumstances (portraiture, audio and video recording are three notable examples), narratives composed by others remain the dominant recourse. However, this then opens up not just the possibility that only certain lives are narrated but also that lives may be subject to distortion and misrepresentation, intentionally or otherwise.[11]

## A new heroine for new times

While there are many parallels in the Chinese case, as will be demonstrated later, there are also other considerations possibly unique to China that add new and intriguing dimensions to this issue. The most obvious of these is the fact that the country has had, and continues to have, one of the world's most highly centralised forms of political control. This, combined with one of the world's most developed propaganda machines, meant that the state has been able not just to oversee, but minutely micro-manage, the production of fictional and non-fictional life stories by and about disabled people for much of the early post-reform era and use these for specific purposes.

The initial appearance of such stories can be seen as the general result of the wide-ranging political and social changes that began in the 1980s. In these early days of reform, the favoured medium of narrating stories of disability was film, and this seems to have been due to the fortuitous combination of a particular director with a personal interest in disability (veteran Xie Jin, whose desire to make a film about disability in 1977 stemmed from his experiences with his own learning-impaired children), with the rapid realisation on the part of the cinema industry as a whole that disability was appealing to audiences on both a visual and emotional level.[12] However, this was followed shortly by the appearance of written narratives, initially about disabled people but later produced by disabled people themselves, and the example that first captured the nation's attention was the remarkable story of Zhang Haidi. Paralysed from the waist down following a battle with a form of cancer that damaged her spinal cord, she had reportedly overcome adversity to become a model worthy of emulation not just by disabled people but also the public at large.

The initial publication of her particular story was very much linked to a political about-face regarding the definition and use of 'heroic models' (*yingxiong mofan*). These had been deployed regularly by the Chinese Communist Party (CCP) propaganda department as part of its programme of socialist education even before the establishment of the People's Republic of China (PRC) in 1949; but it was the initiation of the campaign to 'Learn from Lei Feng' (*Xiang Lei Feng xuexi*) in 1963 that saw the programme reach new levels of intensity. Model citizens such as Lei Feng were intended to reinforce morale building and guide behaviour, not just amongst their own communities (which in Lei Feng's case was the Army), but also amongst society in general.[13] Youthful fighters, cadres and production types dominated and were characterised not just by their correct 'working style' but also increasingly by their progressive thoughts and feelings.[14] These thoughts and feelings were initially revealed, more often than not, through their diaries, which were deemed to have superior didactic potential due to their personal and frequently soul-searching nature.[15]

As with all things, the Cultural Revolution saw romantic idealist tendencies reaching a climax. Its 'cult of youth' effectively ensured that all heroes (by this time predominantly Red Guards) had to be not just zealous followers of Mao Zedong thought, but they also had to be at their physical and mental peak.[16] Such an emphasis on physical and mental perfection essentially disqualified, therefore, anyone with a disability and so during this period the cultural representation of people with impairments that were not the direct result of military or revolutionary action was practically non-existent.[17] The early years of reform that followed, however, saw a rapid move away from such heroes to newer models, most notably intellectuals and other specialists. With high moral standards *and* levels of education, these were considered by the state to be the vanguard of the new trend towards the construction of 'socialist spiritual civilisation', which in effect has meant the promotion of a socialist morality based on self-development and self-sacrifice. Since the late 1980s, it has been an important part of the Party's humanist-inspired method of countering the self-interest inherent in market economics; but, with its use of popular exemplars, it clearly has its roots in the pre-reform campaigns.[18]

In addition to high moral standards and levels of education, it was also often the case that these new heroes, although exemplary in one or more key aspects, were not the 'picture-perfect' models of old, and this emphasis on diversity and pluralism allowed the inclusion of formerly overlooked disabled members of society should they possess the qualities required of these new models.[19] Zhang Haidi was identified as one such person. Her story initially appeared in the *People's Daily* (*Renmin ribao*) in January 1981, but it was not until 1983 when she was awarded the title 'Outstanding Communist Youth League Member' (*Youxiu gongqingtuanyuan*) by the Central Committee of the

Communist Youth League of China[20] that she was styled the 'New Lei Feng of the 1980s' (*Bashi niandai de xin Lei Feng*) and elevated to a level of national prominence equivalent to that enjoyed by Helen Keller in the United States.[21] Deng Xiaoping is reported as having urged the population to 'Study Zhang Haidi and become a new communist with revolutionary ideals, sound morals, good education, and a strong sense of discipline,' while her image and deeds were widely publicised in newspapers and magazines, as well as on propaganda posters and murals (see Figure 7.1).

One of the lengthier expositions regarding Zhang Haidi's life and achievements published around this time appeared in *Dazhong ribao* on 8 March 1983. Entitled 'China's Modern-day Pavel[22] – Zhang Haidi (*Zhongguo dangdai Bao'er – Zhang Haidi*)', the article relates key events from her life and describes in further detail the prominent aspects of her character as highlighted by Deng Xiaoping. The content and the form of the article itself make for interesting reading as both were later to become typical of writings about disabled people in the Chinese media. The most noticeable of these is that at the very outset

*Figure 7.1* 'Study Comrade Zhang Haidi, the Lei Feng of our time'
Source: From the private collection of Alice de Jong.

we are provided with a detailed description of her disability and its severity.[23] Her disability directly frames our reading of her story and this forms something of a contrast to her own semi-autobiographical novel, as we shall see later. Even the most intimate details are revealed during the course of the article; for example, she apparently refrained from drinking or consuming liquid-like food to avoid soiling herself (she had no control over these functions) to the extent that the total amount of urine she produced a day was only a fifth of that produced by a normal person, and her own health suffered as a consequence.[24]

The article then proceeds to relate her outstanding academic achievements: how, without ever going to school, she mastered the primary and middle school curricula, taught herself English (by the time her story was published she had already translated around 160,000 characters) and began to study Japanese, German and even Esperanto. We are also told that she was able to contribute to commune life by initially teaching the local children while everyone else went out into the fields to labour, and then later by teaching herself medicine so that she could become the local physician. Although the article manages to gloss over many of the personal difficulties faced by Zhang Haidi growing up during the Cultural Revolution (more of which are depicted in her own retelling of this period in her life), they do reveal that she had attempted suicide in 1973 when she was 19, but that this 'defect' was mitigated by the fact that she had come to her senses and revived herself at the last minute. Of this event, she is reported as saying: 'I'd rather be in the situation where I had to get back up 110 times, even though this would mean that I'd fallen down 100 times; for as long as I can get back up, then I'm moving forward, and not back.'[25] The inclusion of this event further reinforces the authors' message that her character was worthy of emulation:

> She never stopped battling on, regardless of the tortuous nature of the life she had to lead. She devoted herself to society in a selfless manner. She was like a fire, burning brightly, keeping others warm, emitting a dazzling light: she truly is a modern-day Pavel. The things she has done should make each and every one of us think...shouldn't healthy people like ourselves not actually be doing that bit extra to study hard, work selflessly, and give more back to society?[26]

*Figure 7.2* 'Study Zhang Haidi and become a new communist with revolutionary ideals, sound morals, good education and a strong sense of discipline!'
Source: From the Stefan R. Landsberger Collection, International Institute of Social History, Amsterdam.

With tributes such as this, Zhang Haidi soon became an iconic symbol of struggle against adversity and success against the odds, and the highly formulaic editorial framing of her biography in these early appearances again highlights the undeniably political and social role of her life story: she was a new heroine for new times, 'a new communist with revolutionary ideals, sound morals, good education, and a strong sense of discipline' (see Figure 7.2). The social and cultural barriers that existed previously and prevented the publicising of a disabled life had been lifted. What is more, the wave of enthusiasm for studying Zhang Haidi and the values attributed to her whipped up by Deng Xiaoping's now famous exhortation continued for some time.

## The Zhang Haidi effect

Although such zeal for studying Zhang Haidi is now diminished among the general public, her reputation and influence among members of the disabled community remains, as is demonstrated by the continued attention she receives in the media in her role as a writer, chair of the China Disabled Persons' Federation (CDPF) (*Zhongguo canjiren lianhehui*) and member of the China Peoples' Political Consultative Conference National Committee.[27] Just as importantly, the model created by early biographical stories of Zhang Haidi's life (including aspects of both form and content) has continued to be applied, while the publication of inspirational stories has been a key method of promoting 'socialist spiritual civilisation'. In short, the way in which her story was first published has influenced how the stories of other disabled people have been told, effectively creating a social rhetoric of disability in China.[28]

To commemorate the twentieth anniversary of the commencement of the nationwide campaign to study Zhang Haidi, for example, the Huaxia Press compiled a collection of life narratives of disabled people from her old hometown, all of whom were inspired to achieve by 'the spirit of Haidi' (*Haidi de jingshen*). According to its editor, Yan Baoyu:

> 'The spirit of Haidi' blew across the land like a spring breeze; it was like a banner. It influenced numerous generations of people, but it was disabled people in particular who really grasped its significance – although life is filled with many beautiful things, you cannot rely on others to give them to you, you have to go and find or create them for yourself. At the same time, it also encouraged a greater sense of self-esteem, self-respect, and tireless self-improvement and hard work; and, because of this, many disabled people have grown up in Haidi's mould. From being social and familial burdens and weights, they have been transformed into those who not only produce but also command the wealth of society; from being overlooked, pitied and consoled, they have become those who build new lifestyles, enjoy equality, create true beauty and enjoy wonderful lives.[29]

Yan Baoyu's emphasis mirrors that of the earlier article 'China's Modern-day Pavel – Zhang Haidi', namely the fact that disabled people should, like Zhang Haidi, work tirelessly to improve themselves so that they can be productive members of the new society. However, it is noteworthy that he also immediately goes on to remind the reader that much of the credit for their achievements has to go to the state and the Party for their 'love' and 'concern' and the fact that disabled issues have formed an integral part of the 'Three Represents' (*San ge daibiao*),[30] and thereby the campaign for 'socialist spiritual civilisation'.[31]

Although the campaign for 'socialist spiritual civilisation' has since extended to all parts of the population in all walks of life, disability and disabled people, possibly due to the highly visible nature of their problems and the often-heroic way in which they and their carers have to deal with even everyday issues, have continued to be an important focus of activities. To be worthy of acclaim, disabled people must demonstrate one, or ideally all, of the following attitudes – self-respect (*zizun* or *zizhong*), self-confidence (*zixin*), self-improvement (*ziqiang*) and self-support (*zili*), collectively known as the 'four selfs' (*si zi*) – as well as contribute, materially or spiritually, to the further well-being of society as a whole (see Figure 7.3). In doing so, they testify to the possibilities that have opened up since the reforms and the adoption of socialist morality as a guiding principle for public behaviour.

International pressures have also had a part to play in this, as many of the disability-related activities in China came about as a specific response to United Nations-sponsored international developments relating to increasing awareness of disability rights, and thereby contributed to state plans to increase China's international image as a civilised country. One of the most significant events that followed was the founding of the CDPF in 1988, which, within a relatively short space of time, became a highly influential vice-ministry with offices across the country, and this was due very much to the fact that the driving force was Deng Xiaoping's disabled son, Deng Pufang.[32] The CDPF has been able to promote (both through its own publishing houses, such as the Huaxia Press, as well as other regional and national organisations) books, publications, feature films, TV and radio programmes. All of them focus on the lives of disabled people, particularly those that have been able to improve their lives through individual hard work and/or with the support of the state, Party and CDPF.[33]

Yet, this sense that people should constantly strive to improve themselves has taken on a new significance with disabled people, and this certainly seems to follow on from the example set by Zhang

人生的意义在于贡献，而
不是索取。

———张海迪

*Figure 7.3* 'The meaning of life rests with contributing and not demanding –
Zhang Haidi'
*Source*: From the Stefan R. Landsberger Collection, International Institute of Social
History, Amsterdam.

Haidi. The recounting of the experiences of Yin Xiaoxing (b.1970)
provides a clear example of this. One of the most recent crop of
disabled models whose stories appear in publications as diverse as
*Public Security Monthly* (*Gong'an yuekan*) and *Healthy Living* (*Jiankang
shenghuo*), his particular story has been reprinted several times under
the title 'Love Finally Finds a Home for the Wheelchair Hero' (*Lunyi
yingxiong, aiqing congci bu liulang*), and embodies many of the characteristics commonly found in writings on disabled peoples' lives.

As in Zhang Haidi's case, from the very title we are left with no
doubt that the person in question, our 'hero', has overcome physical and possibly other obstacles to achieve something out of the
ordinary. We are told that a childhood episode of polio resulted in
him using a wheelchair for independent mobility. Yet, in 1991, he

set out on a solo wheelchair expedition with only 500 *yuan* in his pocket and spent the next 12 years traversing China relying wholly on his 'unswerving determination and steadfast belief', an adventure that earned him various titles including 'Wheelchair Hero' (*Lunyi yingxiong*) and 'China's Forrest Gump' (*Zhongguo de Agan*).[34] Yin's rationale for undertaking such an adventure, he explains in interview, is that, although he had been an excellent student and had taken on various jobs in an attempt to support himself as he did not want to 'be an encumbrance to his family or a burden on society', his dream was to be a writer so that he could 'describe all the various emotions and feelings of disabled people'. His trek around China was one way of proving that he was 'unwilling to submit to his fate of being unable to walk', and his diary is cited directly for further elucidation: 'A life that is weak still has the right to sing in the sunshine. I want to use my own particular method to tell people that, regardless of whether they are disabled or not, they *can* fly just as long as they have a dream in their hearts.'[35]

Despite the fact that the state, principally through the CDPF and its numerous publicity channels, has made great use of disabled life narratives in its attempt to raise awareness of the lives of people with disabilities, and, thereby, incorporate them into mainstream society, the way in which this has been done has often further accentuated the fact that disabled people are different. Identity politics has been a key factor in these developments for the political acceptance of the Western concept of disability in China in the 1980s resulted in the adoption of a new label, 'the disabled' (*canjiren*).[36] This label has subsequently been applied to a vast range of people with disabilities and illnesses and one of the main outcomes of this is the creation of, in the minds of the public, a somewhat homogenous group that is identifiable by a physical or mental difference to 'normal people' (*zhengchangren*). While much of this stems from the innumerable newspaper reports that disabled people are to be pitied and need help and assistance, equally so, it seems to stem from the labelling of social models as 'disabled' and the emphasis pinned on the out-of-the-ordinary aspects of their character or actions that have singled them out for acclaim. Ironically, therefore, the identification of Zhang Haidi and others as disabled has tended to reinforce their distinctness, not just as individuals, but also as a group, thereby exacerbating their marginalisation.

In the Western context, too, life writing in the 'empire of the normal' has generally been associated with distinction, celebrity or success in a chosen field to the extent that it is almost a prerequisite. With regard to disabled autobiography, Couser argues:

> The situation of disabled individuals is that their most obvious 'distinction' is one that may disqualify them as autobiographers – unless it can somehow be made the focus of the book, the hook for the reader. But if the disability becomes the whole subject of the story, there is some risk of reducing autobiography to case study – reifying disability and thus reinforcing marginaliza-tion... We are left with the paradox that those individuals with disabilities who represent themselves in autobiography may not in fact be very representative – in other words, typical – of those with disabilities.[37]

And it certainly seems to be so in the Chinese case. Zhang Haidi and Yin Xiaoxing are two prominent cases that exemplify the way in which many of those disabled people who have been seen to be deserving of a public life story have had to do more than make up for the physical effects of their disability. In Zhang Haidi's case this was professionally and intellectually, while in Yin Xiaoxing's case this was physically. The overriding message from the stories written about them is that these people have, with superhuman effort, actu-ally gone further and achieved more than 'normal people' could ever have done. Yet, further to this, the reported rationale for them under-taking such activities has been so that they can avoid being a burden on their families and become active contributors to the new society.

## Reclaiming a life

In her own semi-autobiographical novel *Dreams from a Wheelchair* (*Lunyiche shang de meng*), which was first published in 1991, Zhang Haidi seemingly begins to reclaim some of the ownership she has lost over her own life story since it first appeared almost a decade previously. Set in the years leading up to, during and following the Cultural Revolution, the novel focuses on the life of a young girl, Fang Dan. Alternating between the first and third person, it incor-porates many of the details of Zhang Haidi's life as told and retold in the Chinese media over the years. What differs, however, is the manner in which the details of her life and the role her disability has played in it are related, and this reveals much of the consequences of diverging agenda of author and subject if the narratives are not self-composed.

Unlike Zhang Haidi's life narratives in the media, Fang Dan's disability is not detailed at the start of the novel. It is initially left to the reader to deduce the reason for the protagonist's seclusion within the four walls of her house where, day-by-day, she sits in terrible loneliness listening to girls playing outside:

> I felt such a terrible sense of despair. Their voices and laughter were so close, yet here I was locked up in my room. I felt bitter that I could not have their friendship and affection, and I felt sad that I had no classmates, teachers or lucky singing group in my life. I saw that I had shed tears, but was this really crying? I often wanted to cry, but I never cried in front of people, let alone sobbed. I always gulped back my tears; yet, I really wanted to have a good cry and made every effort to do so, the way you can do when you are on your own. I didn't want to hear people say that I was brave, as I wasn't, not a bit. I was crying on the inside. I always wanted to force myself to do it and I thought that it would be nice. I wanted to cry in a happy way...I wanted to get to know those girls, but how could I let them know that I even existed?[38]

Even when she realises that she can draw their attention by singing, she decides to try and cover up her disability when they first meet for fear of a negative reaction. But her fears are unfounded and she soon becomes the focus of the group's friendship, which in turn becomes the focus of her life.

The descriptions of her disability and how it affects her life are intermingled throughout with concerns about her friendships with neighbourhood children, relationships with her family members and interactions with the local community. For example, in one episode, her new friend Heping brings around her ballet shoes and the girls take turns to try them on. Fang Dan initially resists, but is eventually talked around:

> Fang Dan hesitantly took the shoes, put them on her feet and tied the laces. 'Beautiful! They're just right!' exclaimed Weina. 'Look, it's almost as if they were made for her!' added Heping. She then

turned and said: 'Fang Dan, look how pretty they are on you!' Fang Dan was too afraid to look at her feet. She knew that they had already become misshapen, but with everyone praising them so she couldn't help but take a peek at them. It was then she saw that the white ballet shoes had transformed her feet into something marvellous. Look, were they not as pointed and straight as when Heping's when she danced? 'I have feet that can dance!' She was so thrilled! She really wanted to stand up and pirouette on points as Heping had done. Before she knew it she had lifted her legs to get off the bed, but then she suddenly stopped. These two legs didn't seem to be hers; they wouldn't stretch out in the way her heart was telling them to do. In that moment, her excitement was crushed. She lowered her head and her face reddened. 'What's the matter, Fang Dan?' Heping quickly asked. All the girls crowded around her. 'I ... I can't dance ... I'm not like you, probably never will ... ' she said.[39]

Moments such as these when her frustration and her fears come to the fore provide a powerful sense of otherness that at times becomes overwhelming. Yet, at the same time, the articulation of personal physical and emotional concerns in this way begins to complicate the standard hegemonic scripts of disability of the time that depicted disability as something to be pitied and/or overcome.

The Cultural Revolution proves to be one of the darkest times in Fang Dan's life and many events are related in great detail here (unlike in the narratives authored by others), providing the focus for much of the novel. From the time her parents are taken away as counter-revolutionaries, she is reliant on the support of her friends, one of whom, Li Jiang, brings her foreign literature at great risk to himself.[40] When her parents finally return, they move from the city to rural Taozhuang, where her father ensures she has a window so she can see the world outside (this had been physically blocked up in the city to try to protect her from the increasing chaos outside). Here, ironically, her sense of isolation and uselessness only increases as she see everyone else go off to work in the fields, a frustration she reveals to the sent-down youth Du Hanming:

When the work bell sounds, I can't help wanting to stand up and go off to work with you all, even though might be hard and tiring, even though it might be filthy and sweaty work. But all I can do is sit here. Do you know? I want to work, I want to work; whatever the job, it doesn't matter.[41]

It is only when she is given the eponymous wheelchair and, shortly after, asked to become the village tutor that she feels some sense of freedom and purpose to her life and this is related in a letter to Li Jiang:

Li Jiang, how I used to wish that I could go to school! Each time my mother would carry me on her back to the hospital past the school gates, I couldn't help crying. How I envied those children sitting in the classrooms. Back then I couldn't imagine that I would become a teacher to the children of Taozhuang. I am so blessed that I can use what I have learned to teach these children and see them make progress. Li Jiang, the happiness I felt when I found out that I could do something for the people of Taozhuang also made me realise that my life was truly meaningful. Taozhuang has enabled me to become someone useful[42]

Her sense of purpose continues to grow as she starts to read medical texts in hope of becoming a doctor and eventually begins to treat, and cure, those in need around her, often at great physical expense to herself and others. On one occasion, her determination to help results in her being pushed in her wheelchair through the snow to a neighbouring village, which is further evidence of her growing influence in the community. In a final letter to Li Jiang she reveals the transformation she has undergone while at the commune:

Li Jiang, can you sense it? I've changed. I'm no longer that young girl, with the white face who dreamed of freedom as she sat all day by the window. It is as if my heart has grown wings and set flight. Now I can say it, the world is my oyster...[43]

And, so, it is through her writing that we can begin to see the individual through the rhetoric surrounding a very public persona. Many of the aspects of Zhang Haidi's life that proved so appealing to the creators of the new social models back in the 1980s appear in the character of Fang Dan – her spirit, strength and determination, her intelligence and, possibility most importantly, her need to be of use to society. This is clearly indicative of a certain amount of internalisation of the standard scripts of disability by the author herself; however, the way in which they are retold demonstrates the beginnings of a gradual process of conscious re-appropriation and, where once her life story was wholly public and political, there are now aspects that are private and personal. Although there are elements to the story that complicate the state-sponsored narrative of disability there remains a great deal of consonance and this is certainly one of the reasons why the novel became the focus of official acclaim, won numerous national awards for literature and was listed among the books for patriotic education.[44]

More recently, other disabled people have turned to writing, both in the form of autobiographical novels as well as autobiography. One such example is Chen Yan (1973–), a blind piano tuner, whose richly illustrated biography *Chen Yan: A World of Sound* (*Chen Yan: erbian de shijie*) from 2004 provides a chronological and pictorial look at her life, from the time she was abandoned to the care of her grandmother as a very young baby once her parents discovered her disability, through her training as a piano tuner and the establishment of her own piano-tuning business, to the many other accomplishments she has worked hard to achieve in spite of the restrictions imposed by her impairment. She tells us of her mastery of the unicycle and her practice of Taekwondo, among other things, and provides us with the photographic evidence of her endeavours.

Although relatively unknown outside the disabled community and without the same backing provided by Zhang Haidi's social or political status, her autobiography has been promoted in a very similar manner due to the inspirational message she expressly and purposefully provides throughout the book,[45] as she herself sums up in the afterword:

> I wrote this book so that more people could understand blind people and the rough and arduous road of self-improvement we blind people have to endure. The process of writing was like walking down a road I had walked down before. The events of the past were revealed one after the other, and often I cried when I wrote of events that were painful. There was too much suffering, too much struggling; yet, it was all real (although I did change the

name of some people). The story of my life was different in many ways, but it was filled with tears and laughter as I made my way along its roads.[46]

These by now familiar themes of tireless self-improvement, battling against the odds and outstanding achievement, are picked up on by both Cheng Kai of the CDPF, who provides the foreword to the book, and the editor, whose words help to close the book. Cheng Kai states:

I believe that the publication of this book will encourage and spur on those people, particularly the disabled, who find themselves in difficulty. Making known Chen Yan's achievements can only further increase awareness of helping others, and promote the establishment of human relationships characterised by equality and friendship, and a society characterised by collaboration and assistance. I have even more reason to believe that Chen Yan's future will be better and that the aims of disabled people of 'equality, participation and sharing' will be soon realised with the Party and State's continued implementation of the scientific development view that puts people first, along with the support of humanitarian activities carried out at every level of society, and the indomitable spirit of tireless self-development held by disabled people everywhere.[47]

Although Chen Yan's autobiography reveals, therefore, many personal details of her life, its highs and its lows, both its editorial framing and Chen Yan's own words ultimately echo the common social and political rhetoric of disability. Its standard 'triumph over tragedy' scenario aided its publication and promotion over and above the stories of other relatively unknown disabled people.[48]

## New technologies and new subjectivities

*Chen Yan: A World of Sound* and *Dreams from a Wheelchair* both provide us with insights into the personal lives of people with disabilities, yet do so in very different ways and, as a consequence, highlight the ways in which traditionally published life narratives may be shaped by editorial forces as well as authorial designs.[49] However, new technologies may now be providing different and less restricted avenues for writing about one's own life. Zhang Haidi, for example, in addition to publishing *Dreams from a Wheelchair*, and numerous other novels and writings besides, has in more recent years used the internet to great effect to relate her own life experiences and this is possibly where we can see the greatest divergence of her public and private self. Since she first set up her personal webpage in 2005, she has populated the site with numerous articles about issues that have affected her and those around her, as well as her own poems, paintings, photographs and blog entries, to name but a few.[50] Although there are references to disability on the site, including a section devoted to 'overcoming illness' (*zhansheng jibing*) and mention of some of the events she has attended as a representative for the disabled both in China and abroad, many of the pages reflect her own personal interests. Her first entry writes:

> Today I now have my very own piece of autumn meadow – my blog! Over the past few years I've had lots of things that I've wanted to share with my friends, such as my writings and my oil and watercolour paintings. I've also got photographs of me doing jobs at home, washing clothes, cups and bowls, not to mention reading and writing...[51]

No longer do we just see the 'Self-improvement Model' (*Ziqiang mofan*) as awarded by the CDPF in 1991 or the 'National Model Worker' (*Quanguo laodong mofan*) as conferred by the State Council in 2000;[52] we are now able to see even more of the private person behind the public persona. And, in similar ways, Yin Xiaoxing and Chen Yan have also explored the freedom offered by a personal website to retell their life stories in their own words, share private thoughts and experiences and link up with friends, old and new.[53]

The internet appears to have enabled these three writers to further reclaim their individuality and, at the same time, build a new community of friends, disabled and non-disabled, around the world. In the Western context, too, the internet has been shown to provide a new world for publishing and writing disabled life stories. It is seen to be a liberating force as it enables people to (re)claim ownership of their life stories and it enables them to tell stories without having to go through the rigmarole of finding a publisher or getting official approval. It has been described as fulfilling a post-colonial function, namely 'the demand to speak rather than being spoken for and to represent oneself rather than being represented or, in the worst cases, rather than being effaced entirely'.[54] The internet has also been shown to assist disabled people in reaching out to others in the same way as it has done for similarly disenfranchised groups.[55]

As a prominent member of the disabled community of many years standing, Zhang Haidi has been in a peculiarly privileged position as her education and political connections have provided her access to the publishing world through which she has been able retell her life story from a more personal perspective, albeit through the form of a semi-autobiographical novel. Yet, it is through the new semiotic tools available online that she has finally been able to divest herself of the rhetoric surrounding her character and actions as disabled model and writer, to give free rein to her personality and subjectivity, and this has been done without compromising her social and political position. Personal websites are now beginning to appear on an increasingly regular basis written by people who do not have the media status of Yin Xiaoxing and Chen Yan or lack the political clout of Zhang Haidi, and it is clear that this relatively new form of life writing in China is beginning to fulfil its counter-discursive potential.[56]

## Whose life is it anyway?

The life stories of people with bodily dysfunction have been shown to have two sides – the personal (which gives voice to the body and how stories are told through the body) and the social (which determines how context shapes the narrative and affects which stories get told and how they are told to others),[57] and it is often the case that the telling of these stories involves 'an extraordinarily complex negotiation between private experience and public expression'.[58] Using the case of Zhang Haidi as a prominent example, this chapter has demonstrated how the production of life writing of and by disabled people in China has transformed over time, closely reflecting general transformations of the socio-political context, as well as specific changes in the conception of the disabled body and individuality. Since the reform era, disabled people have increasingly been the subject of life narratives, sponsored by the state as part of its policy to both demarginalise them and at the same time provide new models of social morality for public acclaim. Ironically, the selection of stories à la 'empire of the normal' has resulted in concentration simply on disabled people who have achieved outstanding successes amidst extreme difficulty and this focus has only further emphasised the fact that they are different. The majority of published life writings of and by disabled people, therefore, have generally continued to serve, intentionally or otherwise, the perpetuation of a hegemonic discourse of disability – a discourse that focuses on the primacy of the community at large over the individual, and the utilisation of personal stories for public ends. It has only been since the appearance of more independent writings and genres, and most particularly since the advent of personal websites and blogging, that some disabled people in China have been able to explore their individuality in a way that is devoid of any political or social intent, and have found avenues to communicate and express their subjectivities and identities as an effective form of cultural redress.

## Notes

1. Sharon L. Snyder et al., eds., *Disability Studies: Enabling the Humanities* (New York: The Modern Language Association of America, 2002), 3.
2. G. Thomas Couser, *Recovering Bodies: Illness, Disability and Life Writing* (Madison: University of Wisconsin Press, 1997), 4.
3. Nancy Mairs, 'Foreword' to *Recovering Bodies*, ed. G. Thomas Couser, xi.
4. Couser, *Recovering Bodies*, 4–5.
5. Anne Hunsaker Hawkins, *Reconstructing Illness: Studies in Pathography* (West Lafayette: Purdine University Press, 1993), 3.
6. Hermione Lee, *Body Parts: Essays in Life-writing* (London: Chatto and Windus, 2005), 4.
7. Mairs, 'Foreword,' xi.
8. Perkins, for example, addresses the ways in which autobiographical narratives 'give voice to oppositional or counterhegemonic ways of knowing'; see Margo V. Perkins, *Autobiography as Activism: Three Black Women of the Sixties* (Jackson: University Press of Mississippi, 2000), xii. Schaffer and Smith demonstrate how life narratives can function as 'a crucial element in establishing new identities'; see Kay Schaffer and Sidonie Smith, 'Conjunctions: Life Narratives in the Field of Human Rights,' *Biography* 27.1 (2004): 6.
9. Snyder et al., *Disability Studies*, 7.
10. G. Thomas Couser, 'Introduction – The Empire of the 'Normal': A Forum on Disability and Self-representation,' *American Quarterly* 52.2 (2000): 305–310.

11. Couser, *Recovering Bodies*, 4–6. Yet, misrepresentation can just as easily occur here, too, as demonstrated by Hevey in his examination of the tenebrous role photography has played in the construction of disabled identities; see David Hevey, *Creatures Time Forgot: Photography and Disability Imagery* (New York: Routledge, 1992).

12. Xie Jin's 1977 film *Youth* (*Qingchun*), which focuses on the experiences of a young deaf girl as she is 'cured' of her disability and given the opportunity to contribute to the communist revolution in a more proactive way, opened the door to a whole raft of films that make reference to disability in a substantial way. See Sarah Dauncey, 'Screening Disability in the PRC: The Politics of Looking Good,' *China Information* 21.3 (2007): 481–506.

13. Stefan R. Landsberger, 'Learning by What Example? Educational Propaganda in Twenty-first Century China,' *Critical Asian Studies* 33.4 (2001): 549–551. See also his comprehensive website collection hosted by the IISH, *Chinese Posters: Propaganda, Politics, History, Art*, http://chineseposters.net/index.php (accessed 8 October 2012).

14. Mary Sheridan, 'The Emulation of Heroes,' *China Quarterly* 33 (1968): 50.

15. Ibid., 52.

16. Ibid., 68–72. See also Tina Mai Chen, 'Proletarian White and Working Bodies in Mao's China,' *positions: asia critique* 11.2 (2003): 365.

17. For an explanation of the way in which military veterans were venerated during this time, see Neil J. Diamant, *Embattled Glory: Veterans, Military Families, and the Politics of Patriotism in China, 1949–2007* (Lanham: Rowman and Littlefield, 2009). For other exceptional cases in the cinematic context, see Dauncey, 'Screening Disability,' 485–488.

18. Dawn Einwalter, 'Selflessness and Self-interest: Public Morality and the Xu Honggang Campaign,' *Journal of Contemporary China* 7.18 (1998): 257–269.

19. Landsberger, 'Learning by What Example?' 551–559.

20. 'CPC Calls for Learning from Zhang Haidi,' *China Report: Political, Sociological and Military Affairs* 429, 10 June 1983.

21. Helen Keller (1880–1968) lost both her hearing and vision as a baby, but learnt to read numerous foreign languages in Braille, wrote nearly a dozen books and was awarded the Presidential Medal of Freedom. Her autobiography, *The Story of My Life* (1903), has been translated into around 50 languages and she was included in *Time* magazine's top 100 most influential people of the twentieth century.

22. Pavel Korchagin, the central character in *How Steel was Tempered*, a semi-autobiographical novel by Nikolai Ostrovsky (1904–1936), is severely disabled during the novel. The strong sense of socialist realism and heroic central character ensured a welcome in China following the story's adaptation to film in 1942. See Tina Mai Chen, 'Internationalism and Cultural Experience: Soviet Films and Popular Chinese Understandings of the Future in the 1950s,' *Cultural Critique* 58 (2004): 107.

23. Lu Tanxian and Liu Deyu, 'Zhongguo dangdai Bao'er – Zhang Haidi (China's modern-day Pavel – Zhang Haidi),' in *Haidi guxiang de canjiren*

(Disabled people from Haidi's hometown) by Yan Baoyu (Beijing: Huaxia chubanshe, 2003), 1.

24. Ibid., 5.
25. Lu and Liu, 'Zhongguo dangdai Bao'er,' 6. Other sources suggest 101 times.
26. Ibid., 1.
27. An outline of her awards and career can be found at 'Zhang Haidi,' http://news.xinhuanet.com/ziliao/2003-01/17/content_694856.htm (accessed 15 January 2010).
28. For a discussion of the 'social rhetoric of illness' in the Western context, see Arthur W. Frank, *The Wounded Storyteller: Body, Illness, and Ethics* (Chicago: University of Chicago, 1997), 21. For the Chinese context, see Deirdre Sabina Knight, 'Madness and Disability in Contemporary Chinese Film,' *Journal of Medical Humanities* 27.2 (2006): 101.
29. Yan, 'Preface' to *Haidi guxiang de canjiren*, by Yan Baoyu, 4.
30. Ibid., 4.
31. Einwalter argues that this campaign continues to be an important part of the Party's claim to political legitimacy; see Einwalter, 'Selflessness and Self-interest,' 257.
32. For comprehensive study of the CDPF and Deng Pufang, see Matthew Kohrman, *Bodies of Difference: Experiences of Disability and Institutional Advocacy in the Making of Modern China* (Berkeley: University of California Press, 2005).
33. One particularly interesting trilogy of writings by disabled authors, from the older established writers to the relatively unknown, is that edited by Wang Xinxian: *Weile shengming de meili* (To the beauty of life) (Beijing: Huaxia chubanshe, 2005); *Fangfei xiwang* (Let dreams take flight) (Beijing Huaxia chubanshe, 2005); and *Shouhuo gandong* (A treasury of emotions) (Beijing Huaxia chubanshe, 2006).
34. Li Jianjun, 'Lunyi yingxiong, aiqing congbu liulang' (Love finally finds a home for the wheelchair hero). *Jiankang shenghuo* (Healthy living) 1 (2004): 38.
35. Ibid.
36. Kohrman, *Bodies of Difference*, 15.
37. Couser, *Recovering Bodies*, 182–183.
38. Zhang Haidi, *Lunyiche shang de meng* (Dreams from a wheelchair) (Beijing: Renmin wenxue chubanshe, 2005), 10.
39. Ibid., 27.
40. He particularly recommends *The Gadfly*, a 1897 novel by Ethel Lilian Voynich, which was well received in early twentieth-century China due to its depiction of revolution, romance and heroism. The main protagonist overcomes illness to fight for freedom and independence, and becomes a potential source of inspiration for Fang Dan. Ibid., 136.
41. Ibid., 244.
42. Ibid., 281.
43. Ibid., 353.

44. 'Zhang Haidi: jixu yong shengming de jiqing lai xiezuo' (Zhang Haidi continues to write inspired by an enthusiasm for life), http://www.gmw.cn/content/2006-11/10/content_506023.htm (accessed 18 February 2008).

45. At her autobiography signing in Beijing, people were reportedly moved to tears. Many children had been brought to see her, the youngest being only three years old; the parents of this particular child hoped that the child would 'study from Auntie Chen Yan and develop a strong willpower and an optimistic spirit.' See ' "Chen Yan: erban de shijie" zizhuan zai Jing qianshou ("Chen Yan: a world of sound" autobiography signing in Beijing),' http://www.00544.com.webdump.org/2004/jiejueshalong/409080001.htm (accessed 25 July 2013).

46. Chen Yan, *Chen Yan: erban de shijie* (Chen Yan: a world of sound), (Yinchuan: Ningxia chubanshe, 2004), 207.

47. Ibid., preface.

48. Couser, 'Introduction – The Empire of the "Normal",' 307.

49. Frank suggests that even the most hardened autobiography may have to make compromises, consciously or otherwise, prior to publication. See Frank, *The Wounded Storyteller*, 21–23.

50. 'Haidi de BLOG' (Haidi's blog), http://blog.sina.com.cn/haidi (accessed 18 February 2008).

51. 'Qin'ai de pengyoumen, dajia hao!' (Hello, dear friends!), http://blog.sina.com.cn/s/blog_46d3fc8f0100009z.html (accessed 18 February 2008).

52. 'Zhongguo yidai qingnian de jiao'ao – Zhang Haidi' (Zhang Haidi – the pride of a generation of China's youth), http://www.wscl.gov.cn/artshow.asp?id=367 (accessed 25 July 2013).

53. See 'yinxiaoxing de boke (yinxiaoxing's blog),' http://blog.sina.com.cn/yinxiaoxingboke (accessed 8 August 2010); 'Chen Yan gangqin diaolü (Chen Yan piano tuning),' http://www.bjpiano.com (accessed 9 November 2007) – Chen Yan's site also acts as a portal for her piano-tuning business.

54. Frank, *The Wounded Storyteller*, 13.

55. Evgeny Morozov, 'Blogs: The New Frontier in Human Rights,' *Transitions Online*, 5 January 2007.

56. For an in-depth discussion of one young writer – Zhang Yuncheng – who has explored the use of memoir and personal website as tools for self-expression and personal redress, revealing a burgeoning sense of disability consciousness that extends beyond urban areas, see Sarah Dauncey, '*Three Days to Walk*: A Personal Story of Life Writing and Disability Consciousness in China,' *Disability & Society* 27.3 (2012): 311–323.

57. Frank, *The Wounded Storyteller*, 2–3.

58. Couser, *Recovering Bodies*, 8.

# 8

# A Look at the Margins: Autobiographical Writing in Tibetan in the People's Republic of China[1]

*Isabelle Henrion-Dourcy*

> *Although one's corpse goes under the earth,*
> *One's story remains above*

(Tibetan proverb)

## Tibetan autobiographies, past and present

The practice of writing one's life was well rooted in pre-modern Tibet[2]: biographies (Tib. *rnam-thar*) and autobiographies (Tib. *rang-rnam*)[3] of religious masters were, and still are, very popular readings, for monks as well as literate lay people. Some of these texts, written in prose, prose interspersed with verse, or entirely in verse, are even often read aloud because of the musicality of their composition. The earliest known examples of autobiographical writing, only a few dozen folios long, date back to the twelfth century, but auto/biography as a historical and literary genre exploded in the seventeenth and eighteenth centuries, both in length and quantity.[4] This was a pivotal historical period, which saw the emergence and consolidation, in Central Tibet, of the regime of the Dalai Lamas, and, in outer Tibetan regions, of large monastic centres. There are at least 150 book-length autobiographical texts that are accessible today,[5] most of which contain several hundred folios.

These auto/biographies are in principle built upon a soteriological narrative frame: they are meant to retrace step by step the exemplary path of the (nearly always male) religious master towards his 'complete liberation' – literal translation of *rnam-thar*, complete liberation from Samsāra. The purpose is religious,[6] so these texts include long lists of religious masters, teachings received, books studied, religious artefacts made, rituals and pilgrimages undertaken, and offerings received. They may also comprise visions, prophecies, magical signs and wondrous stories, all very popular among Tibetans. These texts are thus best described as hagiographies, didactic tales for religious edification and inspiration. But the genre is actually quite diverse: some writings delve into otherworldly contemplation, while some others are annalistic, anecdotal, quasi-secular in their outlook. Some are factual and unadorned, others are 'pyrotechnic displays'[7] of complex poetics, while rare ones explore the intimate layers of the self, or rather multiple selves.[8] All are marked by a moral tension between 'conflicting social norms: one requiring that persons refer to themselves with humility and the other that religious teachers present themselves as venerable exemplars'.[9] Authorship is also problematic, as scribes have often edited or embellished the diaries of their masters. The heterogeneity of pre-modern Tibetan autobiographies thus precludes easy generalisations. The nature and purpose of these texts, where history and myth are not separate conceptual categories, are at odds with the current methodological standards of scholarship, yet they are one of the most important sources of information for historians today.[10] They help Tibetanists build chronologies, networks of personal relations across vast geographic distances, and social and economic contexts for the major events described in other genres of writings.

This chapter is however concerned with 'modern' Tibetan autobiographies, that is, those written after the Chinese take-over of Tibetan regions in the wake of the founding of the People's Republic of China (PRC) in 1949 – and only those written in Tibetan. In quantity, content, style and authorship, they depart from the traditional genre in important ways. Not radically so, but in varying degrees: these texts are also heterogeneous, as authors from different educational backgrounds unevenly draw from various (traditionally Tibetan, Western or Chinese) compositional models. Modern autobiographies are indeed not considered to pertain to the same literary category as the traditional ones (Tib. *rnam-thar, rang-rnam*) and they don't pursue the same soteriological aspirations. They are rather considered to belong to the genre of history, or chronicle (Tib. *lo-rgyus*), a term that sometimes appears in the titles. If one sets apart the few autobiographies written by present-day religious masters along 'traditional' lines, modern authors are now generally lay people. Several texts among the earlier ones were produced by former officials or aristocrats, but many have since emerged from social strata that were not empowered to write history in pre-modern Tibet: from relatively uneducated political prisoners or from ordinary people from remote regions of the Tibetan plateau. In several ways, these accounts provide an alternative writing of history on two simultaneous fronts: an alternative to the pre-modern Tibetan elites' construction of collective memory and an alternative to post-1950s Chinese official rhetoric on Tibet.

First-person narratives have actually played a significant role among Tibetans since the Chinese take-over. As much in the PRC as in exile, they have been instrumental in the local and international politics of representing Tibet, past and present. On both sides of the Himalayas, though with different rhetoric and mediums, accounts of personal experience have been officially encouraged and held as evidence to counter the other side's ideological claims. Autobiographical writing has thus shifted from a predominantly religious purpose in the pre-modern era, to a political one since the 1950s.

In sketching this very broad overview of Tibetan autobiographical writing since the 1950s, the most salient feature is the stark contrast, in quantity and literary genre, between the texts published in the PRC and those produced in exile. First, in numbers: the ongoing inventory that I have been compiling since 2005 comprises at present 157 book-length autobiographies published in exile in South Asia or in the West (61 of which are in English[11] or, rarely, in other Western languages), and only 17 in the PRC. One can therefore speak of an 'autobiographical craze' in exile that is unknown in Tibet. As for genre, each side has been heavily influenced by two culturally foreign models: the Western style of 'testimony' on one side, for the autobiographies published in exile; and the revolutionary practice of self-criticism and thought-training on the other side, for those published in the PRC. Some texts have actually crossed the Himalayas (the entering of exile texts being far more difficult and risky than the reverse), but it is difficult to assess the stylistic and thematic influences exerted from each side. The Dalai Lama's biography[12] and autobiography[13] have circulated undercover since the early 1980s in Tibet, where they have had a huge emotional and political impact. Conversely, some autobiographical texts from Tibet have circulated in exile: a few short accounts translated into English in the mid-1980s[14] and the courageous autobiography of Nags-tshang Nus-blo, *The Joys and Sorrows of the Boy from Nagtsang Family*.[15] This text directly confronts painful memories of state repression and blood-shed in the author's area during his childhood in the 1950s, has been translated from the Amdo regional dialect into modern literary Tibetan (in India in 2008) and is due to appear in English.[16]

It is the Dalai Lama who blazed the trail for all modern autobi-ographical writing with his 1962 *My Land and my People*. He then asked his fellow Tibetans to write down their memoirs in order to carry out a 'duty of memory' in the wake of the vanishing of 'old Tibet'. Those who wrote their accounts, hailing mostly from priv-ileged classes because of the level of literacy required, thought of this life writing practice as an 'offering' to the Dalai Lama. When the second wave of Tibetan refugees started arriving in exile from 1979 onwards, the Dalai Lama again urged these witnesses freshly come out of Tibet to write down their harrowing experiences under the PRC government. These texts were meant to inform the Tibetan community and the world about living conditions very little known outside of China, and to ensure that those experiences would not be forgotten. Most of the accounts in English are ghost-written by Westerners and many consist of evocations of life before the Chinese take-over or prison memoirs. Those in Tibetan tend to be concerned with resistance to the military occupation in the 1950s and 1960s, or the documentation of local history, the social system and daily life prior to the Chinese take-over. All explicitly aim to oppose the bleak Maoist description of Tibet's past as 'hell on earth'. The following broad categories will give a sense of the variety of these exile writ-ings, although some autobiographies cross over these loosely defined groupings. One finds autobiographical accounts by religious figures (15 in Tibetan, 15 in English or other Western languages); by for-mer officials, former members of the elites or officials in exile (27 in Tibetan, 15 in English); by guerrilla fighters from eastern Tibet (18 in Tibetan, 4 in English); by political prisoners that have come out of Tibet since the end of the 1980s and evoke prison, labour camps and repression since the Cultural Revolution (30 in Tibetan, 15 in

English); by ordinary folk detailing daily life and/or local history (1 in Tibetan, 8 in English); by exiles narrating their life experiences in the West (3 in Tibetan, 4 in English); and finally by Tibetan exiles who decided to return to the PRC (2 in Tibetan).

As for the autobiographies published in the PRC, the agenda has been very different. During the radical Maoist years, telling of one's life story, whether verbally or in writing, was a compulsory public practice. It was used as an effective tool of thought-control to achieve total individual obedience to the state.[17] As Uradyn Bulag remarked, 'modern China is an oral-history regime, in which everyone has been trained to vocalise their subjectivity, voicing their loyalty to the Party and hatred to a changing array of enemies'.[18] This compulsory practice of telling one's life developed into two opposed scripts according to the author's social background: either the 'speaking bitterness' (Chin. *suku,* Tib. *sdug-bsngal bshad-pa*) narrative, where the exploited members of the pre-revolution society vented their rage at their former oppressors; or the 'confession' (Chin. *zhaogong,* Tib. *rang-skyon brjod-pa,* self-criticism) narrative, whereby these oppressors repented of their social and political crimes, reworking themselves into modern socialist selves and pleading allegiance to the new government. Out of the 17 autobiographies published in Tibetan in the PRC listed above, seven fall into this 'confessional' category. The other accounts comprise: three texts by important religious figures of Amdo (in Qinghai province) who wrote either in a rather traditional style about their religious and secular activities[19] or wrote their account in Chinese;[20] the independently written[21] *Joys and Sorrows* by Nags-tshang; one literary evocation of the author's childhood;[22] and at least five autobiographies written by religious figures in a traditional style, primarily about religious experiences. These works by charismatic leaders are independently produced in local religious centres and are aimed mainly at disciples. It is difficult to compile an exhaustive survey: one has to travel to each individual centre to know of their existence, and there are probably many more such religious 'traditional' life writings. The same difficulty is met in exile: many autobiographical accounts, especially those produced in the last 15 years, are privately produced, either in vanity press or printed and bound at a local facility, with neither publication details nor distribution. One needs to have heard about these accounts and then it is necessary to hunt them down in order to lay a hand on them.

Having set the overall context of modern Tibetan autobiographical writing, I will now turn to the purpose of this chapter. I am concerned here with Tibetan autobiographies published in the PRC, more specifically in Central Tibet and Lhasa, where most of my research has been carried out. Life writing is a political tool at the disposal of the state: the autobiographies I will study were all commands (7 out of the 17 autobiographies in Tibetan I am aware of). As it turns out, the politics of personal memory among ethnic minorities of the PRC, in the specific context of the post-Mao State-sponsored local and oral history project, is anchored in a particular book series, the *Selected Materials on History and Culture*. As for any kind of autobiographical writing, we have to ask ourselves: who are the authors recounting their lives for? Who requests those texts and who benefits from them? In the Tibetan case, we have to understand the specific conditions in which the *Materials* are produced, the way personal and collective memory are shaped, the institutional constraints weighing on the authors, the model narratives that they are expected to follow and the literary conventions that organise their writing. After a presentation of this collection, I look in detail at two autobiographies, the first and the last one (to date) that were published in the collection. Is life writing totally constrained politically, or is there a margin for manoeuvring where authors manage to reclaim part of their personal and/or collective identity? How do personal motives cross with the official enterprise of producing history? Do the authors succeed or fail to conform to the master narrative laid in front of them? Do they add elements that are not part of the prescribed narrative? What aspects of life are pushed forth to reach certain agendas, and what are those important agendas? In both of these accounts, I will try and assess the part of compliance and strategy that organises those endeavours.

## The series *Selected Materials on History and Culture*[23]

The *Materials* represent a vast and unique collection of historical data produced by Research Committees on History and Culture throughout the PRC. These committees are constituted within various administrative units (at the national, regional/provincial, prefectural, county or city levels) of the Chinese People's Political Consultative Conference (abridged to PCC[24]). The PCC is itself an organ of the United Front[25] Work Department, an agency directly under the central committee of the Communist Party and managing relations with high-profile non-Party figures. These are mostly members of the social and political elites before the communist revolution, as well as important intellectuals, artists, businessmen or overseas Chinese. It seeks to promote national unity by ensuring that these individuals, who are potentially hostile to the Party, bring their support to the government. The United Front has been instrumental in the management of religion and minority nationalities in the PRC. These dimensions are critical to the Tibet issue, and this agency has played a crucial political role in this restive region. It is therefore quite surprising that, while the politics of writing history in the PRC has received colossal attention, very little has been geared to the specific historical work undertaken by the United Front through its PCC-based committees.[26]

The *Materials* enterprise was first envisioned by Zhou Enlai in 1959, as a means to archive the memory of elder members of the PCC, thus elites who had not participated in or had even opposed the Revolution but whose personal role in local pre-communist history was significant. The series had a time frame: from the last years of the Qing dynasty to 1949. It also had a guiding principle, the 'three first-hands' (Chin. *san qin*):[27] the events recollected had to be 'experienced, seen and heard first-hand' by the authors. A special emphasis was put on collecting 'raw materials', presented as a scientific and objective history: personal experience was held as evidence, and the accounts were posited as accurate and unadulterated. The *Materials* project came to a halt during the Cultural Revolution, and was rekindled at the end of the 1970s. It was considered a useful way to mobilise local and oral history to achieve national pacification and reconstruction in the aftermath of radical Maoism.[28] What is interesting about these *Materials* is that they represent 'history written by the vanquished',[29] the deposed former elites. These have either written accounts of events in which they personally participated; or they have been interviewed by PCC researchers, who then compiled articles or books from these 'raw' oral data. There does not seem to have been any consistency throughout the PRC in the quality of the data gathered, the training of the interviewers or the formatting of the written accounts. Produced at different administrative levels of the PCC and with different standards of quality, and purporting a variety of points of views, this vast collection is thus heterogeneous.

Under their academic pretence, these *Materials* are actually performative acts of political compliance, and have often been dismissed as straight propaganda. They are obviously edited, although it is difficult to know exactly through which processes and whether or not the interventions are the same throughout the whole collection.[30] For the Tibetan case, some of the depictions of the past as presented in the *Materials* have irked exile intellectuals so much that a former minister-in-exile, Wangdü Dorje, wrote a 125-page rebuttal of two volumes of the collection.[31] Sifting through the propaganda, the familiar reader does find in this collection a wealth of information unavailable elsewhere, sometimes even reprints of original historical documents. The two major works of historical scholarship in the West have actually used these publications to some extent.[32]

Although the *Materials* is a national project, it has some specificities in Tibet.[33] It was only launched in 1980 in the Tibet Autonomous Region, whereas other Tibetan areas of the PRC[34] had already published a few volumes in the 1960s. Until its ninth volume (1988), the collection was intended for (Party) internal circulation (Chin. *neibu*), after which the books were sold to the public.[35] In most Tibetan areas outside the TAR (autonomous prefectures and counties in Qinghai, Gansu, Sichuan and Yunnan provinces), the collection is published at provincial as well as at local levels, though apparently at irregular intervals. In TAR, however, most of the *Materials* are published at the regional-level PCC, while only a few are published sporadically in lower-level PCC offices. Moreover, all the *Materials* produced in the TAR have been first written and published in Tibetan, since the old generation was not so conversant in Chinese. They have then been translated into Chinese after two years or so. Yet, other Tibetan areas in the PRC produce materials directly in Chinese (then translated into Tibetan), or in Tibetan.

Within the *Materials*, autobiographical accounts are a small but significant part: 7 accounts amid the 28 volumes published in the TAR. These memoirs are of course not representative of mainstream Tibetan experiences. But this tiny former-elite-minority is a significant one, because among the privileges of the nobles was access to literacy and authority for speaking about Tibet as a whole, prerogatives that they have to some extent recovered since the end of radical Maoism.[36] All of these modern autobiographies were compulsory writings because their authors were holding honorary positions in the PCC. Nearly all of them hailed from the regional-level PCC, but one of them, the second autobiographer we will examine shortly (Lobsang Tenzin) was a member of the Lhasa city-level PCC. Both authors examined below were born in the early twentieth century (1914 and 1916), but have known very different life courses. They both composed their autobiographies themselves, and in the mid-1980s, but the first one was published in 1993, whereas the second one was published much later, in 2004. I was able to interview the second one but not the first one because of his high status – permissions being nearly impossible to secure unless one goes through Beijing offices and plans well ahead. Yet I did manage to interview people involved in editing his autobiography.

## Lhalu Tsewang Dorje: The autobiography of a high-profile politician

The first autobiography[37] is more formal and overtly political than the second one because of the high profile of the author. As Lhalu Tsewang Dorje (1914–2011)[38] was the most prominent Tibetan member (one of the vice-chairmen) of the PCC at the TAR level, his memoirs were certainly thought of as an important political document. His account is indeed the first autobiography published in the 16th volume of the Tibetan *Materials*. In the same manner as it did in other minority areas such as Inner Mongolia,[39] the PCC in Tibet was probably attempting to entice the most emblematic political figure of the conquered region to write a confessional narrative of his life and plead allegiance to the new government. The honour, or rather the assignment, befell Lhalu, although there were more likely prominent candidates such as the Panchen Lama (1938–1989) or Ngapö Ngawang Jigme (1910–2009),[40] head of the Tibetan delegation that signed the 17-point agreement with the PRC in 1951 and member of the national-level PCC in Beijing. The publication of Lhalu's autobiography was thus highly symbolic for the Chinese government and diplomatically sensitive for the author, who had to take a stance on a number of issues in which he was personally involved, such as the arrest of Regent Reting, for example. The manuscript was thus very cautiously crafted and carefully edited: about a fifth of the original manuscript has reportedly been taken out.

The text is first an important historical document. The author starts by retracing the history of the lineage of the Lhalu family, into which he married as an 'adopted husband'. Lady Lhalu, who was much older than him, had actually been his father's long-time mistress. The Lhalu family ranked into the highest of the four aristocratic strata after having produced two incarnations of the Dalai Lamas (the 8th and the 12th). The author goes on to evoke his father Lungshar, a major political protagonist of the early twentieth century, a minister and favourite of the 13th Dalai Lama (1875–1933). Lungshar and his wife were sent to England in 1913 to accompany four Tibetan teenagers gaining education in engineering and the sciences and, unofficially, to try and meet the king, offer him presents and evoke the political situation of Tibet. This covert mission does not seem to have yielded much result, as the couple hurriedly went back to Tibet in 1914. Lungshar's wife was pregnant, and they claimed to believe that if she gave birth in England, the boy would be blond, with blue eyes and a long nose, as a pretext for leaving Britain. They arrived in the Himalayas just in time for Tsewang Dorje's birth, in Darjeeling. Lungshar, his father, had been extremely impressed with London and the British political system. He urged the 13th Dalai Lama to make political and social reforms in Tibet, encountering strong opposition from the conservative monastic establishment. In 1934, just a few months after the death of the 13th Dalai Lama, Lungshar was accused of state treason and enucleated, an exceptional punishment that had not been implemented for several decades. He was demoted, his estate was confiscated and all of his descendants were banned from both inheriting a noble title and working for the government.

By all accounts, Lhalu proved to be, as was his father Lungshar, a very astute politician. He manoeuvred his way back into the circles of power by claiming that Lungshar was not his biological father, and by paying huge bribes. The Lhalu family into which he married was at that time the richest lay aristocratic estate owner in Tibet. He resumed official service in 1937 and climbed the ladder while serving in several positions, until becoming the governor-general of the Kham province in east Tibet (1947–1950). This was a critical appointment given the Chinese pressure mounting on Tibet's eastern frontiers. The Lhasa government was then employing Robert Ford, a British radio operator, to facilitate communication between the post in Kham and Lhasa, and who recalls his encounters with Lhalu in his own autobiography.[41] It is Ngapö who took over from Lhalu in Kham, surrendering to the People's Liberation Army in 1950. In March 1959, during the Lhasa uprising against Chinese rule, Lhalu was the commander-in-chief of the Tibetan army. He was captured, put in the Drapchi prison with all senior officials and subjected to struggle sessions as one of the wealthiest nobles of Tibet.[42] That was his second major downfall. He came out surprisingly early from prison, in August 1965, on the eve of the Cultural Revolution, and worked as a farmer for the next 12 years. During this period, a great number of former upper-class Tibetans died or barely survived in prison or labour camps. Again, he made his way back into favourable circles. He was reinstated in 1983 and his positions have been merely honorary, mostly in the TAR-level PCC and in the parliament. One of the interesting features of his autobiography, at least as it was put to me by a reader in Lhasa, is that it tells contemporary Tibetans of all the intrigues in which the aristocracy were engaged in order to maintain itself, pre- and post-1950s, and of all the strategies they developed in order to survive through difficult periods. While these provide in themselves remarkable details concerning the workings of the upper class, they also tally with the '*Materials*' [insistence on describing] internal conflicts, seen as a sign of the Tibetan governing classes' decadence.[43]

## A confessional narrative with a 'folkloristic' touch

The autobiography was well received by the general public, except by his former rival aristocratic peers, who contended the accuracy of some of the events described. All agree on its particularly elegant writing style. By all accounts, Lhalu wrote the manuscript himself and made the changes himself, after receiving suggestions from the editors at the PCC. Since he was the first prominent politician from Central Tibet to write his memoirs in the PRC, one wonders what could have been the specific scripts that framed his writing. He does not explicitly refer to a master narrative, but it is quite obvious from the tone and contents of the book that his account is in the line of neither the pre-modern Tibetan autobiographies, even those from lay ministers (which he was undoubtedly familiar with), nor of the modern historical chronicles,[44] nor of the oppositional autobiographies written by Tibetan exiles that may have found their way into Tibet.

One has to look at other influences, from within the PRC, that shaped his account. As Di Feng and Shao Dongfang state, there have only been three model narratives for all political autobiographies in the PRC, two of which referred to common class subjects newly empowered by the communist regimes.[45] For authors of Lhalu's rank the model narrative was predictably a product of the PCC (in Beijing), and none other than the autobiography of the uppermost deposed individual of pre-revolutionary China: *The First Half of My Life* (later translated as 'From emperor to citizen'), by Aisin-Gioro Pu Yi, the last emperor of the Qing dynasty.[46] Uradyn Bulag termed this narrative 'the greatest coup of China's oral history',[47] acknowledging the masterful recasting of the destiny of the last emperor into Marxist teleology. Informants in Lhasa confirmed that Lhalu was indeed very familiar with this narrative, which had been translated into Tibetan in the early 1960s. Until the 1970s, upper-class prisoners in the PRC spent a great deal of prison time studying this book and compiling, time and again, their own life story in the same self-critical vein, from age eight onwards.

It is thus probable that Lhalu was expected to produce a narrative demonstrating his successful thought-reform. In Marxist teleology, modernity is conceived as the triumph of the socialist society, consciously shaped by a mass of awakened, rational and liberated men – the collective good being reframed as the nation in China. It is the newly empowered working class that fashioned history, yet the disempowered elites were entitled to participate in the new history insofar as they not only upheld the ideological rift between tradition and modernity, but also (and paradoxically) constructed an imaginary continuity from past to present. They had to show how their demise was a necessary step to build modern China and how they could now contribute to the common good. In the same way, Lhalu's text had to somehow simultaneously oppose and relate past and present: Tibet without the Chinese and Tibet with the Chinese. He had to make history more legible, to make the current evolution of Tibet appear as both logical and necessary.

The master narrative of Pu Yi was explicitly used in Inner Mongolia. Prince De, the most powerful local prince, had told his life story to PCC editors in the 1960s. Modelled on Pu Yi's narrative frame, it came out as a book in 1984 under the title *Demchugdongrub in His Own Words*.[48] This is the period when Lhalu was writing his own memoirs, a period less radical than the ideological times of Pu Yi. The PCC probably intended to replicate this literary and historical coup in Tibet, but it hasn't been as successful as in Inner Mongolia. Lhalu's autobiography is not a story of national integration such as Prince De's. The political priorities in Lhasa in the mid-1980s, somewhat more relaxed in ideology, were rather geared towards the frenzied 'emergency rescue'[49] campaign to archive memory and tradition before their vanishing. The new political agenda, throughout the various government offices dealing with 'culture', was folkloristic, whether in the realm of arts and crafts, or in the realm of oral history. So, from this angle, the state's expectations that weighed on Lhalu's text were to display a rich and colourful past, but of course oriented by necessity, as with the 'confession' narrative, towards the modernist political project of the PRC. Lhalu's life story is indeed rife with interesting details about the daily life of the aristocracy. Tsering Yangdzom, in her study of Tibetan aristocratic families in the early twentieth century, makes ample use of Lhalu's autobiography to explain the system of residence names (pp. 145–147), the nobility's marriage patterns (pp. 172 *sqq.*) and wedding ceremonies (pp. 182–196), the education system and the youth (pp. 230–239) as well as New Year ceremonies (pp. 242–245).[50] In the same vein, Lhalu was also the subject of a 45-minute documentary movie,[51] where his life was exemplary of the particulars of the lives of the aristocracy and the changes undergone since the Revolution.

## Compliance and strategy: Management of the past and genealogy

Lhalu was expected to perform his loyalty to the state, and he did so to a large extent. The way he has rendered the major political events of Sino-Tibetan relations in which he took part, the interspersing of his text with assertions that Tibet is an integral part of the motherland and his gratefulness for the PRC government's kindness are all important commitments. Yet, a closer look at his text reveals that he falls short of the narrative that he 'could' have produced. He pleads allegiance to the state, but in a formulaic manner that is not organically woven into the text, and ultimately appears not to have been put into practice during his life course. His tale is definitely not a contrite socialist confession for the emancipation of

the poor classes, and his life path is not exemplary of national ethnic integration as was the case with Mongolian Prince De's account.
Thought-reform and reworking of oneself into a modern self serving
the PRC is non-existent. Moreover, instead of a unity of the nation
in the past and the present, the reader sees clearly in his account
the accretion of two mutually unintelligible temporalities: the Tibet
he knew before the 1950s and everything from then on. His way
of depicting the traditional life of the nobility seems unrevised. He
describes in great detail all his former estates and the way he collected taxes from his subjects, without a single line of political guilt.
His reference to religious values is carefully scant, but significant. The
reader discovers that, as the Chinese take over Tibet, three of his sons
are being recognised as incarnate lamas (Tib. *sprul-sku*), thereby mark-
ing a strong allegiance with the Buddhist establishment. Moreover, in
such a politically framed autobiography, he could have 'easily' made
disparaging remarks about the Dalai Lama and his former colleagues
who had fled to exile. As a cabinet minister and commander-in-chief
of the Tibetan army in 1959, he was supposed to be well aware of
the Dalai Lama's security. But was he actually informed of his escape?
Could it be that he was deliberately left behind, for some unclear
personal reasons?[52] His account is elegant: it shows only restraint
and respect, pointing instead to the young age of his children for
his decision to stay in Lhasa. He never went to visit Tibetans in
exile, probably because of his conspicuously high status at the PCC,
but his wife did visit Dharamsala and Tibetan settlements in South
India on at least two occasions. Navigating allegiances between both
sides of the Himalayas is a vexed question for an autobiographer in
his position, and his account shows a remarkable sense of political
astuteness.

As proposed by Martin Fromm, it is irrelevant to try and think
of the *Materials* collection (in its second wave, from the 1980s
onwards) in terms of domination by and resistance to the state.
These accounts of personal experience are co-constructions, with
on one side the state imperatives and far-reaching thought-control
exerted over decades, and on the other side subjective positionings
in multiple webs of social relations. What allows for flexibility and
subjectivity are, Fromm argues, the inherent contradictions in the
demands put by the PCC on the authors. The autobiographers 'creatively draw on the fissures of the post-Mao ideological terrain'.[53]

They need to weave their lives into three competing imperatives: the Party's revolutionary legacy, the market reforms and national integration. In the case of the Tibetan authors co-opted by the PCC, those contradictions were to balance being persecuted before 1978 with being celebrated and enlisted to support the government after 1978. This had to be done through the mobilisation of local histories – yet those local histories threatened to disrupt the Party's narrative for national integration. The compilation of folkloristic details therefore proved to be a viable avenue for Lhalu, to position himself in both the official 'raw materials' history project and his own personal history. This careful and strategic attitude is congruent with Patrick French's comment about Lhalu, whom he met briefly and by chance at a Lhasa hospital in 1999. He wasn't able to speak with him because Lhalu wanted to secure the approval of the PCC secretary to avoid any risks. But French met with a woman close to him, who told him that Lhalu 'was hoping the best for Tibet', and that his contribution to the PCC was an attempt 'to control the excesses of China'. 'Tibetan intellectuals in Lhasa draw a clear distinction between the likes of Phagphala, who was seen as a committed traitor, and Lhalu, whose treachery was believed to be conditional and pragmatic.'[54]

This careful navigation between compliance and strategy allowed Lhalu to convey his own points in making his memoirs available to the public eye. These transpire, to my sense, in the very title of the book: *The History of the Lhalu Family and a Brief Account of My Story*. Tibetans have a well-known penchant for genealogies, in the local or political domain (families) as well as in the religious realm (lineages). Genealogy, oral or written, is a powerful tool for legitimising order (social order at the village level, or among prominent families), legitimacy (in the case of religious lineages) and identity, both personal and collective.[55] Lhalu seems to have approached the state-imposed exercise of the autobiography with a traditional Tibetan spin: this book also allowed him to bequeath to his family an empowering genealogy, especially for one of his sons, now vice-chairman of the TAR, and his grandchildren who are successful businessmen. Patrick French also 'suspect[ed] that Lhalu ... was concerned primarily for his own family, hoping that the next generation would not be consumed by suffering and ideology, as his had been'.[56] Lhalu's narrative is thus hybrid. It is multi-layered, fulfils different functions and provides for different audiences at once.

## Lobsang Tenzin: A life spanning three different Tibetan regimes

The second autobiography is remarkable for a number of reasons. These reasons are the exceptional longevity (1916–present) and rich experience of the author; his relatively modest social background (he hailed from a commoner family of good status, unlike the aristocratic lineage of the autobiographers of the *Materials*); and, most strikingly, the fact that this narrative cuts across the Tibet/exile divide. Here is a man who has not only lived for many years on both sides of the Himalayas, but who moreover managed to publish his life story in 2004 simultaneously in Beijing and in Dharamsala.[57] This is the only political-literary occurrence of this kind that I am aware of. The existence of a second version in exile, unrevised and unedited, allows for a comparison with the book published in the *Materials*. This yields important insights into the editing processes at work in this collection. The version published in the PRC is actually quite 'daring', by Lhasa standards. Many Tibetan readers, upon seeing the content of the book, were incredulous that this book obtained official approval. The author describes in some detail life in exile and his frequent encounters with the Dalai Lama. In contrast, any mention of the exiled leader is taboo in public discourse in the PRC, and very strictly monitored in official publications. He further tells how he took monastic vows with the Dalai Lama, which implies a binding personal relationship with the hierarch.

'The bhiksu' (Tib. *dge-slong*) Lobsang Tenzin, as his name as an author appears on the cover, has had an extensive experience of, and engagement with, the administrative centres of three Tibetan worlds: pre-modern Tibet, early exile and post-Mao Tibet. He occupied middle-range official positions in Lhasa until 1959, in exile in Dharamsala and Delhi from 1959 to 1979, then again in Lhasa since 1980. Nowadays, Tibetans going back and forth across the border is not a rare phenomenon, but for Tibetan public figures of his generation, it was sensational. To my knowledge, he is the only one among these rare returnees to have written and published his memoirs in the PRC.[58]

Lobsang Tenzin was born on the auspicious occasion of the full moon of the Sa-ga month (on the 15th day of the 4th lunar month, commemorating the birth, enlightenment and *parinirvana* of the

Buddha) in 1916 in a village near Medrogungkar, some 40 miles east of Lhasa. His father worked as a clerk for the district officer, and his family, though a common family of tax-payers[59] attached to an aristocratic estate, was relatively well-off. He received a formal education in a private school in Lhasa, and entered government service as a low-ranking clerk at age of 17, while being bestowed as an adoptive husband in a good family of Lhasa. His whole career, from 1933 to 1959, was done within the Treasury Office, and he steadily climbed up the social ladder in his consecutive positions.

His first appointment was to be a carrier of the Dalai Lama's sedan chair. He was one of the palanquin carriers who brought the infant Dalai Lama from his native north-eastern province of Amdo (in today's Qinghai province) to be enthroned in Lhasa in 1939. This duty required extreme physical endurance, and he is retrospectively grateful for all those harsh years, that granted him physical and mental resistance and a healthy long life.

He was then appointed as grain collector in a district in south-western Tibet for some years. In 1954, he was part of the delegation that accompanied the Dalai Lama on his visit to mainland China. On the order of the Chinese authorities, he then taught for some time in a Lhasa middle school. He again travelled abroad in 1956, as he accompanied the Dalai Lama to India for the celebrations of the 2,500th *parinirvana* of the Buddha. His last appointment was that of chief tax collector in Tsona, in southern Tibet, which was a fairly important position in the pre-modern administration. He was in Tsona in March 1959 when he met the escaping Dalai Lama and his entourage rushing to India. He was requested to follow the court. He complied with some dismay, as he had to leave behind in Lhasa his wife and nine children, including his youngest girls, triplets who were barely two years old.

Upon arrival in India, he continued to work as a servant of the government (-in-exile), mainly coordinating the reception and organisation of the Tibetan refugees. As he was an accomplished musician and singer, he was appointed by the Dalai Lama to set up, as early as 1959, the institution that would later become the Tibetan Institute of Performing Arts (TIPA). He was one of the five founders of the TIPA and later headed the institution. In 1962, he surprised the whole Dharamsala community by taking the monastic vows of *bhiksu* with Yongzin Trijang Rinpoche, one of the two tutors of the

Dalai Lama. He later took the full ordination (more than 360 vows, which represents a huge commitment) with the Dalai Lama himself. As he owes full allegiance to his master, this is a worthwhile detail to keep in mind as we follow his tracks to Lhasa afterwards, and as he takes a stance on Tibetans in exile. Already when he was young in Tibet, he aspired to devote the last part of his life to the practice of religion and he had told his family about his plans. Throughout the later part of his autobiography, he lists the various teachings that he has received and how he practiced them. He then became Secretary of the Education Department and supervised schools established in the settlements. He went on to work at the All-India Radio in Delhi,[60] then, still in Delhi, at the Tibet Office for a few more years. At that point, at the request of the Education Department, he accepted to resume charge of the TIPA, which had by then nearly fallen in ruins.

This was in 1979, and the liberalisation policies had just started in Tibet. Two of his sons came over from Lhasa to meet him and pressed him to return back home to look after his nine children. In early 1980, he left Dharamsala without notice, went on pilgrimage to various sites in Nepal, crossed the border and reached Lhasa. In 1980, this was astounding. Actually, he was one of the earliest Tibetan returnees.[61] Moreover, he was not just any 'ordinary' exile Tibetan, but one with extensive knowledge about the culture and politics of exile, who had himself been involved in reshaping Tibetan customs in India. He writes that he originally wanted to stay for only six months, but that the authorities didn't allow him to go back and forth, so he settled in Lhasa. Because he was branded by the authorities as a 'patriotic Tibetan',[62] a returnee who had come back to the motherland, his move fed the strategies of propaganda. He was immediately looked after, and later co-opted, by the city-level PCC. He received a good government salary and engaged in the works and duties that were expected of him: to tell his story to journalists from Lhasa and Beijing, to do some research with his colleagues at the PCC, and to sit at various meetings and banquets.

His first years back in Tibet were difficult, as he met with rejection from both sides: those in Tibet couldn't understand why he had come back, and his former acquaintances in Dharamsala were infuriated, publishing pamphlets branding him as a 'Marxist *bhiksu*' or a traitor. He kept very much to himself and pursued his own agenda: the restoration of the meditation dwelling of Tsongkhapa in Chöding near the Sera monastery, the repairing of medicinal hot springs and the sponsoring of elementary schools. Nowadays, he lives with family members in Lhasa, meeting frequently with his nine children and many grandchildren, and practising religion continuously. Among those who read Tibetan books in the city, his autobiography has sold well and was favourably received.

## A cursory comparison between the two versions

The introduction of the Dharamsala version, absent in the Beijing version, states that he was urged repeatedly by various institutions linked to the United Front to write his life story, and he names the individuals who asked him to do it. He repeatedly tried to dodge the task, using the self-deprecating trope very common among traditional Tibetan autobiographers:[63]

> For an ordinary and crude person like me, who does not know anything, who does not possess an ounce of either innate or acquired knowledge, to write a *rnam-thar* story doesn't bring any benefit whatsoever. Suppose I wrote it, needless to say that the learnt ones, since I am an ordinary and crude person, would see it as nothing else than a cause for laughter (p. 2[64]).

One page below, he even calls himself a 'senile old man'. Yet, with the guarantee that he needn't be 'afraid nor suspicious, because there will be no corrections, suppressions, nor change of any sort' (p.3) to his text, he had no choice but to comply with his duty as a member of the PCC. He wrote his account entirely himself,[65] starting in 1983 and, after a series of back and forth with the editors at the PCC, he finished the manuscript on 6 July 1990 – which is, incidentally, the birthday of the Dalai Lama, an event that Tibetans particularly enjoyed celebrating publicly, but which has since been forbidden.

The manuscript was not deemed suitable for publication and didn't come out. After waiting for more than ten years, he sent a copy out to his relatives in India who published it in vanity press, so that the book would be out before he dies. Eventually, unbeknownst to him, the TAR-level PCC proceeded with the publication, sent it to Beijing for printing and in the end both books came out in 2004.

Broadly speaking, the two versions look similar, but there are notable differences, starting with a disparity in volume: 578 pages for the Dharamsala edition, 361 pages for the Beijing one. The layout and the size of the font are so different in both editions that the amount of cut material is difficult to assess. There do not appear to have been any additions made in the Beijing edition. It is most likely that both texts have stemmed from the same manuscript, but one was edited, whereas the exile version was published as received. The fact that whole passages were deleted from the Beijing version explains the considerably reduced size of the book. In order to get a sense of where the cuts were made, I compared both versions based on the time divisions of the Dharamsala edition. As is shown in Table 8.1 below, it is mostly in his account of life in India that the cuts have been made.

Both versions, however, convey a sense of straightforwardness, honesty, balance and dignity on the part of the author, for example when he is irked by Tibetan officials misconduct in both pre-modern Tibet and exile, but he treads much more cautiously when describing his experiences in Lhasa after 1980. A cursory glance reveals five most striking differences between the two versions. First, in the title itself: 'The Life of the *Bhiksu* Lobsang Tenzin' in the Indian version, versus 'The Story of Me, the *Bhiksu* Lobsang Tenzin, and Related Facts about Society' in the Beijing one. Second, the tables of

*Table 8.1*  Comparison of the content of the Dharamsala and Beijing editions

|  | DHARAMSALA (578 pages) (%) | BEIJING (361 pages) (%) |
| --- | --- | --- |
| 1) Childhood and teens (1916–1933) | 4.2 | 3.7 |
| 2) His work at the Treasury Office and other official positions in pre-modern Tibet (1933–1959) | 28.2 | 28.8 |
| 3) Period in India (1959–1980) | 40 | 32.5 |
| 4) Return to Tibet (1980–1990: autobiography ends in 1990) | 23 | 30.5 |
| 5) Appendices (previously published articles on holy places, market prices, etc.) | 4.6 | 4.5 |

contents are different: a mere thumbnail 11 lines in the Beijing version, with short titles that do not evoke precise time frames,[66] versus five detailed pages in the Dharamsala edition, with a division into five chronological periods, comprising sub-sections with long and precise titles. Third, the names of the institutions of both pre-modern Tibet and the exile government are, in the Beijing edition, changed to the names they bear in official PRC documents. For example, the pre-1959 Tibetan government becomes 'the local government',[67] the government-in-exile becomes 'the so-called "government-in-exile"', with quotation marks implying a denial of its legitimacy. Fourth, passages about the Dalai Lama and politics in exile, deemed unsuitable by the Lhasa editors, have predictably been removed, for instance accounts of the Dalai Lama's activities and speeches. The autobiographer sometimes quotes them extensively, as they were his everyday life as an officer in India. The removed passages also include allusions to political routines of exile institutions, such as declarations about the independence of Tibet, raising the national flag, singing the national anthem and speeches to school children about the 10 March uprising. Finally, the traditional reverential way of addressing the Dalai Lama and religious masters has been abridged to mere name citing, such as 'Taley Lama' (phonetic for Dalai Lama, never used by Tibetans but borrowed from Manchu by the Chinese), or more often 'Taley', which is felt like an insult by Tibetans. Likewise, his quotations of the public advice given by the Dalai Lama on special occasions have also been removed, but his descriptions of teachings received and practised have been kept as such.

## Compliance and strategy: Loyalty and genealogy

Lobsang Tenzin wrote his life account only to comply with the state's command, and he makes it clear how demanding the writing process was for him. In the colophon, for example, he insists on perseverance: 'While writing, it has been laborious to put together the story of an ignorant man like me, and it is devoid of any fundamental meaning. Nevertheless, because it was an order from the TAR authorities, because they urged me greatly, again and again, I made efforts and persevered...'[68] And a few lines down: 'I wrote it, being neither idle nor relaxed'. As he confided to me, the task was daunting and he had to engage in purificatory practices before setting himself to pen and paper. He had no documents to work from and had to rely on his memories alone – and they were still very crisp, as I could see in my interviews in 2005. For the seven years that writing lasted, he totally withdrew socially and wrote in reclusion. He went to visit holy places, and started each writing session with prayers and mantras to have a clear mind and sharpen his memory. The book would expose him to the gaze of several audiences at the same time, within and outside Tibet, and they all had different, maybe even opposing expectations.

Beyond the constraints, the author probably tried to get across his own points as well, as can be seen in his text. First, he portrays himself as a faithful government servant, showing commitment to his tasks for whichever administration he had to work for. This trope is in continuity with pre-modern autobiographies written by lay aristocratic officials.[69] Yet he is cautious to state time and again that he has never taken part in any counter-revolutionary activities and that he had no choice but to leave with the Dalai Lama to India. In several instances, his statements are congruent with PRC ideology, as when he assesses favourably the 'modern' situation of Tibet in the 1980s. His allegiance is again, as with Lhalu, very formulaic, and not organically woven into the text. At the same time, he repeatedly pleads the government to give him back his former house and heirloom, which was promised to him as a returnee who had not been a counter-revolutionary. It is reasonable to assume that a first strategic aim of the author is to perform an act of loyalty to the State, and a proof of his inoffensive behaviour, in order to regain access to his lost property, among other benefits – a strategy that has not been successful until now. A second important aspect concerns the relationship with his children. In the Dharamsala version, he expands profusely on his family history and on individual advice to each and every one of his nine children, according to their personality and their weaknesses. As with Lhalu, but at the level of his humbler origins, we see here again a wish to bequeath to his nine children a memory and a genealogy of their origins. The third point may actually be the most important: he gives extensive quotations of the speeches he made not only when he was a government employee in exile, but also when he was summoned to make public declarations upon his return to Lhasa. These are aimed at his former friends and acquaintances in Dharamsala: setting the record right about the exact nature of his activities as a 'patriotic Tibetan' gone back to the PRC. He probably wished to show that he had not forgotten his time in exile, nor the binding relationships that he had established there. And this is why he wanted the book to come out while he was still alive: to prove to the other side that he had not been a traitor in Tibet.

## Conclusion

Further ethnographic study in Lhasa would be useful to assess the impact of these texts on a readership of diverse ages and backgrounds, and see whether the multiple layers and reclaimings present in these texts are understood, or even approved, by Tibetan readers. In the limited scope of this presentation of autobiographies published in the *Materials* collection, I have tried to show that these life stories are performances rather than literary texts. They are public acts of personal allegiance to the government, a 'United Front strategy ... to win friends to the Party [and] to neutralize the enemies'.[70] Autobiography on duty produces reminiscences of a public past rather than a private past. Except for their childhoods and families, where authors show more warmth in their descriptions, one does not find in these writings many personal, emotional, let alone existential reflections. Expressing publicly these aspects of the self is considered largely shameful (Tib. *ngo-tsha*, 'hot face') among Tibetans.

These autobiographies are remarkable *tours de force* in that they try to balance the expectations of multiple readerships: the PCC who requested, edited and published the texts, the protagonists of the events described or Tibetans with similar experiences (who may disagree with the account), and the future generations of Tibetans who will judge the deeds of the author. *Double entendre*, in hidden references and targets in passing comments, is used by Lhalu, for example, but not so much by the more straightforward Lobsang Tenzin. These accounts are carefully crafted multi-layered narratives. It is unsure whether they succeeded in achieving the goals set for them by the PCC. Being rooted in memory, testimony and personal experience, they do not explicitly confront the social and political transformations in Tibet. They reconstruct at length a past Tibet where there was no Chinese (more than 80% of Lhalu's book), and thereby pinning their names and their experiences onto parts of their lives that they could control from a literary point of view.

Although the constraints weighing on this genre of political writing are always visible, the inherent contradictions in the imperatives put forth by the PCC committee allowed the authors to 'creatively draw on the fissures of the post-Mao ideological terrain' and strategise their compliance to this duty. The two accounts studied here have shown concerns for three similar agendas: presenting oneself as a good civil servant, pre-emptively defending oneself against possible accusations, and finally and maybe most importantly, establishing a family genealogy and offering a legacy to one's descendants. These three concerns are actually in line with the concerns of pre-modern Tibetan auto/biographers: the narratives tend to be apologetic, and work often as testaments, or genealogy.[71]

These two accounts were produced by an older generation of Tibetans: the first wave that was co-opted in the PCC. The folkloristic drive of experiential history in the 1980s allowed this older generation, whose foundational intellectual training was solely in Tibetan with virtually no Chinese, to share images of a world gone by, full of the 'strange' elements of the past. As Stevan Harrell and Li Yongxiang have shown for a somewhat younger generation of ethnic minority intellectuals among the Yi, the fact that they had been intellectually trained in Chinese allowed for this new 'sophisticated, bicultural minority elite'[72] to produce alternative regimes of historicity in minority areas. In Tibet, this generation has not yet produced accounts in the *Materials* collection. A new chapter will have to be written when this generation will have to strategise its compliance within official political narratives.

## Notes

1. This research was funded by a Belgian American Educational Foundation Scholarship and carried out at Harvard University, thanks to the warm welcome of Leonard van der Kuijp and Janet Gyatso. I am indebted to Tashi Tsering (Amnye Machen Institute, Dharamsala) for the treasured wealth of sources and insights shared over the course of this project.

2. The most extensive studies include Janet Gyatso's seminal book *Apparitions of the Self: The Secret Autobiographies of a Tibetan Visionary* (Princeton: Princeton University Press, 1998); Janet Gyatso, 'Autobiography in Tibetan religious Literature: Reflections on its Modes of Self-Presentation,' in Shōren Ihara and Zuihō Yamaguchi, eds., *Tibetan Studies, Proceedings of the 5th Seminar of the IATS, Narita 1989, Volume 2* (Naritasan Shinshoji: Monograph series of Naritasan Institute for

Buddhist Studies, 1992): 465–478; Kurtis Schaeffer, *Himalayan Hermitess: The Life of a Tibetan Buddhist Nun* (Oxford: Oxford University Press, 2004); Kurtis Schaeffer, 'Tibetan Biography: Growth and Criticism,' in Anne Chayet, Cristina Scherrer-Schaub, Françoise Robin and Jean-Luc Achard, eds., *Edition, Éditions: l'Écrit au Tibet, Évolution et Devenir* (Collectanea Himalayica 3) (München: Indus Verlag, 2010), 263–306.

3. These two terms are the most frequent and are associated most closely with the literary category of personal narratives. However, a variety of other terms appear in the titles of life writings, such as *rtogs-brjod* (lit. an account of what is fully grasped [from a Buddhist point of view], which translates the Sanskrit *avadāna*), *byung-ba brjod-pa* (lit. an account of what happened), *rang-tshul brjod-pa* (lit. an account of one's natural disposition), or *lo-rgyus* (chronicle). These taxonomies seem to refer to distinct literary categories, depending on the content of the account, but there is much overlap and it is thus difficult to isolate specific characteristics for each genre.

4. Schaeffer, 'Tibetan Biography,' 263.

5. Gyatso, *Apparitions of the Self*, 101, from a count that she made in 1989. It is likely that there are many more such writings, starting with shorter autobiographical accounts included in larger texts. Such embeddings are very frequent and not all of those large texts contain tables of contents. Producing an inventory of pre-modern autobiographies is thus rather difficult. Moreover, many autobiographies have probably been destroyed in the havoc of radical Maoism and so we will never know how many such writings were produced before the Chinese take-over. Schaeffer has found in the Tibetan Buddhist Resource Center database 1,225 known auto/biographies for the pre-modern period, but he does not specify how many of these are autobiographies; see 'Tibetan Biography,' 267.

6. There have been very few autobiographies written by lay people and these have been aristocrats who enjoyed a high level of education. A special mention should be made of the fourteenth-century *Situ's testament* (Tib. *Si-tu bka'-chems*), as studied by Leonard van der Kuijp, 'On the Life and Political Career of Ta'i-si-tu Byang-chub rgyal-mtshan (1302–1364?),' in Ernst Steinkellner, ed., *Tibetan History and Language. Studies Dedicated to Uray Géza on His Seventieth Birthday* (Vienna: Arbeitskreis für Tibetische und Buddhistische Studien Universtät Wien, 1991), 277–327. Situ was a monk with an aristocratic background, a head of state who wrote an account with secular motives. The earliest known lay autobiography has been studied by Lauran Hartley, in 'Self as Faithful Public Servant: The Autobiography of mDo-mkhar-ba Tshe-ring dbang-rgyal (1697–1763),' in Gray Tuttle, ed., *Mapping the Modern in Tibet, PIATS 2006: Proceedings of the Eleventh Seminar of the International Association for Tibetan Studies. Königswinter 2006* (Bonn: International Institute for Buddhist Studies, 2011): 45–72. rDo-ring bsTan-'dzin dpal-'byor's autobiography (Tib. *rDo-ring Pandita'i rnam-thar*), composed in 1806, comprehensively studied by Li Ruohong, *A Tibetan Aristocratic Family in the Eighteenth Century:*

A *Study of Qing-Tibetan Contact* (Ph.D., Harvard University, 2002). See also Elliot Sperling, 'Awe and Submission: A Tibetan Aristocrat at the Court of Qianlong,' *The International History Review* 20.2 (1998): 325–335. Sheldkar gling-pa's autobiography, *Telling the Account of my Life, a Means to Pass the Long Days of Spring* (Tib. *Rang-tshul brjod-pa'i gtam dpyid kyi nyiring phud thabs*), composed *ca.* 1912, seems to be the latest example of life writing by a lay minister in pre-modern times.

7. Schaeffer, 'Tibetan Biography,' 264.
8. In the case of accomplished tantric masters. See Gyatso, *Apparitions of the Self.*
9. Ibid., 105.
10. Leonard van der Kuijp, 'Tibetan Historiography,' in José Ignacio Cabezón and Roger R. Jackson, eds., *Tibetan Literature: Studies in Genre* (Ithaca: Snow Lion Publications, 1996), 40; Schaeffer, 'Tibetan Biography,' 263.
11. For a first survey and content analysis of 12 of those in English, see Laurie Hovell McMillin, *English in Tibet, Tibet in English: Self-presentation in Tibet and the Diaspora* (New York: Palgrave, 2001), 113–232.
12. A Chinese translation, intended for restricted circulation (Chin. *neibu*) but rapidly leaked among Tibetans, of John Avedon's *In Exile from the Land of Snows: The Definitive Account of the Dalai Lama and Tibet since the Chinese Conquest* (New York: Knopf, 1984).
13. *My Land and My People* (Tib. *Ngos yul dang ngos kyi mi-mang*) (Darjeeling: Freedom Press, 1963).
14. K. Dondhup, *The Water-bird and Other Years: A History of the Thirteenth Dalai Lama and After* (Delhi: Rangwang Publishers, 1986), 147–218.
15. Tib. *Nags-tshang zhi-lu'i skyid-sdug*, first privately printed in Xining, 2007, then published later that year at Blue Lake Publishing House in Xining. For a preliminary study of this autobiography and its reception among Tibetan readers, see Xenia de Heering, 'Les pratiques de lecture dans l'Amdo contemporain,' *Monde chinois* 31 (2012): 64–70.
16. As of summer 2012, the English translation is under review at Duke University Press.
17. See Ann Anagnost, *National Past-Times: Narrative, Representation and Power in Modern China* (Durham: Duke University Press, 1997); Charlene Makley, ' "Speaking Bitterness": Autobiography, History, and Mnemonic Politics on the Sino Tibetan frontier,' *Comparative Studies of Society and History* 47.1 (2005): 40–78. Between 1949 and 1966 alone, more than 500 such biographies were published in China, see Di Feng and Shao Dongfang, 'Life-writing in Mainland China (1949–1993): A General Survey and Bibliographic Essay,' *Biography* 17.1 (1994): 34.
18. Uradyn Bulag, 'Can the Subalterns Not Speak? On the Regime of Oral History in Socialist China,' *Inner Asia* 12 (2010): 95–111.
19. Muge Samten (1914–1993) and Tseten Shabdrung (1910–1985). See Nicole Willock, 'Rekindling the Ashes from the Dharma and the Formation of Modern Tibetan Studies: The Busy Life of Alak Tseten Zhabdrung,' *Latse Library Newsletter* 6 (2009–2010): 2–25.

20. Huang Zhengqing, *Huang Zhengqing Yu Wushi Jiamuyang* (Huang Zhengqing and the Fifth Jamyang Shepa) (Lanzhou: Gansu Minzu Chubanshe, 1989). Translated into Tibetan as A-pa A-blo, *A-blo spun-mched kyi rnam-thar* (Beijing: Nationalities Publishing House, 1994). Thanks to Charlene Makley for this reference, as well as for pointing out that the Chinese version was compiled from oral interviews of the author done by researchers of the *Materials* collection of the Gannan Tibetan Autonomous Prefecture (within Gansu province).

21. This means that the author compiled his life account spontaneously, prompted by neither the state nor disciples, as in the case of religious masters.

22. mKhas-grub, *The Flight of the Orphan: Autobiography of my Early Life* (Tib. *Tshe-stod kyi rang-rnam dva-phrug gi gshog-rtsal*) (Beijing: Nationalities Publishing House, 2003).

23. Chin. *wenshi ziliao xuanji*; Tib. *rig-gnas lo-rgyus dpyad-gzhi'i rgyu-cha bdams-sgrigs.*

24. Chin. *zheng(zhi) xie(shang)*; Tib. *chab(-srid) gros(-tshogs).*

25. Chin. *tongzhan bu*; Tib. *'thab-phyogs gcig 'gyur.*

26. On the *Materials* in the PRC and especially the autobiographies published in this collection, see Hu Chi-hsi, 'Une Mémoire Collective d'un Demi-siècle: La Collection des *Wenshi ziliao*,' *Études chinoises*, 4.1 (1985): 113–120; Martin Fromm, *Producing History through 'Wenshi Ziliao': Personal Memory, Post-Mao Ideology, and Migration to Manchuria* (Ph.D., Columbia University, 2010); Bulag, 'Can the Subalterns Not Speak?'

27. Fromm, *Producing History*, 5, n. 2. Tib. *mthong thos myong gsum.*

28. Fromm, *Producing History.*

29. Hu, 'Une Mémoire Collective,' 114.

30. Fromm evokes the editing processes of the collection in Manchuria and the specific relationship between the editor, the interviewer and the interviewee; see *Producing History*, 47–50.

31. dBang-'dus rDo-rje, *Bod kyi rig-gnas lo-rgyus rgyu-cha bdams-sgrigs 'don-thengs dang-po dang brgyad-pa'i nang khungs-med nor-'khrul mang-dag cig 'dug-gshis phyi-rabs blo-gsar rnams mgo-bo mi rmongs-pa'i ched dngos-byung nor-bcos gsal-bshad* (Because there were very many groundless inaccuracies in the 1st and 8th volumes of the *Selected Tibetan Materials On History and Culture*, I expound [here] the corrected reality, so that the youth in the next generation are not fooled) (Dharamsala: Department of Information and International Relations, 1989). I am grateful to Leonard van der Kuijp for having informed me about this document and shared his copy.

32. Melvyn Goldstein, *A History of Modern Tibet, 1913–1951: The Demise of the Lamaist State; A History of Modern Tibet, Volume 2: The Calm before the Storm, 1951–1955* (Berkeley: University of California Press, 1989, 2007); Tsering Shakya, *The Dragon in the Land of Snows: A History of Modern Tibet since 1947* (New York: Columbia University Press, 1999).

33. On the *Materials* in Tibet, see Gling-dbon Padma skal-bzang, 'Bod-rang skyong ljongs srid-gros nas bton-pa'i "Bod kyi lo-rguys rig-gnas dpyad-gzhi'i rgyu-cha bdams-bsgrigs" skor mdo-tsam gleng-ba,' (Short introduction on the 'Selected Tibetan Materials in History and Culture' of the Tibetan PCC) *Bod-ljongs zhib-'jug (Tibetan Studies) Anniversary volume 1965–2005* (2005): 108–114; Benno R. Weiner, 'Official Chinese Sources on Recent Tibetan History: Local Gazetteers, wenshi ziliao, and CCP Histories,' http://library.columbia.edu/content/dam/libraryweb/libraries/eastasian/Weiner_Local_Tibetan_Gazetteers.pdf (accessed 25 July 2012); and Alice Travers, 'La Fabrique de l'Histoire au Tibet Contemporain. Contours et Articulations d'une Mémoire Collective dans les *Matériaux pour l'Histoire et la Culture du Tibet*,' (paper presented to the Colloque Société Asiatique/Collège de France, 'Les matériaux de l'historien,' 29 May 2012).
34. See Weiner, *Official Chinese Sources*, 12–17, for a list of the *Materials* in Chinese in Qinghai province and Tibetan autonomous administrative units of Gansu, Sichuan and Yunnan.
35. Gling-dbon, 'Bod-rang skyong ljongs srid-gros nas bton-pa'i,' 110.
36. See Heidi Fjeld, *Commoners and Nobles: Hereditary Divisions in Tibet* (Copenhagen: NIAS Monographs, 2004).
37. lHa-klu Tshe-dbang rdo-rje, 'Dang-po/Yab-gzhis lHa-klu'i khyim-tshang gi lo-rgyus skor // gNyis-pa/Phran Tshe-dbang rdo-rje rang-nyid kyi byung-ba rangs-rim brjod-pa (Part 1: On the History of the Yabshi family Lhalu; Part 2: Account of my story, Tsewang Dorje), in *Bod rang-skyong ljongs srid-gros lo-rguys rig-gnas dpyad-gzhi'i rgyu-cha u-yon lhan-khang, Bod kyi lo-rguys rig-gnas dpyad-gzhi'i rgyu-cha bdams-bsgrigs, no. 7 (spyi'i 'don no. 16)* (Beijing: Mi-rigs dpe-skrun-khang, 1993).
38. For evocations of Lhalu in historical scholarship in English, see Goldstein, *A History of Modern Tibet*, 210 *sqq*; and Tsering Yangdzom, *The Aristocratic Families in Tibetan History, 1900–1951* (Beijing: Intercontinental Press, 2006), 18–24.
39. Bulag, 'Can the Subalterns Not Speak?' 107.
40. I heard during a field trip in Lhasa in 2005 that he had completed his autobiography, but it still awaits publication.
41. Robert Ford recalls Lhalu 'as typical of the more progressive Tibetan officials. They knew they were backward, and genuinely wanted to learn and to modernize their country – so long as no harm was done to their religion.... [H]e was keenly interested in the outside world and studied the pictures in [Ford's] illustrated magazines. He wanted to know about tractors and other agricultural machinery and about industrial processes in the West.' *Captured in Tibet* (Oxford: Oxford University Press, 1990 [1957]), 23.
42. The American communist journalist Anna Louise Strong was in Lhasa at the end of the 1950s and she personally witnessed Lhalu's struggle sessions. She recounted them in the 8th chapter, 'Lhalu's serfs accuse', of her book *When Serfs Stood up in Tibet* (Beijing: New World Press, 1960), 168–190.

43. Travers, 'La Fabrique de l'Histoire,' 10 (*my translation*).
44. For example, his former colleague Shakabpa's *Political History of Tibet*, which was published in the 1960s in India and was smuggled secretly into Tibet in the 1980s.
45. Chen Guangsheng, *Lei Feng (1940–1962): Chairman Mao's Good Soldier* (Beijing: Zhongguo Qingnian Chubanshe, 1963); Mu Qing, Feng Jiang and Zhou Yuan, *Jiao Yulu (1922–1964): A Model of County Party Secretary* (Beijing: Renmin Chubanshe, 1966). See Di and Shao, 'Life-writing in Mainland China,' 35.
46. Aisin-Gioro Pu Yi, *From Emperor to Citizen: The Autobiography of Aisin-Gioro Pu Yi*, tr. W.J.F. Jenner (Oxford: Oxford University Press, 1987 [First published in English: Foreign Languages Press, Beijing, 1964–1965]) [In Chinese: *Wo de qianbansheng* (Beijing: Chunzhong chubanshe, 1960)]. The text was actually ghost-written by Li Wenda.
47. Bulag, 'Can the subalterns Not speak?' 107.
48. Ibid.
49. Tib. *myur-skyobs* (Gling-dbon, 'Bod-rang skyong ljongs srid-gros nas bton-pa'i,' 109).
50. Tsering Yangdzom, *The Aristocratic Families*.
51. *Tibetan People – Former Tibetan Aristocrat Lhalu Cewang Doje* (Beijing, 2007), DVD.
52. One indeed wonders about the differential treatment, in exile, of Ngapö Ngawang Jigme's death in 2009 (which spurred many comments and even official eulogies) and Lhalu's death in 2011 (which did not inspire a single public comment).
53. Fromm, *Producing History*, 1.
54. Patrick French, *Tibet, Tibet: A Personal History of a Lost Land* (New York: Knopf, 2003), 202.
55. Gyatso, *Apparitions of the Self*, 117. My findings therefore differ from Laurie Hovell McMillin, who had concluded that 'Tibetan-ness constructed in these texts is closely associated with exile, with Buddhism and with nationalism'; see, *English in Tibet*, 122.
56. French, *Tibet, Tibet*, 202.
57. dGe-slong blo-bzang bstan-'dzin, *dGe-slong blo-bzang bstan-'dzin gyi mi-tshe gcig* (A life, that of Bhiksu Lobsang Tenzin) (Dharamsala: n.p., 2004); dGe-slong blo-bzang bstan-'dzin, *Phran dge-slong Blo-bzang bstan-'dzin rang-nyid kyi lo-rgyus dang 'brel-ba'i spyi-tshogs kyi don-dngos 'ga'-zhig* (The story of Bhiksu Lobsang Tenzin and a few related facts about society), in *Bod rang-skyong ljongs srid-gros lo-rguys rig-gnas dang mi-rigs chos-lugs 'khrim-lugs u-yon lhan-khang, Bod kyi lo rgyus rig gnas dpyad gzhi'i rgyu cha bdams bsgrigs, vol. 24* (Beijing: Mi rigs dpe skrun khang, 2004).
58. The other two returnees to have written memoirs are Alo Chönzay (A-lo chos-mdzad), *Bod kyi gnas-lugs bden-rdzun sgo phye-ba'i lde-mig* (The key that opens the door to the truth to the Tibetan situation) (privately distributed in Chatswood, Australia, 1983); the author went back to Tibet for two years, spent a few years in Beijing, then escaped to Australia;

and Tashi Tsering, *The Struggle for Modern Tibet: The Autobiography of Tashi Tsering* (Armonk: ME Sharpe, 1997).
59. Tib. *khral-pa*. Social category in pre-modern Tibet that indicates the status of a commoner but rather well-to-do family, whose links of bondage are not too constraining and who have some rights over the land they cultivate.
60. All Tibetans who lived in India in the 1970s vividly remember his voice, esp. when he read out the 'Prayer on remembering impermanence' (Tib. *Mi-rtag dran-bskul snying gi thur-ma*), by Pabongka Dechen Nyingpo (1868–1940). His style was apparently very striking.
61. According to the '100 Questions and Answers about Tibet' published on China Tibet Information Center's website, the total number of returnees who have settled in Tibetan areas of the PRC since 1979 (until the publication's release, approximately in 2002) is about 2,000; in contrast, the number of Tibetan 'compatriots' who have visited their relatives for a short period in the PRC and have then gone back to exile is estimated at 60,000: see http://www.tibetinfor.com/tibetzt/question_e/5/094.htm (accessed 25 July 2012).
62. Tib. *rgyal-gces mi-sna*.
63. Gyatso has elaborated on this trope in *Apparitions of the Self*, 102–114. Schaeffer has translated the opening lines of the fifth Dalai Lama's autobiography which carries the same self-deprecating ideas; see 'Tibetan Biography,' 273–274.
64. All the page numbers in the text refer to the Dharamsala version, unless otherwise specified.
65. Interview, Lhasa, 2005.
66. Such as 'Tasks to be accomplished in one year at the Treasury Office' or 'About the position of collecting grain in gTing-skyes' [place name].
67. Tib. *sa-gnas srid-gzhung*, translating the Chin. *dangdi zhengfu*. For the Tibetans, their government was not 'local', since it was not conceived as being at the periphery of another government.
68. Dharamsala version, 577; Beijing version, 360.
69. Hartley, 'Self as Faithful Public Servant,' 57.
70. Bulag, 'Can the Subalterns Not Speak?' 106.
71. van der Kuijp, 'On the Life and Political Career of Ta'i-si-tu,' 278; Schaeffer, 'Tibetan Biography,' 266; Hartley, 'Self as Faithful Public Servant,' 58.
72. Stevan Harrell and Li Yongxiang, 'The History of the History of the Yi, part II,' *Modern China* 29.3 (2003): 364.

# Bibliography

Aisin-Gioro Pu Yi. *From Emperor to Citizen: The Autobiography of Aisin-Gioro Pu Yi*, translated by W.J.F. Jenner. Oxford: Oxford University Press, 1987.

Alo Chönzay (A-lo chos-mdzad). *Bod kyi gnas-lugs bden-rdzun sgo phye-ba'i lde-mig* (The Key that Opens the Door to the Truth to the Tibetan Situation). Privately distributed in Chatswood, Australia, 1983.

Anagnost, Ann. *National Past-Times: Narrative, Representation and Power in Modern China*. Durham: Duke University Press, 1997.

Apter, David E. and Tony Saich. *Revolutionary Discourse in Mao's Republic*. Cambridge and London: Harvard University Press, 1994.

Arnold, David and Stuart Blackburn, eds. *Telling Lives in India: Biography, Autobiography and Life History*. Bloomington: Indiana University Press, 2004.

Avedon, John. *In Exile from the Land of Snows: The Definitive Account of the Dalai Lama and Tibet since the Chinese Conquest*. New York: Knopf, 1984.

Ayers, William. "Current Biography in Communist China." *Journal of Asian Studies* 21.4 (1962): 477–485.

Bai Jianwu. *Riji* (Diary). Nanjing: Jiangsu guji chubanshe.

Barlow, Tani E., ed. *Gender Politics in Modern China: Writing and Feminism*. Durham: Duke University, 1993.

———. *The Question of Women in Chinese Feminism*. Durham and London: Duke University Press, 2004.

Bauer, Wolfgang. *Das Antlitz Chinas: die Autobiographische Selbstdarstellung in der Chinesischen Literatur von ihren Anfängen bis heute* (The Face of China: autobiographical self-representation from its origins to the present). Munich: Carl Hanser Verlag, 1990.

———. "Time and Timelessness in Premodern Chinese Autobiography." In *Ad Seres et Tungusos: Festschrift für Martin Grimm zu seinem 65. Geburtstag am 25. Mai 1995*, edited by Lutz Bieg, Erling von Mende, and Martina Siebert, 19–31. Wiesbaden: Harrassowitz, 2000.

Birch, Cyril. *Scenes for Mandarins: The Elite Theater of the Ming*. New York: Columbia University Press, 1995.

Boorman, Howard L. and Richard C. Howard, eds. *Biographical Dictionary of Republican China*. New York: Columbia University Press, 1967.

Bossler, Beverly J. *Powerful Relations: Kinship, Status, and the State in Sung China (960–1279)*. Cambridge: Harvard University Press, 1998.

Braester, Yomi. *Witness Against History*. Stanford: Stanford University Press, 2003.

Brook, Timothy. *The Confusions of Pleasure: Commerce and Culture in Ming China*. Berkeley: University of California Press, 1998.

———. "Capitalism and the Writing of Modern History in China." In *China and Historical Capitalism: Genealogies of Sinological Knowledge*, edited by Timothy

Brook and Gregory Blue, 110–157. Cambridge: Cambridge University Press, 1999.

Brownell, Susan. *Training the Body for China: Sports in the Moral Order of the People's Republic.* London: University of Chicago Press, 1995.

Bulag, Uradyn. "Models and Moralities: The Parable of the Two 'Heroic Little Sisters of the Grassland'." *China Journal* 42 (1999): 21–41.

———. "Can the Subalterns Not Speak? On the Regime of Oral History in Socialist China." *Inner Asia* 12 (2010): 95–111.

Campbell, Duncan. *Kuang Lu's Customs of the South: Loyalty on the Borders of Empire.* Wellington: Victoria University of Wellington, 1998.

Cao Lüji. "Shou Ruan Zhuweng nianbo (qi san) (For the birthday of "uncle" Ruan Zhuweng, no.3)," *Bowang shanren gao* (Manuscript by the mountain man of Bowang). In *Siku quanshu cunmu congshu* vol.185, edited by *Siku quanshu cunmu congshu* biancuan weiyuanhui. Jinan: Qilu shushe, 1995–1997.

Carlitz, Katherine. "Shrines, Governing-Class Identity, and the Cult of Widow Fidelity in Mid-Ming Jiangnan." *Journal of Asian Studies* 56.3 (1997): 612–640.

———. "Lovers, Talkers, Monsters, and Good Women: Competing Images in Mid-Ming Epitaphs and Fiction." In *Beyond Exemplar Tales: Women's Biography in Chinese History*, edited by Joan Judge and Hu Ying, 175–192. Berkeley: University of California Press, 2011.

Casebeer, William D. "Moral Cognition and Its Neural Constituents." *Nature Reviews. Neuroscience* 4.10 (2003): 840–47.

Chang, Jung. *Wild Swans.* London: Harper Press, 2012.

Chang, Kang-i Sun and Haun Saussy, eds. *Women Writers of Traditional China: An Anthology of Poetry and Criticism.* Stanford: Stanford University Press, 1999.

Chaves, Jonathan, tr. and intr. *Pilgrim of the Clouds: Poems and Essays by Yüan Hung-tao and His Brothers.* New York and Tokyo: Weatherhill, 1978.

Chen Baichen. *Xiankou riji* (Keeping-mouth-shut diaries, 1966–1972, 1974–1979). Zhengzhou: Daxiang chubanshe, 2005.

Chen Guangsheng. *Lei Feng (1940–1962): Chairman Mao's Good Soldier.* Beijing: Zhongguo Qingnian Chubanshe, 1963.

Chen Jiru. "Hanfeng Ruan Zhongcheng waizhuan" (Unofficial biography of Minister Ruan Hanfeng). *Chen Meigong xiansheng quanji* (Complete works of Chen Meigong), Ming edn. Shanghai Library, 38.12a–38.19b.

Chen Shaotang. *Wan Ming xiaopin lunxi* (Discussion and analysis of late Ming "xiaopin"). Hong Kong: Bowen shuju, 1980.

Chen, Tina Mai. "Proletarian White and Working Bodies in Mao's China." *positions: asia critique* 11.2 (2003): 361–393.

———. "Internationalism and Cultural Experience: Soviet Films and Popular Chinese Understandings of the Future in the 1950s." *Cultural Critique* 58 (2004): 82–114.

Chen Yan. *Chen Yan: erbian de shijie* (Chen Yan: A world of sound). Yinchuan: Ningxia chubanshe, 2004.

"'Chen Yan: erbian de shijie' zizhuan zai Jing qianshou" ("Chen Yan: a world of sound" autobiography signing in Beijing). http://www. 00544.com.webdump.org/2004/jiejueshalong/409080001.htm (accessed 25 July 2013).

"Chen Yan gangqin diaolü" (Chen Yan piano tuning). http://www.bjpiano. com (accessed 9 November, 2007).

Ch'en Shih-hsiang. "An Innovation in Chinese Biographical Writing." *Far Eastern Quarterly* 13.1 (1953): 44–62.

Cheng, Nien. *Life and Death in Shanghai*. London: Grafton, 1986.

Chia, Lucille. *Printing for Profit: The Commercial Publishers of Jianyang, Fujian (11th-17th Centuries)*. Cambridge: Harvard University Press, 2002.

China Internet Network Information Center. *[29th] Statistical Report on Internet Development in China*, 2012. http://www.apira.org (accessed 28 August, 2012).

China Tibet Information Center. "100 Questions and Answers about Tibet." http://www.tibetinfor.com/tibetzt/question_e/5/094.htm (accessed 25 July 2012).

Chiu-Duke, Josephine. "Mothers and the Well-being of the State in Tang China." *Nan Nü: Men, Women and Gender in China* 8.1 (2006): 55–114.

Chou Chih-p'ing. *Yüan Hung-tao and the Kung-an School*. Cambridge: Cambridge University Press, 1988.

Chow, Kai-wing. *Publishing, Culture, and Power in Early Modern China*. Stanford: Stanford University Press, 2004.

Chua, Emily Huiching. "The Good Book and the Good Life: Best-selling Biographies in China's Economic Reform." *China Quarterly* 198 (2009): 364–380.

Coble, Parks M. *Facing Japan: Chinese Politics and Japanese Imperialism, 1931–1937*. Cambridge: Council on East Asian Studies, Harvard University, 1991.

Cohen, Paul. *Speaking to History: The Story of King Goujian in Twentieth-Century China*. Berkeley: University of California Press, 2009.

Couser, G. Thomas. *Recovering Bodies: Illness, Disability and Life Writing*. Madison: University of Wisconsin Press, 1997.

——. "Introduction – The Empire of the 'Normal': A Forum on Disability and Self-representation." *American Quarterly* 52.2 (2000): 305–310.

——. *Memoir: An Introduction*. Oxford: Oxford University Press, 2011.

"CPC Calls for Learning from Zhang Haidi." *China Report: Political, Sociological and Military Affairs* 429, June 10, 1983.

Crawford, Robert. "The Biography of Juan Ta-ch'eng." *Chinese Culture* 6.2 (1965): 28–105.

Cui Xianghua. "Cong tongyangxi dao nü jiangjun" (From child bride to woman general). In *Zhongguo nü jiangjun* (Chinese women generals), edited by Cui Xianghua et al., 1–36. Beijing: Jiefangjun wenyi chubanshe, 1995.

Dalai Lama. *My Land and My People* (Tib. *Ngos yul dang ngos kyi mi-mang*). Darjeeling: Freedom Press, 1963.

Dauncey, Sarah. "Screening Disability in the PRC: the Politics of Looking Good." *China Information* 21.3 (2007): 481–506.

——. "*Three Days to Walk*: A Personal Story of Life Writing and Disability Consciousness in China." *Disability & Society* 27.3 (2012): 311–323.

dBang-'dus rDo-rje. *Bod kyi rig-gnas lo-rgyus rgyu-cha bdams-sgrigs 'don-thengs dang-po dang brgyad-pa'i nang khungs-med nor-'khrul mang-dag cig 'dug-gshis phyi-rabs blo-gsar rnams mgo-bo mi rmongs-pa'i ched dngos-byung nor-bcos gsal-bshad* (Because There Were Very Many Groundless Inaccuracies in the 1st and 8th Volumes of the *Selected Tibetan Materials on History and Culture*, I Expound [here] the Corrected Reality, so that the Youth in the Next Generation Are Not Fooled). Dharamsala: Department of Information and International Relations, 1989.

de Bary, William T. and Irene Bloom, eds. *Sources of Chinese Tradition*, vol. 1. New York: Columbia University Press, 2000.

de Heering, Xenia. "Les pratiques de lecture dans l'Amdo contemporain." *Monde chinois* 31 (2012): 64–70.

de Welles, Theodore. "Sex and Sexual Attitudes in Seventeenth-Century England: The Evidence from Puritan Diaries." *Renaissance and Reformation* 24.1 (1988): 45–64.

dGe-slong blo-bzang bstan-'dzin. *dGe-slong blo-bzang bstan-'dzin gyi mi-tshe gcig* (A Life, that of Bhiksu Lobsang Tenzin). Dharamsala: n.p., 2004.

dGe-slong blo-bzang bstan-'dzin. *Phran dge-slong Blo-bzang bstan-'dzin rang-nyid kyi lo-rgyus dang 'brel-ba'i spyi-tshogs kyi don-dngos 'ga'-zhig* (The story of Bhiksu Lobsang Tenzin and a few related facts about society). In *Bod rang-skyong ljongs srid-gros lo-rguys rig-gnas dang mi-rigs chos-lugs 'khrim-lugs u-yon lhan-khang, Bod kyi lo rgyus rig gnas dpyad gzhi'i rgyu cha bdams bsgrigs, Vol. 24*. Beijing: Mi rigs dpe skrun khang, 2004.

Demiéville, Paul. "Hou Che. Tchang Che-tschai sien cheng nien p'ou." *Bulletin de l'École française d'Extrême Orient* 23 (1924): 478–489.

——. "Chang Hsüeh-ch'eng and his Historiography." In *Historians of China and Japan*, edited by W.G. Beasley and E.G. Pulleyblank, 167–185. London: Oxford University Press, 1961.

Di Feng and Shao Dongfang. "Life-writing in Mainland China (1949–1993): A General Survey and Bibliographic Essay." *Biography* 17.1 (1994): 32–55.

Diamant, Neil J. *Embattled Glory: Veterans, Military Families, and the Politics of Patriotism in China, 1949–2007*. Lanham: Rowman and Littlefield, 2009

Ding Chen, ed. *Qinli Zhongguo Gongchandang de 90 nian* (Personal Experiences of 90 Years of the Communist Party of China). Beijing: Renmin chubanshe, 2011.

Dolezelova-Velingerova, Milena and Lubomir Dolezel. "An Early Chinese Confessional Prose: Shen Fu's *Six Chapters from a Floating Life*." *T'oung Pao* 58.1/5 (1972): 137–160.

Dondhup, K. *The Water-bird and Other Years: A History of the Thirteenth Dalai Lama and After*. Delhi: Rangwang Publishers, 1986.

Dooling, Amy D. and Kristina M. Torgeson. *Writing Women in Modern China: An Anthology of Women's Literature from the Early Twentieth Century*. New York: Columbia University Press, 1998.

Dryburgh, Marjorie. "Rewriting Collaboration: China, Japan and the Self in the Diaries of Bai Jianwu." *Journal of Asian Studies* 68.3 (2009): 689–714.

Duara, Prasenjit. *Rescuing History from the Nation.* Chicago: University of Chicago Press, 1995.

Durrant, Stephen. "Self as the Intersection of Traditions: The Autobiographical Writings of Ssu-ma Ch'ien." *Journal of the American Oriental Society* 106.1 (1986): 33–40.

Eakin, Paul John. *How Our Lives Become Stories: Making Selves.* Ithaca: Cornell University Press, 1999.

——. "Autobiography, Identity and the Fictions of Memory." In *Memory, Brain and Belief,* edited by Daniel Schacter and Elaine Scarry, 290–306. Cambridge: Harvard University Press, 2000.

——. *Living Autobiographically: How We Create Identity in Narrative.* Ithaca: Cornell University Press, 2011.

Eber, Irene. "Hu Shih and Chinese History: The Problem of *Cheng-li Kuo-ku.*" *Monumenta Serica* 27 (1968): 169–208.

Ebrey, Patricia, ed. *Chinese Civilisation: A Sourcebook,* 2nd ed. New York: Free Press, 1993.

——. "Empress Xiang (1046–1101) and Biographical Sources beyond Formal Biographies." In *Beyond Exemplar Tales: Women's Biography in Chinese History,* edited by Joan Judge and Hu Ying, 193–211. Berkeley: University of California Press, 2011.

Egan, Susan Chan. *A Latterday Confucian: Reminiscences of William Hung (1893–1980).* Cambridge: Council on East Asian Studies, Harvard University, 1987.

Einwalter, Dawn. "Selflessness and Self-interest: Public Morality and the Xu Honggang Campaign." *Journal of Contemporary China* 7.18 (1998): 257–269.

Elman, Benjamin A. *From Philosophy to Philology: Intellectual and Social Aspects of Change in Late Imperial China.* Cambridge: Council on East Asian Studies, Harvard University, 1984.

——. "Political, Social, and Cultural Reproduction via Civil Service Examinations in Late Imperial China." *Journal of Asian Studies* 50.1 (1991): 7–28.

Elvin, Mark. "Female Virtue and the State in China." *Past and Present* 104 (1984): 111–152.

Esherick, Joseph. *Ancestral Leaves: A Family Journey through Chinese History.* Berkeley: University of California Press, 2011.

Feng Jicai. *Ten Years of Madness: Oral Histories of China's Cultural Revolution.* San Francisco: China Books and Periodicals, 1996.

Field, Jesse. "Taking Intimate Publics to China: Yang Jiang and the Unfinished Business of Sentiment." *Biography* 34.1 (2011): 83–95.

Fjeld, Heidi. *Commoners and Nobles: Hereditary Divisions in Tibet.* Copenhagen: NIAS Monographs, 2004.

Fludernik, Monika. "Time in Narrative." In *Routledge Encyclopedia of Narrative Theory,* edited by David Herman, Manfred Jahn and Marie-Laure Ryan, 608–612. London and New York: Routledge, 2005.

Ford, Robert W. *Captured in Tibet*. Oxford: Oxford University Press, 1990 [1957].

Fogel, Joshua. "On the 'Rediscovery' of the Chinese Past: Cui Shu and Related Cases." In *The Cultural Dimension of Sino-Japanese Relations: Essays on the Nineteenth and Twentieth Centuries*, edited by Joshua Fogel, 3–21. Armonk: M.E. Sharpe, 1995.

Fong, Grace. "Inscribing a Sense of Self in Mother's Family: Hong Liangji's (1764–1809) Memoir and Poetry of Remembrance." *Chinese Literature: Essays, Articles, Reviews* 27 (2005): 33–58.

Foxe, John. *The Unabridged Acts and Monuments Online* (HRI Online Publications, Sheffield, 2011). http://www.johnfoxe.org/ (accessed 28 July, 2011).

Frank, Arthur W. *The Wounded Storyteller: Body, Illness, and Ethics*. Chicago: University of Chicago, 1997.

French, Patrick. *Tibet, Tibet: A Personal History of a Lost Land*. New York: Knopf, 2003.

Fromm, Martin. *Producing History through 'Wenshi Ziliao': Personal Memory, Post-Mao Ideology, and Migration to Manchuria*. Ph.D., Columbia University, 2010.

Gergen, Kenneth J. and Mary M. Gergen. "Narratives of the Self." In *Memory, Identity, Community: The Idea of Narrative in the Human Sciences*, edited by Lewis P. Hinchman and Sandra K. Hinchman, 161–184. Albany: State University of New York Press, 1997.

Gling-dbon Padma skal-bzang. "Bod-rang skyong ljongs srid-gros nas bton-pa'i «Bod kyi lo-rguys rig-gnas dpyad-gzhi'i rgyu-cha bdams-bsgrigs» skor mdo-tsam gleng-ba" (Short Introduction on the "Selected Tibetan Materials in History and Culture" of the Tibetan PCC). *Bod-ljongs zhib-'jug* (*Tibetan Studies*), Anniversary volume 1965–2005 (2005): 108–114.

Goldstein, Melvyn. *A History of Modern Tibet, 1913–1951: The Demise of the Lamaist State*. Berkeley: University of California Press, 1989.

——. *A History of Modern Tibet, Volume 2: The Calm before the Storm, 1951–1955*. Berkeley: University of California Press, 2007.

Golley, Nawar Al-Hassan, ed. *Arab Women's Lives Retold: Exploring Identity through Writing*. Syracuse: Syracuse University Press, 2007.

Goodman, Bryna. "The New Woman Commits Suicide: The Press, Cultural Memory, and the New Republic." *Journal of Asian Studies* 64.1 (2005): 67–102.

Goodrich, L Carrington. *The Literary Inquisition of Ch'ien-lung*. New York: Paragon, 1966.

Grant, Beata. *Eminent Nuns: Women Chan Masters of Seventeenth-century China*. Honolulu: University of Hawaii Press, 2009.

Greenbaum, Jamie. *Chen Jiru (1558–1639): The Background to, Development and Subsequent Uses of Literary Personae*. Leiden: Brill, 2007.

Greenblatt, Stephen. *Renaissance Self-fashioning: From More to Shakespeare*. Chicago: University of Chicago Press, 1980.

Gu Jiegang. *The Autobiography of a Chinese Historian*, translated by Arthur Hummel. Leiden: Brill, 1931.

Guo Jiulin. "Zhongguo zhuanji wenxue fazhan gailun" (Introduction to the Development of Chinese Biography. *Wenyi baijia* (Arts Forum) 7 (2010): 101–107.

Guo Moruo. *Guanzi jijiao* (Collected annnotations to the "Guanzi"). Beijing: Kexue chubanshe, 1955.

Gusdorf, Georges. "Conditions and Limits of Autobiography." In *Autobiography: Essays Theoretical and Critical*, edited by James Olney. Princeton: Princeton University Press, 1980.

Guy, R. Kent. *The Emperor's Four Treasuries: Scholars and State in the Late Ch'ienlung Era*. Cambridge: Harvard University Asia Center, 1987.

Gyatso, Janet, "Autobiography in Tibetan Religious Literature: Reflections on Its Modes of Self-Presentation." In *Tibetan Studies, Proceedings of the 5th Seminar of the IATS, Narita 1989, Volume 2*, edited by Shōren Ihara and Zuihō Yamaguchi, 465–478. Naritasan Shinshoji: Monograph series of Naritasan Institute for Buddhist Studies: 1992.

———. *Apparitions of the Self: The Secret Autobiographies of a Tibetan Visionary.* Princeton: Princeton University Press, 1998.

"Haidi de BLOG" (Haidi's Blog). http://blog.sina.com.cn/haidi (accessed 18 February, 2008).

Hamilton, Nigel. *Biography: A Brief History*. Cambridge: Harvard University Press, 2007.

Han Wo. *Kai he ji* (Record of opening up the waterway). In *Jingming keben Gujin yishi* (Ancient and modern unofficial histories, facsimile edition) vol.35, edited by Wu Guan. Shanghai: Shangwu yinshuguan, 1937.

Hardie, Alison. "Conflicting Discourse and the Discourse of Conflict: Eremitism and the Pastoral in the Poetry of Ruan Dacheng (c.1587–1646)." In *Reading China: Fiction, History and the Dynamics of Discourse. Essays in Honour of Professor Glen Dudbridge*, edited by Daria Berg, 111–146. Leiden: Brill, 2007.

Hardy, Grant. *Worlds of Bronze and Bamboo: Sima Qian's Conquest of History.* New York: Columbia University Press, 1999.

Harrell, Stevan and Li Yongxiang. "The History of the History of the Yi, part II." *Modern China* 29.3 (2003): 362–396.

Harrison, Henrietta. *The Man Awakened from Dreams: One Man's Life in a North China Village, 1857–1942*. Stanford: Stanford University Press.

Hartley, Lauran. "Self as a Faithful Public Servant: The Autobiography of Mdo mkhar ba Tshe ring dbang rgyal (1697–1763)." In *Mapping the Modern in Tibet. PIATS 2006: Proceedings of the Eleventh Seminar of the International Association for Tibetan Studies. Königswinter 2006*, edited by Gray Tuttle, 45–72. International Institute for Buddhist Studies, Bonn, 2011.

Hawkins, Anne Hunsaker. *Reconstructing Illness: Studies in Pathography*. West Lafayette: Purdine University Press, 1993.

He, Jiangsui. "Death of a Landlord: Moral Predicament in Rural China, 1968–1969." In *The Chinese Cultural Revolution as History*, edited by Joseph W. Esherick, Paul G. Pickowicz and Andrew G. Walder, 124–152. Stanford: Stanford University Press, 2006.

He Liyi. *Mr China's Son: A Villager's Life*. Boulder: Westview Press, 1993.

Hershatter, Gail. "The Gender of Memory: Rural Chinese Women and the 1950s." *Signs: Journal of Women in Culture and Society* 28.1 (2002): 43–70.

———. "Forget Remembering: Rural Women's Narratives of China's Collective Past." In *Re-envisioning the Chinese Revolution: The Politics and Poetics of Collective Memory in Reform China*, edited by Ching Kwan Lee and Guobin Yang, 69–92. Stanford: Stanford University Press, 2007.

———. "Getting a Life: The Production of 1950s Women Labor Models in Rural Shaanxi." In *Beyond Exemplar Tales: Women's Biography in Chinese History*, edited by Joan Judge and Hu Ying, 36–54. Berkeley: University of California Press, 2011.

Hevey, David. *Creatures Time Forgot: Photography and Disability Imagery*. New York: Routledge, 1992.

Hinsch, Bret. "The Textual History of Liu Xiang's *Lienüzhuan*." *Monumenta Serica* 52 (2004): 95–112.

———. "Review Article: The Genre of Women's Biographies in Imperial China." *Nan Nü: Men, Women and Gender in China* 11.1 (2009): 102–123.

Ho, Clara. *Overt and Covert Treasures: Essays on the Sources for Chinese Women's History*. Hong Kong: Chinese University Press, 2012.

Holzman, Donald. *Poetry and Politics: The Life and Works of Juan Chi, AD 210–263*. Cambridge: Cambridge University Press, 1976.

Hovell McMillin, Laurie. *English in Tibet, Tibet in English: Self-presentation in Tibet and the Diaspora*. New York: Palgrave, 2001.

Howard, Richard C. "Modern Chinese Biographical Writing." *Journal of Asian Studies* 21.4 (1962): 465–475.

Hsü Kai-yu. *Wen I-to*. Boston: Twayne Publishers, 1980.

Hu Chi-hsi. "Une Mémoire Collective d'un Demi-siècle: la Collection des *Wenshi ziliao*." *Études chinoises* 4.1 (1985): 113–120.

Hu Jinwang. *Rensheng xiju yu xiju rensheng: Ruan Dacheng yanjiu* (The comedy of life and a life in comedy: a study of Ruan Dacheng). Beijing: Zhongguo shehui kexue chubanshe, 2004.

Hu Shi. *Hu Shi wencun* (Preserved writings). Taipei: Yuandong tushu gongsi, 1953.

———. *Hu Shi yanjiang lu* (The lectures of Hu Shi). Shijiazhuang: Hebei renmin chubanshe, 1999.

Hu Wenkai. *Lidai funü zhuzuo kao* (Research on Chinese women's writings through the ages). Shanghai: Guji chubanshe, 1985.

Hu Ying. *Tales of Translation: Composing the New Woman in China, 1899–1918*. Stanford: Stanford University Press, 2000.

———. "Naming the First 'New Woman'." In *Rethinking the 1898 Reform Period: Political and Cultural Change in Late Qing China*, edited by Rebecca Karl and Peter Zarrow, 180–211. Cambridge: Harvard University Asia Center, 2002.

Huang, Martin. *Literati and Self-re/presentation: Autobiographical Sensibility in the Eighteenth-century China Novel*. Stanford: Stanford University Press, 1995.

Huang, Philip C.C. "Rural Class Struggle in the Chinese Revolution: Representational and Objective Realities from the Land Reform to the Cultural Revolution." *Modern China* 21.1 (1995): 105–143.

Huang Shang. "Guanyu Zhang Zongzi" (On Zhang Zongzi). In *Haoshou xueshu suibi: Huang Shang juan* (Essays by senior scholars: Huang Shang). Beijing: Zhonghua shuju, 2006.

Huang Zhengqing. *Huang Zhengqing yu Wushi Jiamuyang* (Huang Zhengqing and the 5th Jamyang Shepa). Lanzhou: Gansu Minzu Chubanshe, 1989.

Huang Zongxi [Tsung-hsi]. *Records of the Ming Scholars*, translated by Julia Ching. Honolulu: University of Hawaii Press, 1987.

Huddart, David. *Postcolonial Theory and Autobiography*. London: Routledge, 2008.

Hummel, Arthur W., ed. *Eminent Chinese of the Ch'ing Dynasty (1644–1912)*. Washington DC: United States Government Printing Office, 1943–1944.

Hung, William. "A T'ang Historiographer's Letter of Resignation." *Harvard Journal of Asiatic Studies* 29 (1969): 5–52.

Huters, Theodore. *Bringing the World Home: Appropriating the West in Late Qing and Early Republican China*. Honolulu: University of Hawai'i Press, 2005.

Idema, Wilt L. "The Biographical and the Autobiographical in Bo Shaojun's *One Hundred Poems Lamenting My Husband*." In *Beyond Exemplar Tales: Women's Biography in Chinese History*, edited by Joan Judge and Hu Ying, 230–245. Berkeley: University of California Press, 2011.

Idema, Wilt L. and Beata Grant. *The Red Brush: Writing Women of Imperial China*. Cambridge: Harvard University Asia Center, 2004.

lHa-klu Tshe-dbang rdo-rje. "Dang-po / Yab-gzhis lHa-klu'i khyim-tshang gi lo-rgyus skor // gNyis-pa / Phran Tshe-dbang rdo-rje rang-nyid kyi byung-ba rangs-rim brjod-pa" (Part 1: On the History of the Yabshi family Lhalu; Part 2: Account of my story, Tsewang Dorje). In *Bod rang-skyong ljongs srid-gros lo-rguys rig-gnas dpyad-gzhi'i rgyu-cha u-yon lhan-khang, Bod kyi lo-rgyus rig-gnas dpyad-gzhi'i rgyu-cha bdams-bsgrigs, no. 7 (spyi'i 'don no. 16)*. Beijing: Mi-rigs dpe-skrun-khang, 1993.

IISH. *Chinese Posters: Propaganda, Politics, History, Art*. http://chineseposters. net/ (accessed 8 October, 2012).

——. *Models and Martyrs*. http://chineseposters.net/themes/models.php (accessed 8 April, 2013).

Israel, John. *Lianda: A Chinese University in War and Revolution*. Stanford: Stanford University Press, 1998.

Jelinek, Estelle C., ed. *Women's Autobiography*. Bloomington: Indiana University Press, 1980.

Ji Liuqi. *Mingji nanlüe* (An outline history of the Southern Ming). Beijing: Zhonghua shuju, 1984.

Jiao Xun, *Jushuo* (On theatre) [1805]. In Zhongguo xiqu yanjiuyuan, ed., *Zhongguo gudian xiqu lunzhu jicheng Vol.8* (Collected works on classical Chinese theatre), 201–202. Beijing: Zhongguo xiqu chubanshe, 1980.

Johnston, Reginald. *Twilight in the Forbidden City*. Oxford: Oxford University Press, 1985.

Jolly, Margaretta. "Approaching the Auto/biographical Turn." Conference report from "The First International Conference on Auto/Biography" at the University of Peking [Beijing], June 21–24, 1999, Unpublished Conference Report.

———. "The Exile and the Ghostwriter: East-West Biographical Politics and the Private Life of Chairman Mao." *Biography* 23.3 (2000): 481–503.

———. "Coming Out of the Coming Out Story: Writing Queer Lives." *Sexualities* 4 (2001): 474–496.

———, ed. *Encyclopaedia of Life Writing* 2 vols. London: Routledge, 2001.

Judge, Joan. "Reforming the Feminine: Female Literacy and the Legacy of 1898." In *Rethinking the 1898 Reform Period: Political and Cultural Change in Late Qing China*, edited by Rebecca Karl and Peter Zarrow, 158–179. Cambridge: Harvard University Asia Center, 2002.

———. "Blended Wish Images: Chinese and Western Exemplary Women at the Turn of the Twentieth Century." *Nan Nü: Men, Women and Gender in China* 6.1 (2004): 102–135.

———. *The Precious Raft of History: The Past, the West and the Woman Question in China*. Stanford: Stanford University Press, 2008.

Judge, Joan and Hu Ying, eds. *Beyond Exemplar Tales: Women's Biography in Chinese History*. Berkeley: University of California Press, 2011.

Kang Daisha. "Yan'an zai xiang wo zhaohuan" (Yan'an was calling me). In *Yan'an zhi lu* (The road to Yan'an), edited by Su Ping and Xu Yuzhen, 20–35. Beijing: Zhongguo funü chubanshe, 1991.

Keren, Michael. "Blogging and Mass Politics." *Biography* 33.1 (2010): 110–126.

Kerlan-Stephens, Anne. "The Making of Modern Icons: Three Actresses of the Lianhua Film Company." *European Journal of East Asian Studies* 6.1 (2007): 43–73.

Kinkley, Jeffrey. "A Bettelheimian Interpretation of Chang Hsien-liang's Concentration-Camp Novels." *Asia Major* IV.2 (1991): 83–113.

Kinney, Anne Behnke, ed. *Traditions of Exemplary Women: A Bilingual Resource for the Study of Women in Early China*. http://www2.iath.virginia.edu/xwomen/intro.html# (accessed 15 August, 2012).

Knight, Deirdre Sabina. "Madness and Disability in Contemporary Chinese Film." *Journal of Medical Humanities* 27.2 (2006): 93–103.

Ko, Dorothy. *Teachers of the Inner Chambers: Women and Culture in Seventeenth Century China*. Stanford: Stanford University Press, 1994.

———. "Thinking about Copulating: An early-Qing Confucian Thinker's Problem with Emotion and Words." In *Remapping China: Fissures in Historical Terrain*, edited by Gail Hershatter et al., 59–76. Stanford: Stanford University Press, 1996.

Kohrman, Matthew. *Bodies of Difference: Experiences of Disability and Institutional Advocacy in the Making of Modern China*. Berkeley: University of California Press, 2005.

Kuang Lu. *Chiya* (Customs of the South). Haixuetang edn. preface dated 1769.

Lachman, Charles. "On the Artist's Biography in Sung China: The Case of Li Ch'eng." *Biography* 9.3 (1986): 189–201.

Landsberger, Stefan R. "Learning by What Example? Educational Propaganda in Twenty-first Century China." *Critical Asian Studies* 33.4 (2001): 541–571.

Larson, Wendy. *Literary Authority and the Modern Chinese Writer.* Durham: Duke University Press, 1991.

——. *Women and Writing in Modern China.* Stanford: Stanford University Press, 1998.

Lean, Eugenia. *Public Passions: The Trial of Shi Jianqiao and the Rise of Popular Sympathy in Republican China.* Berkeley: University of California Press, 2007.

Lee, Hermione. *Body Parts: Essays in Life-writing.* London: Chatto and Windus, 2005.

——. *Biography: A Very Short Introduction.* Oxford: Oxford University Press, 2009.

Leibold, James. "Blogging Alone: China, the Internet, and the Democratic Illusion?" *Journal of Asian Studies* 70.4 (2011): 1023–1041.

Lejeune, Philippe. *On Diary,* edited by Jeremy Popkin and Julie Rak, translated by Katharine Durnin. Honolulu: University of Hawaii Press, 2009.

——. "Le Moi est-il International?/Is the I International?," translated by Jean Yamasaki Toyama. *Biography* 32.1 (2009): 1–15.

Li Jianjun. "Lunyi yingxiong, aiqing congci bu liulang" (Love finally finds a home for the wheelchair hero). *Jiankang shenghuo* (Healthy living) 1 (2004): 38–39.

Li Qing. *Sanyuan biji* (Notes from three government departments). Beijing: Zhonghua shuju, 1982.

Li Ruohong. *A Tibetan Aristocratic Family in the Eighteenth Century: A Study of Qing-Tibetan Contact.* Ph.D., Harvard University, 2002.

Li, Wai-yee. "The Representation of History in *The Peach Blossom Fan.*" *Journal of the American Oriental Society* 115.3 (1995): 421–433.

Li Zhanzi. "Di er ren cheng zai zizhuan de renji gongneng" (The interpersonal function of second-person address in autobiography). *Waiguo yu* (Journal of foreign languages) 6.6 (2000): 51–56.

——. "Zizhuanzhong fenshen biaoda de renji yiyi" (The interpersonal significance of reflexive expression in autobiography). *Waiyu jiaoxue* (Foreign language education) 22.3 (2001): 7–13.

——. "Xianzai shi zai zizhuan huayu zhong de renji yiyi" (The interpersonal significance of the present tense in the language of autobiography). *Waiyu yu waiyu jiaoxue* (Foreign languages and their teaching) 154 (2002): 3–7.

——. "<Fayu ke> yuyan xide, wenhua shenfen he zizhuan sucai" (French lessons: language acquisition, cultural identity and autobiography) *Sichuan waiyu xueyuan xuebao* (Journal of the Sichuan Institute of Foreign Languages) 21.4 (2005): 70–74.

Li Zhen. "Cong tongyangxi dao nü zhanshi" (From child bride to woman soldier). In *Xinghuo liaoyuan: Nübing huiyilu* (A single spark can start a prairie fire: recollections of women soldiers), edited by Xinghuo liaoyuan bianjibu (Editorial staff of the [series] Xinghuo liaoyuan), 61–68. Beijing: Jiefangjun chubanshe, 1987.

Liang Heng. *Son of the Revolution*. London: Fontana, 1984.

Liang Qichao. *Yinbing shi heji: wenji* (Writings from the ice-drinker's studio: collected works). Shanghai: Zhonghua shuju, 1936.

—— (Liang Ch'i-ch'ao). *Intellectual Trends in the Ch'ing Period*, translated by Immanuel C.Y. Hsü). Cambridge: Harvard University Press, 1959.

Link, Perry. "A Brief Introduction to Chang Hsien-liang's Concentration Camp Novels." *Asia Major* IV.2 (1991): 79–82.

Liu, Fengyun. "Liang Duan." In *Biographical Dictionary of Chinese Women*, edited by Clara Ho, 127–128. Armonk: M.E. Sharpe, 1998.

Liu, Jianxin. "Gendered performances and norms in Chinese personal blogs." *Gender Forum* 30 (2010). http://www.genderforum.org/ (accessed 12 August, 2012).

Liu, Lydia. *Translingual Practice: Literature, National Culture, and Translated Modernity – China, 1900–1937*. Stanford: Stanford University Press, 1995.

Liu Yun et al., eds. *Huaining xianzhi* (Gazetteer of Huaining County) [1686]. In *Zhongguo fangzhi congshu: Huadong difang*, vol.730. Taipei: Chengwen chubanshe, 1985.

Liu Zhizhong. "Ruan Dacheng jiashi kao" (Family history of Ruan Dacheng). *Wenxian* 3 (2004): 193–204.

Loftus, Ronald P. *Telling Lives: Women's Self-writing in Modern Japan*. Honolulu: University of Hawaii Press, 2004.

Lu Rong. *Yige Shanghai zhiqing de 223 feng jiaxin* (223 letters home from a Shanghai educated youth). Shanghai: Shanghai shehui kexue chubanshe, 2009.

Lu Tanxian and Liu Deyu. "Zhongguo dangdai Bao'er – Zhang Haidi" (China's modern-day Pavel – Zhang Haidi). In *Haidi guxiang de canjiren* (Disabled people from Haidi's hometown), by Yan Baoyu, 1–9. Beijing: Huaxia chubanshe, 2003.

Lu, Tina. *Persons, Roles, and Minds: Identity in Peony Pavilion and Peach Blossom Fan*. Stanford: Stanford University Press, 2001.

Lu, Weijing. "Faithful Maiden Biographies: A Forum for Ritual Debate, Moral Critique, and Personal Reflection." In *Beyond Exemplar Tales: Women's Biography in Chinese History*, edited by Joan Judge and Hu Ying, 88–103. Berkeley: University of California Press, 2011.

——. "Personal Writings on Female Relatives in the Qing Collected Works." In *Overt and Covert Treasures: Essays on the Sources for Chinese Women's History*, edited by Clara Ho, 411–434. Hong Kong: Chinese University Press, 2012.

Lu Xun. *Diary of a Madman and Other Stories*, trans. William Lyall. Honolulu: University of Hawaii Press, 1990.

Lufrano, Richard. *Honorable Merchants: Commerce and Self-Cultivation in Late Imperial China*. Honolulu: University of Hawai'i Press, 1997.

MacKay, Elaine. "English Diarists: Gender, Geography and Occupation, 1500–1700." *History* 90.298 (2003): 191–212.

Mair, Victor, ed. *The Columbia Anthology of Traditional Chinese Literature*. New York: Columbia University Press, 1994.

Mairs, Nancy. Foreword to *Recovering Bodies: Illness, Disability and Life Writing*, edited by G. Thomas Couser, ix–xvi. Madison: University of Wisconsin Press, 1997.

Makley, Charlene. " 'Speaking Bitterness': Autobiography, History, and Mnemonic Politics on the Sino-Tibetan frontier." *Comparative Studies of Society and History* 47.1 (2005): 40–78.

Mann, Susan and Yu-yin Cheng, eds. *Under Confucian Eyes: Writings on Gender in Chinese History*. Berkeley: University of California Press, 2001.

Mann, Susan L. "Women in the Life and Thought of Zhang Xuecheng." In *Chinese Language, Thought, and Culture: Nivison and His Critics*, edited by Philip J. Ivanhoe, 94–120. Chicago and La Salle, Ill: Open Court, 1996.

——. *Precious Records: Women in China's Long Eighteenth Century*. Stanford: Stanford University Press, 1997.

——. *The Talented Women of the Zhang Family*. Berkeley: University of California Press, 2007.

——. *"AHR Roundtable*: Scene-setting: Writing Biography in Chinese History." *American Historical Review* 114.3 (2009): 631–639.

Mao Xiang. *Yingmeian yiyu* (Reminiscences from the Shaded Plum Study). In *Fusheng liu ji (wai san zhong)* (Six records of a floating life), by Shen Fu, edited by Jin Xingyao and Jin Wennan. Shanghai: Shanghai guji chubanshe, 2000.

Marcus, Laura. "The Newness of the 'New Biography'." In *Mapping Lives: The Uses of Biography*, edited by Peter France and William St Clair, 193–218. Oxford: Oxford University Press, 2002.

Marx, Karl. *A Contribution to the Critique of Political Economy*, translated by N.I. Stone. Chicago: Charles Kerr, 1904.

McDermott, Joseph. *A Social History of the Chinese Book: Books and Literati Culture in Late Imperial China*. Hong Kong: Hong Kong University Press, 2006.

McDougall, Bonnie S. and Anders Hansson, eds. *Chinese Concepts of Privacy*. Leiden: Brill, 2002.

Miles, Steven B. "Strange Encounters on the Cantonese Frontier: Region and Gender in Kuang Lu's (1604–1650) *Chiya.*" *Nan Nü: Men, Women and Gender in China* 8.1 (2006): 115–155.

Mitter, Rana. *The Manchurian Myth*. Berkeley: University of California Press, 2000.

——. *A Bitter Revolution*. Oxford: Clarendon Press, 2005.

mKhas-grub. *The Flight of the Orphan: Autobiography of my Early Life* (Tib. Tshe-stod kyi rang-rnam dva-phrug gi gshog-rtsal). Beijing: Nationalities Publishing House, 2003.

Moloughney, Brian. "From Biographical History to Historical Biography: A Transformation in Chinese Historical Writing." *East Asian History* 4 (1992):1–30.

Moloughney, Brian and Peter Zarrow, eds. *Transforming History: The Making of a Modern Academic Discipline in the Twentieth Century*. Hong Kong: The Chinese University Press, 2011.

Moore-Gilbert, Bart. *Postcolonial Life-writing: Culture, Politics and Self-representation.* London: Routledge, 2009.

Morozov, Evgeny. "Blogs: The New Frontier in Human Rights." *Transitions Online,* January 05, 2007.

Morris, Andrew D. *Marrow of the Nation: A History of Sport and Physical Culture in Republican China.* Berkeley: University of California Press, 2004.

Mu Qing, Feng Jiang and Zhou Yuan. *Jiao Yulu (1922–1964): A Model of County Party Secretary.* Beijing: Renmin Chubanshe, 1966.

Mühlhahn, Klaus. " 'Remembering a Bitter Past': the Trauma of China's Labor Camps, 1949–1978." *History and Memory* 16.2 (2004): 108–139.

Nalbantian, Suzanne. *Memory in Literature.* Basingstoke: Palgrave Macmillan, 2003.

Nansha sanyushi (Wang Zhongqi). *Nan Ming yeshi* (Unofficial history of the Southern Ming). Shanghai: Shangwu yinshuguan, 1930.

Ng, Janet. *The Experience of Modernity: Chinese Autobiography of the Early Twentieth Century.* Ann Arbor: University of Michigan Press, 2003.

Ng, On-cho and Q. Edward Wang. *Mirroring the Past: The Writing and Use of History in Imperial China.* Honolulu: University of Hawaii Press, 2005.

Nivison, David. "Aspects of Traditional Biography." *Journal of Asian Studies* 21.4 (1962): 457–463.

———. *The Life and Thought of Chang Hsüeh-ch'eng (1738–1801).* Stanford: Stanford University Press, 1966.

———. "Replies and Comments." In *Chinese Language, Thought, and Culture: Nivison and His Critics,* edited by Philip J. Ivanhoe, 267–341. Chicago and La Salle: Open Court, 1996.

Ōki Yasushi. "Textbooks on an Aesthetic Life in Late Ming China." In *The Quest for Gentility in China: Negotiations beyond Gender and Class,* edited by Daria Berg and Chloë Starr, 179–187. London and New York: Routledge, 2007.

Ong, Chang Woei. *Men of Letters Within the Passes: Guanzhong Literati in Chinese History, 907–1911.* Cambridge: Harvard University Asia Center, 2008.

Parke, Catherine. *Biography: Writing Lives.* New York and London: Routledge, 2002.

Passerini, Luisa. "Introduction." In *Memory and Totalitarianism,* International Yearbook of Oral History and Life Stories, vol. 1, edited by Luisa Passerini, 1–19. Oxford: Oxford University Press, 1992.

Perkins, Margo V. *Autobiography as Activism: Three Black Women of the Sixties.* Jackson: University Press of Mississippi, 2000.

Perkins, Maureen, ed. *Locating Life Stories: Beyond East-West Binaries in (Auto)biographical Studies.* Honolulu: University of Hawaii Press, 2012.

Pilling, David. "Lunch with the FT: Han Han." *Financial Times,* April 21, 2012.

Pollard, David, tr. and ed. *The Chinese Essay.* London: Hurst & Co., 2000.

Portelli, Alessandro. "History-Telling and Time: An Example from Kentucky." *Oral History Review* 20.1&2 (1992): 51–67.

Qian Chengzhi. *Suo zhi lu* (Record of what I know). Hefei: Huangshan shushe, 2006.

Qian Nanxiu. "*Lienü* versus *Xianyuan*: The Two Biographical Traditions in Chinese Women's History." In *Beyond Exemplar Tales: Women's Biography in Chinese History*, edited by Joan Judge and Hu Ying, 70–87. Berkeley: University of California Press, 2011.

Qian Qianyi. *Liechao shiji xiaozhuan* (Brief biographies of poets from all the reigns). Shanghai: Zhonghua shuju, 1961.

Qian Zhongshu. *Fortress Besieged*, translated by Jeanne Kelly and Nathan K. Mao. London: Penguin, 2004.

Qu Qiubai. *Superfluous Words*, translated by Jamie Greenbaum. Canberra: Pandanus Books, 2006.

Quan Zhan. "Shiji zhi jiao: Zhongguo zhuanji wenxue de liu da redian" (At the turn of the century: Six key points in Chinese biographical literature) *Huaibei zhiye jishu xueyuan xuebao* (Journal of the Huaibei Professional and Technical Institute) 1.1 (2002): 34–36.

——. "Minzu jingshen, minjian lichang, pingminhua shijiao: xin shiji pingmin zhuanji zonglun" (National spirit, grassroots standpoint and common people's perspective: A review of common people's biographies in the new century), *Zhejiang shifan daxue xuebao* (Journal of Zhejiang Normal University) 31.6 (2006): 7–13.

Quanguo funü lianhehui bangongting, Fujian sheng funü lianhehui (Bureau of the National Women's Federation and Women's Federation of Fujian Province), ed. *Qingchun zai zhanhuo zhong* (Youth in the flames of war). Fuzhou: n.p., 1996.

Rickett, W. Allyn. *Guanzi: Political, Economic, and Philosophical Essays from Early China*. Princeton: Princeton University Press, 1985.

Rigney, Ann. *The Rhetoric of Historical Representation: Three Narrative Histories of the French Revolution*. Cambridge: Cambridge University Press, 1990.

——. "The Point of Stories: On Narrative Communication and Its Cognitive Functions." *Poetics Today* 13.2 (1992): 263–283.

Ropp, Paul. *China in World History*. Oxford: Oxford University Press, 2010.

Rosenthal, Gabriele. "Geschichte in der Lebensgeschichte" (History within life stories). *Bios – Zeitschrift für Biographieforschung, Oral History und Lebensverlaufsanalysen* 2 (1988): 3–15.

Ross, Michael and Anne E. Wilson. "Constructing and Appraising Past Selves." In *Memory, Brain and Belief*, edited by Daniel Schacter and Elaine Scarry, 231–258. Cambridge: Harvard University Press, 2000.

Rousseau, Jean-Jacques. *Les Confessions de J J Rousseau. Tome Premier*, London, 1786. Eighteenth Century Collections Online (accessed 1 August, 2011).

Rowe, William T. *Saving the World: Chen Hongmou and Elite Consciousness in Eighteenth-century China*. Stanford: Stanford University Press, 2001.

Ruan Dacheng. *Hexiaoji* (Harmonising with a flute). Hand-copied facsimile of Ming edition, Tianyige Library, preface dated 1614.

——. *Yonghuaitang shi* (Poems from the Hall of Chanting what is in my Heart). Taipei: Taiwan Zhonghua shuju, 1971 [1928 edition].

——. *Yanzi jian (The Swallow Messenger)*. Shanghai: Shanghai guji chubanshe, 1986.

——. *Ruan Dacheng xiqu sizhong* (Four Plays by Ruan Dacheng), edited by Xu Lingyun and Hu Jinwang. Hefei: Huangshan shushe, 1993.

——. *Yonghuaitang shiji* (Collected poems from the Hall of Chanting what is in my Heart), edited by Hu Jinwang and Wang Changlin. Hefei: Huangshan shushe, 2006.

Ruan Ji. "Daren xiansheng zhuan" (Biography of the great man). In *Ruan Ji ji jiaozhu* (Annotated works of Ruan Ji), edited by Chen Bojun. Beijing: Zhonghua shuju, 1987.

Sang Fengkang. "Zhuanji zaoyu shuangrenjian – zai shichang jingji tiaojian xia de zhuanji xiezuo" (A double-edged sword – writing biography in a market economy). *Jingmen zhiye jishu xueyuan xuebao* (Journal of Jingmen Technical College) 20.2 (2005): 1–5.

Schaffer, Kay and Sidonie Smith. "Conjunctions: Life Narratives in the Field of Human Rights." *Biography* 27.1 (2004): 1–24.

Schaeffer, Kurtis. *Himalayan Hermitess: The Life of a Tibetan Buddhist Nun*. Oxford: Oxford University Press, 2004.

——. "Tibetan Biography: Growth and Criticism." In *Edition, éditions: l'écrit au Tibet, évolution et devenir* (Collectanea Himalayica 3), edited by Anne Chayet, Cristina Scherrer-Schaub, Françoise Robin and Jean-Luc Achard, 263–306. München: Indus Verlag, 2010.

Schneewind, Sarah. "Reduce, Re-use, Recycle: Imperial Autocracy and Scholar-Official Autonomy in the Background to the Ming History Biography of Early Ming Scholar-Official Fang Keqin (1326–1376)." *Oriens Extremus* 48 (2009): 103–152.

Schneider, Laurence A. *Ku Chieh-kang and China's New History: Nationalism and the Quest for Alternative Traditions*. Berkeley: University of California Press, 1971.

Schwarcz, Vera. *The Chinese Enlightenment: Intellectuals and the Legacy of the May Fourth Movement of 1919*. Berkeley: University of California Press, 1986.

——. *Bridge across Broken Time: Chinese and Jewish Cultural Memory*. New Haven: Yale University Press, 1998.

Scott, Joan W. "The Evidence of Experience." *Critical Inquiry* 17 (1991): 773–797.

Shakya Tsering. *The Dragon in the Land of Snows: A History of Modern Tibet since 1947*. New York: Columbia University Press, 1999.

Shao Dongfang. "Transformation, Diversification, Ideology: Twentieth Century Chinese Biography." In *Life Writing from the Pacific Rim: Essays from Japan, China, Indonesia, India, and Siam, with a Psychological Overview*, edited by Stanley Schab and George Simson, 19–39. Honolulu: East-West Center, 1997.

Sharpe, Kevin and Stephen Zwicker, eds. *Writing Lives: Biography and Textuality, Identity and Representation in Early Modern England*. Oxford: Oxford University Press, 2008.

Shen Fu. *Six Records of a Floating Life*, translated by Leonard Pratt and Chiang Su-hui.London: Penguin, 1983.

——. *Six Records of a Life Adrift*, translated by Graham Saunders. London: Hackett, 2011.

Shen, Grant Guangren. *Elite Theatre in Ming China, 1368–1644*. London: Routledge, 2005.

Sheridan, Mary. "The Emulation of Heroes." *China Quarterly* 33 (1968): 47–72.

Smith, Paul Jakov. "Impressions of the Song-Yuan-Ming transition: the Evidence from *Biji* Memoirs." In *The Song-Yuan-Ming Transition in Chinese History*, edited by Paul Jakov Smith and Richard von Glahn, 71–110. Cambridge: Harvard University Press, 2003.

Smith, Sidonie and Julia Watson. *Reading Autobiography: A Guide for Interpreting Life Narratives*. Minneapolis: University of Minnesota Press, 2001.

Snyder, Sharon L., Brenda Jo Brueggemann, and Rosemarie Garland Thomson, eds. *Disability Studies: Enabling the Humanities*. New York: The Modern Language Association of America, 2002.

Spakowski, Nicola. *"Mit Mut an die Front." Die militärische Beteiligung von Frauen in der kommunistischen Revolution Chinas, 1925–1949* ("Courageously to the front." Women's military participation in the Chinese Communist Revolution, 1925–1949). Cologne: Böhlau, 2009.

Spence, Jonathan. *Return to Dragon Mountain*. London: Quercus, 2008.

Sperling, Elliot. "Awe and Submission: A Tibetan Aristocrat at the Court of Qianlong." *The International History Review* 20.2 (1998): 325–335.

Standen, Naomi. *Unbounded Loyalty: Frontier Crossing in Liao China*. Honolulu: University of Hawaii Press, 2007.

Strassberg, Richard E. "The Authentic Self in 17th Century Chinese Drama." *Tamkang Review* VIII.2 (1977): 61–100.

Strong, Anna Louise. *When Serfs Stood up in Tibet*. Beijing: New World Press, 1960.

Struve, Lynn A. "History and *The Peach Blossom Fan*." *Chinese Literature: Essays, Articles, Reviews* 2.1 (1980): 55–72.

——. "Huang Zongxi in Context: A Reappraisal of his Major Writings." *Journal of Asian Studies* 47.3 (1988): 474–502.

——. *The Ming-Qing Conflict, 1619–1683: A Historiography and Source Guide*. Association for Asian Studies Monograph No. 56. Ann Arbor: Association for Asian Studies, 1998.

——. *Voices from the Ming-Qing Cataclysm: China in Tigers' Jaws*. New Haven: Yale University Press, 1998.

——. "Chimerical Early Modernity: The Case of 'Conquest-Generation' Memoirs." In *The Qing Formation in World-Historical Time*, edited by Lynn Struve, 335–380. Cambridge: Harvard University Asia Center, 2004.

——. "Confucian PTSD: Reading Trauma in a Chinese Youngster's Memoir of 1653." *History and Memory* 16.2 (2004): 14–31.

——. "Dreaming and Self-search during the Ming Collapse: The Xue Xiemeng *Biji*, 1642–1646." *T'oung-pao* 92 (2007): 159–192.

——. "Self-Struggles of a Martyr: Memories, Dreams, and Obsessions in the Extant Diary of Huang Chunyao." *Harvard Journal of Asiatic Studies* 69.2 (2009): 73–124.

Summerfield, Penny. *Reconstructing Women's Wartime Lives: Discourse and Subjectivity in Oral Histories of the Second World War*. Manchester and New York: Manchester University Press, 1998.

Tang Xianzu. *Tang Xianzu xiqu ji* (Collected plays of Tang Xianzu), edited by Qian Nanyang. Shanghai: Shanghai guji chubanshe, 1978.

Tang Xiaobing. *Global Space and the Nationalist Discourse of Modernity: The Historical Thinking of Liang Qichao*. Stanford: Stanford University Press, 1996.

Tashi Tsering. *The Struggle for Modern Tibet: The Autobiography of Tashi Tsering*. Armonk: ME Sharpe, 1997.

*Tibetan People – Former Tibetan Aristocrat Lhalu Cewang Doje*. Beijing, 2007. DVD.

Todd, Margo. "Puritan Self-Fashioning: The Diary of Samuel Ward." *Journal of British Studies* 31.3 (1992): 236–264.

Travers. Alice. "La Fabrique de l'Histoire au Tibet Contemporain. Contours et Articulations d'une Mémoire Collective dans les *Matériaux pour l'Histoire et la Culture du Tibet*." Paper presented at Colloque Société Asiatique/Collège de France, "Les Matériaux de l'Historien", 29 May 2012.

Tsai, Kathryn Ann, ed. and tr. *Lives of the Nuns: Biographies of Chinese Buddhist Nuns from the Fourth to the Sixth Centuries. A Translation of Pi-ch'iu-ni chuan, Compiled by Shih Pao-ch'ang*. Honolulu: University of Hawaii Press, 1994.

Twitchett, Denis. "Chinese Biographical Writing." In *Historians of China and Japan*, edited by W.G. Beasley and E.G. Pulleyblank, 95–114. London: Oxford University Press, 1961.

——. "Problems of Chinese biography." In *Confucian Personalities*, edited by Arthur Wright and Denis Twitchett, 24–39. Stanford: Stanford University Press, 1962.

——. "Introduction." In *The Cambridge History of China Vol. 3: Sui and T'ang China, 589–906 AD, Part 1*, edited by Denis Twitchett, 1–47. Cambridge: Cambridge University Press, 1980.

——. *The Writing of Official History under the T'ang*. Cambridge: Cambridge University Press, 1992.

van der Kuijp, Leonard. "On the Life and Political Career of Ta'i-si-tu Byang-chub rgyal-mtshan (1302–1364?)." In *Tibetan History and Language. Studies Dedicated to Uray Géza on His Seventieth Birthday*, edited by E. Steinkellner, 277–327. Vienna: Arbeitskreis für Tibetische und Buddhistische Studien Universität Wien, 1991.

——. "Tibetan historiography." In *Tibetan Literature: Studies in Genre*, edited by José Ignacio Cabezón and Roger R. Jackson, 39–56. Ithaca: Snow Lion Publications, 1996.

Vernon, Alex. "No Genre's Land: The Problem of Genre in War Memoirs and Military Autobiography." In *War, the Military, and Autobiographical Writing*, edited by Alex Vernon, 1–40. Kent and London: Kent State University Press, 2005.

Wachter, Phyllis E. "Annual Bibliography of Works about Life Writing, 1999–2000." *Biography* 23.4 (2000): 695–755.

———. "Annual Bibliography of Works About Life Writing, 2009–2010." *Biography* 33.4 (2010): 714–846.

Wakeman, Frederic, Jr. "Romantics, Stoics, and Martyrs in Seventeenth-Century China." *Journal of Asian Studies* 43.4 (1984): 631–665.

Waldron, Arthur. "China's New Remembering of World War II: The Case of Zhang Zizhong." *Modern Asian Studies* 30.4 (1996): 945–978.

Waltner, Ann. "Life and Letters: Reflections on Tanyangzi." In *Beyond Exemplar Tales: Women's Biography in Chinese History*, edited by Joan Judge and Hu Ying, 212–229. Berkeley: University of California Press, 2011.

Wang Daxiang. http://www.wangdxx.com/ (accessed 15 September, 2012).

Wang Jianshuo. http://home.wangjianshuo.com/ (accessed 17 September, 2012).

Wang Jing. *When "I" was Born: Women's Autobiography in Modern China.* Madison: University of Wisconsin Press, 2008.

Wang Lingzhen. *Personal Matters: Women's Autobiographical Practice in Early Twentieth Century China.* Stanford: Stanford University Press, 2004.

Wang Ning. "The Making of an Intellectual Hero: Chinese Narratives of Qian Xuesen." *China Quarterly* 206 (2011): 352–371.

Wang, Q. Edward. *Inventing China Through History: The May Fourth Approach to Historiography.* Albany: State University of New York Press, 2001.

Wang Siren. "Shicuoren chundengmi ji xu" (Preface to the *Spring Lantern Riddles or Ten Cases of Mistaken Identity*). In *Ruan Dacheng xiqu sizhong* (Four plays by Ruan Dacheng), edited by Xu Lingyun and Hu Jinwang, 169–170. Hefei: Huangshan shushe, 1993.

Wang Xinxian, ed. *Fangfei xiwang* (Let dreams take flight). Beijing: Huaxia chubanshe, 2005.

———. *Weile shengming de meili* (To the beauty of life). Beijing: Huaxia chubanshe, 2005.

———. *Shouhuo gandong* (A treasury of emotions). Beijing: Huaxia chubanshe, 2006.

Wang Ying. "Shi lun Ruan Dacheng xingxiang de suzao" (On the portrayal of Ruan Dacheng). *Shenyang Shifan Xueyuan xuebao: sheke ban* (Journal of Shenyang Normal College: social science edition) 1 (1995): 64–67.

Wang Zhonghan. *Qingshi xinkao* (New studies on Qing history). Shenyang: Lianning daxue, 1990.

Watson, Rubie S. "Memory, History, and Opposition under State Socialism. An Introduction." In *Memory, History, and Opposition under State Socialism*, edited by Rubie S. Watson, 1–20. Santa Fe: School of American Research Press, 1994.

Webster, Tom. "Writing to Redundancy: Approaches to Spiritual Journals and Early Modern Spirituality." *The Historical Journal* 39.1 (1996): 33–56.

Wechsler, Howard J. "The Founding of the T'ang dynasty: Kao-tsu (reign 618–26)." In *Cambridge History of China 3: Sui and T'ang China, 589–906, Part I*, edited by Denis Twitchett, chap. 3. Cambridge: Cambridge University Press, 1979.

Weigelin-Schwiedrzik, Susanne. "Party Historiography in the People's Republic of China." *Australian Journal of Chinese Affairs* 17 (1987): 77–94.

Weiner, Benno R. "Official Chinese Sources on Recent Tibetan History: Local Gazetteers, *wenshi ziliao*, and CCP Histories." http://library.columbia.edu/content/dam/libraryweb/libraries/eastasian/Weiner_Local_Tibetan_Gazetteers.pdf (accessed 25 July, 2012).

Wells, Matthew. *To Die and Not Decay: Autobiography and the Pursuit of Immortality in Early China*. Ann Arbor: Association of Asian Studies, 2009.

*Wenshi ziliao xuanji (Selection of Cultural and Historical Materials)*. Beijing: Zhongguo wenshi chubanshe, 1986.

Widmer, Ellen. "The Rhetoric of Retrospection: May Fourth Literary History and the Ming-Qing Woman Writer." In *The Appropriation of Cultural Capital: China's May Fourth Project*, edited by Milena Doleželová and Oldřich Král, 193–221. Cambridge: Harvard University Asia Center, 2001.

———. *Beauty and the Book: Women and Fiction in Nineteenth Century China*. Cambridge, MA: Harvard University Asia Center, 2006.

———. "Women as Biographers in Mid-Qing Jiangnan." In *Beyond Exemplar Tales: Women's Biography in Chinese History*, edited by Joan Judge and Hu Ying, 246–261. Berkeley: University of California Press, 2011.

Widmer, Ellen and Kang-i Sun Chang eds. *Writing Women in Late Imperial China*. Stanford: Stanford University Press, 1997.

Williams, Philip F. "'Remolding' and the Chinese Labor-Camp Novel." *Asia Major* IV.2 (1991): 133–149.

Williams, Philip F. and Yenna Wu. *The Great Wall of Confinement: The Chinese Prison Camp through Contemporary Fiction and Reportage*. Berkeley: University of California Press, 2004.

Willock, Nicole. "Rekindling the Ashes from the Dharma and the Formation of Modern Tibetan Studies: The Busy Life of Alak Tseten Zhabdrung." *Latse Library Newsletter* 6 (2009–2010): 2–25.

Winter, Jay and Emmanuel Sivan. "Setting the Framework." In *War and Remembrance in the Twentieth Century*, edited by Jay Winter and Emmanuel Sivan, 6–39. Cambridge: Cambridge University Press, 2000.

*Wo de jianzheng: 200 wei qinli kangzhan zhe koushu lishi* (My testimony: 200 oral histories based on personal experience of the War of Resistance). Beijing: Jiefangjun wenyi chubanshe, 2005.

Wu Mi. *Riji* (Diary) 10 vols. Beijing: Sanlian, 1998–1999.

Wu Mi. *Riji xu bian* (Diary: second series) 10 vols. Beijing: Sanlian, 2006.

Wu Pei-yi. "Self-Examination and Confession of Sins in Traditional China." *Harvard Journal of Asiatic Studies* 39.1 (1979): 5–38.

———. *The Confucian's Progress: Autobiographical Writings in Traditional China*. Princeton: Princeton University Press, 1989.

———. "Childhood Remembered: Parents and Children in China, 800–1700." In *Chinese Views of Childhood*, edited by Anne Behnke Kinney, 129–156. Honolulu: University of Hawaii Press, 1995.

Wu, Yenna. "Women as Sources of Redemption in Chang Hsien-liang's Labor-Camp Fiction." *Asia Major* IV.2 (1991): 115–131.

Wu Yingji. "Liudu fangluan gongjie" (Proclamation to Prevent Disorder in the Secondary Capital). In *Guichi ermiao ji* (Records of two notables of Guichi), *juan* 47. Qing edition in Bibliothèque Nationale, Paris.

Xie Guozhen. *Ming Qing zhi ji dangshe yundong kao* (On factional activity in the Ming-Qing transition). Shanghai: Shanghai shudian, 2004.

Xie Wei. *Zhongguo lidai renwu nianpu kaolu* (Catalogue of chronological biographies of historical personalities). Beijing: Zhongguo shuju, 1992.

Xu Linjiang. *Zheng Xiaoxu qian ban sheng pingzhuan* (Critical biography of Zheng Xiaoxu: his early life). Shanghai: Xuelin chubanshe 2003.

Xu Weiyu. *Lüshi chunqiu jishi* (Collected notes to "Master Lü's 'Spring and Autumn Annals'"). Beijing: Guoli Qinghua daxue, 1935.

——. "Hao Lan'gao (Yixing) fufu nianpu" (Chronological record of Hao Yixing and his wife). *Qinghua xuebao* (Qinghua Studies) 10.1 (1936): 185–233.

Xu Xingwu. "Qingdai Wang Zhaoyuan *Lienüzhuan buzhu* yu Liang Duan *Lienüzhuan jiaozu duben*" (Wang Zhaoyuan's "Commentary on the 'Biographies of women'" and Liang Duan's "Annotated reader of 'Biographies of women'" during the Qing period). In *Ming Qing wenxue yu xingbie yanjiu* (Studies of literature and gender in the Ming Qing periods), edited by Zhang Hongsheng 916–931. Nanjing: Jiangsu guji, 2002.

Xu Zi. *Xiaotian jinian fukao* (Annals of an era of small prosperity, with annotations), edited by Wang Chongwu. Beijing: Zhonghua shuju, 1957.

Yao Mingda. *Zhang Shizhai xiansheng nianpu* (Chronological biography of Zhang Xuecheng). Shanghai: Shangwu yinshuguan, 1929.

Yao Ping. "Good Karmic Connections: Buddhist Mothers in Tang China." *Nan Nü: Men, Women and Gender in China* 10.1 (2008): 57–85.

——. "Women's Epitaphs in Tang China (618–907)." In *Beyond Exemplar Tales: Women's Biography in Chinese History*, edited by Joan Judge and Hu Ying, 139–157. Berkeley: University of California Press, 2011.

Yagoda, Ben. *Memoir: A History*. New York: Riverhead Books, 2009.

Yang Liensheng. "The Organization of Chinese Official Historiography: Principles and Methods of the Standard History from the T'ang through the Ming Dynasty." In *Historians of China and Japan*, edited by W.G. Beasley and E.G. Pulleyblank, 44–59. London: Oxford University Press, 1961.

Yang, Rae. *Spider Eaters*. Berkeley: University of California Press, 1997.

Yang Ye, ed. and tr. *Vignettes from the Late Ming: A Hsiao-p'in Anthology*. Seattle: University of Washington Press, 1999.

Yang Zhengrun. *Xiandai zhuanji xue* (A modern poetics of biography). Nanjing: Nanjing daxue chubanshe, 2009.

Yangdzom Tsering. *The Aristocratic families in Tibetan history, 1900–1951*. Beijing: Intercontinental Press, 2006.

Yeh Wen-hsin. *The Alienated Academy: Culture and Politics in Republican China, 1910–1937*. Cambridge: Council on East Asian Studies, Harvard University, 1990.

——. "Historian and Courtesan: Chen Yinke and the Writing of *Liu Rushi Biezhuan*." *East Asian History* 27 (2004): 57–70.

"yinxiaoxing de boke" (yinxiaoxing's blog). http://blog.sina.com.cn/yinxiaoxingboke (accessed 8 August, 2010).

Yu Shiling, ed. *Lu Ji, Lu Yun nianpu* (Chronological biography of Lu Ji and Lu Yun). Beijing: Renmin chubanshe, 2009.

Yu Yingshi. "Changing Conceptions of National History in Twentieth-century China." In *Conceptions of National History: Proceedings of Nobel Symposium 78*, edited by Erik Lönnroth, Karl Molin, Rognar Björk, 155–174. Berlin and New York: Walter de Gruyter, 1994.

Yuan Hongdao. "Xu Wenchang zhuan" (Biography of Xu Wenchang). In *Yuan Zhonglang suibi* (Random notes by Yuan Zhonglang), edited by Li Ren, 216–218. Beijing: Zuojia chubanshe, 1995.

Yuan Zhongdao. "Ruan Jizhi shi xu" (Preface to the poems of Ruan Jizhi). In *Kexuezhai ji* (Collected works from the Kexuezhai), edited by Qian Bocheng. Shanghai: Shanghai guji chubanshe, 1989.

———. *Youju feilu* (Notes made while travelling and at repose). Shanghai: Shanghai yuandong chubanshe, 1996.

Zarrow, Peter. "Meanings of China's Cultural Revolution: Memoirs of Exile." *positions: asia critique* 7.1 (1999): 165–191.

Zhang Aifang. *Lidai funü mingren nianpu* (Chronological biographies of famous women in history). Beijing: Beijing tushuguan chubanshe, 2005.

Zhang Dai. "Da Yuan Tuo'an" (Replying to Yuan Tuo'an). In *Langhuan wenji* (Langhuan Anthology). Changsha: Yuelu shushe, 1985.

———. "Ruan Yuanhai xi" (Plays of Ruan Yuanhai). In *Tao'an mengyi, Xihu mengxun* (Dream memories of Tao'an, Dream recollections of West Lake), edited by Li Ren. Beijing: Zuojia chubanshe, 1995.

———. *Shikuishu houji: Ma Shiying Ruan Dacheng liezhuan* (Supplement to Book for a Stone Casket: biographies of Ma Shiying and Ruan Dacheng). In *Yonghuaitang shiji* (Poems from the Hall of Chanting what is in my Heart), by Ruan Dacheng, edited by Hu Jinwang and Wang Changlin, 509–512. Hefei: Huangshan shushe, 2006.

Zhang Haidi. *Lunyiche shang de meng* (Dreams from a wheelchair). Beijing: Renmin wenxue chubanshe, 2005.

———. "Qin'ai de pengyoumen, dajia hao! (Hello, dear friends!)" http://blog.sina.com.cn/s/blog_46d3fc8f0100009z.html (accessed 18 February, 2008).

"Zhang Haidi: jixu yong shengming de jiqing lai xiezuo" (Zhang Haidi continues to write inspired by an enthusiasm for life). http://www.gmw.cn/content/2006-11/10/content_506023.htm (accessed 18 February, 2008).

"Zhang Haidi." http://news.xinhuanet.com/ziliao/2003-01/17/content_694856.htm (accessed 15 January, 2010).

Zhang Pengyuan. "Hu Shi and Liang Qichao: Friendship and Rejection between Intellectuals of Two Different Generations." *Chinese Studies in History* 37.2 (2003–2004): 39–80.

Zhang Shujun et al., eds. *Jianzheng lishi: Zhongguo 1975–1976* (Historical testimony: China 1975–1976). Changsha: Hunan renmin chubanshe, 2009.

Zhang Tingyu, ed. *Mingshi* (Ming History). Beijing: Zhonghua shuju, 1974.

Zhang Youkun et al., eds., *Zhang Xueliang nianpu* (Chronological biography of Zhang Xueliang) 2 vols. Beijing: Shehui kexue wenxian chubanshe, 2009.

Zhang Xianliang. *Ganqing de jilu* (The record of emotion). Beijing: Zuojia chubanshe, 1985.

———. *Zhang Xianliang xuanji* (Selected Works of Zhang Xianliang) Volume I. Beijing: Baihua wenyi, 1985.

———. *Xiguan siwang* (Getting used to dying). Hong Kong: Jiaodian wenku, 1989.

———. *Wo de putishu* (My bodhi tree) Part I. Beijing: Zuojia, 1994.

———. *Lüshu shu* (Mimosa). In *Zhang Xianliang jingxuanji* (Best selected works of Zhang Xianliang). Beijing: Yanshan, 2006.

Zheng Hui, ed. *Xu Yun heshang nianpu* (Chronological biography of the monk Xu Yun) 5 vols. Zhengzhou: Zhongzhou guji chubanshe, 2009.

Zheng Wei, comp. *Sui shu* (History of the Sui). Beijing: Zhonghua shuju, 1973.

Zheng Xiaoxu. *Riji* (Diary) 5 vols. Beijing: Zhonghua shuju, 1993.

Zhong Fuguang. "Huangpu junxiao Wuhan fenxiao nüshengdui de yi duan huiyi" (Some recollections of the women's team in the Wuhan Branch of the Huangpu Military Academy). In *Da geming hongliu zhong de nübing* (Women soldiers in the mighty torrent of revolution), edited by Zhonghua quanguo funü lianhehui and Huangpu junxiao tongxuehui (All-China Women's Federation and Alumni Association of the Huangpu Military Academy), 31–38. Beijing: Zhongguo funü chubanshe, 1991.

Zhonghua quanguo funü lianhehui (All-Chinese Women's Federation), ed. *Zhongguo funü yundong shi* (History of the Chinese Women's Movement). Beijing: Chunqiu chubanshe, 1989.

"Zhongguo yidai qingnian de jiao'ao – Zhang Haidi" (Zhang Haidi – the pride of a generation of China's youth). http://www.wscl.gov.cn/artshow.asp?id=367 (accessed 25 July 2013).

Zhou Dongbing. "Women shi nü zhanshi" (We are women soldiers). In *Xinghuo liaoyuan: Nübing huiyilu* (A single spark can start a prairie fire: recollections of women soldiers), edited by Xinghuo liaoyuan bianjibu (Editorial staff of the [series] Xinghuo liaoyuan), 80–86. Beijing: Jiefangjun chubanshe, 1987.

Zhu Xichen. "Zhongguo xiandai nüzuojia zhuanji xiezuo zongshu" (Overview of biographies of women writers in modern China). *Xueshujie* (Academics in China) 5 (2006): 270–274.

Zurndorfer, Harriet T. *China Bibliography: A Research Guide to Reference Works about China Past and Present.* Leiden: E.J. Brill, 1995.

———. "China and 'Modernity': the Uses of the Study of Chinese History in the Past and the Present." *Journal of the Economic and Social History of the Orient* 40.4 (1997): 461–485.

———. "Wang Zhaoyuan." In *Biographical Dictionary of Chinese Women*, edited by Clara Ho, 227–230. Armonk: M.E. Sharpe, 1998.

———. "Gender, Higher Education, and the 'New Woman': the Experiences of Female Graduates in Republican China." In *Women in China: The Republican*

*Period in Historical Perspective*, edited by Mechthild Leutner and Nicola Spakowski, 450–481. Münster: Li Verlag, 2005.

——. "Regimes of Scientific and Military Knowledge in Mid-Nineteenth Century China: a Revisionist Perspective." Paper presented to the Ninth Meeting of the "Global Economic History Network", held at Wen-chou College, Taipei, 2006.

——. "The *Lienü zhuan* Tradition and Wang Zhaoyuan's Production of the *Lienüzhuan buzhu*." In *Beyond Exemplar Tales: Women's Biography in Chinese History*, edited by Joan Judge and Hu Ying, 55–69. Berkeley: University of California Press, 2011.

# Index

Note: Locators with 'fn' refer to notes.

Printed and bound in the United States of America